This one is for my beloved children
Luke, Joe and Georgia
xxxxxxx

Published by Accent Press Ltd – 2006
ISBN 1905170572

Printed and bound in the UK by
Cox & Wyman Ltd,. Reading

Cover Design by Anna Torborg

The publisher acknowledges the financial support
of the Welsh Books Council

Acknowledgements

Accepted wisdom has it that writers should always write about what they know.

Rubbish. If I did that, all I'd have to show for my endeavours would be several lengthy tomes of unbelievably dull twitterings, plus the odd *exposé*, for which I'd probably get sued. The trick is to cheat; to look upon your friends as a research archive, and to write about what they know instead.

My first thanks, therefore, go to Rachel Hurford, who, as well as being a dear friend, is also an optometrist, which handily provided Sally with a sensible job. To Kiran Kapur, Anne Catchpole and Adrian Magson, who, unlike me, have all done that 'Outward bound' thing and who sent all the emails that informed chapter seven. Thanks, mates. To the 8th Penge and Beckenham North Venture Scout unit, which may well be no more, but lives on in my heart. To Della Galton, who first posted the Sherlock Holmes email – okay, so almost everyone in the world has now heard it, but it stays because – well, because it made Sally laugh. To the lovely folk at both Labour Party Headquarters and Charing Cross Police Station – I'm so, so sorry I didn't write down your names. To Merlin, wherever you are these days – woof woof! To Philips, for inventing the Planisphere – *so* clever. And finally, (though he doesn't, as yet, even know it) to Patrick Moore, who wrote Philip's 'Night Sky' and so gave authority to my ill-informed passion for looking at the stars and going 'Wow! Look at that!'. How spooky that it should have a photo of the Pleiades on the cover. Must have been written in the stars…

Prologue

It is five twenty seven in the morning. And some thirty-nine thousand feet over the north Atlantic, an aeroplane is heading swiftly and silently towards Gatwick airport. Aboard it, and crick-necked beneath his itchy red blanket, Nick Brown has spent much of what passes for night on this flight path trying, and failing, to sleep. His legs, which are long, are rammed hard against the seat-back in front of him, and his head, which feels woolly, against the cream cabin wall. He should be in business class. He should be in an aisle seat. But life, as it seems to a lot for Nick lately, has conspired to relieve him of any expectations of comfort: the plane he should have boarded is grounded at LAX, and this one, on which he has just scraped a passage, could only offer him row twenty-seven, seat A. Thus he has shared ten or so tortuous hours with a small boy called Luke, and his sister, Georgina. And sporadically, their mother, plus ripe smelling baby, who are seated, *when* seated, in Row twenty-six.

The plane heaves on eastwards. The captain announces their imminent descent. Resigned now, Nick abandons his blanket, but the sleep that's eluded him since tea-time on Thursday now engulfs him with a sudden and irresistible force. He is a chronic insomniac, and this is its pattern. His eyelids are heavy now. Closing despite him. Ensuring that, come the long wait in Arrivals, he will move as in treacle and feel like the pits. The small child beside him has a foot in his groin and one sticky hand on his new silk tie. He'd like to remove it but doesn't want to wake him. He looks so very like his own son did at that age.

In twenty or so minutes the plane will touch down. He's not only not slept, he has not eaten either. As the plane begins to make its final approach, his stomach lurches unpleasantly. He feels for his shoes with cold, sluggish feet and because they have told him to, squirms very gently, retrieves the warm buckle from under him, and does up his belt. He rubs his eyes and looks down at the quilt of landscape beneath him, bisected by a seaside rock ribbon of traffic, and punctuated, here and there, with small huddles of trees. Far beneath him grow clumps now of roofscape and garden. The odd swimming pool, stable, and pale, gravelled drive. The *faux*-rural backdrop of this part of Sussex. Scenery all at once familiar yet strange. They sink lower still. The rock splinters. Becomes car lights. The gardens get flowerbeds. The windows get curtains. He stretches his arms, scans the houses below him. It is five fifty two. Dawn is coaxing the sun up. He sees, very clearly, a light snapping off.

As the plane swoops silently over the north Sussex countryside, carrying Nick Brown to his tryst with a crisp cotton pillowslip in the North Terminal Meridien Hotel, Sally Matthews, chilly in a T-shirt and knickers, switches off the light and pads back to her bed. She has lain wide-eyed on the single bed in the spare room since three thirty, but must return to bear witness to the alarm clock, which will buzz its sharp greeting in seventy-eight minutes. By which time, she knows, she will be deeply asleep.

'Nnnnggch,' says her husband, Jonathan, exhaling. He has spiralled the duvet, swiss-roll style, around him.

Sally eases the remaining flap over her goose-pimpled legs. There is no duvet inside this bit of cover because the two are incompatible, the former a generous John Lewis cover, the latter a rather scant Debenham's quilt. The resultant deficit – a good twelve-inch strip along one side (always *her* side) – barely covers one leg. Were she to move across the bed and snuggle her cold body up to that of her husband, she could have filled duvet cover aplenty. But she can't do that or she will wake him. And if she wakes him he will be in a mood. And if he gets in a mood he will stay in a mood. So she stays where she is at the edge of the mattress, breathes lightly and quietly and tries not to fidget.

She lies there and looks out. Their bedroom, which is cool, spacious and full of heavy old pine furniture, has a large picture window. It doesn't afford quite the view of the skylight in the spare room, but from her place on the left of the marital bed, Sally can still see a big chunk of the night sky. It's cloudless and black and peppered with stars. Stars and planets and, presumably, comets. There's movement now, up there. Tiny, but actual. She fancies, as she tends to most nights, that she'll see one. A shooting star, shooting… to wherever stars shoot. But, no. Not tonight. There's a red light. An aircraft. Making arrow-straight progress across her window pane vista. A jumbo, she guesses. On its way into Gatwick.

It winks at her now as it passes.

Chapter I

It was magnificently starry, that Friday-night sky. A sky so densely studded with twinkles and sparkles and heavenly bodies that even the most dour and unimaginative person might find themselves pausing to draw breath in wonder. To marvel at the miracle of the universe before them. To muse on the breathtaking brilliance of space.

And there was me, Sally Matthews, forty one, very sleepy, slightly damp, somewhat peevish, forging my weary way along the B-roads of the Sussex countryside, to retrieve my darling daughter from her friend's house. Stargazer that I was, heavenly body I was not. Pausing to wonder I most *definitely* was not.

I remember I was very tired. Tired and rather irritable, to be honest, as I had been rudely interrupted from one of those aromatherapy candlelit baths magazines are always banging on about, and was not very pleased to be trolling across the county with still-soggy hair, a whiff of burned wax about me, and the remnants of a passion-fruit exfoliating face pack still clinging like bogies to all the chinks in my face.

I had taken Jonathan's car. Not because it made any difference, but partly because mine didn't have a lot of petrol in it, and mainly – OK, *wholly* because he didn't like me to drive it. It was an act of irritable defiance, because the two of us had just had a row. The sort of row you have when your teenage daughter phones you at God knows what hour in the morning and entreats you, in that special way daughters have, to please please please please please please *pleeeease* come and fetch her. Like *now*. You know the kind of thing.

'What the hell is she doing calling us at this hour?' he'd said.

'She wants me to go and pick her up.'

'What? *Now*? At this hour?'

'At this hour. She's had some sort of row with Amanda and wants to come home.'

'Well, she can't. I'm not having you traipsing off out at this hour.'

'So *you* go, then.'

'*Me* go? I've had best part of a bottle of claret!'

'Well one of us has to. I told her I would.'

'Well you can just go and untell her. She's nearly seventeen, for God's sake. She can stay there and lump it.'

'But I can't just leave her. She sounded upset.'

'Well tough, frankly. Sal, she'll *get over it*.'

'But I can't –'

'Yes you *can*. She runs rings round you. Why on earth did you say yes? She's got to learn that she can't expect –'

'I know I know I *know*! But she sounded really upset, and I don't want to think of her –'

'And doesn't she know it! Don't you realise –'

'Don't you *care*? Jonathan, don't you *care* that –'

'Oh, for God's sake, don't start! *Go*, then, Sal. *Go*. Do what you like!'

That kind of thing.

So I had thrown on pyjamas and a pair of battered Reeboks, and, pausing only to snatch up Kate's dreadful black cardigan, had stomped off into the night feeling martyred and angry while Jonathan stayed put and huffed in his chair.

The road was big, wide, empty, dark. All the sorts of things country roads generally are at night. It was flanked by tall trees, almost all in full leaf now, a dense black filigree against deep inky blue. I passed the garden centre, the garage that sells those dreadful flapjacks, and Mr Chip's olde worlde rocking-horse factory, before pulling off on to the long sinew of road that connected the real world to the chocolate-box village where Amanda's family lived. It's a road I've travelled many times over the years. Kate and Amanda having been friends all their lives. Hmm. Yeah, right. Until now.

I took the dog, of course. If I had to go galumphing about the countryside in the small hours on my own, it made sense to have something more ferocious on board than just the smell of Jonathan's sweaty cricket kit.

So there I was, muttering the sort of things mothers mutter when they know they've been slaves to their kids because they're slaves to their hormones, and fastening vaguely mutinous thoughts on my recalcitrant husband. And I didn't see him coming. Didn't see *it* coming. And if that sounds ambiguous and slightly portentous that's because, looking back, it's just how it was.

I had rounded a bend in the road, the trees giving way to an undulating hedgerow, and the tarmac now climbing, it seemed, right to the horizon and beyond. So much so, in fact, that at first I mistook the light on the brow of the hill for a star. I blinked at it. No, no. Not light. *Lights*. Another car, then. I flipped my headlights to dipped. The lights burned brighter, blotting the world out. Squinting now, I eased off my speed a little and waited for the other driver to switch their full beam off as well. But they didn't. Didn't seem to, at any rate. The illumination grew stronger. Whiter. The damp hair at my neck began to prickle. What on earth were they doing? I slowed even more. I could not see the road now – could not see a thing bar the twin orbs that were rapidly approaching, their halos growing brighter and increasingly blinding, second by shimmering second.

It was then that it struck me, with terrifying clarity: I was going to die. I was going to die at any moment. I was going to die, moreover, in a pair of tartan pyjamas and a grubby black cardigan. For whatever was attached to the headlights in front of me was actually driving on *my side of the road.*

I don't recall quite what it was that I did, only that self preservation must have kicked in and wrestled some sort of sense from the flapping of my arms. At any rate, a squeal, a swerve and a couple of bumps later, and I'd come to a shuddering ABS-enhanced stop, amid the wide swathe of lush and exuberant foliage that formed the verge that ran down the side of the road. The lights ahead vanished, having slewed off themselves now, and the carriageway appeared again, way over to my right.

For some seconds I stared at it, fish-eyed and speechless, then swivelled my head around and braced for the sound of an impact. The other car, for car it was, careered wildly but briefly, then came to an untidy stop at the edge of the other carriageway. Its tail lights burned a ruby glow on to my retinas. Merlin, displaced but apparently unmoved by his near-death experience, had hoisted a leg up and was scratching his ear.

'Jesus!' I squeaked to him. 'Ohmygod! Crikey! Jesus!' and lots of other stuff along the same lines. The car had stalled and I fumbled for the ignition. The headlamps both flickered as the engine roared briefly but, try as I might, I couldn't make it go. I could hear the wheels whizzing but the car *wouldn't go*. My hands and my legs had begun to shake uncontrollably. I looked back down the hill again. Nothing. No movement. No sound.

What should I do? I craned my neck to see. No impact. No visual evidence of a crash. Should I do something? Phone someone? Get out and go see? In my *pyjamas*? On my *own*? No, no. Phone someone. That was best. Call the police. God alone knew what sort of maniac was out there. A drunk driver most probably. That was it. So this was best. Don't get out. Getting out *very* stupid. Call the police. Stay in the car. Lock the car. Wait till they come. I unbuckled my seat-belt with trembling hands and groped in the passenger footwell for my bag. Call the police. That would be best. I rummaged in my bag in the darkness for my mobile, but my fingers were all wibbly and wobbly and useless. Where *was* the damn thing? I hauled my bag on to my lap. I was sure it was in there. I had definitely had it in there earlier. I looked behind me again. Still nothing. No movement. No sound. I threw the bag on the seat in disgust. And no *phone*. What now, then? Oh, God. What next? What next with no phone and a car that wouldn't go? And then a new thought popped up to fuel my rising panic further. Supposing the other driver was injured or something? Dead, even? Yikes. Supposing it wasn't a maniac at all? Supposing it was an old person? Supposing it was a septagenarian in a flat cap? Who'd *had a heart attack*? Or an epileptic fit? Or a stroke? Oh, God.

I could see the headline. 'Heartless Woman Leaves Injured Pensioner For Dead'. 'Merlin,' I said, reluctant but decided. 'We've got to get out. We've got to go and see if they're all right. Act fierce. Just in case. *Fierce*, OK? *Dangerous*.'

Merlin, ears pricked enquiringly, cocked his head to one side. I opened the car door. 'Go grrr. OK? Got it? "Grrrr". Nice and loud. Show your teeth.'

The night air was chilly and damp against my bare shins. Merlin, clearly pleased with the development of this unscheduled adventure, bounced out and sniffed the ground appreciatively. How I envied him his easy confidence. His complete lack of worry. So it was night time. What of it? Same as day time only darker. Oh, to be a stupid dog. I'd driven this road a thousand times before but for me it seemed suddenly unrecognisable. More bleak. More Jurassic. More remote. More dark.

More *scary*. I could see another headline: 'Defenceless Woman In Questionable Nightwear Raped and Pillaged and Left to Die in

Lane'. A weapon. I should at least have a weapon. I remembered Jonathan's cricket bat would be in the car too. His bat would do it. That would knock them for six. I ran around and hauled it from the boot.

'Right,' I hissed, clamping one hand around Merlin's collar and the other round the neck of the bat. 'You stay *right* by my side, OK? *Heel* and all that.'

It was only when we'd started off down the fifty or so yards of roadway to the other car that I noticed that something tangible had changed: the driver's door, previously closed, had swung open, and that the person inside seemed to be thrashing about. Person? Or *persons*? It was too dark to tell. There could be a car load. Of drug addicts, criminals, people having sex. I closed my fingers tighter still round Merlin's collar. He was straining against it and pulling me with him – keen to get to his quarry and lick them to death, no doubt. The thrashing continued. I could make out an elbow. Maybe, I thought, in appalled fascination, the driver was having a heart-attack *now*.

God, I hoped not. I drew a little nearer. Near enough to see, with some relief, that the struggle taking place was not so much medical or sexual as one of a basically technical kind: the unmistakeable jerking and pulling and grunting of someone who couldn't get their seat-belt undone. I drew nearer still, Merlin whining beside me, and heard 'bloody thing! Wretched – bah! Will you – Jeez!' Then an elbow shot out, then a leg, then another and, with a clunk and a scuffle, the driver got out.

A *male* driver. Oh, cripes. I was very, very frightened. What now, then? I wondered. Set the dog on him? Run for it? Stand in the middle of the carriageway and scream? Running seemed foolhardy (I had not laced my trainers) and screaming was pointless. Who the hell was going to hear? So I opted for releasing my hand from Merlin's collar and adopting a baseball-style stance with the bat .

The man (who was man-like – that is, substantially taller and stronger than I was, which was all I really needed to know) came loping towards me, saying 'Please! It's OK! Don't panic!' while Merlin bounded in energetic circles around him, in the hope, I suspected, that he might have a stick.

'Don't *panic*?' I yelled, swishing the willow around and trying to sound fierce on Merlin's behalf. 'What the hell d'you think you were doing? You could have killed me!'

He stopped a prudent few feet from me, bathed in shadow. 'I know. I'm so *sorry*. Are you all right?'

What do you do? What do you do when you're standing in the middle of the road in the middle of the night in the middle of nowhere with no one around and a man, who just drove down your side of the road and nearly killed you and who looks big and strong and who might be a lunatic, is standing there and saying 'are you all right?' and all you're in is a pair of ridiculous pyjamas and an undertaker's cardigan and your dog thinks he's got a bit-part in *The Waltons*? What do you *do*? I could hear Merlin's tail thumping enthusiastically against the leg of the man's jeans. The man himself stood and waited – brow slightly furrowed, arms hanging – for whatever he had coming. Be it sensible answer or thwack on the head.

I clutched the bat tighter. 'Of course I'm all right!' I snapped. 'I'd hardly be standing here if I wasn't, would I?'

'Well, that's a relief, at least. But your car,' he glanced past my shoulder. 'Is your car all right? It seems to have run off the road.'

'Of course it's run off the road! You were driving straight at me! MERLIN! HEEL! What on earth did you think you were *doing*?'

The man, who looked even bigger and stronger at this range, came a step closer. I could see him better now.

'I don't *know,*' he said, pocketing his car keys and spreading his palms in apology. 'I got lost. I *am* lost. I took a wrong turn half an hour back and I've been driving round and round ever since. Jeez, it's like a maze round here. No signs. No lights –'He drew the back of his hand across his forehead '– and, well, I 'm just plain tired, I guess. I think I must have forgotten where I was. I don't know. I really don't. I'm *so* sorry. Thank God you're OK, is all. Look, shall I come and take a look or something?' He eyed the bat nervously. 'You *sure* you're OK?' His accent was strange. I couldn't quite place it. Not local. Merlin licked his hand.

'I'm OK,' I said, lowering my weapon a fraction. My terror was beginning to quieten a little. He didn't *look* like he wanted to kill me. And, anyway, what choice did I have? 'Actually, no,' I said. 'I'm not OK. I'm stuck. I mean the car is stuck. In the mud, I think. So, yes. Would you do that, please?'

'Absolutely. Right away,' he said. He nodded and started off back up the road, giving the bat a wide berth.

OK. So he wasn't going to kill me, but things still didn't look promising. The verge was one of those ones thoughtfully flagged up by signs saying 'soft' to dissuade drivers from using them to picnic and frolic and so on. Those lucky enough not to have been barged into one, that is. It was wide and deep, curving down away from the road towards what looked like a brook or a stream and, at this time of year, a profusion of meadowgrass, cow parsley and prehistoric bindweed. All very pretty, all very pastoral, all somewhat unsuited to two tons of car.

'Hmm,' he said, frowning, as I joined him among the dewy stalks. The air was thick with midges and heavy with scent. It had rained heavily in the last few days, and the ground beneath my feet felt swampy and squelchy. I bent to tuck in my trainer laces, in case a slug or spider tried to hitch a lift. His mouth twitched in amusement.

'Look, why don't you get back in?' he suggested. 'You must be frozen in those.'

I pulled the edges of my cardigan together with a huff and got back into the car.

He moved away, round to the far wing, folding his cuffs back as he went. Tan jacket. I thought. Suede. Pale jeans. Tall. About six two. Six three. A stone coloured shirt. He crouched down. Dark hair. A definite wave. Fairly short. Square jaw. Should I write this all down or something? He stood up again. Absently ruffled Merlin's head. A thick metal watch strap gleamed at his wrist. Then he was back at the window. Late thirties. Early forties. Not drunk. Not disorderly. Insane? I didn't think so. Except in the matter of steering, perhaps.

I pressed the button and lowered the window.

'Yup,' he said. 'It's your nearside wheel that's the problem. Pretty boggy down there.' No gust of alcohol. A faint trace of some sort of aftershave, perhaps. 'It looks well bedded in. I've rammed a bunch of grass and stuff under the wheel. D'you want to hop over and let me to have a try for you, maybe?'

Did I? Should I? Was it safe? Wasn't there even now the tiniest chance he might speed me away and rape me? Kill me? And then slay Merlin too? Surely not. *Surely* not. His shirt was from Gap.

But even so…'No, no,' I said. 'I'll do it.'

'OK, hang on,' he said, stepping back and hopping around to the front again as I fired the ignition. I put the car into gear and eased off on the clutch. The wheels did a lurch and the tyre went *zzzzwweeeee*. Mud flew in quantity. The car didn't move.

Seconds later he was back at the window, the look on his face grim, the scene on his jeans grimmer still. They looked like a post-modern art installation. 'No go,' he said, appearing not to notice. 'It's really swampy down there. That's just made it worse. We need better traction. I'll go and see what I can find.'

Traction? Of course. I wasn't thinking straight. For the tyre to grip. Without another word, he straddled the stream and plunged off into the undergrowth. I could make out his tall form disappearing into a gap in the hedgerow. I was growing anxious now about the time. I checked the clock on the dashboard. Twenty past one. A good forty minutes since Kate had called me. She'd be fretting by now. And if she fretted too much, she'd call home. And Jonathan, assuming he bothered to wake up at all, of course, would start fretting and flapping as well. There was no sign of the man and no sign of Merlin. Where had they gone to? Brazil?

He emerged moments later with two big armfuls of twigs and stems and God knew what. He looked a little like a trapper on a trap-setting jaunt. Merlin, who was a pointer and had jaws built for no-nonsense pheasant retrieval, was trotting alongside, log in mouth. What a fine old time he was having. I could see the tip of his tail – I'd refused to have it docked – flip-flapping, wiper style, while the man crouched down to tuck the foliage under the wheel. I continued to sit, in my pyjamas and cardigan, and ponder the hopeful possibility that I was dreaming.

'OK,' he said at last. 'That ought to do it. You want to give it another try? While I get round the back and push?'

He looked so much the good – if somewhat grubby – Samaritan, that I almost found myself apologising for inconveniencing him. He braced his hands against the boot. I gave it another try. The wheels spun some more.

'Whoah!' he called. I took my foot off the accelerator.

'No good,' he said, back at the window once more. 'We need better grip. This stuff is all soaking. It's just turning to mush. And I don't have enough strength on my own to give it any momentum. Hmm…'

'Could I come round the back and help push, maybe?'

He looked at me sideways and grinned. 'Er, not unless Merlin here has his driver's licence, I don't think.'

'No, no,' I said. 'I meant couldn't we take the handbrake off and just, well, push it a little way with the engine off?' I didn't mean this at all. A car this size? In a hole? Up a hill? Him and puny little me? It was a ridiculous suggestion. But not quite as ridiculous as my actual one so it would have to do.

'We-ell, *may*be' he said politely. Then, 'Got it! Car mats. Rubber. That'll do it.'

'Car mats?'

'Car mats! I'll go off and get them. Stay right there.'

Yeah, *right*. As if I was going anywhere. I got back into the car and glanced at the clock again. Almost one thirty now. And getting colder as well. The dew had seeped into my trainers and the bottoms of my pyjama legs felt like soggy wallpaper against my shins. I saw him returning in the wing mirror, the mats from his car flopping heavily at his side. He went straight around to the side of mine and crouched down to arrange them. His profile, sharp against the light from the headlamps, was angular, masculine. The sort of profile that would work well at the helm of a ship. The sort of profile that gets labelled 'heroic'. I shivered. This was really not pyjama weather. I hoped the rest of the package was too.

'That's it,' he called at last, opening the passenger door. He braced his shoulder against the door frame. 'Right. D'you want to give it another try? Nice and slowly this time, OK? Slow as you can.' I started the engine again and pressed down gingerly on the accelerator. The wheel spun briefly and I slammed on the brake.

''S OK,' he said, leaning out to make an inspection. 'That's just the mud on the wheel there.' His hand was clamped around the top of the door and I could see a fat gold band on his little finger. 'OK,' he said. 'Go again. You're almost there.'

I pressed down the accelerator, millimetre by agonising millimetre, and was rewarded by forward motion at last. Conscious of his shoulder still braced against the door frame, I eased all four wheels slowly back up on to the road. The passenger door clunked shut and I waited, engine idling, while he moved to my side of the car. He opened the rear door to let Merlin scramble in.

'There you go,' he said, leaning in and adopting the sort of expression men just can't help adopting when they've prevailed, in their manly way, over disaster. His hands, I noticed, were wet and streaked with mud too, and there were grass flecks and burrs all over his jacket and shirt. He looked about as menacing as Worzel Gummidge. The only danger he'd be, I decided, was to a washing machine filter.

'Oh, dear. You're filthy,' I said. 'Do you want a Wet One?'

His brows lifted. 'A *what*?'

'A wipe,' I said, reaching into the glove compartment. 'To clean your hands up a bit.'

He smiled at me, then, revealing perfect white teeth. I always notice teeth, Jonathan being a dentist. Along with eyes, naturally, and his were very striking, even in the darkness. Forget-me-not blue. Thick, heavy lashes. 'No, no. No problem,' he said, rubbing his palms vigorously against his already filthy jeans. 'I'm just fine. Really. Look, d'you want to take a note of my number or something? I don't think there's any damage, but you might have a scratch or two underneath all the mud. Difficult to tell in the dark.' He shook his head and then looked straight at me. 'Jesus, I am *so* sorry.' He looked it too. Looked appalled, all of a sudden. As if the enormity of what might have been had suddenly slapped him around the face. He looked, I decided, like an OK kind of person. I wondered, for all his no-nonsense can-do efficiency, if he wasn't a little in shock.

'Well,' I said, allowing a small smile to reassure him. 'No harm done. But yes. You're right. I should take your number.'

He nodded. 'I'll go fetch my insurance details, shall I? Be right back.'

I watched him stride off to his car again. Merlin yawned extravagantly from the back seat. The crescent moon looked on benignly. I could see Betelgeuse peeking at me through a gap in the distant trees. I wondered where he had come from. I wondered where he was going. I *think* (though I suspect this is hindsight in action) that I wondered, even then, about life's chance encounters, and how strange it was to think that I'd probably never see him again.

'There you go,' he said, handing me the torn away top half of a copy of a car-rental agreement. His writing was upright and spiky. A hired car. He obviously wasn't local, just as I'd thought. 'There's my name,' he said, pointing. 'And that's my mobile number there, and that number on the top is the rental-firm agreement number, I think. Anyhow, if you need the insurance, I'm sure they'll sort it out. Shall I take yours?'

Jonathan was paranoid about giving out our home phone number, so I gave him my mobile number instead. He wrote it down carefully on the copy in his hand. 'Right,' he said. 'Any problems, just call me, OK?' He proffered his hand through the window. I shook it. It was strong and cool.

'Nick,' he said. 'Well, like I say, I'm really sorry.' He grinned wryly. 'But it's certainly been a pleasure to meet you.'

'Sally,' I said back, feeling strangely discomfited by the way he was looking at me. 'Yes,' I said, returning his gaze for half a second longer than my brain had been expecting. 'You too. Nice to meet you as well.'

'So,' he said. 'Like I say, *any* problem, just call.'

'OK,' I said. 'I'll do that. Thank you.'

And then he was gone. And it was only when I was almost at Amanda's house that I realised I hadn't given him any directions. That he still didn't know how to get where he was going. That he was still lost.

It played on my mind. Not a lot. Just a little. Just enough that perhaps I should have read something into it. But I wouldn't have, would I? Not at that point I wouldn't. Because at that point I didn't have the benefit of hindsight. If I had, I might have realised what now seems so obvious. That, as of that starry night, I was lost too.

Chapter 2

'What the hell have you been doing with my car?'

So. Here we were again. Saturday morning. Saturday morning in the jolly Matthews household.

Ah. And Jonathan was up.

By the time I had collected Kate and driven us home, it was getting on for half past two in the morning. I had told her what had happened, I had ranted at her selfishness, I had blathered on about responsibility, I had wittered about consideration and I had droned about inches and miles and all the other dreary parenting staples I'd always promised I wouldn't utter but which spewed unbidden from my lips with ever more depressing frequency these days. Mainly I had pointed out that her father would be furious, and serve her right if he grounded her for what was left of the weekend. But by the time we swung into the driveway, the house was in darkness and Jonathan was in bed. No surprise there, then, I remember thinking fleetingly. Did he never worry about us? Me? Ever? At all?

But a good night's sleep, at least; just the one hour awake. Clearly an adrenaline-filled off-road experience with a handsome stranger was just the ticket, insomnia-wise. I flipped the duvet from over my face and squinted away the sunshine. He was standing at the foot of the bed, holding two mugs of tea and scowling at me. 'Well?'

I shuffled reluctantly up to a sitting position. Not quite eight thirty yet. Saturday morning. Some cricket match or other seemed to ring a distant bell. Along with Morgan's wedding – an ever present tinkling. I had, I recalled dimly, a cake woman to see.

'I had an accident,' I said. I wanted to add 'not that you much cared, obviously.' But I didn't. Because to do so would simply etch a cluster of new lines to join the ones already drawn over his shaggy iron brows. He was bear-like. Grizzly. Although he spent much of his life wielding a drill, his young female patients fell in love with him, always. As had I once. It seemed a long time ago.

A grizzly bear with a chronically sore head. 'An *accident*?' he said, switching from scowl to incredulous stare. The lines re-convened into train tracks on his forehead. 'Accident?' he said again. 'Christ! What sort of accident?'

'An accidental sort of accident. A minor accident. Not even an accident at all, in fact. I was just run off the road and the car got stuck in the verge.'

'Run off the *road*?'

I told him what happened.

He shook his head and puffed out his cheeks. I hadn't heard him shower but he obviously had, for he was already dressed. He had the good grace to look concerned, even if largely, I suspect, for the welfare of the car.

'Well,' he said, putting his mug on the ottoman and showering the floor with the athlete's foot powder he sprinkled all over the place every morning for the fairy dust-queen to deal with. 'I just hope you realise that's *exactly* why you shouldn't have gone out to fetch her in the first place. Ridiculous to put yourself in such a vulnerable position. You could have been killed. Why on earth didn't you phone me?'

In every event, a lesson. I laid supplicant's hands on the duvet in front of me. 'What good would that have done? You couldn't drive. You said so. Anyway, I didn't have my phone.'

Stupid admission. I never seemed to learn. 'Didn't have your *phone*?' He rolled his eyes. 'Sally, how could you even *think* of charging off in the middle of the night without your phone? God! That's exactly why you should have listened to me in the first place! You could have been out there all night! God only knows what might have happened to you! I mean the man might have been some sort of lunatic! IS some sort of lunatic, by the sound of it.'

'I don't think so. He was very helpful, as it happens.'

'Very *helpful*? I'll give him helpful! I hope you got his number –'

'I got his number.'

'Because I've a good mind to get on to him right now and give him a piece of my mind!'

Though grateful for his concern, I found myself more than a little anxious to forestall such an event. 'Please don't do that, Jonathan. It was an accident. He was very sorry.'

I picked up my mug and took a sip of the contents. It was tepid and treacly.

'I should damn well think so! And all because you will insist on running around after that girl all the time! She runs rings round you! At her beck and call every moment of the day. It's no wonder she takes advantage.'

At least some of this was true so I didn't even bother to try and formulate a response. Which was fine, because he hadn't finished ranting at me anyway.

'What *is* it with her?' he rattled on. 'We never had all this nonsense with Morgan!'

Morgan being our eldest. Or more specifically, *his* eldest, Jonathan having been married before. His first wife, Tricia, had died in a car accident. Morgan had been three when Jonathan and I met. Just four when I became her new mum. And he was right. We *hadn't* had these problems with Morgan. Because Morgan was an altogether different kind of girl. Not better. Just different. Just less headstrong and feisty. And not the youngest, which everyone knew made a difference. I glowered into my mug and knew exactly what he was thinking. That Kate was only more trouble than Morgan because of her complement of renegade genes. I glowered at him too. 'She's just a *teenager*, Jonathan. For goodness' sake, that's what they're *like*.'

'Only because you spoil her,' he huffed. 'What that girl needs is to learn her lesson once in a while. So she can bloody well get her backside out of bed and go down and clean my car for me. *Kate*!'

He marched out of the bedroom and stomped across the landing.

'And I broke both legs, thank you for asking,' I muttered. I turned over in bed and tried to go back to sleep.

Chapter 3

They say that all sorts of things are written in the stars. Which is an appealing idea, but more than a little woolly in the facts department. Stars are beautiful, heart-stopping, stunningly mysterious. But the notion that life is somehow celestially governed is something I never had much truck with.

It was beguiling, certainly, to think that my brush with mortality that Friday night had a whiff of the supernatural about it, enticing to think that my chance meeting with a handsome stranger was something other than, well, simple chance. But pondering such abstracts simply because a certain someone has fetched up in your thoughts rather a lot is kooky and daft. Goodness, I thought, as I drove into work on Monday morning, I'd be reading my horoscope next.

Or maybe not. Fate was for fatalists, not pragmatists. And I was most definitely the latter. I became an optometrist, for instance, not because of any celestial career guidance, but because I had developed a debilitating crush on a boy called Kevin in the sixth form at school, and optometry just so happened to be what *he* was going to do. Dreadful to think that such major life choices are often made in such a haphazard and arbitrary way. As it was, he didn't get a place on the course, and by that time I had grown weary of carting so much unreciprocated adoration around with me anyway. But it turned out OK. I liked my job, as it happened. I liked the way it was so complex and interesting and varied, yet still so reassuringly day-to-day samey.

Or had been, until just lately.

I worked at a place called Amberley Park, some six or so miles from Gatwick airport. Originally the site of a minor stately home, it was now home to a stately state-of-the-art retail development, which had risen phoenix-like from the ashes of aristocracy and had everything the proletariat could hope to find in such a place. The biggest stores, the biggest car park, the biggest food court, the biggest fountains, the biggest (the *vilest*) plastic palm trees imaginable, all stylishly stashed under one cavernous roof. Specifically, it was home to the biggest branch of Sandals the chemists, in which Sandals Opticians resided. Of which, at that moment, I was senior optometrist. Perhaps not the loftiest of career peaks, admittedly, but I was happy enough. Or had been. We'd recently been swallowed up (though their words had been 'merged with') by the Drug U Like group, an aggressively expansive American chain, who had all sorts of plans for our retailing future, ambitions that it seemed did not necessarily include me.

'The R word,' hissed Ruth, when we met up in the cloakroom. 'It's been said. It's for definite, mark my words.'

She announced this dramatically, as was entirely usual. My friend Ruth, in her spare time, was a writer of fiction. When she wasn't stocktaking, or doing contact lens fittings or (more usually) chatting up reps, she was busy selling stories to women's magazines. I sometimes wondered if she didn't live her whole life practising snatches of portentous dialogue.

'R word?' I asked. I was busy checking the list in the back of my diary. '*Speak to caterer/ think table plan/ arrange date for b.maid fitting (v.imp!!!)/ buy dog food.*' I was just trying to work out quite why it was that I'd recently scribbled down '*ring my MP'*.

Ruth loomed in front of me. '*Redundancy*, Sally.'

I glanced up now. 'What? You're kidding.' I recalled the letter I'd been sent by Drug U Like the previous week. It had alluded to the prospect of changes, certainly. But career options, it had said. Not redundancy. Redundancy had never occurred to me.

She shook her head. 'Wish I was, but I'm not, I'm afraid. Russell heard Dennis banging on about it in the staff room on Friday.'

Russell was one of the other three optometrists. In his words, a chick magnet. In mine, a big wuss. But a nice enough one. We got along OK.

Ruth slammed her locker door shut and moved away to the basins, twisting up a fat plummy lipstick as she went.

'So that's me, then,' she added, puckering her generous lips at the mirror. 'Last in, first out, is my guess.'

I didn't want Ruth to go. Ruth didn't have a job title as such. She'd been originally brought in as an optical assistant, but in the three years she'd been here, she'd taken over pretty much everything not done by one of us, and a good bit of that stuff as well. Without her, the practice would soon collapse into chaos.

'But they can't do that,' I said. 'I'm sure they can't do that. There was that agreement, wasn't there? I'm sure there was.'

She jiggled the lipstick lid at me. 'Oh, yes. But that's not worth the paper it's written on. You watch. It'll be all jolly-pals-from-across-the-pond stuff this evening, but you mark my words. Give it a month and it'll be "off you go, then", or a stint on the tills down in Sanitary Protection. No thank *you*. No. I'll take the redundancy money and go write my novel. You'll be all right, though.' She made a kiss at the mirror. 'They'll hang on to you. You're not sales staff, of course. Mind you, I wouldn't rule out rollerblades.'

'Rollerblades? What on earth are you talking about?'

'Well, you know Americans. Anything you can sell you can sell faster on wheels. Mark my words. Just a matter of time.'

To help facilitate the forward momentum of the Sandals/Drug U Like union, the entire staff of Sandals' southern division had been asked to attend an evening meeting at a swanky hotel just outside Horley. A team-building (oh, how I would come to rue that expression) meeting, to enable, so the memo had enthusiastically promised, us 'folks' to get to know each other better.

We'd arrived, in wary dribbles, and been welcomed effusively. There were no wheels in evidence, but there was instead a reception, which was useful in that it enabled us folks to understand that the Drug U Like folks had deemed us the sort of people for whom the cocktail onion and the Twiglet would be the snack foods of choice. This would be followed, we were told, by a short presentation, which presumably would also be useful in that it would enable the Drug U Like folk to ease us gently along the rocky road to retail enlightenment without the need for leg irons or prescription drugs. To that end, we were ushered into some sort of conference facility with floor to ceiling, wall to wall midnight blue drapes, behind which pinpoints of light twinkled gaily. Things didn't look promising. At our seats were some shocking pink Drug U Like folders. Plus a Drug U Like pencil and Drug U Like pen. There was also a shocking pink Drug U Like bum-bag, which proved, once unzippered, to be positively bursting with similarly hued and badged Drug U Like stuff. A Lip U Like chapstick, some Sun U Like suncream, a Smooth U Like razor and some Legs U Like tights.

In American tan, naturally.

‘Christ,’ observed Russell, who was rummaging beside me. ‘What’s this thing then? A Shag U Like jonnie?’

A head swivelled in front of us. ‘You’re kidding,’ I said.

‘I sure hope so,’ he answered, fingering it gingerly. ‘No, no. Don’t panic. Another girl-thing I think. A ‘breathable Soft U Like scented whisper,’ it says here. A *what?*’

I pulled mine from my bum-bag.‘It’s a panty pad, Russell.’

‘So why can’t it say so?’

‘Because it’s American,’ said Ruth. ‘Americans,’ she explained, ‘for all their in-yer-face manner are actually the most Victorian people on the planet. Everyone knows that. Hold up, guys. Here comes the posse.’

A group of half a dozen men and women with clipboards and perfect teeth were beginning to take their seats on the stage, behind a long table which was dotted with flagons of water and swathed in a monogrammed shocking pink cloth. Around us a laser-driven Drug U Like logo was drifting bumper car-style off the walls and floor. The lights began to dim. Strident music began to play. I began to regret my last tumbler of juice.

Plunged into sudden blackness, it occurred to me that this was a little like a Disneyland ride. Perhaps the floor would move. Perhaps dinosaurs would poke heavy green heads from the folds in the curtains and snort corpse-flavoured breath into the audience. Russell groaned. ’Stand by. It’s Crap U Like showtime.’ He started idly unwrapping his Teeth U Like gum.

But there were no dinosaurs. Just a short film about Drug U Like’s illustrious (boring) history, and a preponderance of rhetoric about how nice they all were. Drug U Like were, it explained to us, everything a Drugstore should be Wholesome. Principled. Uncompromising on pricing.

And, of course, pink.

The presentation over, the lights blinked back on again, and a short man in a pink shirt took up his place at the podium. He thanked us all warmly for coming along. We would, he hoped, work with our Drug U Like colleagues to ensure a smooth and comradely transitional phase. There was no mention of redundancies, though lots of other R words. Like rationalization, re-organization, remits, re-structuring, reconnaissance and rout, which were plopped into his speech at regular intervals, seemingly regardless of whether they’d fit.

‘So,’ he said, beaming at the largely stupefied audience. ‘It’s question time now, folks. Who’s going to be first up?’

There was a lengthy silence, overlaid with a variety of tracheal manoeuvres.

‘Come on, guys. Shoot!’ he tried. Nobody shot.

‘How’s about a –’

A hand surfaced up in the front row.

‘Yes, *sir*,’ he said brightly, flapping his clipboard.

‘I was wondering if your plans encompass any initiative for installing a new vending machine in the gent’s toilet,’ a man said.

Nobody tittered. Somebody sneezed.

‘I’m glad you asked that,’ he said, with admirable earnestness. ‘We have a focus group, right now, on to human resource management. Staff welfare is one of our number one thrusts.’

Finally, We were allowed out, and encouraged to return to the function room, where we were split into more focus groups, where there would be an opportunity to put questions in a less formal environment. Hopefully, one that wasn’t pink. We would then re-convene for the vast buffet supper that was already being trolleyed in around us.

Russell sniffed his way past it. ‘Well, that was pretty excruciating, wasn’t it? I don’t know about you guys, but I need a decent drink. Shall we slink off and get a beer at the hotel bar?’

It was our habit to go for a drink after work on Mondays. On Monday night Jonathan always stayed up in London, and Kate rehearsed with her dance troupe.

‘Ooh, I don’t know,’ said Ruth, who was becoming rather pink herself and had affixed her bum bag around her middle as a gesture of support. ‘I’d quite like to stick around here for a while, actually. Can’t hurt to get a better look at the enemy, can it? Sal? You staying here? Yes? Get me one in while I zip to the loo.’

I left Russell to ferret out a Foster’s pump somewhere and headed back to the function room. By now, lubricated by wine and free toiletries, people were beginning to mill with markedly more enthusiasm. Edging my way towards the already crowded bar area I wondered about Ruth’s observation that I was not sales staff. It seemed to me she was wrong on that count. Everyone seemed to be sales staff in the Drug U Like culture. Everyone united with the single ambition of getting our wares sold and cash in the till. I wondered about the likes of some of our elderly patients. All the pensioners, clutching their NHS vouchers, for whom a trip for new glasses was a rare day out. What would happen to the service we provided for *them*? Shoved in, back to back, between sunglasses promotions and two for one frames deals and contact-lens sales. I spotted our manager, Dennis, deep in conversation with the blonde from the podium. His gentle nudges about productivity seemed suddenly rather benign.

Ruth, impatient with my shuffling progress towards the tepid *vin de pays*, grabbed two glasses of some murky fruit cocktail from a circling waiter and downed half of hers at a stroke. 'Well isn't this jolly?' she said. 'I'm kind of warming to all these thrusting Americans, aren't you? Oh, I know the bottom line is going to be hassle and ridiculous sales initiatives and the demise of the entire Anglo-Saxon culture as we know it and everything, but it makes a change, doesn't it? All grist to the novelist's mill.'

I didn't know about grist, but I wasn't sure about the making of changes . I didn't like change as a rule.

'Anyway, she went on, 'lets mingle, shall we? You can't deny there's some decent talent knocking about here. Let's put ourselves about a bit, shall we? I think the optoms are meeting in that room over there.' She gestured. 'Oh, and guess what?' She gave me a nudge. 'I've already clocked the prototype model for the Hunk U Like range.'

'The what?'

'A vision,' she said, scouring the headscape and grinning like a mad person. 'A vision of what?'

She sighed extravagantly. 'A vision of *utter* shagability, Sal. Let's just say,' she added, dipping her glistening lips to my earlobe, 'that he can bundle me into a darkened room and check out my prescription *anytime*.' 'Ah! Look sharp,' she hissed suddenly, poking me. 'If I'm not mistaken, it's heading our way.'

'*What's* heading our way? '

'The guy I just saw, stupid! Hunk U Like, Shag U Like, Snog U Like – uh oh! And coming up behind you. Ten past two.'

What? She thrust out an arm. 'Hello. Ruthie Preston, optometry sales management.'

Ruthie? Optometry sales management? Eh? I was just wondering quite where she dredged that one up from, when a long male, suited arm extended from behind me.

I swivelled. 'Hello there,' he said. 'I'm Nick Brown.'

It took about two seconds for the name and face to register. One more, at any rate, than it took him to say, 'Well, well! We meet again, Sally!' Then, 'Is Sally OK with you?' with that sing-song, unusual accent he had. I extended my own arm and he shook my hand firmly. 'What a very, very pleasant surprise!'

He'd remembered my name. 'Sally's fine,' I said, feeling myself go the colour of the punch. For what reason I knew not. But go it I did.

'Oh! You two know each other, do you?' said Ruth, looking confused and a little peeved. I was still blinking under the intense blue of his gaze.

'In a way,' he went on. 'We met on Friday night. Though I have to say, Sally, I almost didn't recognise you with your clothes on.'

I couldn't think of anything witty to say in response to this, so I ended up just smiling stupidly at him while the blush slithered on down my neck.

'Actually, that's not true,' he went on, gesturing towards me with his glass and grinning. 'I recognised you straight away. But I couldn't place you. No cricket bat tonight. It was the absence of a cricket bat that had me stumped.'

'Gracious!' said Ruth, spluttering though her mouthful of drink and gaping in mock horror. 'Shouldn't you carry a licence for jokes that bad? And is someone going to fill me in here, or what?'

'Ruth, Nick's the man I told you about. The accident?'

'Aha!' she said. 'What a turn up! So it was *you*, was it?' She poked him.

'Guilty as charged,' he said, dipping his head. His hair ran in waves across the top of his head. Like sand once the tide's out, only glossy and milk-chocolate brown.

'You found your way home then?' I said.

'Eventually,' he answered. 'By way of Croydon and Horsham.'

'Croydon? You're kidding!' I said.

He sipped his drink and winked.

'Ri-ight,' said Ruth, poking at the ice in her glass now instead and pushing her chest out a bit. 'American. Got it. So that would explain why you were driving on the wrong side of the road.'

I was still two seconds behind. Of course. Of *course*. He nodded and flicked his eyes back and forth between us. I felt suddenly rather awful that I'd told Ruth about it. As if I'd broken a confidence. Talked about him behind his back.

'Kind of, I guess,' he said ruefully. 'Though I'm not American, as it happens. English by birth. I've been out there twenty odd years now, though.' Which would explain his strange accent. 'And here I am. Back. Another drink, anyone, before we go in?'

Our focus group – the eight staff that made up Sandals Opticians at Amberley park, together with those from our neighbouring branches – clustered self-consciously in the small conference room that was to play host to our meeting. As well as Nick Brown, who was introduced formally as their UK Optometry Human Resources Development Co-ordinator (which was why his badge just said Nick Brown, I supposed), there was an Area Director, who introduced himself as Donald, and who started by reassuring us all firmly that nothing dreadful was about to happen. Which, we quietly agreed, meant it probably was.

But I recall little of what he said after that. I will confess that even at this early stage I was so distracted by the strange sensation that had come over me as a consequence of meeting Nick Brown again, that I took no notice whatsoever of anything that was said and had to have Ruth fill me in via whispers. I didn't see it like that *then* of course. But it's all too obvious now.

He caught up with me again back in reception.

'Everything OK with your car, then?' he asked me.

I nodded, feeling shy. 'The car is fine.'

'And you too?'

'Yes. Quite OK, thanks.'

'And here you are again.' His eyes narrowed as he smiled. 'And you work for Sandals. Your friend is right. What a turn up.'

I gestured at his pink badge. 'And you work for Drug U Like.'

'Hmm. Guilty again.'

'Guilty?'

He cast an eye over the sea of heads. 'I'm not getting a terrifically good vibe here this evening. I'm not sure the UK is quite ready for the Drug U Like approach to retail.'

'It's just the uncertainty, I suppose. No one's really sure what's going to happen. What *is* going to happen? Is it true about there being redundancies?'

He narrowed his eyes further. His suit, I noticed, was of some soft floppy fabric, and his tie wasn't pink, but the colour of his eyes . 'I probably know no more than you do,' he said. 'A lot will depend on what happens with the pilot stores. There'll be some relocations, no doubt. But that's not my primary remit. '

Corporate speak. More of those R-words. Good. I felt a whole lot less flustered talking shop. 'And your remit is what?'

'To set up the new optom division here, initially. Rationalise our resources. Team-build. Put systems in place. Bring a little good ol' Drug U Like magic to the unsuspecting people of Sussex.' He grinned. 'That kind of thing.'

His tone, I noticed, was ironic. 'So. Rollerblades it is, then,' I said, draining my drink.

'Rollerblades?'

'My friend Ruth seems to think the Drug U Like culture will involve spectacle sales on wheels. Please tell me it isn't true.'

'Ah,' he said, frowning. 'No can do, I'm afraid. We set a lot of store by innovation. It's what keeps us one step ahead.' I wondered if this might be a good moment to ask where he stood on the business of our role in delivering a healthcare service, and quite where he felt aggressive sales initiatives might play a part in the nation's optical health. 'It's a tight market,' he went on, answering my question. 'Complacency is not a sound business strategy.'

I twiddled my glass, unsure whether he was teasing me or not. 'So it's not as outlandish a suggestion as I thought, then?'

'Not at all.' He sounded like he meant it. 'Which is not to say I'm about to put it to committee. But believe me, I've seen way more radical initiatives. And where's the problem anyway? I mean, not roller blades specifically, but where's the problem with providing a first rate service at a competitive price? That's all we're about really, you know.'

'Not multi-million dollar profits, then?'

He looked entirely unfazed. Even a little amused. He waved an arm expansively. 'Sure, profits. We're a business. But I don't see why that has to be at odds with a public service ethos. And, hey, let's not be disingenuous here. Sandals are a profit making concern too, you know. And you work for a salary, don't you?'

'Yes of course I do. But I also think there's a danger of people like myself becoming ever more compromised by commercial imperatives. It's already happening as it is.' I stopped then, because I was beginning to sound like a crusty old bag. He was nodding politely and waiting for me to say more. I couldn't think of anything. I was suddenly all at sea again.

'Absolutely,' he said helpfully. 'I see what you say. Though I have to tell you, I'm *sure* you'll like the uniform. It's shocking pink of course, and perhaps a *little* on the short side, but eye-catching certainly, and it comes with this little embroidered name badge on the pocket, and –'

'Uniform?' I spluttered. 'But I'm an optometrist! I don't wear a uniform!'

'Ah,' he said, scratching his chin thoughtfully. '*Ah*. So they didn't tell you about that?'

'You're kidding!' I said. 'You can't *seriously* expect –'

He looked at me gravely. 'Do I *look* like I'm kidding?' He frowned again. 'Oh, forgive me, Sally. Can I get you another drink? Something to eat?'

'Um…yes. Yes, OK. A drink. Some more juice.' I handed him my glass. 'But you *are* kidding, aren't you?'

'Of course,' he said, winking. 'Don't move. Be right back.'

I watched him weave smoothly through all the bodies to the bar.

A strange tingle passed through me. The hand of destiny, maybe? No. That was rubbish. It was simple coincidence. But rather nice, rather thrilling, for all that.

Chapter 4

'So your maniac motorist's an optometrist too, is he?' asked Ruth, as we hurtled over the Gatwick flyover and surged down to join the traffic on the road back towards East Grinstead . It was just beginning to get dark and the street lamps were burning salmon against the greying sky.

'I don't know, as it happens. I suppose he might be. But I don't think so. He's Human Resources, isn't he? Which I suppose means personnel.'

'Well, whoopy-do! Our lucky day then, methinks. *My* lucky day, at any rate. He can push me off the straight and narrow any old time he likes.' She screeched to a halt at the traffic lights and stretched her neck to check her lipstick in the rear view mirror. 'So what else did he say? Married? Kids? Significant other?'

I'd already wondered that, which addled me somewhat. Dolly Daydream, I thought. Time to rein myself in. 'Significant excess of commercial zeal,' I said firmly. 'And I'm not sure I much like being considered a human resource.'

'But is he *married*?' she persisted.

'God! I don't know, Ruth! It's hardly the sort of thing I'm going to be asking him, is it?'

'First thing I would have. Did you get a look at the size of those shoulders? And what an amazing co-incidence that he should be the guy who nearly hit you!'

Yes. I thought. That was all it was. Thrown together by fact. Not fate. 'Not specially,' I said. 'He's staying at the Meridien at the moment. He'd only flown in that morning, apparently, and he'd been to some meeting somewhere. Jet-lagged, I suppose.'

'But even *so*. Anyway, hope you told him what a whiz I am in the stock room. Hmm. Things are looking up. I can feel a conquest coming on. When's he start, then?'

'I don't think it works like that. I think he moves between branches. But I think he's coming in on Friday, isn't he? There's some Drug U Like lunch meeting or something, isn't there?'

She checked the mirror again.

'Yum yum! Better get my hair done, then.'

*   *   *

When I got home, Kate was already there, and the kitchen, as ever, was strewn with mess I hadn't made. She was sitting in her usual slumped position at the kitchen table, engrossed in some reading. Her empty plate was perched on a stack of magazines, half a dozen wizened disks of pepperoni from a microwave pizza fanned neatly around the rim.

'Good rehearsal?' I asked her.

'Nope. Good meeting?'

'Instructive, I suppose. You've eaten, then?'

In answer, she nodded and shunted the plate a little further away from her. I picked it up, scraped it and deposited it by the sink. She grunted an acknowledgement. Grunted, at any rate.

'Oh, there's some messages, by the way. Dad called to say Morgan's got a couple of days off and is coming down with him tomorrow to talk to you about the dresses.' She pulled a face. 'You have told her how I felt about the lilac, haven't you?'

I hadn't, in fact. Because there was little point. There were all sorts of colours that looked good on bridesmaids. But sadly, for Kate, none of them were black. 'Oh, and Gran called as well,' she added. 'Wanted you to ring her back when she gets in from *t'ai chi*.'

I looked at the time. It was almost ten. 'Right,' I said, pulling down the front of the still-full dishwasher and frowning. 'I'd better get on and do that, then. Did she say what about?'

Kate shook her head and returned to studying the thick clump of A4 sheets she had on the table in front of her.

'What's that?'

'Bah!' she said. 'Don't ask, OK? Just don't ask.'

I didn't ask. She followed me out into the hall.

'God! I mean, Mum, tell me *honestly*. Do I *look* like a dining car to you?'

This was a perfectly normal exchange in the Matthews household so I plopped myself down on the chair by the phone and raised my eyebrows enquiringly. 'A dining car?'

'Yes!' she looked at me with disdain and flapped the papers she still had in her hand. 'I should have been Diesel. Lynsey *knew* I wanted to be Diesel. It's all because that cow Athena's turned up. "Oh, *I* know the part!"' she screeched, '" I was Diesel in the

Whyteleafe Hotsteppers production, of course! I could do it *blindfold* blah blah blah". She thinks she's so good, but she dances like a duck. *I* should have been diesel. I've a good mind to quit altogether. Dinah indeed!'

'Dinah?'

'Dinah the dining car, of course! It's a crap part. *Crap*. Oh, I'm *so* mad.'

'Part in *what*?'

'God, Mum! *Starlight Express*, of course. *God!* Don't you know *anything*?'

I had always thought *Starlight Express* was done on skates. But not in this town, obviously. Kate's boots banged seven bells out of the stair treads and I dialled my mother's number in the faint hope of slightly less strenuous conversation.

But didn't get it.

I wondered what I would do once I retired. Would I opt for *t'ai chi* classes? Go to bingo on Thursdays? Collect limited edition decorative plates?

'How was it?' I asked my mother, who did all of these things and who, though abysmal at bingo, seemed to get a great amount of fulfilment and pleasure from being in permanent angry correspondence with the Franklin Mint. Among other things. 'Pah,' she answered.

'I thought you decided you were going to stick with the yoga.'

'Yoga? I gave that up yonks ago.'

'I thought you enjoyed your yoga classes.' More than she seemed to enjoy *t'ai chi*, at any rate.

'Initially,' she corrected me. 'But it went off a bit.'

'Went off?'

'Went off. It may suit Dorah Bryan, but there comes a time in a woman's life when the prospect of being able to bend over far enough to view your own undercarriage holds more dread than appeal, quite frankly.'

'And what's in prospect if you stick with the *t'ai chi* then?'

'Mental stillness, of course!'

I wondered if, in my mother, the teacher had taken on more than they could chew.

'In *theory*, at any rate,' she sniffed. 'A lot of my meridians are still pretty blocked up, but Cos thinks I'm showing great potential.

'Cos?'

'As in lettuce. He's from Bognor, but I think he's a Buddhist. Anyway, dear. I didn't want to talk about *t'ai chi*. I was ringing about the refuge. Did you have any luck with your MP?'

Ah. Her other current project.

My mother, like many of her age and situation, lived in quiet gentility in a well maintained Victorian house in Eastbourne. One that had been converted into retired women's flats. She had a perm, a lot of ornaments, and a stand on French apples, but there was where her similarity to most other people's mums ended. Next door to my mum's place was a women's refuge, which was run by a scary ex-hippy called Polly, and filled with an itinerant and unhappy population of women and children who'd escaped violence at home. That they had nowhere else to go was an ironic kind of juxtaposition, really, because the lease was running out and the landlords were being difficult. They wanted the refuge out so that the house could be sold. And then, no doubt, converted into a whole bunch of new flats, for people who didn't get in punch ups.

The sort of situation my mother excelled in. My mother always enjoyed a good protest.

The note in my diary made sense: I was supposed to ring my MP and hound him about it.

'Mum, look, I'm sorry, but I really didn't get a moment to do anything about it today. It's been really busy, what with –'

'No matter,' she said gleefully. 'Because *I* did.'

'You did?'

'Yes. I've not heard back from *my* MP yet, but I spoke to this ever so nice man at the *Evening Argus* and he's going to come round and talk to us about it on Friday. I was talking to Polly earlier and she thinks we're definitely on the right track. Media Exposure is what we need.'

'But what about the council? Wasn't Polly going to see if she could get the council to fund things temporarily? I thought there was some talk of them getting an extension on the lease.'

My mother clucked down the phone at me. 'Hmmph! And pigs might fly. They're a useless bunch the lot of them. I've told them, you know. On their own heads be it. They won't find themselves so dismissive when they have half a dozen homeless families on their hands, will they? Anyway, we're getting up a petition, and hopefully that piece in the paper, and then perhaps someone will sit up and take some notice. Anyway, the main thing is to keep bashing away at it, isn't it? So I've written a letter outlining the situation and popped it in the post to you.'

'To me?'

'Of course! I thought you could type it up on your computer for me. Then we can send it out to everyone influential we can think of and start making some serious waves.'

I noted the 'we'. Another thing for the list in my diary.

I would have to get a bigger one, I thought.

Chapter 5

I got into work on Monday morning to find Ruth on her knees in the middle of the shop floor, pulling all our own-brand sunglasses from their holes in the carousel racks. 'No longer wanted on voyage,' she said, sliding a pair into a bubble-wrap bag and dropping it into a box on the floor. 'I've got crate loads of Drug U Like shades out the back. This lot are bound for the depot.'

'Goodness,' I said, privately wondering whether the racy wrap-around pair I'd rather fancied would now be subject to a substantial price reduction. 'They don't let the grass grow, do they?'

She hauled herself upright and smoothed the front of her skirt. 'This,' she said gravely, 'is simply the tip of the iceberg, let me tell you. Go and check out the pink carpet sample in the office.'

I had to concede that since the Drug U Like lunch meeting with Nick Brown, the idea of shaking off our rather staid suburban image was at least injecting a little frisson of novelty into the working day. At least, I *told* myself it was the meeting. Nothing whatsoever with *him*. Not at all.

Ruth picked up the box of sunglasses and followed me through to the office. 'And guess what else?'

I flipped through the ridiculously long list of tests that had been booked in, and noticed a couple of familiar heart-sink names. 'What else?'

'Training.'

'Training? Training in what?'

'Well, not so much training, as *re*training.' She fanned her fingers and jiggled them about a bit. 'Retraining The Drug U Like way.'

Ruth invariably got in before me in the morning. It was, she said, the best way to maximise her social life and still keep her novel on track. I often thought of her when awake in the small hours. Perhaps *I* should start a novel. A page a night. God knew, I spent enough of it awake these days. It also meant she was generally more privy than most to the machinations of the store's assistant manager, with whom these days she often shared the early riser staff breakfast and had not so long ago shared a bed for a while. Though, thankfully, he was now back with his wife.

'I was talking to Michael earlier, and he said there's a memo going round today about it. There's to be a series of training camps coming up –'

'Camps?'

'Yes, you heard me right. Camps. With a capital C. Or no – with a capital B and S. As in bloody great bug-fest and squelch. They've organised a programme of team-building induction weekends, apparently, in order to better, well…induct us, I suppose. Whatever *that* means.'

Being inducted sounded somewhat sinister. I had a vision of fat pinstripe-suited American gangsters, engaged in the business of coercive practices on unsuspecting pharmacists in remote shacks. Or indeed, thin ones. With toffee suede jackets and forget-me-not eyes. Could it be? I plucked some shades from the rack.

'Er, camps where, exactly?'

She split the tape from another Drug U Like box with her ball point and tutted at the contents.

'Look at this crap,' she said, poking the pen back into her hair. 'Who on earth is going to buy these? Eighty-nine pounds ninety-nine! Jesus! Oh, he wasn't sure. Wales, somewhere, he thought. Somewhere wild and unsavoury, at any rate. He thinks we're in the first cohort, too, so better get your billy can scrubbed up.'

'Billy can?' I said. 'That sounds exciting.'

'Exciting?' she snorted. 'I think not, Sal. Sounds much more like something we should be worrying about.'

My worries, generally, are nebulous confections. Like things that you see from the corner of your eye but can't quite get into focus. Ruth's however, were entirely tangible. She plonked herself down in our usual corner of the pub and groaned. 'Look at me!' she said. 'An hour on my knees on the floor and my back is killing me! So sod this bloody Scouts lark.'

Russell dropped the three bags of crisps he had clamped in his teeth. 'An hour on your knees on the floor, Ruth? Thought that would be just up your street. Dib dib dib,' he said. 'Dob dob dob.'

'Dib sodding dob yourself, Russell,' she said now, scowling as she accepted the pint he was holding out to her and gulping a good two inches from the top. 'What the hell does that mean anyway?

And I mean, can you imagine? *Me*? Bounding about in a cagoule? Wearing track suit bottoms? Not wearing mascara? *Running*?' She put her glass down and cycled her arms.

Russell re-routed his gaze to her chest and opened his crisps.

'Er, no, frankly, Ruth. I went out with an Akela once,' he announced. 'Very hands-on. Very capable. Not as hot as you in the chest department, I'll grant you, but she could tie a mean sheepshank.'

Ruth looked at him disdainfully. 'Well I don't think I could shank a sheep if my life depended on it,' she announced, with some feeling. 'The nearest I've got to being under canvas was when I lost a contact lens at a party last year and took out a barbecue awning.'

'It's not tents,' I said. 'It's cabins, Dennis said. And the memo said nothing about nautical pursuits.'

The memo had said nothing of substance at all, in fact. Just advised us of a series of upcoming dates and urged us to decide which ones suited best. None, regrettably, in my case. I'd already checked Jonathan's diary.

'Tents, cabins. What's the difference? It's all rustic, isn't it?' she growled. 'All a million miles from hot water, radiators and watching *EastEnders*. What else do you need to know?' She stared moodily into her beer. 'And there's bound to be climbing – I mean, why else go somewhere so hilly? And stuff in boats, Sal, you mark my words. There's *always* stuff in boats. Kayaks or canoes at the very least. Perhaps I should develop hydrophobia or something. And they always do that swinging-off-rocks thing as well – what's it called? Wassailing?''

'Abseiling.'

'Exactly. *That*. I've *seen* that Julie Walters film. I know what's coming, believe me. Pant wetting territory, for definite.'

The Drug U Like bum bag took on a whole new significance.

'I doubt it'll be anything of the sort,' I reassured her. 'Probably no more than a bit of hiking and having to make a raft out of two oil drums and a plank without anyone punching anyone else on the nose. That kind of thing. Jonathan went on one once. Russell's right. It'll be just like Scouts, but without all the woggles and community singing. I think it might be rather fun.'

Ruth slapped her hand on the table. 'That was it! That survival programme! They had to sleep under banana leaves for a week and dig their own toilet and eat buffalo testicles for dinner! Oh my Lord! It makes my blood run cold.'

'There are no buffalo in Wales,' Russell told her. 'Only sheep.'

'Sheep? *Sheep?* God! That's even worse! At least you know where you are with a testicle.'

'What a load of nonsense,' observed Jonathan when I got home from work and told him about it the following day. He looked hollow eyed and tired, and like he'd run out of anything happy to think about, which these days was often the norm. As well as the surgery in Oxted he worked at, he was a partner in a rather swank practice in Wimpole Street, and on Mondays and Tuesdays he worked up there, and had done for almost five years. I wondered, often, how much he really enjoyed it. The rigours and stresses of celebrity dentistry were encroaching ever more on his humour, to my mind. He was still in his suit and his overnight bag was standing in the corner, where it would sit until such time as I did something with it.

'Maybe so,' I said. 'But compulsory nonsense. So I rang and checked with Lydia earlier and I've put myself down for the one on the twenty-fifth. It's only three days. I'll be back on the Tuesday.'

He was hacking the end off a baguette, and bacon was spitting under the grill. He had a pathological unease about me speaking to his secretary, in case, I presumed, we ganged up on him. But as he'd been in London it made sense to circumvent him. He didn't like being called while tinkering between the lips of B-movie actresses and bleaching the teeth of his boy band pubescents. He paused in his sawing.

'The twenty-fifth? You can't go then! That's the weekend my parents are coming, isn't it? What on earth possessed you to put yourself down for those dates? What am I supposed to do with them all weekend?' he started sawing again. 'You'll have to change it.'

I shook my head. His face was stony.

'I can't,' I said. 'There were only three options, and the other two were no good. One of them's when Morgan's down to sort things out with the dressmaker, and the other one clashes with Bob and Androulla.'

Truth be known, everything clashed with Bob and Androulla. Principally because *I* clashed with Bob and Androulla. Or more specifically, Androulla. By virtue of things I could do nothing about. I clashed with Bob and Androulla because I was not Tricia, didn't play bridge, was married to Jonathan, and was not Morgan's mum. Androulla, however, was Morgan's fairy Godmother. And therein lies a tale or six. But to dwell on it's bad for my health, so I don't. Suffice to say that I would have sped off to Wales like a shot to avoid Bob and Androulla. But as neither Russell or Ruth could make those dates, I had traded off Bob and Androulla avoidance for the almost comparably joyous occurrence of not having to schlep around all weekend after Jonathan's mother. A happy, happy clash, all told. A win-win situation. I folded my arms across my chest and wondered quite when this combative streak had taken hold of me.

'Oh,' he growled, flipping his bacon over and frowning. 'That's great, then.' He turned to direct a flinty look at me. 'Can't you get out of it? Can't you just tell them it isn't convenient? People have commitments. They may be American, but they can't expect everyone to just drop everything at their say-so.'

Which was rich given that in the not too distant past we had done exactly that for Bob and bloody Androulla. I'd got two precious tickets for *Miss Saigon*, but, oh no, Bob and Androulla, who resided these days in a villa-with-four-toilets just outside Fuengirola, were going to be in the country for the weekend. A one-time-only not-to-be-missed offer. Couldn't *possibly* miss them. Our plans weren't so much dropped as fired floorwards like scuds.

Though it had said as much on the form. And, yes, it had crossed my mind that had I asked to be excused then not a soul would have castigated me for it. But Jonathan's mother. Bob and bloody Androulla. Way too tempting by half. And besides, this was my career, wasn't it? I never made a hint of a squeak of a murmur at any of *his* lofty pan-global trips.

'I know that,' I said, judging the temperature and finding it salad drawer chilly. 'But it's important I go. They're well aware that people have commitments. Of course they are. But what about my commitment to my job? My *career?* It's not going to look very good if the senior optom can't be bothered, is it? I have to *impress* these people.'

Jonathan, obviously far from impressed at the notion that my job might be anything other than an optional extra, pulled out the grill pan again and stabbed irritably at the bacon, shaking it off on to his slabs of baguette.

'And it's only three days, Jonathan. I will get all the food in. I will make up the beds. I will plan all the meals. And Kate will be here, don't forget. It's hardly as if you're being abandoned.'

And they *were his parents*. I lifted the grill-pan from where he'd dumped it on the work surface and took it over to the sink. 'And what about dinner?' I asked him. 'Is that all you're having? And where's Morgan? Wasn't she coming down with you tonight?'

'She's taken the dog out with Kate. And I've got tennis coaching. It's Tuesday, remember?'

His tone was accusatory. Silly me. Tuesday, *ergo* tennis, *ergo* rush back from London, *ergo* tennis gear, sandwich and doughnut required. *Ergo wife* required. And wife, of course, late home. Well, *God!* Frankly. Quite apart from the utter ridiculousness of a man of fifty-two spending his time being coached in something, period, it was always something. If not tennis, then cricket, or bridge, or bloody golf. I wondered if I shouldn't have a summer schedule posted up somewhere, like TV stations do.

'Of course,' I said, refusing to feel guilty, but looking it nevertheless because my face was so used to it. 'I'd forgotten. Shall I see if there's a KitKat somewhere?'

His eyes flicked up in response to the edge in my voice then he bent and reached into the fridge for the bottle of ketchup.

'I'm perfectly capable,' he said, unscrewing the lid and jerking a thick red coil onto his plate. He screwed it back on again, grim faced and rigid, then poured himself a mug of tea. 'Oh, you go off on your camp,' he whined as I stood and watched him put the cosy back on it. 'Don't you worry about us. We'll cope.'

Marriages are like wasps. Or black Spanish bulls. Irritable creations, inclined to quick temper. A little like Jonathan, in fact. I watched him gather his tea and his sandwich and I wondered, not for the first time just lately, why it was that women were so hopelessly drawn to men who were so remote and testy. The Mr D'arcy effect? The Heathcliff moment? Was that what had done it for *me*? Why were men-with-a-problem so attractive to young women? Sure, it made for good fiction, with all the swooning and uncertainty, but was it such a good blueprint for longevity in marriage? Forget the grand passion – shouldn't niceness be part of the deal? What a twat Jonathan was. What a blind, stupid fool. Had he made the tiniest, the teeniest, the most infinitesimal gesture towards being nice to me, towards accepting-with-good-grace that I had a right to a life, I would have probably – no, *definitely* – have decided not to go.

In any event, once he'd departed into the garden with his tea I spent a vaguely enjoyable couple of minutes seething and scowling and making faces at his back out of the kitchen window. No one offered to make *me* a cup of tea. No one offered to make *me* a bacon sandwich or iron my tennis shorts or remember that I had a suit awaiting collection at the dry cleaners or that I might just be tired and in a bad mood and in need of careful handling or for someone to be nice to me now and again.

'Bollocks, then,' I said to the teapot. 'I'm going.' And I poured myself a large Pimm's instead.

Chapter 6

I though, then, long and hard, about the wisdom of *actually* going away for the weekend. I had so much else to do, what with the wedding, and my mother's on-going save-the-refuge campaign, and the business of getting Kate to her dance class rehearsals, not to mention the creation of no less than five Starlight Express costumes, a job pressed on me on the rather dubious credentials of having run up a couple of hasty tutus last year . It would, I knew, be rather fun to escape for a couple of days – apart from one or two overnight Continuing Education courses, I hadn't been off and done anything on my own for years. It felt rather exciting to be Someone With Career Commitments. Jonathan was always swanning off somewhere and I was always the one left behind holding the iron. We always used to say how nice it would be once the children were older and I could accompany him on conferences, but I sometimes wondered if I actually remembered that right, because somehow it never seemed to happen. Perhaps it was just me that had thought it. Because he never seemed particularly enthused if I mentioned it these days, and in any case, there always seemed to be something, or someone, who needed me to stay at home.

I was busy. Required. Indispensable. Needed. Shouldn't things like that make me feel *good*? An image of Nick Brown's face swam across my dutiful thoughts. But there *was* a wedding to get organised. A scant four months off now. And I was the one who was doing it.

Not that I minded, really. If there was one single thing that marked me down as the suburban middle-class woman I strenuously tried not to be, it was my absolute and completely barking-mad conviction that planning Morgan's wedding would be fun.

Morgan and Kate used to play Barbie flat share together. They would set out little rooms for the dolls, walled in by paperbacks, and I would bring them little cups of milk, and tiny jam sandwiches and cut up Cadbury's fingers and fragments of crisps, which I would decant into tiny bags made out of sweet wrappers, and which they would both fall upon with rapturous delight. But that, I thought now, was a long, long time ago.

Because there was to be, it seemed, no easy girly camaraderie round the kitchen table today. A kitchen table that I had fondly looked upon as the hub – nay the very pinnacle, of happy, fulfilling family life. What could be nicer? Saturday afternoon, Jonathan exiled to the drive with bucket and chamois, and me and my gals, all smiles and enthusiasm, doing girl-stuff and frippery and guest lists and flowers. Or not. Half an hour into favours and typefaces and cake permutations, and a perceptible tension had settled over the proceedings. Kate was wearing her tales-from-the-crypt frock. It lent a certain macabre chill to her words.

'What, *that*? You're joking, right?'

'No, Kate,' said Morgan, in a tight, clipped voice. She had already weathered Kate's rant over the issue of her chignon, and now it seemed she must brace herself for more. She had extracted a photograph from one of the files in front of her, and had placed it under Kate's disdainful gaze. 'Of course I'm not joking. This is the dress –' she lay the photo on the table and pointed '– and you have a circlet of freesias for your hair. And this really cutesy little embroidered drawstring bag. And I've seen these *gorgeous* little brocade ballet pumps and –'

'Hang on. Hang on,' said Kate, animated enough to cantilever forward the better to glare at the glossy picture in front of her. 'You mean this is the dress *I've* got to wear?'

Morgan blinked at her. 'Yes. Of course. What did you think it was?'

Kate didn't elaborate as to quite what she thought it might be because she was now too busy gaping in horror. 'And ballet pumps?' It was more spit than speech. '*Ballet* pumps? You're not serious. You *cannot* be serious!'

Jonathan, who was supposed to be outside and not getting under our feet and so on, had wandered into the kitchen in order to rinse out his chamois leather at the sink. 'You *cannot* be *seeeeerious!*' he said, with uncharacteristic gaiety and in a very silly voice. It was nice to see him smiling for a change.

'Oh, shut *up*, Dad. It's not funny,' snapped Kate, with sudden animation. 'She *cannot* be serious. You cannot be serious, Morgan. No.'

Oh, the joy of wedding preparations. Morgan snatched the photograph back from her sister and whipped the look-at-me-I'm-getting-married-and-isn't-life-just-peachy expression from her face . It had begun to droop anyway. She slapped on a big-sisterly menace one instead. 'I am *deadly* serious, Kate. Deadly. This *is* it and you *are* wearing it.'

'You'll look lovely,' I chipped in hopefully from my end of the table, wondering if this might be the time to go and unload the washing machine or worm the dog. Merlin, who was ever alert to a possible slaughter situation, click-clacked over the quarry tiles to lay in wait in the utility room.

'Lovely?' Kate shrieked, stabbing at the photo with a black talon. 'Lovely? In that! I'll look like an old lady's knicker drawer! How can you possibly imagine anyone could look lovely in a dress that looks like it's been made out of nursing home curtains? It's hideous! It's ghastly! It's all ribbony! It's gross!' She slapped the back of her hand against the photo in disgust. 'It looks like a cake, Morgan! It looks like a pair of bloomers. Ye-arrrrgh! Ye-uurg!' (or something like that.).

Jonathan, chastened, flapped his leather in the air. It made a loud snapping sound and shot drips all over the table.

'Oh! Tsk! Da-*ad!*' said Morgan.

He gathered it into a lump again and peered over his younger daughter's shoulder to squint at the picture. 'For goodness' sake, Kate. You only have to wear it the once. Only for a few hours. It's hardly going to kill you.'

She nodded at him thoughtfully. 'Hey, yeah, *right*, Dad. But who'd know the difference if it did? Because I'll look like a crematorium flower arrangement anyway.'

At which point he glowered and scuttled back to the garage. Morgan, clearly more than a mite peeved at this flagrant dismissal of her sartorial acumen, started gathering all her photos and colour copies together and bustling them into order on the table top. 'Hmm,' she said, darting a look of disdain at her sister. 'Which will be an improvement in my opinion. Right now you just look like a crematorium. Besides, what do *you* know about style anyway? Sancha thought it was really pretty.'

Sancha, the other bridesmaid, was Cody, the groom's, niece. We'd met her just the once, at their engagement party. Though she had a Smartie coloured brace and an eating disorder she also had a baguette bag and an account at Harvey Nicholls. Morgan was very taken with details like that.

Kate was not. 'Morgan, Sancha is twelve, for God's sake. Twelve year olds know nothing about anything. Twelve year olds don't *mind* being trussed up like comedy toilet roll holders. Twelve year olds don't have breasts and – and – and well, *feelings!* She might think she'll look a babe in a bloody Bo-peep ensemble, but more fool her, I say. I mean, *look* at it, will you? It's got *puffed sleeves* for God's sake!'

Which juncture was the one at which I would normally have bustled in and inserted a tart 'Don't swear, please, Kate,' or 'enough of that, thank you, young lady' or similar, but my precise form of words was arrested mid-think by what Morgan said next, which was 'Yes, Kate. I *know*.'

Or, to be accurate, not so much *what* she said, but the way she said it, which was somewhat akin to the passage of a lone tumbleweed across a bleak plain. Kate, obviously either oblivious to the sudden and dramatic drop in temperature, or too busy with her own internal ranting to notice, answered, 'But *why?* I mean, what are you *thinking* of? Do you really hate me that much?'

In actual fact,' Morgan said, suddenly all expansive and smiling, 'there *was* another style I rather liked, as it happens. A shift dress. In satin. Very nice, in fact. But, alas, no good.'

'No good?' I asked, knowing this was leading somewhere unsavoury, but not entirely sure where that place was.

'No,' she went on, turning her eyes from her sister and smiling again, at me this time. 'Because it was *sleeveless*, you see.'

'Sleeveless?' I said.

'Yes,' she responded. '*Sleeveless*.'

I was just about to ask what sleeves or a lack thereof had to do with anything, when Kate's expression suddenly reconfigured itself. Into something approximating the expression you might adopt if you'd just discovered you'd swallowed a slug . She blinked at her sister, she blinked at me, she blinked at the dog and then she narrowed her eyes. 'Oh, I *get* it,' she muttered. Morgan said nothing.

I did. I said, 'And what's the problem with that, then?'

'You'll have to ask her,' said Morgan, with some asperity.

'You cow,' hissed Kate.

'Now, *hang* on –' I spluttered. With some feeling. What on earth, I thought, was going *on* here?

'You cow,' Kate hissed again. 'You absolute *cow*.'

Morgan said nothing. Just carried on riffling through her file in the manner of a person who has not a care in the world. Well, almost. Her fingers, I noticed, were trembling slightly.

'Look –' I began.

'Anyway!' Morgan chirruped suddenly. 'That's about it, then, I think. Shall I put the kettle on, or open that bottle of Chablis? Hmm? Mum? Wine?'

Kate, who might, on recent experience, be reasonably expected to leave the room *avec* much drama, remained, waxy-faced, in her seat.

'*Look*,' I said again. 'What's going *on*, girls?'

Morgan got up from her chair and started bustling at the worktop behind me. I looked at Kate.

'Well?'

'Nothing.'

'I'm not completely stupid, Kate. If it's nothing, then why do you look like you've just been slapped by a haddock?'

'Nothing, OK? Nothing,'

'Kate, it's *not* nothing. Now will you please tell me what exactly is going on around here before I –'

'Look, mum, it's *nothing*, OK?'

This was Morgan, still behind me, and now, presumably, uncorking the bottle of wine. I could hear the dry squeak of a corkscrew in cork. Kate's gaze snapped up over my shoulder and back again. Then she scraped back her chair, pulled her trailing skirt to attention and stormed out, finally, as if prompted by a stage-hand, slamming the door hard for good measure.

'*Morgan!*' I said, as the air quivered around us. 'What *was* all that about?'

Morgan plucked out the cork and began untwisting the corkscrew. '*Nothing*, mum. *Really*.' she said.

The one thing a mother knows above all others is that 'nothing' is as loaded a word as exists within the familial lexicon, so I was not to be fobbed off lightly. But just at that moment, Jonathan called from the garage. I gave Morgan a stern don't-move-until-I-come-back kind of look and took myself off to see what minor domestic tragedy had befallen him. It was, as ever, a Hozelock drama,

Jonathan being utterly inept at couplings, so by the time I got back into the kitchen, Morgan, who was, of course, twenty-four and therefore not remotely impressed by the unspoken edicts of matriarchal superiority, had shot off.

'Merlin,' I announced, 'something's afoot here.' And I took myself stealthily up the stairs.

I'm not normally given to lurking at keyholes, and, in any case we didn't have any on our upstairs door knobs, so I positioned my head flat against Kate's bedroom door and pressed my right ear to the wood.

They were talking at each other in the sort of tone that would have been a full-on shoutathon were it not for the minor inconvenience of having to be very, very quiet. I could barely make out what they were saying.

'You cow,' Kate was hissing. 'You promised me you wouldn't tell her – you promised! How could you *do* that?'

'Do *what*?' Morgan protested. 'I never said a word! And besides, that wasn't the deal! The deal was that *you'd* tell them. The deal was that you'd tell them six weeks ago. And you didn't. Are you completely stupid? You've *got* to tell them! How long do you think you can go on hiding it? *Well?*'

There was a silence, then the sound of a window being opened. And a plop as my stomach turned over. Oh, God.

'Well mum *isn't* stupid,' Morgan continued. 'So if I were you I'd get my backside off that bed and get down there and tell her, before she finds it out for herself. And she will you know. As will Dad. God! You are *such* an idiot, Kate! What were you *thinking*?'

Oh, God! It all fitted! Her mood swings! Her temper! Her refusal to eat! Her refusal, moreover, to use the communal fitting room when I'd bought her that new Diesel T-shirt last month! She'd got off the bed. I could hear her boots clomping. 'Oh and you're Mrs bloody goody two shoes, then, are you?' A pause. 'Yeah, right. And I could tell a tale or two, so don't start preaching at *me*! It's my life. It's my *body*. OK?'

Her body??? God, *sleeves*. I'd been sidetracked by sleeves. Were sleeves a euphemism for empire line, maybe? For dresses that would fail to accommodate the gentle swell of…..Oh, oh, oh! This was looking seriously bad. Go in? Stay out? Confront them? Keep listening? Make notes? I really wasn't sure what. A silence had fallen. A bedspring went boiing. Keep listening, then. Just for a bit…

'Sally, what on *earth* are you doing?'

Jonathan's voice. *Bad.* Because whatever appalling thing it was that Kate was being exhorted to admit to me (and I was quite sure by now that it was something about which I'd be seriously appalled) would, I was quite, *quite* sure, be best digested and given-serious-thought-to before being given an airing to her father. But here he was anyway. We must do this together.

'Shhh!' I hissed at him. 'I'm listening.'

'Listening? To what?' He still had the chamois in his hand. He cocked an eyebrow.

'To the *girls,* of course. There's something very bad going on, and they won't tell me what, so I –'

'What sort of bad? Are they fighting?'

'No! But rowing about something. I think…I'm not sure…. but Kate…' I was groping for words.

'Oh for goodness sake!' He exhaled and approached the bedroom door. And then knocked on it. *Rattattatat!*

And I prepared to be appalled.

There are, of course, degrees of appallingness. Bracing myself for the news that my still-pubescent daughter was with-child (by her exploding faced werewolf of a boyfriend? Heaven preserve us), I followed Jonathan into the bedroom. To find – oh, joy! – that no, she wasn't pregnant, that no, she didn't have an intravenous drug habit either, and that no, she hadn't signed up to join a faux-religious closed-order hippy encampment just outside Poona. Ergo, I was not as appalled as I might have been. Oh, no. Just relieved. Relieved beyond belief. What she did have, however, and it took mere seconds to discover it, was a slim tangle of blackly-inked barbed wire-type squiggles circumnavigating her upper right arm.

I was dismayed, yes. Disappointed, certainly. But appalled? How *on earth* could I find space to be appalled when I was so busy giving thanks to the Lord?

Which didn't help much, because feeling thus (which is one of the very few fringe benefits of having such a manic and fertile maternal imagination) led me, quite naturally, to adopt the voice of calm-in-a-crisis, which, even more naturally, made Jonathan cross. His dudgeon was plainly as high as the Eiger and he wanted me up there as well.

So I shut up.

'Only a tatt*oo*?' he spluttered. '*Only* a TATTOO!!!' True to type, and never having displayed much sense of perspective in the matter of teenagers and what they got up to (and, admittedly, a little professional exposure to frizzled septums and The Priory etc.) he was going a nice shade of sun dried tomato.

Which looked all the more arresting for being highlighted by the shaft of warm sunshine that was wafting merrily through the window, and in whose tender caress he now stood. He slammed his chamois down on Kate's desktop. It sat there, weeping moistly, like a small pickled brain.

'Yes, Dad!' Spat Kate, who was now nose to nose with him and yanking her sleeve back down. 'It's only a Tattoo! God! That's *all!* Chill, can't you? What's the matter with you?'

Which (unconvincing) display of insouciance was a bit disingenuous, given that it occurred to me now that I'd not seen Kate sleeveless in best part of two months. Must step up on the vigilance, I thought.

'What's the matter with *me*?' he barked. 'The *matter*? Kate, you have disfigured yourself! You are sixteen years old and not only have you disfigured yourself for life, but you have also branded yourself as someone brainless and stupid and ignorant. AND you have lied to us.' He stabbed a finger in the general direction. 'Who did it? Who did this to you? Because so help me, I'll see him charged. This is exactly the sort of –'

'Dad, you're being ridiculous! It's *just* a tattoo, for God's sake! Everyone has them these days. *Everyone*.' Which struck me as ill-judged. And struck me correctly. Jonathan's face was now red pepper red.

The finger jabbed the air again. '*You* are not everyone. *You* are my daughter, young lady. And I am appalled and disgusted. As you will be once you're adult enough to realise what a stupid, immature thing it is that you have done. What about your career? What about the rest of your life? What about all the years to come in which you will be ashamed of your own body? (Which I thought was overdoing it a tad) And don't even *think* of giving me a catalogue of celebrity icons (he waved a hand around the room here) who are similarly disfigured. I don't *care* if Madonna or that bloody Aminem lout has one. Because if these are the sort of people you look up to and respect, then God help us, my girl.'

He then dropped his voice to a terrible whisper. 'I thought I could expect better from my daughter.'

Morgan and I stood like a couple of shop window dummies while Jonathan continued to exude deep disappointment and the dust motes danced round his head. Kate, in a corner so tight now that she couldn't manoeuvre, and having had her last counter blow pre-empted so cruelly, did the only thing one can reasonably do in such circumstances, and burst into big gulping sobs.

'It's that boyfriend,' Jonathan announced grimly, over supper, once the girls had gone off with the dog. They'd made up and were friends again, but it occurred to me as it had often lately, that the age gap between them seemed to be growing ever wider. The more assured and grown-womanly Morgan was becoming the more distant and uncommunicative Kate seemed to be.

Calm, of a sort, had at least been achieved. After numerous petitions from both myself and Morgan, Jonathan had refrained from dragging Kate down from the bedroom (where she had elected to stay, in order to better consider the general unfairness of life, parents and western post-feminist society, presumably), and, more importantly, given that I was chief henchman, from impetuously imposing sanctions on her social life in perpetuity. But the feeling that a big and terrible milestone had been reached hung over the rest of the afternoon and early evening, and would do so, I suspected, for days. Thank God he was back off to London tomorrow and could take his deep disappointment along with him.

He curled his lip, as if he was chewing on a bluebottle. 'She's been a different girl since she started hanging about with that Carl yob. I'm quite sure it was him that put her up to it. We're going to have to start keeping her in a bit more.'

By 'we're' he meant me, naturally, for it would be me that would have to cope with all the tears and the shouting. Me that would have to do all the dirty work.

'He looks worse than he actually is,' I lied smoothly. 'And anyway, I'm quite sure she'll grow out of him soon enough on her own.'

This much was, I felt, true. One thing I did know was that for the sixteen year old Sally Bradshaw (also blessed with a father of Dickensian tendencies) there was nothing so compelling as the company of a boyfriend of whom her father violently disapproved.

Loyalty, I knew, was a different country for a teenager. The more Jonathan ranted, the more she would dig in her heels. And he wasn't *that* bad. His mother was perfectly pleasant. He just wasn't quite good *enough*. That was all.

'Hmmph!' said Jonathan. 'That's not much of a comfort. What else is she going to get up to before that happy day dawns? Eh?'

And so the evening and his huffing and puffing rumbled on. I cleared away the dishes (God! Young people today!), I loaded the dishwasher (bring back National Service, I say), I put a machine load of washing on (he'll be on drugs too, I imagine), I fed Merlin (and shouldn't she be at home revising anyway?) I gathered up the newspapers from their basket and put them in the recycling bag (you're too lax with her generally), I took it out to the dustbins (silence. Bliss), and I sat down, eventually, to watch some TV.

'And that's *another* thing,' announced Jonathan, 'I'm sick of this wretched wedding. It's causing nothing but arguments. And it's still four months off! I had no idea there would be this much hassle and grief and rowing involved. Why can't people simply go off and get themselves married without all this stupid, tedious fuss? Hmm? *Why*?'

It was a rhetorical question, so I didn't try to answer. And though I could have, with feeling, I was now way too tired.

Ours, for all sorts of important reasons that I could now not recall, most, if not all of which were nothing to do with me, had been a well attended but rather low-key affair. My mother, who had had all sorts of reservations about the wisdom of taking on a man with another woman's young daughter, had, to her credit, thrown herself into things wholeheartedly. She made my dress herself – in ivory silk – and she had made Morgan's, too. We made such a pretty pair. But what I do recall, and with feelings I'm still not sure I've quite come to terms with, was the strange undercurrent of almost memorial sadness that had hung like a billowy veil over the day. The streams of people I'd barely yet come to know, who were unfailingly pleasant and jolly and friendly, but who had known and loved Trisha and been at her funeral less than eighteen months previously, and who seemed – to me, anyway – to be connected by the occasion to a hotline to the feelings of grief they'd all shared. It seemed to overlay everything. The gentle hands that patted Morgan's little head. The faces that smiled. The moment when I'd heard someone speaking to Jonathan, saying 'how has she been? Is she finding this difficult? It must be such a terrible strain on you all.'

Most of all, Tricia's parents, a shadowy presence, whom Jonathan, in his wisdom, had browbeaten into coming, because they were, as he'd pointed out, Morgan's grandparents, after all. These were the stuff of my memories of that day. Of the same streams of people that had appeared shiny faced and in confetti coloured clothing in the photo that had sat like a talisman on Jonathan's piano until the day and the row came that saw it finally off. Off to where it lived now, at the top of his wardrobe, along with the rest of his Tricia-shrine stuff.

I had no bad feelings about Jonathan's first wife – I had never, of course, met her – but, oh, how I envied Morgan her freedom from Tricia-awareness. In every way other than biology, it was I and not Tricia who was the mum in her life. I who would make sure her wedding was perfect. Joyous. Sublime. The one that I hadn't quite had.

'Because,' I said now, 'that's not what most people do. People get married as a celebration. They want to *share* it with people. Not sneak off and do it on their own.'

'Hmmph.' he growled, flinging his newspaper at the basket. 'Well I suppose I should be grateful she's not marrying some yob. At least Cody's respectable and upstanding and *clean*. Why can't Kate find someone like that?'

I woke, that night, at three twenty seven, and I decided I *would* go on the Drug U Like weekend. Because all of a sudden I felt old. It suddenly seemed to me that my time at the familial helm was getting close to being up. That our little girl was no longer a girl, but a woman. That in a few short years, she'd have left us and gone, and would be able to make all the mistakes she wanted. I tiptoed into her room, rubbing my arms against the chill – Kate always slept with all her windows open – and peering down at the young woman sleeping before me. Her tattoo, no longer clandestine beneath T-shirts and nighties, was etched cleanly and prettily across her long slender arm. I wondered if she *would* regret it twenty years down the line. Look back and wonder what on earth she'd been thinking. What would she be, I wondered? A dancer? An actress? She so wanted that. She'd be good at it, too. Then married, perhaps. Children.

Middle class lifestyle. She stirred in her sleep, her long lashes quivering. I smiled to myself. Regret? I thought not.

Chapter 7

We had arrived at the Porth Merthyr Management Training centre on a wet and unprepossessing Saturday afternoon, whereupon, having had it helpfully explained that Porth meant gate and Merthyr meant martyr (ho ho ho), we were almost immediately instructed to get kitted up, go off to an assault course, and perform life-threatening stunts without benefit of having the remotest idea quite what it was we were supposed to be doing. Or, indeed, why. But this was the nature of teambuilding, apparently. It didn't seem to have a point other than to assess our responses to its pointlessness. Not that I cared. I wasn't washing or ironing or vacuuming bedrooms or negotiating with caterers or running up costumes or cooking any meals or, indeed, haranguing any MPs. I wasn't altogether sure what it was that I *was* doing, but this little point didn't worry me unduly. Because neither was anyone else.

And now it is Monday, and in the same spirit of bemused incomprehension that has been largely evident across the whole range of activities other than the procurement of large quantities of alcohol and obscure crisp selections at the bar in the evenings, we have been shepherded off to a shack in the woods, many miles from human habitation.

On the plus side, I am not with Ruth, because she's ducked out of this one. She is big-time sick and hungover today. Which is good because I do not wish to have to deal with vomit. Also on the plus side, I am not with the man from Horsham with the alarming hair and the whistling front teeth. On the minus side I am with Russell, who generally effects dismay at the prospect of finding his way to the contact lens cupboard, let alone doing 'outside' without wheels and some shades. And on the oh-so-very-plus side that I am beginning to feel that it might just turn out to be a serious minus, we have Nick Brown as our very own Hike U Like representative; here to help shepherd our feckless duo to success. He arrived at eight thirty this very morning – a vision in khaki – and since then, it must be said, I have somehow metamorphosed from happy-but-cynical forty something on a beano to Baden Powell's newest and most exhilarated recruit.

The shack is reasonably well-appointed, as shacks go, but it strikes me, for perhaps the tenth time this weekend that this (and my part in it) will not inform a reading glasses prescription in the least. I think, momentarily, of Jonathan. I think of his rumbling disappointment with Kate. I think of him forgetting to take the Victoria sponge from the freezer. I think of him telling his mother for the umpteenth time that a duvet will not give her contact dermatitis or lice. I think of him trailing around Marks and Spencer with her while she pummels skirt fronts to see how much they crease. I think of *him*, period, and how much fun this break is. And then I think about Nick Brown and I concede that perhaps there is a purpose to this madness. My sanity. My freedom. My feeling like a teenager. Little unimportant details like that.

Anyway, ten past three and the only little detail nudging my consciousness right now is the fact that I only have seven travel tissues left in my packet and that weeing al fresco is not high on my list of favoured leisure pursuits. Which is pertinent, because the deal is that this afternoon, by way of light relief, we are going to go orienteering. Orienteering is (apparently) simple, fun, challenging, healthy and not in the least dangerous as long as you tuck your trousers in your socks. It's very straightforward. You gather into little gaggles of orienteerers (is there a collective noun for orienteerers? An enthusiasm? An uncertainty? A corduroy?) and are taken off in small groups, at large intervals, to some remote spot. Once there, you get given a map and a compass and a sheet of clues and all you have to do is work out where you are. Easy. Then, by virtue of your undoubtedly superior deductive and observational skills you will find your way via said clues en route from point A to point B, at which location (another shack, presumably) you will be patted warmly on the back, given a hunk of Kendal Mint Cake, and you will feel all jolly and pleased with yourself. Simple. Orienteering is FUN.

Ten past six. No it's not. It's pants. Total pants. No, that's not true, either. It's not orienteering that's pants. It's *us* who are pants. Us as in Russell and I, at any rate. Nick (who I must concede is in no small way a disorientating factor) is otherwise engaged in doing whatever people like him have to do, i.e. not being very helpful and making little covert notes on a pad. Anyway, by virtue of the fact that we are pants at orienteering, it is now way past teatime and we are not even half way through our list of clues. And I have gone *right* off Russell.

Scene 1. Somewhere in South Wales (possibly). Enter Russell, stage left.

'Sal, you are wrong. *There* is the bridle path. The *only* bridle path. It *has* to be that way.'

Russell's voice, I noticed, had taken on a rather petulant quality. I could see him glance at Nick for corroboration.

'Russell,' I tried again. 'It can't be that way. You must be reading the compass wrong –'

'I am not reading the compass wrong, Sally.'

Correction. Aggressive quality.

'Look,' I began again, growing increasingly irritated at both his superior tone and Nick's dogged refusal to take charge and take the bloody compass off him – a bullet point, no doubt, in his wretched teambuilding guidelines. The girl guide in me had long since departed. I was tired and fed up and I needed a wee. No way was I yomping any further across eighteen inch scrub in the wrong direction. I needed serious undergrowth and I needed it soon. 'The thing is,' I went on, 'that if you follow that contour line North West you'll see it gets to a point where there are lots of other contour lines all close together, in a circle. See? Which means a hill. Which means –' I pushed the map pouch under his nose again, 'a *steep* hill. Look that way now. No hill. There would be a hill. But there's no hill. So that way can't be North West, can it? The hill is over *there*.'

Assuming, that was, that we were standing where we thought we were standing, which, by this stage, was no longer certain. Nothing was certain in this bleak and peculiar landscape. Where I came from there was countryside and there was seaside. The former characterised by sweet smelling herbage, picnic areas and cows, the latter by pebbles and promenades and chips. The distinction, in this place, was muddied and uncertain. Here a tree, there a sand dune, here a sheep, there the sea. And not a sniff of a chip shop anywhere.

Russell shifted his weight on to his other foot and glared intently at the compass. Nick was still fiddling with his mobile.

'Perhaps we should go Sally's way anyway, Russell,' he suggested. He had obviously now decided to abandon his *laissez faire* methodology in favour of getting something more constructive done than simply standing around looking rugged. 'At least we might stand a chance of getting a signal up there. I mean, I take your point about the bridle path, but given that it's going to get dark in an hour or so and that it won't be long before we can't make out any of the landmarks anyway, I'm just a bit worried that if we can't get a signal then we're well and truly stymied. What d'you think?'

'I take your point too, Nick,' Russell said in a tone altogether different to the one he'd just bestowed on me. A tone of blokey fraternity and after-match shower rooms and androgen-flavoured deodorant and sweat. 'But if we're all agreed that we've just travelled three miles North – which we are, aren't we?' He glared at me now. 'Then we should be one and a half miles south east of *there*. Which means the ruined castle will definitely be –'

'There are *two* castles on this map, Russell. Two. And I don't think the one we are supposed to be finding – '

'I think,' said Nick, clearly spotting the word 'diplomacy' on his tick sheet and feeling the need to leap in and be aggressively uncontentious, 'that we'd better cancel any plans to reach the castle today. Don't you guys? I think we should really be thinking in terms of trying to establish our position and, having done so, in terms of bypassing the rest of the landmarks and working out which way the meeting point is.'

We were meant to get lost. That was it. This was hitherto undisclosed mettle testing component. That the quality of our responses to being up shit creek would decide who got slapped on the back and promoted and who simply got slapped. I would quite like to have slapped Russell just then.

'Which is what I am trying to *do*, Nick,' he reminded him in what I thought was a rather daringly abrasive tone. 'Only until we can reach some sort of agreement about our position –' He stopped. Contemplating small scale genocide? Who knew?

I pulled the map out from its plastic pouch and slapped *it* instead. 'Look,' I said again. (Being an optometrist, I suppose.) 'Let me just run this by you again. This is where I think we are. Woods, here. Hill, there. Bridle path possibly *there,* I do appreciate, but given that there isn't a stick in the ground to say so, and given that we can see *two* other landmarks that definitely correspond to the map, I think we should go with my reading of it. Which puts us roughly here. OK? Which means we are about, oh I don't know, a mile or so south west of this mound here. On that basis, we should make for the hill. The castle – *the* castle – should be visible pretty soon after we get up it a way. The meeting point is here. Therefore, if we head towards the hill, we should be able to drop down over the footpath there, and we'll be on our way back by default. See?'

Nick nodded. Russell sniffed. He closed the cover on the compass. Click.

'Right,' he said. 'Fine,' he said. 'Whatever,' he said. 'Five minutes in the bloody scouts and you clearly know everything. Fine. Let's go then.'

'For God's *sake*, Russell! Can't we discuss this without you getting in such a strop for once?'

But Russell wasn't listening. He was already ten yards ahead and striding out like Mallory up some bleak Himalayan moraine.

'Hmm,' said Nick, shouldering his backpack and winking at me.

'And don't *you* start,' I snapped.

But I smiled, all the same.

So we walked, strung out like a circus tightrope act, for another forty minutes or so, the air growing colder and the wind growing stronger and the whole afternoon disintegrating into exactly the sort of sulky stand-off that Drug U Like had no doubt wished to encourage, the better to hone us into crack spectacle retailers. The landscape, always undulating, was growing increasingly hilly. We were following the line of the coast now and the scrubby uneven ground was more sand than soil. The reassuring string of street lights that had wound beyond the trees to the north of us were, now, I realised, nowhere to be seen. But our route was at least taking us down a dip in the landscape, and the vegetation was at last growing thicker.

I was just pondering my pathetic anxiety about calling for a wee stop in such aggressively willy-endowed company (and its possible consequences for my managerial style profile) when Russell, who was still way out front and apparently not talking to either of us, turned around and stomped back.

'Great,' he said, as we approached. 'Now what?'

We formed another fairy ring around his precious compass. The wind was piling in off the sea now, and blowing sand into our eyes.

'What?' asked Nick.

Russell gestured ahead of us. 'We have a river, is what. Any suggestions?' He was looking very pleased with himself.

'A river?' I asked.

'Yes. It's a long wide wet thing. You may have come across one. Though not on that map of yours, obviously.'

I lifted the map and scrutinised it carefully.

'There's no river marked here. Not that I can see, anyway.' I traced my finger along the line of our route.

'May I?' asked Nick. I pulled the cord from around my neck and handed the map pouch to him. He took the map from inside it and unfolded it, then scrutinised it himself for a few minutes. Russell stood about a bit more with one hand on his hip and his compass aloft.

'There's a river here,' he said at last, pointing to a blue line on a different part the map. 'Leading down into this estuary. Perhaps we're not where we thought we were. Perhaps we're here. Look, if you follow the route of the river in relation to that hill, then it's possible – yes. Look. There's the farm buildings we were supposed to have passed. Perhaps we should have taken that footpath after all.'

I peered at the map. 'Which footpath?'

'When we were at that milestone an hour or so back.'

'Oh,' piped up Russell. 'You mean the one *I* said we should take?'

'No, not that one,' answered Nick. 'The one before that. The one when we were at that fork. By the sheep field.'

Hah! The one *I* said we should take, in fact. Though clearly not strenuously enough. But there was no satisfaction in saying so, because I'd most probably get a black mark for having been such an acquiescent wimp. I said nothing. Russell spat a midge from his mouth. Nick wrestled with the now flapping map.

'So I guess,' he said, having folded it into some sort of submission,' that it's probable we are, in fact, *here*.' He pointed. 'Which means –'he scanned the hillside and traced a finger along the paper. '– that we need to head west.'

Russell tutted. 'Across the river.'

Nick nodded. 'Across the river.'

So much talk of water. I couldn't stand here any longer. 'Hang on,' I said. 'I have *got* to find a bush.'

*   *   *

When I re-emerged, minutes later, they both seemed in markedly better spirits, having shared the last of Russell's contraband whiskey, and having decided, possibly as a result of the former, that they both now knew exactly where we were. I, meanwhile, had struggled with both my knickers and my conscience. Was the pink plastic packaging from my Drug U Like whisper even now choking a hapless wagtail to death?

'OK?' asked Nick. I assumed the question was rhetorical and not really a request for details. Even so, there was a note of mild amusement in his voice. I looked down at my boots for splash marks.

'Fine,' I said, feeling myself colour. 'So. What's the plan?'

Nick handed me the map and heaved his back pack back on to his shoulders. 'We're going to head up alongside the river for a bit, till we find a good place to cross.'

'*Is* there a good place to cross?'

'We think so. According to the map the source is no more than a couple of miles away, so we reckon it'll narrow down fairly rapidly. If it doesn't, we'll just have to keep going till we get there. There's a bridle path that skirts the edge of the hill and seems to join a road further along.'

I really didn't want to argue with someone whose smile made various bits of me feel so mushy, but needs must . 'Are you sure it wouldn't make more sense to try and head back to the start point?' I said. 'I mean, we didn't cross a river earlier, did we? And we're still not *entirely* sure we know where we are.'

Nick shook his head, narrowing his eyes against the wind. 'No point. There'll be no one there, will there? And it was a pretty remote spot itself.'

I began re-folding the map to fit back into the pouch. 'I suppose. But are we sure the meeting point is the best place to aim for now? I mean, aren't there any villages or anything we could head for on this side of the river?'

'Not within walking distance,' said Russell. I opened up the map again to check for myself.

Which proved to be about the stupidest decision in a day full of stupid decisions, because no sooner had I done so than the wind, now obviously intent on a no holds barred ruck with our collective spirit, snatched it from me and whisked it away into the air. Russell made a grab for it and fell over a tussock, forcing Nick to hurdle both as he set off in pursuit.

It didn't travel far, as the crow flies. But none of us being crows, it might just as well have. We caught up with Nick and peered up into the foliage. The map had finished up wedged among the boughs of a fat oak that was growing by the riverbank.

'Bugger,' said Russell. 'That's that then. Now we really *are* lost.'

'No more lost than we were five minutes ago,' I offered.

'But with every possibility of getting more lost by the minute.'

'And it's beginning to get dark,' observed Nick. 'But I can get it anyway. If you give me a leg up, Russell.'

The river ran through in a small gorge. The ground fell away sharply to the right of the footpath, the tree in which the map was lodged rising up from the steep slope and branching only slightly above our heads. But the map, infuriatingly, was still just out of reach.

'Is there really any point?' I asked him.

He nodded. 'I don't see how we're going to find our way back without it. Once it gets dark we could be going round in circles all night. It's not that high –' He began shrugging off his back pack once more, his can-do expression in place. '– just a question of a couple of feet, really. Give us a hand here, Russell, and I'll try and make a grab for it.'

Russell laced his fingers and cupped his hands at knee height. His hair was all tufty from the now swirling wind, and he looked like a chimpanzee. Nick put his foot in and said 'brace yourself. Ready?' then, one hand splayed firmly on the top of Russell's head, he launched himself upwards and stretched to get hold of the nearest branch.

But failed to. Just a twig, which immediately snapped off in his hand. Russell grunted as Nick teetered, flailing wildly for a hand hold, before crashing back down, knocking them both off their feet.

Which would have been fine – the tree could keep the bloody map, then – except that, in attempting not to stamp on Russell's head, Nick did the splits, careered over backwards, and shot off in a muddle of limbs down the slope.

I could hear him say 'yow!' then a flurry of leaf litter, then an 'oof!' then an 'ouch!' then a couple of loud snaps. Horrified, I sank to my knees at the edge of the footpath.

'Oh, Christ!' I said, peering into the darkness. 'Nick? Nick! Are you all right?'

'Er…no,' came the distant answer. 'I've hurt my side and I think I've done something to my ankle.'

Russell scrabbled across to join me. The canopy of leaves was so thick and complete that we could barely make Nick out. A swathe of flattened foliage marked his route and a strong smell of soil filled the chilly air. He was about twenty feet below us. Close to the water. *In* it, in places, even.

'What sort of something?' asked Russell. 'Have you broken it?'

'I don't know,' he called breathlessly. 'I twisted it when I fell.'

He groaned and rolled over. He'd been brought to a stop by a thick fringe of bracken and saplings. Had they not been there, he'd have fallen straight in over the bank.

I turned to Russell. 'I think we're going to have to climb down and help him up,' I said anxiously.

'God! Orienteering is the pits,' he replied.

We slithered carefully down. The slope was steep and deceptively treacherous. The jumble of spring growth and half-rotted leaves camouflaged numerous outcrops of rock. Russell got to him first, and squatted beside him. I scrambled across. Even in the semi-darkness, Nick looked grey. Both his feet were wet and he was splattered with soil and decomposing leaves.

'How bad is it?' I asked, fairly stupidly. I was beginning to feel seriously fed up now, and not a little anxious. He gritted his teeth and smiled weakly up at me. 'Let's just say I'm not going to be instigating any rollerblading initiatives in the near future. Jeez. What a stupid thing to do.'

It seemed to take forever to haul him back up the slope. By the time we reached the top again, sweating and panting, it was almost fully dark, the first stars glimmering shyly above us and just a low strip of pink left on the horizon to usher out the remains of the day.

'Right,' he said, taking charge once again as we re-convened and sat down on the grass back up at the path's edge. There was a gleam of sweat on his forehead, and he was breathing heavily. He looked as if he was in serious pain. 'We need to make a plan,' he said. 'Best bet, I think, is that I stay here, and you two retrace your steps back up as far as the milestone. Yes. That'll be best. One thing we do know is that the footpath there eventually connects with a road. The road they brought us in on, right?'

He paused. We waited.

'Right?' he said again.

'Right,' we both echoed.

'OK,' he went on. 'Once you're on the road there's bound to be a car along eventually, or, if not, a house, a farm or something. Somewhere you can get help from at any rate. And you have your mobile, don't you, Russell? I'm sure once you've gotten a little higher, you'll be able to get a signal anyway, in which case, you can call up the centre and get them to come out and meet you. Meantime, I'll hobble a bit higher up this hill, so I can keep an eye out for you. OK?' His face was beginning to look as if it had been clingfilmed. He was blinking a lot. 'And you'd better take the torch,' he mumbled 'Oh, and the number of the centre, of course. In my…in my….'

And then he groaned and his head flopped down between his knees.

'Oh, *Jesus*!' bleated Russell. 'Jesus! What now?'

Nick didn't move, though I could still hear his breathing. I could see the downy hair on the back of his neck was wet.

'Russell, get the bag. There's some water in there.'

Russell fished in the back pack and pulled out the tepid remains of the bottle of Volvic.

'Shall I throw it on him?'

Nick's head snapped up again. 'Don't you dare bloody throw it on me! I'm fine, OK? Just felt a bit dizzy, is all. Shit, but my side really hurts.'

I took the bottle from Russell, opened it and handed it to Nick.

'Here, drink some,' I told him, more than ever anxious now to have him in one piece. 'It's probably the pain. And you're probably dehydrated too. Better?'

He nodded. Though I wasn't sure he was. Any half-formed wild hopes I'd harboured about this being the point where he'd tell us everything was all right and that he had flares or a field telephone or an emergency fold-away four by four in his pocket had long since disappeared. The expression on his face was beginning to scare me.

He looked like he really was going to faint. Perhaps we should get him up on his feet. I had visions of one of those dreadful movies where if the hero isn't kept walking up and down, he'll die. I never quite worked out why, precisely, but it frightened me all the same.

I jiggled his arm. 'You've hurt yourself badly, haven't you? *Where* does it hurt? Which side? Shall I have a look? Oh, God! *Bloody* map.'

He grimaced again as he gestured. 'Here. Yes. My ribs. I think I landed on my mobile.'

'Oh, my God, Russell! He might have broken some ribs! There might be internal bleeding. Try not to move, Nick. Stay as still as you can, OK?' I looked across to Russell. 'We can't leave him. We can't leave him here on his own, can we?'

Russell's forehead creased. 'So what do we do?'

'I don't know.'

'I'm fine,' said Nick. '*Really*. Just –'

I turned back to him. 'Just what?'

'Just, well, just that if you could loosen your grip on my wrist a little it might improve my circulation, is all.'

I hadn't even realised. I gave him his arm back. He looked like a ghost.

'We can't leave him,' I said again.

'No,' Russell conceded. 'But we have to do something. How about one of us stays here with Nick and the other one goes? Like, well, I suppose, like me, maybe?'

He looked like he'd rather lick the asphalt off a newly tarred road, but I could tell he could see it was the only thing to do. Unless I went, of course. He was looking very anguished. Who knew what big fears lurked within his veneer of machismo? I felt rather sorry for Russell at that moment. He seemed suddenly terribly young.

'Or me,' I said, mentally crossing my fingers. '*I* could go.'

'No way,' said Nick, with encouraging firmness. Perhaps he wasn't about to die after all. Then he added, 'You can't go off on your own, Sally,' which comment would, in any number of alternative circumstances, have had me bristling with feminist pique. But not this one. Oh, no. No veneers with me.

Russell caught my eye. 'No, no, Nick's right,' he agreed quickly. 'Be better if I go. You stay with Nick and do the nursey TLC bit.'

'If you can just find somewhere high enough,' suggested Nick, while I went radish, 'you should be able to get a signal.'

I felt frightened for him. Frightened for all of us. It was dark. What if Russell had an accident too? I spread my hands. 'But how will they find him? He won't know where he is, will he?'

Nick shook his head. 'It doesn't matter. They'll send out a search party. They'll find us.' He looked into the gloom. 'Eventually.'

We half carried, half dragged Nick up the footpath a little further, to where a gap in the scrub formed a steep thistled pathway that gave us access to a pale expanse of dune. I gave him three paracetamols with the last of the water, and we settled ourselves on the ground. We'd attached Russell's white baseball cap to a branch by the footpath, and could do nothing now but await his return.

We watched him stride off with the torch and the back-pack. And then there we were. All alone.

Chapter 8

Alone *together*.

What a day. It's been six or seven hours now since we set off from the centre, and it feels like even more. I am damp, I am cold, I am hungry, I am tired, I am bashed, I am battered, I have sand in my boots. And yet, here I am, standing on the crest of a sand dune, a vista of picture-postcard beauty below me, and a moon of impossibly detailed perfection, slung low, like a beach ball, in a cloudless night sky. So what do I feel? I feel alive. Alive in a way I haven't in a long time. I'm not sure why, but I do, all of a sudden. Perhaps there is something to this lark after all.

Scene 2. Somewhere else in South Wales. Stage right.

'Ahoy there!'

Nick had hobbled off down a dune a little way to 'make use of the restrooms' as he put it. I fretted briefly about the vague embarrassment I'd feel if I could hear him doing a wee (why?) but the silence in his absence was complete and unbroken. It was almost as if I'd found myself marooned in another time. The only solid evidence of the twentieth century was a solitary light that burned way over on the other side of the estuary, high on the hillside, beyond the far shore. The tide had gone out and the crescent of bay was a smooth bed of sand now. Waiting to be walked on and pummelled by bare toes.

'I'm right here,' I called, turning to scan the darkness behind me. His shape reappeared as a solid block against the skyline. I trotted across to help him back up.

'You're bad for my health, you are,' he observed, as I linked my arm in his to help him. 'I was just thinking. You know, every time I come into contact with you some disaster or other seems to happen.'

'What! Well, that's charming, I must say. It's *me* who should be worried. You're a walking calamity.'

'You got us lost.'

'*Russell* got us lost. And it was *you* who had the bright idea to try and shimmy up a tree trunk, as I recall. In my book that makes *me* the innocent victim, not you.'

He nudged me with his elbow.

'Ah, but it's a vibes thing. Must be some sort of aura you've got going or something. If I had any sense, I 'd give you a pretty wide berth. Yeeow! You *see*? You just took me straight down a pot hole! Like I say, bad for my health.'

For all that, he was looking much better. The painkillers had long since kicked in, and my panicky fears for his gradual slide into coma had long since melted away. Taking my hand for support, he eased himself gingerly back down on to the thick grass, then tucked the arm on his good side carefully behind his head and grinned up at me.

'What we really need,' he said chattily, 'is a whistle.'

I lowered myself down beside him. The grass was all spikes and thorns. I yanked on a length and started idly stripping it. 'A whistle? What for?'

'First rule of orienteering. Always carry a whistle.' He grinned again. 'In case you lose your map.'

'And what's the second rule?'

'Um…pass. Don't know. Probably always carry a bicycle. Or orienteer only in a built up area. Or, no. Probably that if you've elected to ignore the first rule, then whatever you do, don't lose your map.'

I sucked on the smooth green stem I'd extracted and listened to the far away hiss of the sea. I wondered, idly, what my family were up to. They seemed a very long way away.

'Is there a wine gum rule?' I asked him.

'I very much doubt it. Why?'

'Because it would be nice to think I've got something right, and I happen to have a packet in my pocket. I've been saving them. Do you want one?'

He raised himself carefully on to one elbow. 'Jeez. I don't think I've eaten a wine gum in two decades. Do they still say port and claret on them? It always felt very grown up to be sucking on something so sinful.'

I ferreted in the folds of my Barbour. 'At least I thought I had – oh, no. I know. I put them in the game pocket.'

He raised his brows. 'The *what?*'

'The game pocket.' I lifted the flap and slipped my hand into it. 'The *detachable* game pocket, in fact. It's where you put your bloody corpses once you've shot them so you don't get entrails spilling out all over your tweeds.'

'Ugh, that's so gross,' he said, rolling slightly to look at me. He lifted his forearm and propped his chin on his palm. There were the beginnings of dark stubble clouding his jaw. He pulled a face. 'No rotting game in there with the wine gums, I hope?'

I shook my head as I pulled out the bag. 'Not unless – hey! That's a thought! I *do* have a whistle! Of course I do!' I ferreted some more. 'God, I'm so stupid! I've got Merlin's whistle! Here!' I pulled it out and handed it to him. 'It's worth a try, isn't it?'

He turned it in his hand and then put it to his lips and blew.

'Except it doesn't work.'

'Oh, no. It does work. It's just you can't hear it because it's the wrong frequency for human ears. But I thought, if there's someone out there looking for us with a dog –'

'Or *just* a dog, maybe. A wild dog. A pack of wild dogs perhaps. Or wolves. They still have wolves in Wales don't they? I think they do in the Appalachians. Should we take cover or something?' His eyes were picking up shards of moonlight and reflecting them back at me. He started laughing.

'Of course they don't,' I said. 'At least I don't *think* they do. No, of course not.'

'But you never know. Perhaps Merlin will hear it, eh? Perhaps he'll come bounding to the rescue.' He laughed. 'Jeez, you know, you gave me such a fright that night. You and your huge dog and your wild hair and that maniac look in your eyes. I thought you were going to slug me.'

'Me? Gave *you* a fright? That's rich! Just stop and think how it must have seemed for me! Tootling along happily, minding my own business and then this crazy man comes storming down the lane straight towards me. I thought I was going to die, for sure.'

'But you didn't. So you obviously weren't on the list that day.' He turned to look at me. 'You believe in fate?'

'I believe in a careful observance of the highway code. It's stood me in good stead so far.'

'No, I mean, *really*.'

'No. Not at all. You make your own luck. Why, do you?'

'I wasn't thinking luck. I was thinking more of serendipity. That kind of thing. But, no. I guess you're probably right. Funny though, us nearly colliding that night, wasn't it? And then you fetching up at the meeting three days later.' He turned the whistle in his hands and chuckled to himself. 'With that 'don't mess with me, pal' look on your face.'

'Cheek!'

'If I was a wolf, I don't think *I'd* mess with you.' He handed it back to me. 'Even so, no point in tempting it, eh?'

'What?'

'Fate, dingbat. Perhaps we'll just stick with the wine gums, yes?' He lay on his back again and chewed his sweet. 'Jeez, it's starry tonight.'

I lay down again also. The sea grass was tussocky and damp underneath me, but the sky was a perfectly smooth wash of ink.

'Very. I wish I had some binoculars.'

'I wish I had a mattress. And a blanket. And a pillow. And a flask of coffee. And some muffins. And some good runny honey. And a TV with five sports channels. Oh, and a bottle of bourbon. Hey. ' He nudged me lightly with his elbow. 'D'you want to hear a joke?'

'Go on, then.'

'OK. Let's see if I remember this right. Sherlock Holmes, OK? And Watson, of course, well, they go on a camping trip. They head out into the countryside, set up their tent, and go to sleep. Some hours later, Holmes wakes up Watson, and says "Watson, look up at the sky and tell me what you see."

'Watson looks up and replies, "I see millions of stars."

" Hmm," says Holmes. "And what does that tell you?"

'Watson thinks for a bit and then he says, "Astronomically speaking, it tells me there are millions of galaxies and potentially billions of planets. Astrologically speaking, it tells me that Saturn is in Leo. Time-wise, it appears to be approximately a quarter past three. Theologically speaking, it's evident that the Lord is all powerful and that we are but small and insignificant beings. Meteorologically speaking, it tells me we will have a beautiful day tomorrow. What does it tell you, Holmes?"

'Holmes is silent for a moment, then speaks.

"Watson, you idiot," he says. "Someone's stolen our tent!"'

I'd heard it before but it didn't seem to matter. It still made me laugh. 'That's a very good joke.'

He smiled with childish pleasure. 'It is, isn't it? My son emailed it me last week. God, but I wish *we* had a tent.' He held up his wrist and squinted at his watch face. 'Jeez. Nearly eleven. D'you think he *has* gotten lost?'

I thought it highly likely. 'Yes,' I said, feeling not the slightest trace of panic. 'But he'll be back soon enough. Another wine gum?'

He took one and held it in the air to inspect it. It glowed amber against the soft gleam of the moon. He popped it into his mouth. 'I don't think Saturn is in Leo right now. I think Uranus is just nudging up alongside Aquarius with a view towards making a stab at Sagittarius. You think?'

'God, I wouldn't know. I know sod all about astrology.'

He laughed.

'Me neither. I just made that up. But there's the Plough, and that's Cassiopeia, isn't it? Over that way?' He pointed. 'Yeah. Yeah, I think it is. That W shape.'

I scanned the sky. 'And that's Perseus. Low, over there. If it was winter you'd be able to see the Pleaides too, but they rise in the day at this time of year.'

'The Pleaides?'

'The Seven Sisters. My favourite stars. Just under Taurus. They're very faint. It's actually easier to see them when you're not looking straight at them. Kind of catch them out of the corner of your eye. Look right at them and they seem to disappear. It's a rods and cones thing. The rods are for monochrome vision and the cones are for colour. And because you have a greater density of rods than cones towards the edges of the retina, when you look at faint things at night, they're clearer at the edge of your visual field. Which is why stars like the Pleaides seem to disappear when you look straight at them.'

'Well, I never knew that.' He turned his head towards me. Even though I couldn't see it, I was aware that he was gazing at me again. It made me feel strange. 'You study the stars a lot then?' he asked.

'Not study, exactly. I wouldn't profess any proper knowledge. But I certainly spend lots of time looking at them.'

'An amateur astronomer, then.'

'Hardly. No. More a professional insomniac.'

I could smell the orangey sweetness of the wine gums between our faces as he exhaled. 'Tell me about it,' he said.

'You too, then?'

'Yeah. Me too. Me *three*. But, hey. *C'est la vie*, and all that. I used to waste a hell of a lot of time worrying about it, but now I've pretty much decided not to bother. Except that it's so maddening that every morning at about six I get sleepy like you wouldn't believe. You know?'

I reached down to zip up my jacket again. 'I know. I know that feeling exactly. I wish I had the knack. I wish I could work out what it is that wakes me up. I've tried all sorts. Baths, milky drinks, exercise, relaxation tapes…' I shrugged. He was nodding.

'And nothing works, right?'

'Nothing.'

'You worry?'

'About not sleeping?'

He shook his head. 'Worry about *everything*. You know. Go over every little thing. Fret. I wouldn't mind so much if I could write a symphony in my head or enjoy a good book or something. But I can't. It's such a lump of dead, unproductive, frustrating time.'

'Oh yes, too right I do. Trouble is, I don't even have anything big *to* worry about. So I worry about rubbish. I worry about running out of dog food. I sometimes wonder what would happen if I *did* have something big to worry about. I doubt I'd sleep at all. But you're right. You get used to it. It's not such a big thing any more. So I sit and I think, and I gaze at the stars, with my little Patrick Moore book by my side.'

'Patrick Moore? He still alive? Jeez!'

'I think so.'

'Well that's all pretty constructive stuff,' he said, smiling and gesturing to the heavens. 'And you've got plenty to gaze at tonight, for sure.'

I tipped my head back and gazed along with him.

'You know, It often occurs to me what a stupefying concept it is that it doesn't matter if I'm home or, say, here, or in France or in Spain, and yet the sky I'm looking it is the very same one. Gives you a real sense of scale, doesn't it? Is the night sky the same in America?'

'In the North, I think. But San Diego's on a different latitude of course, so I guess the stars would be in different positions at different times.' He tucked a hand behind his head again. 'Been a long time since I've looked at this patch of sky.'

'Is that where you live, then? Why did you go there? Was it work?'

He nodded. 'Sort of. I got a post- grad exchange after I finished my MBA. I couldn't wait to leave Britain. Which led on to the offer from Drug U Like. I've been with them fifteen years now.'

'And now you've been sent back here again. Full circle. Does it feel strange?'

He continued to stare at the sky. 'It feels very strange, as it happens. I mean, I've done a lot of travelling in the States with my job, and I get back here once or twice a year. Family visits and so on – my mum lives in Reigate , but I dunno. Yeah, I guess. Strange. I feel a bit disconnected. I miss my son a lot. Though he's at college now so I guess I'd be missing him anyway, huh? And friends, of course. But I've got a lot of difficult domestic stuff going on right now so I guess this placement was probably the right thing to do. For the moment.' He shook his head then, not, it seemed, in negation of anything, but almost as if he wanted to shake some snow from his shoulders. Talk about something else, maybe. It occurred to me, right then, how lonely he might be. I thought I should trundle something bland and light and conversational into the silence in case he thought I was waiting for him to elucidate – hmm. Like Kate's tattoo, maybe? Maybe not. Not right now. But before I could think of anything else he moved his hand, then thrummed his fingers against his chest and smiled at me again.

'Boy, but this ground's uncomfortable, though, isn't it? And cold.' He glanced across at me. 'You're shivering. And that wind's getting up again. You think we should maybe move down the dune a bit? Sit on the sand instead?'

He hauled himself back up to a sitting position and cast around him, the wind, which was indeed getting stronger, carving furrows through his hair. 'Down there, maybe?' He was pointing to where the grassy summits of two dunes dipped to form a slight gully. 'Guess he'd find us just as readily down there, wouldn't he? And they'll have lights. What d'you think?'

Sitting up again myself, I felt the full force of the strengthening breeze. It would make sense. It was a clear night. It could only get colder. 'I think you're right. Let's go down there, if you think you can manage. At least there'll be a little more shelter. Here, let me help you up.'

I took hold of his arm as he eased himself upright, wincing a little from the pain in his side, and again as he placed his injured foot on the ground. I could feel the hard swell of his bicep beneath his jacket. A solid, reassuring chunk of muscle.

'Lean on me,' I told him, bringing my arm around his back to support him. 'That's it. Let me take your weight. Is it very painful still?'

'It's a bitch. Yeeow! Shit, that was *not* a good move. That *hurts*!'

'Then try not to put too much weight on it. Take it slowly. No rush.'

'Sally, rushing,' he said, making his first careful move, 'is not on the agenda tonight.'

He lifted his own arm around my shoulder and we made hesitant progress over the crest of the dune, moving carefully down through the shifting sand. His weight against me made it difficult to balance. His jacket smelled woody and fragrant. I picked my way cautiously as the slope began to steepen, conscious of his warm bulk against my side. The dune here fell away sharply in great concave swathes. It was a curious, alien landscape.

'This looks OK,' I said, glancing around to pick out a suitable nook and scanning the ground for debris. 'If we sit here we're out of the wind, but we can still see some way back up along the valley. See a light, at any rate, when it comes.' I helped him back down to a sitting position against the sand bank and climbed back up a few paces for another glance around. '*If* it comes,' I added. 'He has been ages, hasn't he? I can't imagine it took him that long to get back to the road. How far could it be? Three or four miles?'

'Hmm,' he said, leaning back against the dune and grimacing as he shuffled his back against the sand and straightened his leg. 'I think that might be a *little* optimistic. More like five is my guess. Difficult to say. We were walking around lost for a fair while. Could be further.'

I slithered back down the slope and sat down beside him again, cosy in the lee of the wind. For all the manifest hassles inherent in our situation, I felt strangely content beneath this big sky. Strangely unperturbed by our predicament. Strangely disconnected from my own domestic 'stuff'. Strangely calm. Strangely happy, even. Alive.

'Oh, well,' I said. 'At least it's a bit warmer down here. Another wine gum?'

'Steady,' he said. 'We might need to ration them.' He leaned forward and rolled up his trouser leg a little. 'God, but I'm not sure if I shouldn't get this boot off my foot for a while. It's really throbbing – and, boy, swollen some, too. Look!' He carefully peeled away the top of his damp sock. His ankle underneath it was bulging inside the boot and the skin looked bluish and shiny. It was deeply grooved from the wet ribbing. I moved up on to my knees to look more closely at it. Even in the moonlight it looked livid.

'God, I wish I knew the first thing about first aid. I don't know. It really does look like it might be broken. And if it's broken, shouldn't you leave it as it is? Won't the boot act as a splint or something?'

He pressed the skin gingerly with his finger. 'I don't know. All I know is that right now it feels like it's on fire, and I can't move my toes.' His brows knitted a little. 'I don't think it's broken, though. I broke my arm when I was nine and it hurt so much I bit a great gouge from my lip trying not to cry.'

'Even so,' I said. 'I think you should leave it as it is. Just in case.'

'You're the boss,' he said, and rolled his trouser leg back down.

'Yeah, right,' I said. 'And you're a potato.'

I needed to make use of the restrooms myself soon after, so I hiked a good way up and along the dunes, scanning the dark tree and seascapes around me for the sound of a car or a light.

But there was nothing. Not a thing. Even the light across the bay had now vanished. I imagined some elderly cottager retiring for the night. Switching off the telly, brewing cocoa or hot milk. Filling a hot water bottle. Creaking up the stairs to bed. Even then, with the elements staking their chilly claim on the spring evening, I found myself curiously excited by this state of affairs. The rush of exhilaration that had replaced my earlier anxiety was showing no signs of abating. I breathed deeply, the salty tang prickling in my nostrils. In the distance, creamy lines of foam nudged the foreshore, moving sluggishly under the moon's rippling reflection and trailing glistening water trains over the beach. I turned and made my way back down the dune again, the sand sucking all sound from my movements and pouring in dark runnels down the slope ahead of me. What a strange situation to find myself in. How distant real life suddenly seemed.

I wondered if real life felt a bit removed for him too. What his difficult domestic stuff was. He raised his arm in greeting.

'You know, you looked just like a prow maiden, standing up there. A mad one, naturally, but very statuesque. Any sign of life?'

I flumped back down beside him in the lee of the wind and gathered my hair into a coil at the side of my neck, then drew my collar around it a little tighter.

'Not a thing. What's the time?'

'Almost midnight. Time for another wine gum, I think.'

I fished in my pocket and pulled the packet out.

'Six left. Black or yellow? Or, yep. There's a red.'

'No green ones?'

'No green ones. You already had the last green one.'

'Yellow, then.' He took it. 'God, Sally, look at the state of your hands!' He took both of them, covering my cold fingers with his warm ones. 'They're so scratched and bashed up. And freezing as well. You'd better put my jacket round your shoulders.'

I had barely noticed. But he was right. They were. Criss-crossed with grazes and tiny red weals. And, yes. Very cold. 'Don't be daft,' I said, feeling rather pleased with myself. Kind of blooded and tough. 'I'm OK.'

'But you're freezing. I insist. I'm supposed to be looking after you, don't forget.' He let go of my hands and began tugging his zip down.

'Oh, no,' I said, childishly pleased by this notion. 'You're wet. And you're hurt. So *you're* the one who has to keep warm. In fact, you should have *my* jacket.'

He forestalled my movement with a hand on my arm. 'Come on! As if! Look, OK, then. Why don't you move a little closer beside me instead? I know I really need to take a shower, but it'll make sense, won't it? Body heat. We'll both feel a lot warmer if we huddle up a bit.'

So we huddled up a bit.

And huddling up a bit was not, I think, a terrifically good idea.

A silence descended. A very big one.

'Well,' he said finally, his awkward tone echoing my thoughts and his arm now heavy around my shoulder. 'This is cosy, isn't it?'

I laughed a nervous little laugh. I felt light-headed. I tried to imagine I was huddled up with Russell to see if it would feel tangibly different from being huddled up, as I very much was now, with Nick Brown. I thought it probably would. I thought my pulse would probably be slower. I thought I would probably be a little less heavy on the palpitations front. 'Very,' I agreed. 'Ha ha. Is it somewhere on the Drug U Like teambuilding plan?'

I could feel him nod beside me.

'Oh, absolutely,' he said. 'Teambuilding is what it's all about, you know.'

'Ri-ight,' I said. 'So do I get extra points then?'

'Extra points?'

'Extra points for keeping the group leader warm. Extra points for the selfless distribution of body heat in the face of orienteering injuries. I suspect I'm pretty light on points right now, what with being so bad for your health and everything, so I could certainly use a few.'

I don't know why I said that. Firstly because it made no sense and was just so much stupid wittering, and secondly because it was a very flirtatious thing to say to a man of staggeringly good looks who has one arm around your shoulder. And who you are finally coming to acknowledge (domestic stuff away with the fairies by now) that you are attracted to in a fairly dramatic and overwhelming way.

I don't think *he* knew why I said that, either. He squeezed his arm against mine slightly and laughed a little laugh. It rumbled between us in that peculiarly intimate way laughs do when you're almost nose to nose with someone of the opposite sex. Then he looked at me. 'Oh, you got those already, believe me,' he said quietly.

I didn't know how to respond to that, laden, as it clearly might have been, with so much ambiguity and unspoken sexual innuendo and implication and so on, but on the other hand he could have been referring to some other aspect of my orienteering skills altogether, which is why exchanges of this nature are such a very tricksy thing to negotiate. Hmm…

I glanced back at him, shy now. Hmm. Assuming, that is, that you were seeing them as something to *be* negotiated, as opposed to the exchanges of a straightforward chat between two people who have no agendas they want to negotiate conversations towards in the first place. In the end I just said, 'Pardon?'

He blinked at me. 'I mean, I mean… sorry,' he said, looking embarrassed now. 'Forget I said that. I didn't mean to say that. But yes. Extra points. Righty-ho.'

But he *did* mean that. I knew he did. And worse, *he* knew I knew he did, so neither of us knew quite what to say next. God, how did this feeling manage to creep up on me like this? How did I not see this coming? I wondered if I should perhaps move away from him a little. Put a bit of distance between us. Because the only real difference between huddling and hugging is a clutch of consonants, after all.

On the other hand, if I moved away from him now it would be like confirming that there was a pretty important reason why we should avoid bodily contact with one another, which would not have done at all.

'Good,' I said instead, staying where I was and trying (if failing) to convey by means of body language that it was just plain old girl-guidey good sense to do so. The silence wandered back down to join us again and engage us in yet more wordless conversation.

'Well,' I went on, interrupting it anxiously. 'At least it's not raining. It would be pretty miserable out here if it was raining, wouldn't it?'

'It would, certainly,' he said, nodding.

'And colder, no doubt.'

'And colder.'

'And, well, wet.'

'And wet.'

'And miserable.'

'*And* miserable. And…well….' He turned away from me slightly. Looked up at the sky. Opened his mouth as if to speak. Then closed it again. Then took a deep, important sounding breath and turned his head to gaze at me. 'Sally,' he began. I took one as well, for insurance. 'Look, it's just that…' he switched his gaze to the the sky again. 'I don't know if this is…well, what I *guess* I mean is that I don't know if I should *really* be saying this, but…' And then he stopped and then started and then said 'Hey! Look at that!'

He was suddenly pointing. And I followed his gaze, relieved beyond belief to have a diversion from the scary seismic rumble that was beginning to undermine the foundations of our small talk again. My temples were thrumming. '*What?*'

'That star up there. See it? The one near the horizon. Good God! Is that moving, or what?'

'A plane?' I suggested.

'No, no,' He dropped his arm from around my shoulder and pushed himself up a little. 'It isn't! It's a star, for certain. And look! It *is*. It's *moving*!'

I raised myself up on to my knees and stared up into the sky. 'God, you're right! And look! Look at the tail on it! God, it's a shooting star! Wow!'

We watched, lapsing into an awed and, this time, less complicated silence, as the pinhead of light, with its fiery white tail, streaked fast, straight and sure across the night sky, till it was lost to us beyond the horizon.

'Wow,' I said again.

Nick whistled through his teeth. 'Wow is right. That was something else, wasn't it?' His enthusiasm was child-like. He squeezed my shoulder. 'That was pretty special, wasn't it? Jeez. I wish Will could see this! What a thing! You know, I've never seen one of those before!'

'Oh, ho! Never seen one of *what*?' came a voice. Russell's. Cutting through the moment like a well aimed machete. We both turned to look. His head bobbed on the skyline. I could hardly believe we hadn't heard him coming. I was suddenly, belatedly, all flustered and shaky.

'Over here!' he called out behind him. 'They're down here.'

He crested the dune and slithered down to meet us, the beam from his torch bouncing before him. He looked very pleased with himself. I was pleased *for* him. And pleased, no – *relieved*, that he'd arrived when he had.

'How's the invalid?' he asked, wobbling the beam at Nick's face. 'They've managed to get the four by four up to the base of the dune back there. D'you think you can hobble it? They've got a stretcher and everything if not.'

'I think I can hobble it,' said Nick, letting us both help him to his feet.

Russell was beaming too. Full of relief. We told him about the shooting star and then we all linked arms and heaved our way back up the sand dune, then over the other side, helped by two of the guys from the centre, and a local paramedic, who took charge of everything with reassuring bonhomie and back slaps all round. Were we feeling OK? Would we like some tea, maybe? Could they get either of us a blanket, perhaps? They fed Nick into the back seat and spent a few moments making a preliminary inspection of his injuries. Like Nick himself, they were pretty sure the ankle wasn't broken, but there were still his ribs to consider, and the ambulance, they told us, had already been organised. No problem, they said. They'd have us back safely in no time at all.

So that was all right, then.

But just as they closed the back door of the Land Rover, Nick caught my eye and he looked carefully at me. With a curious expression and big, questioning eyes.

I got into the front seat, made mute by the sudden butterflies taking wing in my stomach. *God.* Didn't know if he should say *what*?

Chapter 9

It had been all right when I went to bed. As I'd lain in my bunk, bathed in the wet flannel smell of the communal bathroom next door and listening to the faint rasp of Ruth's breathing, I had everything all clear and sorted in my head. I loved my husband. Yes, I was attracted to Nick Brown but I *did* love my husband. Didn't I? Yes. Of course I did. What a stupid question. I was happily married. The thing with Nick Brown – no, the *not-quite*-thing with Nick Brown, the *could-have-been-but-wasn't* thing with Nick Brown was exactly that. An attraction. A flirtation. A very pleasant flirtation, certainly – it felt nice and right and life-affirming and *good* to be fancied by someone you fancied back so wholeheartedly, especially when you spent half your life being groped by myopic old men. But that was all it was. One of those grown up but basically insignificant encounters that proper grown ups are wise to. Everything was all right. No need to fret. No need to feel guilty. No need for the thought police. Perish the thought. Nothing – but *nothing* – had changed.

Except now it's seven fifteen on a hazy Tuesday morning, and nothing seems to fit very well after all. I have slept quite well. I have slept unusually well, but have woken to the pounding of some hitherto undiscovered organ in my body. Not sexual. Not a heart string. Not anything I can recognise. Just a small leaping sensation as I contemplate the day. I wish I could switch it off, but I can't. I'm lying here, in my fusty top bunk. Close to the rafters and all the small nameless scurrying things that have made their homes here and I am a little sodium bomb, itchy beneath the hairy plaid blanket. I am listening to Ruth chattering about vest tops and bra straps but already I am wondering if he's back.

I grab for prosaics as I contemplate my feelings. Jonathan's sandwiches. Kate's tattoo. The prospect of saving-the-refuge with my mum. But they refuse to re-assure me. Refuse, because *I'm* changed. I've just seen my first shooting star.

Shooting stars are not stars at all, of course, but meteors. Tiny, tiny dust particles, that move at great speed, and which burn up on entry to the atmosphere. Amazing to think that something so tiny can produce such a spectacular effect.

'God, Sal, look at the state of you! What d'ya do? Get in a punch up with a porcupine?'

This had been Ruth, last night, back at the centre. They must have phoned ahead to let them know we were on our way, because by the time the Land Rover crunched noisily into the forecourt, there was already a small gathering of people outside, in various states of abandonment and dishevelment, all clapping and cheering us home. An ambulance was parked just off to the side, to transport Nick, as they'd told us, to the nearest hospital, in order to X-ray his chest and foot.

He was dispatched without delay, and I was led gratefully off for a shower. Despite the sudden intensity of our parting – no, no, *because* of it, maybe – I felt a bit high. A bit happy, in fact. A bit like I'd just been shot through with adrenaline. Or an arrow perhaps? A little gold one?

Ruth slopped wine into a plastic beaker and passed it to me through the shower curtain. The bathrooms were primitive. A row of six showers, a couple of toilets, some lockers, a battered slatted wood bench.

I looked. Ruth was right. The scratchy hands were just the tip of the iceberg. My shins were both similarly decoratively etched, and there was a crusty three inch cut along the outside of my thigh. The hot water was beginning to make them all hurt.

'You're right,' I said, making an inspection. 'And bites as well. Blimey, Ruth, I'm covered in them. Look at this – ' I stuck out an ankle for inspection. A collection of hard red lumps formed an impromptu bracelet. There were similar bumps on my neck. I stood and let the water stream over my body for a while, and the warm wine infuse inside.

I could hear Ruth sloshing more wine in her mug.

'Hmm. I'm *almost* glad I bunked off now,' she said. 'That guy from Horsham won, of course, and there's been one hell of a ding-dong between those two hags from Worthing. Almost came to blows, apparently. Russ seemed pretty chirpy. But what a balls up, eh?'

'Let's just say I shan't be in any great rush to do that *particular* exercise again.' Which was such a wild and crazy load of rubbish.

Right then I rather thought I'd like to go and live in the woods. Spear salmon for breakfast. Chop trees. Make fires.

'I shan't be in a great rush to do *any* of this again, quite frankly,' she said. 'You know I'm being pursued by that Pharmacist from Redhill now, don't you? And I have a horrible feeling I gave him my phone number last night. He's been offering me mint imperials all day.'

I stuck my head out.

'And your email address, if I remember rightly.'

'Oh, *God*. This is all too much! What a klutz I am! And *God!* There's me, stuck here and fending off the slithery advances of contemptible old men with ear hair and liver spots , and there's *you* – out there –' She gestured. 'All on your lonesome with the Anglo-American treaty. You! Who couldn't care less! Not fair. Not *fair*. What a missed opportunity! If only I'd known he was coming this morning! Shit, Sal, I wish he'd get a move on and ask me out.'

I retreated behind the curtain again to contemplate the alarming rush of blood this statement sent whooshing to my head.

'But he's married, Ruth,' I said.

'Separated,' I heard her say. 'So don't give me any of that moral indignation crap.'

'With a child,' I added.

'Hardly. He's at college. And so what?'

I turned off the water and pulled the curtain back again. I wondered how she knew all this. 'So everything!'

'So *nothing*! He's three thousand miles away, for God's sake!'

'That's not what I meant.'

'What *did* you mean, then?'

I stepped out of the shower and wrapped my towel around me. Ruth was pouring herself some more wine. I felt wilted, all of a sudden. 'I just meant…well, do you need those sort of complications in your life? Really? I mean, yes, he's attractive and all that, but you're young, and you're single. Do you really want to get involved with someone who's probably in his forties and who is everything but?'

She blinked at me. I was glad to be pink from the shower.

'Hey, I'm not talking a joint pension plan here, Sal. Only shagging. Only fun.'

I wished she wouldn't say things like that. It always put me in mind of copulating yaks. She was worth more than that. So, I thought, was he. 'Besides,' she went on. 'He's only here for a while anyway. What is it – a few months?'

Away from his difficult domestic stuff. 'I'm not sure,' I said.

'So we're not talking a long term heavy relationship-type scenario. I just fancy him like buggery, that's all. Where's the harm in that?'

I began gingerly rubbing myself dry through the towel. There were so many ways in which Ruth's cranky life-plan were causing her harm that I would have been at a loss to know how to respond to that one even if I hadn't just had fairly unequivocal (and now physiological – I was *burning*) evidence that Nick Brown wasn't interested in her. For all her thrusting post-feminist pursuit of here-and-now gratification, and her ballsy vocabulary of shagging and drinking, she was lonely and insecure and not terribly happy. She had no family to speak of – no brothers or sisters. Just her Dad, who I knew wasn't terribly well. But she spoke of him little, and I didn't like to press her.

'No harm,' I agreed carefully. 'But not much good either. I guess I just don't understand why you'd want to start another relationship that's going nowhere, that's all. I mean, I know you say you're not thinking long term, but aren't you going to at some point in your life?'

She stood up and snorted.

'Hang on, Sal!' she said, waggling a finger at me. 'Who says it *wouldn't* turn out to be long term? Eh?'

'But you just said –'

'Well of *course* I just said. I'm not stupid, you know. I do know how things work. But who's to say?' She spread her hands and the wine slapped against the side of her mug. 'Who's to say he *won't* fall madly in love with me and want to whisk me back to New York or wherever –'

'San Diego.' It had a dreamy ring about it.

'San Diego, then. It could happen. And – well, for Christ's sake, Sal, allow a girl her little daydreams, won't you?' She grinned at me, but there was something defiant in her eyes. 'I mean,' she said. 'Come on, who *knows*? Why *not*?'

I had no answer to that so I shrugged instead. Which she must have taken as disapproval, because she then said,

'Hey! What's with the face?'

'What face?'

'*That* face. You look like you're sucking on a lemon. Ha! Goodness, Sally Matthews, if I didn't know you were a happily married woman, I'd think you were after him yourself!'

Chapter 10

Nick didn't return. There had been a break, as it turned out. Not his ankle – he'd cracked one of his ribs. Nothing they could do for a cracked rib, apparently, but they'd kept him in hospital for what was left of the night, and then was driven back to his flat in Oxted by the Area Manager, who had to get back early for some meeting. The rest of us stayed at the centre for a de-briefing, then headed off for home, in my case, at some speed, as I had elected to travel with Ruth.

It was a little after one in the afternoon when she dropped me, and as I didn't have to go into work I decided I'd ignore the heaps of washing and shopping (and housework and drudge and arrangements and answerphone messages and *hassle,* frankly) and instead take myself and Merlin off on an afternoon jaunt down to my Mother's. Catch up with her news. Have a nice walk, perhaps. I wasn't done with outdoors. I wasn't done with this *feeling*. I didn't want to be Mrs Matthews again just yet.

But I *am* Mrs Matthews. As Ruth has already pointed out. I am Mrs Matthews, happily married woman. Well, I am, aren't I? To all intents and purposes, in every way visible, as far as anyone can see, is concerned, gives a fig about, I am not an *un*happily married woman, therefore I must be a happily married woman. Mustn't I?

I was a happy bride, certainly. I keep hanging on to that. I was a happy new mother, a happy young wife. Yet the years have rolled by and I don't think I have ever really paused to consider things properly. To step back and take stock. Was I really happy then? Am I really happy *now*? I look at Jonathan sometimes and I struggle to bring it back. The intensity of feeling that I had for him once. To re-engage with it, recall all its nuances and distractions. How enigmatic and protecting and powerful he'd seemed. And yet how vulnerable. Was that part of it? His stoical suffering? Which even now jolts me with sudden compassion. But I wonder if perhaps I should be feeling something different. Something more equal. Something less complicated. I think of him now and I feel no stirring of desire. But up to now I haven't worried. This is normal, is it not? Married people can't possibly keep all that stuff up for so long. I have no money worries, no health worries…and yet….

…and yet if that is so, then why am I feeling so strange right now? Why am I suddenly examining my happiness, as if it's something I can tot up as points on an index, hoping I'll reach the reassurance of achieving an acceptable score?

My mother, I think, is happy. When my father died ten years ago, my mum, holding on to the retirement dream they'd both cherished, sold their semi in Crawley and bought the little ground floor flat she's in now. It's only a short walk to the seafront from here, which is nice because my mum loves to walk. Loves to go to the shops, too, and it's near those as well. Thus she has everything she might want. Mind you, given the situation next door, perhaps a few things she might not want as well. But pulling up outside I see a poster in her window. 'Save number twenty-seven!' it proclaims, in felt tip. Yes, I decide, as I let Merlin out of the car. Overall, I think she's pretty happy.

If not right at this moment. Goodness me, but my Mum's got a bee in her bonnet this afternoon.

'Useless, useless, useless!' she announces as she ushers me into her flat. She marches across the living room and switches off the television.

'Who's useless?' I ask her as I flop down on her sofa. I have aches and pains in all sorts of unlikely places. Unlikely flutterings in others.

'Everyone!' she exclaims, hands on hips in the middle of the little room. 'I thought there would be a huge response once we'd got the piece in the paper – did I show you, by the way?'

'No, you didn't.'

She crosses the room and shunts her tapestry stand out of the way. She's been doing this tapestry for more than a decade. She bought it when Dad was ill and she'd sit up at night with him. All these years on, and it's still only half done. She pulls a file from a pile of papers on the side table behind it. Everyone seems to have a file on the go right now. Perhaps I should start one. *Top Secret. The Nick Brown Affair*. The thought brings a smile to my lips. Then the smile brings a lurch to my stomach. Mum hands me the paper. 'But nothing!' she says. 'Not a dicky bird! And as for all that twaddle that journalist gave me about mounting his media campaign or whatever he called it – nothing! He's not even returning my phone calls now. Probably thinks I'm just some meddlesome old nuisance. Why doesn't anybody *care?*' She stabs a finger in the general direction. 'It's on page eleven. Cup of tea?'

'Yes, please,' I say, flicking through the pages.

'And a biccie for you, Merlie?' She ruffles his head, and he trots off to the kitchen behind her.

The photo is rather good, in fact. My Mother, left of centre, holding a hastily scribbled placard, and a woman in big boots who I recognise as Polly, standing beside her and holding an oversized cheque for £100. There's a gaggle of my mum's neighbours clustered around the entrance, and to the edge a small girl with impossibly big eyes, holding a Barbie doll by the leg.

'Who's the cheque from?' I call out.

'Oh, one of the shoe shops in the Arndale Centre, bless them. One of the mums, Kayleigh, is working there part time. But it's a drop in the ocean. If Polly's any hope of raising a deposit to buy the place, we're going to need to raise thousands.' She comes back in, wiping her hands on a tea towel. 'Did you read the piece?'

'*Buy* the place? Is that what she's hoping to do?' Mum nods. 'Seems rather ambitious to me. I mean these houses must be worth a couple of hundred thousand at least. Quarter of a million even.'

'I think she's hoping for a lottery grant. She's applied. You never know.' She sits down on the sofa beside me. 'Oh, I know it's probably all pie in the sky, but if we could just get people *interested* – find a few benefactors – these poor women, Sally. It really makes you count your blessings that you married a decent man. And those poor little kiddies, what they've been through – it makes your blood run cold.' She pokes a finger at the picture. 'That's little Megan, that one. Tracey's daughter. She's such a sweetheart. Anyway. We've decided it's no good relying on the press, so we're going to start up a petition. Get thousands and thousands of signatures.'

I picture my mum harrying shoppers outside Debenhams. It certainly wouldn't be the first time.

'That's a good idea, mum,' I say. 'That the sort of thing will get you lots of publicity. And it'll carry some weight with your MP as well.'

She shakes her head and grins at me, before getting up again and heading back to the kitchen. I follow her in. The kettle has boiled now, wreathing the tiny room with steam. The windowsill, as ever, is crammed with flowerpots on saucers, all playing host to

African Violet cuttings in various stages of carefully nurtured growth.

She pours milk into mugs. 'Oh, I'm not going to bother with *him,'* she says. 'I'm going straight to the top. I'm going to deliver it to Tony Blair.'

I grin back. 'Just like that?'

'Just like that,' she says firmly. 'In person. Right. Cup of tea, and then we'll go for that walk. And you can tell me all about your trip.'

When I got home, Jonathan's car was already in the drive, and he was Hoovering it. Jonathan Hoovering was always a bad sign. Jonathan could not Hoover and be happy. Jonathan Hoovered in the same way as other people took their frustrations out on squash balls or punch bags or post office queues. Were he happy he'd be sitting in the garden with the sports pages. I had spoken to him only briefly since returning from Wales, and that had been on the phone before I left for my Mother's. And as much of our short interaction was shot through with my sudden, alarming, and very distracting conviction that my voice sounded so strange he would surely notice, I had still not addressed the fundamental I was staring at now. That here was my husband. The man I was married to (wielding a Dustbug and growling aggressively at some minor tar-based transgression on his footwell carpet) – the man I had been married to for almost eighteen years and all I could think of was how absolutely catastrophic it was that I should be feeling this way, at this time, in this *life*.

Merlin, who had been dozing in the back of the car for much of the journey, now gathered his long limbs into order and loped across the drive to greet him. Jonathan looked up. I rallied.

'Hello!' I said cheerfully. 'How are you?'

'Ah,' he said, plopping the mat on the ground and running the back of his hand over his brow. 'Ah. You're back then. How's your mother?'

Why not 'how are *you*?' Why not? I pulled on Merlin's cashmere ears.

'Agitated,' I told him. 'About the refuge. She's decided the best course of action right now is to go and pay a visit to Tony Blair.'

He rolled his eyes. '*What*?'

I shrugged as I pulled my bag from the car.

'You know mum,' I said. 'Never one to do things by halves.'

'Regrettably, I do,' he said, with some asperity. 'Does she really think she's going to be able to just stroll up Downing Street and collar him?' He shook his head and went back to bashing one of his mats.

'Yes,' I said, irritated by his attitude all of a sudden. 'Yes. She does. And I'm quite sure she will. And at least she's doing something *useful.*'

'Whatever,' he said, returning his attention to his Dustbug. 'Nothing would surprise me where your mother is concerned. Any chance of some tea, by the way?'

Chapter 11

'My God my God my God my GOD!'

'Ruth, you are not a religious person. Why are you chanting at deities?'

It was the following Tuesday lunchtime. It had been a busy morning. Since Drug U Like's time and motion attack on the appointments book, we'd become more frenetic than ever. Which was frenetic in any case at this time of year because everyone wanted prescription sunglasses. A fact that Drug U Like were anxious to exploit, by giving hundreds of pairs away free. I knew my precious twenty minutes in the staff canteen would mean an even more frenetic afternoon. Ruth clunked her tray up against mine and reached for a glass.

'Did I say that?' she asked, yanking a fiver from her bulging Bagpuss purse and thrusting it at the cashier. 'Well, I lied, Sal. I have a true and sincere and utterly unshakeable faith.'

The woman at the till sniffed. I carried my lunch to the nearest table and sat down carefully. My bottom was still hurting. A whole week on and my bottom was still hurting. My bottom was still hurting and worse than that, my head was in an even worse mess.

'Since when?' I asked.

Ruth twisted her wrist to look at her watch. Her bosom, ever privy to conversations these days, was a threatening, quivering mass. Like popcorn extruding from a fairground popcorn machine. She put down her tray and pulled out the chair opposite. She was breathless and beaming. 'Since five minutes ago. I know I'm still a novice and covered in sins and all that but I can see a life of spirituality and good deeds and early nights and sensible footwear beckoning even as I speak. I might even take up church. Yes. I might just do that.' She bit into her baguette and chomped on it hungrily, the rapturous smile never leaving her face. 'Well,' I said. 'I just hope church knows what it's letting itself in for. But *why*, exactly?'

Ruth put the baguette down and slapped a few bread shards from her cleavage.

'Why'd'ya think, you dozy mare? He's just been in. Didn't you *see* him? For some meeting or other. And guess what? He has asked me out. He has *asked me out*! Oh, joy! Oh happiness! Oh unbridled lust!'

Ah. *Him*. No I didn't. Something unexpected and small and spiky punched my stomach. Hard. 'Who has?' I said anyway.

'Oh, Sally. You big klutz! Nick Brown! Who else? Just now. Just then. Just –' she stuck her wrist out at me, 'God, Sal. Pinch me. Pinch me hard. I might have dreamt it, mightn't I? Hard. Now.'

I pinched her. 'Don't be so daft,' I said, hoping she had. 'So. Right. When? Where?'

'Friday. For lunch. He said – oh, happy day, Sal! – he just came up to me in the office and said " Ah, Ruth. I've been looking for you." He was all sheepish. Well, not sheepish exactly. But, you know, a bit shy? A bit…oh, you know that look, don't you?' I did. 'And he said. "Look, I just wondered if you had any plans for Friday lunchtime" to which I said – *God*, No. What do *you* think? No I didn't say that. Don't worry. I said, I'm not sure, let me see. I don't think so. No. I'm free. Why? And *he* said "Are you free for lunch then , maybe?" you know, in that lovely way he has. "mebbe?" you know?' I knew. 'And before you say it – and you *were* going to say it, weren't you? – it's not work. It's not a meeting or anything.'

I put my face in my coffee and tried to rationalise away the huge lump of anguish that had settled inside me as being a perfectly reasonable and understandable response given the circumstances, even if those circumstances were completely *un*reasonable given that I was married and he was more-or-less married and I didn't believe in infidelity anyway and so it was really no business of mine to be fantasising about him and mooning about him and perfectly reasonable for Ruth to do any amount of those kinds of things given that she fancied the pants off him and was a free woman who hadn't – thank the Lord – the faintest idea how I felt about him, and every right to want to go out with whoever she damn well pleased. Oh, this was becoming such an unpalatable and unpleasant and horrible thing. Why couldn't I stop it? Why?

'Because I *asked* him,' she went on, in the manner of someone anticipating a ten point analysis of possible alternative reasons and daring her interrogator to just try it. 'I said "oh, is there a meeting or something?" and he said no. He said "no, *not* a meeting. Nothing like that. Just lunch. Just the two of us. If that's OK?" in a *completely* obvious way.

'Anyway, so I said yes, of course, and he said "great. That's great. And then he said he wasn't going to be around on Friday morning so would it be OK if he stopped by to pick me up from here at around twelve-thirty. To pick me up, Sal! Wow! And take me out! And I said, "ooooh yes!". Well, not quite "ooooh yes!" – I kept my cool, of course – and that's it! Lunch! Friday! Happiness!'

And shagging? This was it, then. This was the day. This was the day that, to the visual accompaniment of a brace of jostling bosoms, I was forced to accept that the small but insistent young ripple I'd been fearing had finally broached the millpond of my marital life. For I believe my main thought at that particular moment was something along the lines of 'you can't shag him! He's *mine*'.

Which was preposterous, plainly. I needed, I thought, to get a grip. A big one. But how could you get a grip on something so slithery, so insubstantial, so ephemeral, so intangible? So *wrong?* I left the rest of my lunch – the sort of omelette that people in canteens rustle up from the scrapings of all the left over breakfasts (and for which, ordinarily, I had a fondness) – and listened patiently to Ruth's lengthy monologue about clothing crises and whether she should blow a ridiculous stash of cash on something new to wear. (She had already exhausted her wardrobe of seductresses stretch T-shirts to the general appreciation of a good chunk of myopic local male-hood, if not, up to now, of the local male in question. By the time we had returned to the relative mayhem of the optic area (we had a mid-season sale on, to boot) I rather anticipated a Friday morning of frightening sartorial excess.

I had not seen him. I had not seen or spoken to Nick Brown since waving off the ambulance the previous Monday night. And then, of course, I did. Only ten minutes later, in the corridor on the way to the stock room. But I was so stressed about the whole thing by this time that I couldn't even bring myself to call out to him and ask him how his rib was. Instead I shot off into the ladies before he could see me, grateful that he was headed in the other direction, even if it did mean I only got to look at his retreating back.. Then I went grumpily off to test a Mr Pleasance, who was not only fairly offensive in manner and but who smelled offensive as well, which was just the sort of day it had been. When I got out of the by now toe-curling environs of my consulting room, it was to be greeted by the news that my mother had phoned and it was imperative I call her back urgently, as she had important news to impart. So I did.

She was breathless too, so I asked her if everything was all right.

'All right?' she panted. 'Everything's fine. Why?'

'Because,' I said, 'you sound like you've just been landing a barracuda.'

'Oh, no, dear. Just been practising my Dragon, that's all.'

'Your what?'

'It's a stance,' she puffed.

'But I thought *t'ai chi* was supposed to be gentle and undemanding and spiritual and so on.'

'Not at my time of life and if you're watching Esther Rantzen, dear. Perhaps I should go back to the yoga. Anyway –'

'Yes. *Anyway*.' I was feeling testy by now. 'What exactly is the panic? I'm at work.'

'Oh, no panic, dear. Just some rather exciting news.'

'Which is?'

'Which is that I *can* go and deliver my petition to the Prime Minister. I've been speaking to a very nice man at the Labour Party, and he said it would be no problem at all.'

'Really?'

'Really. I have to sort it out with the police and everything first, of course, but –'

'The police?'

'Yes, at Charing Cross. He's given me their number and it's all very straightforward apparently – the main point is that we need more signatures! Which means as many pairs of hands as we can get. So I was wondering if you were working this Saturday. Are you?'

'Well, no, as it happens, but –'

'Brilliant! You don't mind popping down do you? You only need do a couple of hours or so. Bring Kate! Bring Merlin! Yes. Definitely bring Merlin. He'll be good, because people will want to come up and stroke him. And if people think it's for the RSPCA they'll sign anything. Oh, isn't this all so *exciting*!'

That night I *did* dream about my mother. I dreamed she was travelling the Great Wall of China in a leotard and footless tights, dispensing home grown African violets and dog biscuits and asking

Tibetan Monks to sign her save-the-refuge petition. And then I woke up.

I wake up most nights, of course, but in a generally uncomplicated manner. If not through a dream, in which case I am catapulted awake, then it's a gradual, unfussy clamber back to consciousness. One minute I'm asleep and the next I'm not. Eyes open, brain sluggish, feet cold.

This was neither. I opened my eyes and scanned the dark room for clues. Something had woken me up.

I lay silently for a minute or two, waiting for whatever sound it had been to trot back along to my short term memory and explain itself to me. But there was nothing. Just the tinny click of my watch on the dressing table and a low hum of distant motorway traffic outside.

But something. It had been something. I slid my legs from underneath what little duvet was covering me and swivelled to sit up on the bed. It was a sticky night. A blue-black sky, lit by a moon I couldn't see, and all the treetops still as statues. Jonathan's bulk shifted beside me as I stood up to look out of the window.

Something. But what? I wasn't afraid. So familiar was I with the night time noises of our home that the night house was no more threatening than the day house. I padded down the stairs and went into the kitchen. Merlin, on twenty four hour alert in case of passing grouse, thumped his tail twice but remained in his basket, his doggy smell stirred by the movement of the air. I leaned to stroke his head and murmur a hello.

Something. Not the phone. Not a rafter. Not a floorboard. The immersion heater, maybe. No. A different kind of noise.

I opened the fridge and pulled out a carton of cranberry juice, the lemon light illuminating the cling-filmed remains of the chicken I'd left out for Jonathan after tennis. When was the last time we'd actually sat down to eat a meal together? Weeks, at least. There was an upturned glass on the draining board so I picked it up and poured some juice into it. Then I spotted my mobile on the work surface, plugged into the charger that sat next to my cookery books. The light spilling in from the kitchen window was falling on it and as soon as I looked at it, something went click in my head. I picked it up. Of *course*. The envelope icon was there. *1 message* it said. Of *course.* The phone. That little five note jingle it played. A message. I replayed the notes in my head then glanced up at the wall clock.

Ten past four. And a text message for me. At *this* time? Who on earth from?

Wondering absently about a nocturnal visitation on my mother by the ghost of petitions past or something, I pressed the little buttons to see. *Menu*, it prompted. *View message.*

And there it was. Beneath a phone number that meant nothing to me.

Mars. To the South. WOW. Worth a look, if you're up.

Then *N.* N for Nick. So it was from *him*. The little thump started up in my stomach again. Without really thinking anything further (this was night, I was fuggy), I obediently picked up my keys and padded through the utility room and into the garden, the phone still clutched in my hand. The sky was thick with stars, the grass dewy and compliant underneath my bare feet. And there it was. Shining clear and strong above me as if just arrived specifically for my inspection and approval.

The thing about looking at stars and planets is not the light as such – light is light, after all, whatever the source – but the mere *fact* of them. Their very existence. The scale. The sheer awesome reality of the universe. What must it have been like to look at the stars a thousand years ago? What would it be like to *be* a star, even, shining down on a world that's so changed?

I stared up at the sky until my neck could hold my head back no longer, then sat down on the bench beneath the kitchen window and weighed the phone in my hand. And now I *did* think. Should I send a message back, I wondered? Should I? The cursor, which had been winking steadily ever since I finished scrolling the message, seemed expectant now. Impatient. Compelling.

Thks, I wrote. *Jst seen it. Wow, indeed. S.*

I looked up into the sky again, the back of my head cooling against the house wall. I found Vega. The Plough. Pegasus. The cursor was still blinking at me, after the *S.* I pressed the key again. *Send?* It asked. Should I? *Dare* I?

God! I didn't know! It suddenly seemed that of all the little things I had done in my life that were foolhardy, reckless, dangerous, and downright stupid, then this one, this single press of a little silver button, would eclipse every last one of them. Or was I being silly? Where was the harm, after all? Where was the harm in sending a text message back to him? Where was the harm in a shared interest in Astronomy? A simple communication? An innocent exchange between two like-minded souls?

I thought of him, sleepless and maybe still looking at the stars himself. Staring up, as I was right now, from his window – his garden? – in Oxted, at the very same patch of sky that was spread so beguilingly over me now. I thought of us having a little typed conversation, connected in our solitude while all around us slept. And then I thought of Ruth. I thought *Lunch*. I thought *Friday*. I thought how I had felt when I'd *heard* about Friday. It told me the answer. I scrolled downwards. *Erase*.

Chapter 12

But, strangely, I didn't think of Jonathan. Not then. Not in the way I really should have thought of Jonathan, i.e. the *right* way .i.e. very, very guiltily *indeed.*

I didn't think of Jonathan in any meaningful sense until two days later, at just after four on the Thursday afternoon, when I got an angry call from him just as I was about to go in to do a test, because he couldn't find his dinner suit anywhere.

That's not strictly true, actually. I did think of Jonathan at the time, but only in a completely self-righteous, dismissive, rather petulant, serve-him-right way, which hardly covered me in glory. Worse, I even resented that he'd made me feel like that. How had our marriage come to this? And worse, how was it that I had *let* it come to this without realising that it was heading towards coming to anything I should be worrying about in the first place? And what exactly was the 'this' in question anyway? Why did I need the rather halting and tremulous half-attentions of a man with an absent wife and God knew what baggage to tell me I was not the happily married little bunny I thought I was? Didn't proper grown up people know these things already? Had I been living life with the colour turned down?

I'd had crushes on men before, of course. Who hadn't? Little oases of fanciful longing were the splashes of colour in long-married life. But never before with this persistent side order of impending catastrophe and fall-out attached. Never before with this constant analysis. This ceaseless angsty dialogue I kept having with myself. They never, in short, involved Jonathan. Ever. But perhaps, just perhaps, that was only because all the men I had idly fancied had no plans for straying, or the ones after me had not pushed the right buttons. *Was* it pure luck, this unexpected conjunction? Serendipity, even, between Nick and I? Had my marriage endured simply through logistics? Simply not having been at the right place at the right time?

God. Too much thinking. The remainder of that night I slept not a jot and sat in the spare room using my now world-beating insomnia as a stick to bash myself up with. What I should have done was go into Jonathan, shake him awake and demand to know how precisely his wife had come so dangerously close to sending a text message to a man who drove women off roads (rails???) in the middle of the night and *in the middle of the night*, no less. In short, I should have dealt with it. But I didn't. For one thing, I couldn't even imagine how such a conversation would get going in the first place, given that it was by now five in the morning and the principle reason I knew how many stencilled daisies ran around the spare room dado rail in the first place (87) was that Jonathan would quite possibly spontaneously combust if I so much as cleared my throat at that hour. For another, what would I say? Would I say 'Jonathan, I'm feeling a bit anxious because I've suddenly started hyperventilating over a man who is not yourself and while I appreciate that there is nothing inherently wrong with happily married women having the odd palpitation over George Clooney or Brad Pitt, say, I'm also conscious that this has more the flavour of something about which we should both be concerned so how's about you and me popping down to Relate on the way home from work tomorrow to thrash things out?'. No. I would not. Because Jonathan would say 'whhaaaaat? before I'd even got past the word 'I'm'.

I could, I supposed, have tackled him over breakfast. I could have handed him his toast and broached the subject of our relationship over the Flora tub. But I couldn't, because he'd have said 'For God's sake, you *know* the sort of day I've got, Sally. Can't we talk about this tonight?' And if I'd attempted to broach the subject when he came *home* from work he would have said 'For God's sake, you *know* the sort of day I've had, Sally. Can't we talk about this some other time?' Or I could have been assertive. Ah. Yes. That one. I could have said 'I have just realised I am not completely happy and I am having dangerous feelings and I don't know what to do about it', and he would have become instantly cross and hurt and defensive and said 'Oh, great. You're not happy and you choose *now* to tell me about it. For God's sake, you *know* the sort of ….and so on and so forth.

Which is why, I suppose, people in ailing marriages don't communicate their difficulties to one another and instead go off and start giving their attentions to other, more communicative relationships instead. QED. They've simply lost the knack.

Some forms of communication, however, seem to improve with longevity.

'Oh God. It's still at the dry cleaners,' I told him now.

'*What?*'

'God, I'm sorry. I completely forgot to pick it up.'

'*Forgot*? How could you forget? I reminded you yesterday!' Which was true. 'Great,' he said. 'Now what am I supposed to do?'

'Um,' I said. 'I don't know. Um, can't you wear another suit?'

'How can I wear another one, for God's sake? I don't *have* another one.'

'Um, rent one or something?'

'How the hell am I supposed to rent one? I'm supposed to be catching a plane in little over an hour!'

'Well, I don't know, then! Buy one at Gatwick, perhaps?'

He made a snorting sound down the phone. 'Don't be so stupid, Sally! God! *Honestly*! How could you just forget? How?'

I didn't know. I wasn't sure. I couldn't answer. 'Look,' I said instead. 'I'm really *sorry,* OK?'

He ignored this. 'Right. You'll just have to leave work early. If you leave now, you can pick it up and then meet me in Departures.'

'I can't do that!'

'You have to!'

'I can't *do* that!' I said again. 'I'm *working*. God, *why* can't you just wear an ordinary suit?'

'Don't you ever listen? This is a Royal College dinner. I'm giving a *speech*, for God's sake. Sally, you *have* to get my suit for me.'

'But why don't you just get it yourself? It'll take me just as long.'

'Because I have to check in, don't I? And I don't even know where the dry cleaners is.'

Now *I* snorted. 'That figures.'

'What's that supposed to mean?'

'It's not *supposed* to mean anything. It means that if you did perhaps, then this sort of thing wouldn't happen, would it? I mean I *do* have a job, you know. I do have other things to think about aside from everybody else's domestic arrangements, you know. I can't remember *everything*. There's your suit, and Kate's tap shoes and the dog's injections and whether we've got any bread and the car insurance and remembering your Mother's birthday and organising your receptionist's leaving party and speaking to the man about the leak in the en suite shower and and and.... It's too *much.* You should have reminded me this morning.'

A silence. Then, 'I reminded you yesterday.'

'Well you should have reminded me *again,* shouldn't you? Then I could have dropped it home at lunchtime, couldn't I? How come it's always *me* that has to remember everything for everybody all the time? I'm not a Palm Pilot, you know.'

'Right,' he said quietly. 'That's fine, then.'

'*What?*'

'Fine. I get the message.'

'*What* message?'

'That it's obviously all far too much trouble for you. *Fine.* Not a problem. You're too busy? Not a problem. Putting upon you? Not a problem. I'll sort my own suits out in future. But it would have been a great deal more helpful if you'd bothered to let *me* know before deciding your schedule was too hectic these days to accommodate insignificant trifles like *looking after your family,* maybe. Then I would have made *other* arrangements, wouldn't I? Now are you going to get my suit for me, or what? It's already ten past four.'

'God! All *right!* I'll get your suit!'

'*Thank* you. I'll be at the BA domestic departure gate. Be quick.' And then he was gone.

Nick Brown wasn't my boss as such, but as my actual boss was nowhere to be seen and as Nick Brown – who had appeared as if out of the mists of Valhalla, where he'd obviously been holed up since Tuesday afternoon – happened to be standing a few feet away from me by this time, and glancing at me in a thoughtful and speculative fashion, I decided I had better plunge on in.

'Look,' I said, instantly remembering his sweet nocturnal text message and feeling crosser than *ever* as a consequence. 'Family crisis. Can I ask a *huge* favour?'

His eyes didn't mention it. 'Shoot.'

'It's just that I have to go and pick something up for my husband. He's got to catch a flight. I wouldn't normally *dream* of taking such a liberty, but would it be OK if I zoomed off for half an hour or so? I mean, it's only to the airport, and I'll be as quick as I possibly can. I've got two more tests booked in, but –'

He'd been blinking and nodding a lot while I spewed all this out, but now he raised a hand to halt it.

'Whoah!' he said. 'No panic, OK? I'm sure Russell will be able to cover.'

'I won't be long. It's only –'

'No *panic*,' he said again, soothingly, which made my eyes start pricking. 'Don't worry about coming back. Go on. Zoom away. We'll see you tomorrow, OK?'

I wanted to say thank you. I wanted to hug him – if carefully. I wanted to tell him that I *had* got his message. That I *had* seen Mars and that, yes, it *was* stunning. But I couldn't. I felt way too teary to risk it. So I just nodded at him gratefully and shot off up the stairs.

I couldn't find the dry cleaning ticket either, of course, so despite the jolly geniality of the dry cleaning lady, it still took ten minutes to rootle Jonathan's suit out. She had dozens of them. Big do at Glyndebourne, she said. It was that time of year.

How dare he? How dare he! How dare he speak to me like that! How dare he just assume, just *blithely* assume, that I would drop everything to pick up a suit that he should have reminded me about in the first place and that he had no right to be dumping on me in the first place given that I had a full time job as well, thank you very much and he not only had a bloody secretary to sort things out for him, but arms, legs, brains, hands and all that same stuff *I* had. So why couldn't he just do it himself anyway? Why did he always assume *I* would do everything for him? And how dare he be so bloody sodding bloody annoying bloody debating society *so* bloody clever with words to make it seem like *I* was the one who was being unreasonable and saying that he didn't have any problem at all about having to go and take his own bloody suits to the cleaners if only I'd let him know I was too busy so he could sort something else out. In short, making *me* in the wrong. And, all right, so I *was* in the wrong, and I shouldn't have forgotten, but did he have to be so bloody *hateful* about it? I'd said I was sorry, hadn't I? So why hadn't he had the good grace to accept my apology and be nice to me? God! He was so *bloody* superior.

By the time I had dumped my car in the set down lane, scribbled a note saying 'Emergency!!!!!!' and stuck it under the wiper, and then galloped across the terminal, Jonathan's flight was a scant fifteen minutes from taking off. He was stomping backwards and forwards in front of the business class fast track bit and looking like he might just deck the next person who came up and asked him if they could help him or anything, as the uniformed woman who was scuttling away from him had, evidently, just done. I wanted to hit him. I wanted to shoulder the suit bag and *hurl* the thing at him. But as soon as he spotted me his expression changed radically. As if he'd been punched in the face by a little ray of sunshine.

'Oh, Sal, what a *saint* you are,' he gushed, taking it from me and giving me one of those enthusiastic hugs that fellow footballers do when one's just scored a hat-trick. 'God, I'm *really* sorry,' he said, patting my back. 'You're right. I should have mentioned it this morning. I nearly *did* mention it this morning. I had every intention of mentioning it this morning, but then what with one thing and another and that early extraction and everything – well,' he stepped back and glanced at his watch. 'Better go catch my plane. I'm sorry to be such a bear. I don't mean to be. I expect way too much of you, don't I? We *all* do.' He chucked me under the chin and smiled ruefully. 'It's your fault, you know,' he said. 'You're just too efficient. Too capable. Too perfect. Too lovely. How on earth do you put up with me? Am I forgiven?'

He leaned forward to pop a little kiss on my cheek, and patted my shoulder again.

'You're forgiven,' I said. 'It was my fault. I'm sorry.'

And though the last bit of that was essentially true, the first bit, worryingly, was not.

Which left me at the airport, and all at sea, at the back end of what had already turned out to be a decidedly unprepossessing day. It was almost five. I wondered if I should go back to work after all. But because the reason I wondered if I should go back to work was more to do with who and not what I'd be likely to find there, I took myself off home instead. Ordinarily on a Thursday I'd do a big grocery shop, but as Jonathan was away now, and there was therefore no pressing need to stock up on KitKats, I was at a bit of a loose end.

There was nothing interesting in the house to eat so I ferreted in the freezer and dug out a pie. Chicken and sweetcorn. I hated sweetcorn. Who'd brought this detestable pie into our house? I assumed Jonathan must have while I'd been away. Or Kate, perhaps. Which struck me as very tangible evidence of our increasing remoteness as a family unit. We never seemed to coincide for food any more. I dumped it in the oven in the certain knowledge that I wouldn't get around to eating it. Sitting by myself, fishing out bits of sweetcorn. But then there was always Merlin.

And apart from the doggy delights of his undemanding and adoring company, I was all alone. Kate was at dance class tonight – they were rehearsing twice weekly now; excitement about the production having reached such a pitch of frenzied excitement that I had even noticed a small poster flapping on the bus shelter down the road. Heady times indeed. But the joy of dance was still some weeks away ,and tonight there was nothing doing. Nothing on TV except that pet hospital hamster-in-crisis programme which I hated, and then Question Time, which I hated even more. I wondered if I shouldn't perhaps phone my mother for a refuge update, but then I thought she'd most probably be at *t'ai chi* and then she'd get in and dial one four seven one and phone me back and twitter manically at me at God knew what hour of the night. No. I wouldn't phone my mother. I would sit and read a book instead.

Fairly predictably, this being late May and the night being warm, I fetched up in the garden. It's a pretty house, ours. Seventy years old and well bedded into its surroundings, it stands in a half acre of gently rolling garden that's adjacent to farmland on two sides. At this time the early clematis was in flower, an explosion of pink petals that smelt strangely of chocolate and which were just now beginning to be snatched away by the breeze to cover the ground with pretty candyfloss snow. Which Jonathan would sweep irritably away soon, no doubt. I looked up at the sky. There wasn't much visible. Though the day had been clear, there was now a fair sprinkling of high cloud, deepening now as the night drew its veil over what was left of the day.

And I thought about whether to send a text message to Nick Brown.

If you're a sensible, rational person, you can think sensibly and rationally about things. You can fast forward to some indeterminate time in the future and easily foresee a situation where a suit – or some other domestic item – is involved, and about which you might well, *most probably* will, be engaged in an argument of some sort.

The details are irrelevant. It's the interplay that's important. Few of us can expect to spend the rest of our lives without rowing, or at least, getting into conflict situations with people about whom we care.

But then again – I was on my third Pimms, and still *very* irritable with Jonathan – our projections, like life assurance performance tables, tend to be based on rather optimistic criteria and are thus as accurate a predictive device as a pair of net curtains. Ergo, I was thinking nothing so sensible and prosaic. I was thinking hypothetically. I was thinking no, no, no no, NO! I would *not* get involved in rows about dry cleaning issues with someone like Nick Brown in my hypothetical prediction, because dry cleaning would not BE an issue between us. Nor would dustbins, Sainsbury's, ant infestations, or, indeed, the correct way to iron a shirt. Nonny nonny no no. Because in the make-believe world of wish-fulfilment I would be all the things I *should* have become during the course of my eighteen year marriage. IE assertive and confident and in charge of my own destiny. And the drudge of the house on *my* terms.

Thus any realistic projections I could have inserted into my rambling thoughts (i.e that people in romantic relationships did not spend eternity mooning about and calling each other bunnikins and instead, in time, had tiffs about cleaning the toilet) were borne away and dumped without ceremony. And instead it occurred to me that even though there was nothing much doing in the celestial department, I could still text Nick Brown. To thank him.

I was just thinking this when the sound of a car heralded Kate's return from rehearsals. She wafted into the kitchen to find me rummaging feverishly in my handbag for my mobile.

'You all right?' she asked, pulling off her sweatshirt and frowning. She seemed to frown all the time at the moment.

'Fine, darling,' I quipped, plucking my hand from my bag as if its actions could betray my guilty thoughts. 'Good rehearsal? Everything progressing OK with the production?'

She shrugged and went over to the fridge.'All is as well as can be expected,' she said gravely. 'As well as can be expected when half the cast have all the fluidity of movement of stick insects.'

She sniffed haughtily. Kate did haughty very well.

She took out a carton of orange juice and upended it to her lips.

'Would you like something to eat?' I ventured. 'There's a pie I could –'

'Ugh. I cannot eat, mother. I have absolutely no appetite at all.'

She lumbered off up the stairs with the no-appetite option of a Twix and a bag of Hula Hoops, and I was able, at last, to lay hands on my phone. Then I went and sat barefoot on the bench in the garden and I sent Nick Brown his message. I wrote, '*thnks for earlier. V kind. And thnks fr lettng me know abt Mars. Was brthtkng. Nt mch out tnite. SM. P.S. How yr rib?* Then I sent it off. I thought the SM was a rather nice touch. Not too familiar. Not too presumptuous. Not too….

'Bbbbzzzzzwwwbbbzzzwwbbbzzz!'

My ring tone right now was something like 'tsetse fly'. Close enough to a proper phone noise so as not to make me sound like a twit, but different enough that I actually took any notice when it rang. A sort of strained, high-pitched, warbling screech. As if a small winged insect had found itself unaccountably marooned in an empty baked bean can and kept sticking to sauce globs while attempting to escape. I put the phone to my ear.

'Sally?'

It was Nick Brown. 'Oh!' I said. 'Oh!'

There was a fuzz of noise behind him. 'Just got your message,' he said back. 'Thanks.'

'Oh!' I said again. Because it had never occurred to me that he might actually ring me.

'Couldn't make much sense of it, mind you. Do you have a downer on vowels or something?'

'Um,' I said, with the sudden realisation that learning how to do text messaging from a sixteen year old might have left gaps in my phone etiquette knowledge. 'Er no,' I said. 'Just being concise.'

'Ri-ight,' he said. 'Anyway. Rib on the mend, thanks for asking. Your crisis sorted OK?'

'Crisis sorted. Thanks for being so accommodating.'

'No problem,' he said. 'Good. Anyway. Nice to hear from you.' A pause. 'So you didn't mind then?'

'Mind?'

He coughed. 'Me texting you the other night. I wasn't sure whether it was appropriate or not, but I knew you'd want to see it, so I figured…and then you didn't say anything about it, so I guess I really should have…'

Appropriate or not. In what sense 'appropriate or not'? 'No, no,' I sang, to accommodate all realms of appropriateness and convey my affirmative to all. 'I didn't mind at all. I was up anyway so I went straight out into the garden and looked. And it was brilliant, wasn't it? I nearly sent you a message back, but then…' Then *what*? '…well. Anyway. No. It was very thoughtful of you. Thank you.'

'You're welcome.' He coughed again. 'It was kind of nice to think there might be someone else out there who'd appreciate it. Nice to share it with someone. Anyway…'

'Anyway…'

'I guess I'd better go.' I could hear voices nearby. I presumed he was in a bar or a restaurant or something. It wasn't that late. 'Just thought I'd call and thank you for your message, and, well, say hello. Still cloudy out?'

Or a cave. 'Still cloudy. But I'm sitting in the garden right now so I'll let you know if anything cosmic and radical happens.' Radical? What did I think was going to happen? That the International Space Station was going to slew off its orbit and come careering to earth on my patio set?

He laughed at this. 'That would be neat.'

'No problem,' I began, groping for something else interesting to say before he signed off and went back to whatever it was he was doing. 'In fact, I'll make a special point of –'

'Actually, Sally,' he said suddenly. 'I'm glad you sent that message. Because I was going to ring you anyway.'

'You were?'

My heart braced itself. He sounded so *serious*. Uh-oh. I took a big gulp of my drink.

'Yes,' he went on. 'To apologise.'

'Apologise?' I asked, puzzled. 'Why? What for?'

There was a tiny pause. I could hear him breathe in. I couldn't imagine what he meant.

He breathed out again. His voice became low. 'Because I didn't realise you were married.'

What? Where did *this* suddenly spring from? 'Um, well…' I said. 'Well, I am.'

'I mean… I guess I should have. I mean, why would you not be? But I just assumed you were separated, or divorced or something… I mean, you don't wear a ring or anything…'

He'd noticed *that*? He'd checked that *out?* I moved the mobile to my other ear and looked down at my hand.

'No,' I started twittering, 'I don't. I lost it in the sea. In Worthing, it was. About five years ago, and then Jonathan –'the name felt suddenly uncomfortable on my tongue '– er, my *husband*, well, he bought me an eternity ring to replace it, and it didn't fit – it was too big. And I didn't want to lose that one as well, of course. Ha ha. So I – well, I was going to get it made smaller, of course, but you never get around to these things, do you? I wear it on my middle finger instead, and…um. Yes. You're right. I'm married.'

Another pause. Should I dunk something else into it? If so, *what?*

'Ri-ight,' he said again. 'Anyway, the point is that I hope you don't think…I mean, jeez, I hope I haven't given you…I mean, I hope you didn't….'

And there was me thinking Americans were such articulate people. I gulped a bit more.

'Hope I didn't *what*?'

'You know. Take offence. I mean it must have been obvious to you that –' He stopped again. Why couldn't he just *say* it? Then he did. Sort of. '– well, you *know*…. but if I'd known you were married, I wouldn't have, you know, come on to you the way I did. I'm really not that kind of guy. I just –'

'Hang on,' I said, running my tongue over my suddenly dry lips. 'You didn't, you know. Not *really*. I mean, you did, *sort* of, I suppose, but then, well, you didn't *really*. Not to any great extent. I mean I got the impression you would have *liked* to (my face exploded into a shocking hot blush here)… which was fine, but I thought…well, I assumed you didn't *because* I was married. I thought…'

What *did* I think? What *had* I thought? What in God's name was I thinking now? What, more importantly, did *he* think I'd been thinking? Blimey! Why did I say 'which was fine'?

'Not at all,' he said. 'It was just, you know, what with my situation and everything. And, well, work. Protocol. I mean, it's not really appropriate for me to be–'

That word again.

'Isn't it?' I said, for reasons of pique and frustration and with a definite squeak of dismay in my voice. 'I mean, it's not as if you're my boss or anything. It's –' God, what was I *saying here*? 'No,' I said, hurriedly. 'I suppose it isn't. It's just that *I* thought…well. There you go.'

‘Yes.’

‘Right.’

He coughed again. ‘Anyway, so no harm done, then.’

This was not an enquiry.

‘No,’ I agreed limply. ‘No harm done.’

No harm done? No *harm* done?? NO HARM DONE???? The conversation drew to a juddering, uncomfortable close, and I pressed the end button with shaking fingers and a big fizzle of crossness thrumming between my ears like a plucked banjo string. I got up and stomped around the lawn. No *harm* done? What was he *thinking* of? I felt very, very harmed indeed. As if I had been scooped up, shaken about, pummelled and prodded and then thrown down and left for the buzzards and flies. Everything inside me was jangling. I wanted to ring him straight back and tell him that yes, he was right. He *had* come on to me. Oh, yes, he had come on to me all right. And that even if the whole ‘coming on’ scenario was a naff, blokey thing and entirely the wrong expression to use in that particular circumstance, (the circumstance of us sitting romantically in the moonlight, on a sand dune, and discussing celestial matters and sharing the breathtaking wonder of our first shooting star together) that even if I didn’t know what the female response to ‘coming on’ should be called, that my status was jolly well one of having *been* come on to, and that it was really, really, *really* important that he understood that this was not one way traffic to be brushed off, no harm done; that I had all sorts of feelings and emotions about the business of having been come on to by him and that almost none of them were even *remotely* appropriate, because I *really, really, really liked him too*. I wanted to send him a text message telling him that I had started thinking about him almost every minute of every day and harbouring wildly unsuitable thoughts about holding him and kissing him and making love to him and having him bloody well finish the conversation he’d started back on that sand dune by taking me in his arms and falling in love with me and telling me he couldn’t live without me, and that it was damn well written in the stars – couldn’t I *see* that? – and that, sorry, but he couldn’t do a damn thing about it. Like in one of Ruths’ stories. Yes. That was it. Not burble on about apologising and appropriateness and telling me NO HARM DONE.

But I couldn't do any of that stuff. I was married. I had a husband. I shouldn't even be *going* there. I had to sit on my bench and feel all guilty and shaky and guilty and anxious and guilty and stricken. And *guilty*. Couldn't. Shouldn't. Wouldn't. I downed the last of my Pimms and considered my position. Exceedingly Drunk. So I shuffled off to bed.

I didn't sleep that night. Not once. Not at all. With the rather unfortunate net result that by the time Kate straggled blearily down to breakfast the next morning, I had done every scrap of washing in the house, including the top she'd been wearing that very evening, which contained the very important hen's teeth type concert ticket for some evil sounding band she liked, for which she had paid a friend at dance class a whole twenty one pounds fifty and if it wasn't *too* much trouble, would I now like to come up with some way to compensate her for her entire life being in tatters around her and the world as we know it having come to a brutal end?

Like, *now*?

This was better. This was normality. *This* was my life. I could cope.

I could cope.

'Blimey!' bellowed Ruth, when I arrived at work at twenty to eight with eyes like a pair of canapé eclairs and a critical mass of nasty tastes in my mouth. 'Have the clocks gone back or something?'

And a banging headache. Must not drink in the week. 'Oh, ha ha,' I said, almost as surprised as she was by my ability to pretend that everything was just rosy. 'No. I'm just showing willing. I had to leave early yesterday, so I thought I'd forestall any frowns of disapproval by coming in early and cracking on with some work. You look nice.'

She did, too. She was wearing a flowery summer dress with a bit of braid round the hemline, and a bodice that was threaded with a run of pink ribbon, which gathered up her excess of boobs. I imagined Nick Brown's face buried between them. I thought I was going to be sick.

'Well of *course* I look nice,' she rattled on, swooshing her hips about and fiddling with the little bow at the front. 'I've spent half the night getting ready.' She looked down at herself. 'Though I'm still not sure about this. Too demure, you think? My satin hipsters seemed too in-yer-face at seven.' I imagined them in Nick's face. I imagined Nick's face in her crotch. Between courses, perhaps. Under the table.

Ruth seemed not to notice that I was turning grey. 'And, well, *lunch*, you know. *Day*light. There's an uphill struggle and a half for you. I generally like them to get a glimmer of my sparkling personality before they get a full on dekko at the grim reality.' Christ – what had she in mind? Sex in the cab? 'But I bought my black vest and those pink pedal pushers, just in case. What d'ya think? I don't want to send out the wrong signals.'

Well, now, I thought. *There's* an expression. But flowery dress, ribbons, the fresh bloom in her cheeks. She looked, God – really, really *pretty*. I decided I hated her. For this morning, at any rate.

'I think you look just right,' I cooed.

When he arrived, a little before twelve thirty, I was out on the shop floor, explaining to the elderly lady I'd just tested that wearing varifocal lenses did not mean you could only see distant things from the kneecaps up. He nodded at me as he passed and indicated that he'd like a word before he went off-a-trysting with Ruth.

I realised with alarm that every time I saw him now, my pulse speeded up and my stomach did a pirouette.

'Just a quick one,' he said briskly as I fetched up, all a quiver, at the counter. He had one hand on the computer mouse and was scrolling through a list of what looked like sales figures on the screen. That done, he glanced up at me and smiled. 'You OK?'

I was fully aware I looked revolting, so the tiny enquiring furrow that appeared on his forehead was entirely superfluous.

'I'm fine,' I said, hugging my clipboard to my chest.

'I just wanted to –' The phone on the desk started ringing. 'Oh, hang on –'He picked it up, smiling at me while he listened. 'Yep. Yep. Sure. Yep. Shoot. Uh-huh. No problem. Tell you what. I'm not the best person to deal with this, I don't think. Let me put you on to one of the Optometrists, OK – 'He put his hand over the receiver. 'Secretary to a Dr Falstaff? Wants to talk to someone about some guy who was in here Tuesday? Glaucoma?' I nodded.

'I remember. It was me that tested him.'

He passed me the phone. I could smell his aftershave on it. 'Catch you after lunch, then. Yes?'

*   *   *

He didn't catch me after lunch, as it turned out, because he was not seen in Optometry again that day. Which, were it the product of foresight, would have been a very shrewd move, because Ruth might have laid waste to him if he had.

'I cannot believe it! The bastard!' was almost the very first thing she said to me when she burst into my testing room a little before three. The first thing she'd said had been 'don't ask', so, naturally, I had.

'Oh dear,' I said, gesturing for her to sit down before she took out my desk fan with her angry flailing. 'Lunch not an unqualified success, then?'

Truth be known, I had decided to give myself a good shaking over the matter of my feelings about her lunch with Nick Brown. Decided to give myself a good shaking generally. I had been off to Waterstones during my break and bought a book; '*Infinite Choices* – a thinking woman's guide to fulfilment in the middle years', which I had flicked through in the shop and which promised such encouraging chapters as 'partner fatigue; reassessing your life-needs", and 'the fallow years – relighting your marital fire'. Depressing, then, that so far it had failed me. I tried to affect a look of anxious concern.

'Lunch an unqualified disaster, as it happens,' she growled at me. '*Bastard.* And Ruth Preston an unqualified twit. God, Sal, how could I have been such a prat?' She plucked a tissue from my box.

'So what *happened,* Ruth?'

'Huh! He's dumped me, the bastard! Dumped me! Just like that! Can you *believe* it?'

I felt the word dumped was a little histrionic seeing as how he'd not actually even been seeing her in the first place. But then again, perhaps theirs had been but a brief affair. Just a starter and main course romance.

'Dumped you?' I parroted back. 'What do you mean, dumped you?'

'Are you deaf!' she squawked. 'What I say! God, I am *such* a dim-wit!'

I wasn't sure quite where to take the conversation next, so I said 'no, you're not,' to be soothing.

'Oh, I am. Thirty two sodding years on the planet and I still can't see higher than a man's dick. I need my head sticking in a bucket of whitebait. I am a brainless, stupid, libidinous fool!' She plucked a whole handful of tissues from the box now and trumpeted extravagantly into them.

'No you're not,' I said again, edging the refractor head away from her a little and thinking how rude the word libidinous sounded. Was that *my* problem? Was I just feeling libidinous? I must check out my book a bit more. 'Look, Ruth. I know he's nice and everything – '

'No he's not. He's a slimy bastard.'

'–and I know you like – *liked* him, but was he really the man for you? I mean, as you say, you're only thirty two, you have everything to look forward to, and you –'

Her eyeballs had expanded so much by now that I thought they might just ping from their sockets and bounce off the walls like a couple of superballs.

'*Whaaattt?*' she shrieked. 'Not *dumped*, you dozy cow! Hah! I should be so fucking lucky! *Dumped*, you fool! As in Dumped! As in Dis*card*ed. As in *Made Redundant. Comprendez?* Dumped. Bugger liking him. He's a bastard. A devious bastard as well.'

I blinked hard to stop my own eyeballs flying out. '*What?* You're kidding!'

'I am not kidding Sal. I do not kid about matters this serious. I do not jest about losing my job. '

My concern was now genuine. 'But why? How? For what reason? When?'

She spread her hands and then dumped then in her lap. The pretty dress now made her seem vulnerable and young. 'Because my job is about to be done by a computer, basically.' She threw her head back, and laughed a humourless cackle of a laugh. 'It's such a bloody cliché it would be funny if it wasn't me, wouldn't it? Rationalization. That's the word he used. Rationalization in that just as soon as Drug U Like can get all their super duper new system fucking fandango in place, they will no longer need people like me in the branches, basically. Everything will be done centrally. By machines. Tick tock. And call centres, which amount to pretty much the same thing. Therefore –'

'But they can't just make you redundant, can they? Not just like *that*.'

'Oh, I think they can. But it wouldn't look so good if they did, I guess. Not so hot for morale. So they don't actually use the word redundant, of course. He's offered me another job instead.'

A glimmer of hope, then. 'Which is?'

'Which is contact lens dispensing in West Worthing,' she spat. 'Frankly, I would rather be dead.'

But he *did* catch me. In the end, he did.

I was in the staff car park, having waved a still tearful Ruth off, and rummaging in my bag for my keys.

'Sally,' he called. He was standing in the shadows a few cars away from me. I shovelled all my stuff in the back while he walked over. 'Is Ruth OK?' he asked, his keys swinging from his hand. He had a hands free mobile dangly bit clipped to his shirt front. 'She didn't seem to take things very well.'

'No and no,' I answered, reflecting that a large part of the anger I now felt was due to the fact that he could still have such a disabling effect on me, when he'd just dis-employed my best friend. I spotted his car. Another Mercedes. His company car then, presumably. He was being pretty well rewarded for putting people out of work. 'And I can't say I'm surprised, frankly. I mean, she had no idea. You could have given her some warning, couldn't you?' I wondered if he had the first idea what her real expectations of their meeting had been. Probably not, I decided. 'I mean,' I went on 'It's not every day people turn up for work and find themselves being made redundant out of the blue now, is it?'

'*Redundant?* Since when was she being made redundant?' He looked genuinely surprised.

I raised my eyebrows. 'Well, isn't she? To all intents and purposes? *Isn't* she? You can use all the corporate jargon you want, but whichever way you dress it up, she's lost her job, hasn't she? Which in my book amounts to pretty much the same thing.'

He opened his mouth as if to start to deny it, but then stopped.

'Listen,' he said, pushing one hand through his hair and grimacing. He looked pretty tired himself, I thought. Perhaps we should compare our latest insomnia remedies. Or perhaps not. He *deserved* not to sleep. 'It really wouldn't be appropriate for me to discuss this with you. I'm sorry. I shouldn't have mentioned it at all. I was just a bit concerned. That was all. Truth is, I hadn't expected Ruth to be quite so negative – '

'Not be quite so *negative*? You mean you expected her to leap on the table and say "yeehah! I lost my job! Well, dang, if I don't just feel like giving y'all a quick rendition of the Star Spangled Banner!" *Really*?' I took a breath to stop any more gushing out and my P45 riding on the crest of it. Then I said, 'Come *on*. I mean, *Worthing?* She lives in Godstone, for God's sake!' His mouth had the temerity to twitch a bit at this unintentional alliteration, which made me feel intensely irritable with him. I was tired. I had had no lunch, and most of all I was frustrated by my inability to stand and have a conversation with him without wanting to leap on him in a bestial way. *Even though* I was so cross with him. How could that be? Was I *ill*?

I folded my arms and glared at him instead.

'Look, Sally,' he said. 'I don't really want to go here with you right now, but, you know, things aren't that straightforward. There are personnel changes that have to be made and right now I'm the guy who's got to implement them. I thought we'd done OK by Ruth – she's a lovely girl and we want to offer her something that'll exploit her skills. If she feels that negative about it, there's little I can do, is there? Hey, I don't run the company, you know.'

I nearly said 'oh, yes? And which skills would those be, exactly?' But I stopped myself. He looked genuinely concerned and I suddenly felt chastened. It couldn't have been one of the highlights of his job, I supposed, being charged with having to prise people out of jobs they'd (naively?) assumed were theirs in perpetuity, any more than it was one of mine to tell people they were losing their sight. But even so, was it *really* necessary? Was this *really* progress? How soon before the likes of *me* got replaced by some computer program? That the patients got their eyes tested by an MRI scanner? Or had to plop them out and send them off in jiffy bags by second class post? I wished he wasn't staring at me so earnestly. It made me want to flop against him and groan into his shirt. *Must* Not Drink In The Week. Must NOT.

'Me next, then, is it?' I snapped instead.

He lifted an arm up then dropped it again. 'Come on,' he said, 'you know you're secure here.'

I got into my car. 'Oh, *good*.' I replied, shutting the door and rolling down the window. 'As long as *I'm* OK.' I whizzed the window back up again. 'No harm done, then, eh? Good*bye*!'

*   *   *

I watched him through the rear view mirror as I left the car park. He was three cars behind me and talking to someone on his mobile phone. But the hands free kit made it look like he was simply a mad person talking to himself. I realised I knew almost nothing about him. That he *could* be a mad person. He could certainly be a bastard. *Was* a bastard, according to Ruth. Yet, no matter how sorry I felt for Ruth at that moment, I knew she was wrong about that . Dear oh dear. I *must* be ill, mustn't I? Ill and *cross.*

I stopped to get petrol and stuffed down a king size Twix, which improved my temper a little. Actually, I thought, he was right. It wasn't his fault. Perhaps I should send him a text message later, to apologise for ranting at him. And maybe I could tell him about the onion cure I'd picked up from the new insomnia site I'd found on the internet, and maybe I could see how his rib was doing, and .....

I was still wrestling with reasons to send Nick Brown text messages and their relative legitimacy and appropriateness in the scheme of things when the matter became academic anyway. It was about an hour after I got home from work by now and Jonathan was in the bath – he was headed off to some Tennis Club party, to which I had been invited but couldn't face. Jonathan's tennis club was full of old people and spotty teenagers who said yar instead of yes. More importantly, full of people that had known him since *he* was a teenager. Trisha had been a member. Their names were on the mixed doubles champions board. 1975. I couldn't play tennis. I had tried, early on – God, I had been so anxious to please Jonathan – I had gone down there with him on a Sunday morning for a time when we were first married. I would fly around the court so enthusiastically, groping hopefully at the balls he lobbed so stylishly at me, hurling myself against the chicken wire and scraping great chunks of skin from my arms. But he always got so irritated with my ineptitude that after a while he stopped taking me.

I hadn't expected my mobile to ring so it was a while before the strange trill that was emanating from my handbag made any sense. There was no name on the display, of course, (Nick Brown had not made my mobile's address book) and as I had been expecting a call from Kate, for a lift, my first – my *only* thought was that it must be her now, from a phone box.

'CLEAR OFF! I'M BUSY!' I bellowed, as per our usual greeting.

'Sally? It's Nick Brown,' he said, without preamble.

'Oh!' I said, as my stomach did a back flip. 'Sorry about that! We always –'

'No problem,' he rattled straight on. 'I'm sorry to bother you at home, but we need to meet up.' He sounded like he was making one of those calls that are recorded or monitored for quality assurance and/or training purposes. He seemed to have entirely lost the knack of doing mumbling half sentences all of a sudden.

'We do?' I asked, now realising two salient points. Married. At Home. Of course. And then another salient point. My snappy dismissal of him not an hour earlier. Was this what he was calling about? 'Look, I said. 'About Ruth. I'm sorry I –'

'Not a problem, Sally,' he said smoothly. 'OK? No, I'm ringing because we need to fix up our appraisal meeting, don't we? We never got around to scheduling it.' Oh, I thought. My turn. *Ri-ight.* I could feel my cheeks growing warm. 'I mentioned it this morning?' he went on. 'But we both got kinda sidetracked, didn't we? And I'm off to Brighton in the morning so I thought I'd get on to it now – you don't mind do you? Me calling you up at home?'

'Er..no,' I said, fanning my face with a take away menu.

'Because I thought we could maybe get together Tuesday morning. I have a big Human Resources meeting at midday. And I really need to meet with you before then. So I thought breakfast. At the Meridien, perhaps.'

'Breakfast? That sounds thoroughly uncivilised. I look like road kill first thing.'

He laughed. I could hardly believe I was having this conversation in my own kitchen at eight on a Friday evening with Jonathan in the bath. Having said that, it was *entirely* legitimate…

'Well that's the two of us, then,' he said. 'Wear dark glasses if you like. It's that kind of place anyway. Say eight? In the foyer? We can easily head on to Amberley straight after. Does that work for you?'

I was still on the dark glasses bit. Should I also wear a scarf, like Grace Kelly?

'I'm not sure the concept of the breakfast meeting will ever truly work for me,' I said, feeling very jaunty all of a sudden. 'But needs must, I suppose. Eight, then?'

'Eight it is. In the foyer. I'm looking forward to it, Sally.'

OhmyGod, ohmyGod, ohmy*GOD*. So was I.

Chapter 13

'Thou shalt not. OK? Got that, Merlin? Thou shalt not harbour lustful and unsuitable thoughts. Thou shalt not spend so much as a moment more in fantasising. Thou shalt not even *think* about committing adultery.' Saturday morning. The South Downs all a-chalky and gleaming and dressed in their endless shorn apple-green gowns. There was a pair of walkers high above me on the hill as I drove into Eastbourne and I thought straight back to Wales, which made me have to say it again. 'Thou shalt not – OK, Merlin? Thou shall not even *go* there.' Oh, but Tuesday morning. Eight am. Breakfast. The Meridien. I was finding it difficult to think of anything else.

Once Jonathan had gone out on the Friday evening, I had dithered for some time about whether to call Ruth. I needed to see if she was OK. Get things straight. But my need to tell someone what was happening to *me* was becoming so acute that I was terrified of speaking to *anyone* just then, least of all someone with Ruth's penetrative powers. But as I might have predicted, she phoned me anyway.

'Look,' she had said, when I asked her exactly what she'd meant by redundant, and was she absolutely sure that was the case. 'The bottom line is that

I have absolutely no intention of going to West Worthing, OK? *Or* Crawley, for that matter'

'Crawley? Where did Crawley come from?'

'They have a job there too, as it happens. In the pharmacy.'

'Well Crawley's not so bad! It's only round the corner. You could – '

'And is now run, you big twat, by Adam Winklehopper. You'd have to yoke me to the back of a dustcart before you'd get me there.'

'Ah,' I had forgotten that. Adam Winklehopper of the terrible rages and the halitosis. She had a point.

'So there's those two jobs for starters. Which means there must be others. Which is hardly the same as being made redundant, is it?'

'Yes it is. I had a job. Soon I will not have a job. I call that being made redundant. What do you call it?'

'Look, well, yes. OK. But it's also an opportunity. Which is not the same thing. Sounds to me as if it's a simple case of relocation.

'Oh, or the Amberley job, of course. '

'What? There's another job for you *here*?'

'Yes *here*. But I really don't want it.'

'What sort of job?'

'I can train to be a dispensing optician, apparently.'

'But that's brilliant, Ruth! How could you not want that?'

'Because I *don't*, Sal. I don't want to start studying and training and having to learn stuff again! I want to write! I don't want a career. I just want my job, don't you see? I want to go to work and come home again, and *write*.'

I started to protest. 'Oh, stop *flapping*, Sal,' she interrupted. 'It's not the end of the world, OK? And, listen. I got home tonight to find I'd sold a story to *Coffee Time* magazine.'

Which had obviously improved her mood no end. I was glad for her. 'Isn't that the one that does the reader's husbands' bottoms?'

'Yep. And lucrative bottoms they are too. Three hundred quid. That's my eighth sale this year, you know. If I could just up my output a little I could earn enough to eat twice a week. Which reminds me. I'm glad you called. I want to ask a favour. My Gunk To Go party.'

'Your *what*?'

'Oh, you know. I gave you the invite weeks ago. I was supposed to be having it on Monday night. God only knows what possessed me but there you go. Veronique's just been round. '

'Veronique?'

'You *know*. Works on the Lancôme counter. Orange face.'

'Oh, yes. I know.'

'Well of course I had completely forgotten about it, and I'm picking my dad up on Sunday – he had a colostomy on Wednesday, so he'll be coming out Monday, and he's going to stay with me for the week.'

I felt awful, suddenly. I'd never even known he was going in in the first place. 'You never said, Ruth. Why didn't you tell me? Is there anything I can do to help?'

'Oh, it's no big deal, Sal. He's pretty chipper. But what with his colostomy bag and everything – well, there's no way I can have it here, is there? So I thought, could *you*?'

'Me?'

'It's no bother. Just nibbles, wine, all the usual stuff, which I'll bring, of course. I've invited about half a dozen from work, plus Demelza – you know – from my writer's group. You could invite a couple of neighbours too, couldn't you? I don't want to let Veronique down because she's got her Botox injections to pay for and I know she really needs the money. You get a gift voucher if you're hostess. Ten quid, I think. Will you? Please?'

My evening's engagement with the more neglected reaches of my body and a few aromatherapy candles faded and vanished before my eyes. But that was possibly not a bad thing in any case. I could certainly do it. No Jonathan, and Kate was sleeping over at Amanda's. *Should* do it. It would help Ruth out and it would save me from myself. And I could buy some…well… gunk, I supposed. 'OK,' I said. 'What time. Eight?'

'Seven thirty. But I'll confirm things Monday, OK?'

'OK.'

'You all right?'

'I'm fine. Why?'

'Because you sound decidedly odd.'

'Do I?'

'Yes. Are you ill?'

And now it's Saturday morning and the sun is shining and Eastbourne is positively creaking under the weight of so many people who can't believe their luck that it's hot and it's sunny and it's Saturday.

And I am standing in the dim reaches of the Arndale Shopping Centre with a somewhat bemused Merlin sprawled on the ground beside me and a save-the-refuge petition in my hand.

'I did ask the lady in the café if we could borrow one of her tables,' said Polly, apologetically, 'but she was having none of it. Nothing like feeling welcome is there?'

I looked at Polly, with her vague air of menace and her tattooed biceps and her uncompromising footwear (I had never seen her in anything other than what looked like army surplus hobnail boots), and I wondered if being made to feel welcome was something she enjoyed a great deal of the time. I thought not. I wondered what sort of personal circumstance had led her to the unselfish life she lived now. I couldn't imagine anyone trying to bash her up. But then what did I know? Perhaps she'd become the person she was now precisely because she had been. I felt slightly humbled by her.

'I'm fine standing,' I assured her. 'Been sitting in the car for an hour, so I'm happy to stretch my legs. I should have thought about bringing a water bowl for Merlin though. He's going to be parched pretty soon.'

'Not a problem,' she said, beckoning one of the other women over. As the girls in the refuge had to keep low profile, my mother had roped in a posse of neighbours. 'I'll ask Hetty to nip along to Shoe Heaven for you. I'm sure Kayleigh'll be able to dig something out for you.'

'Thanks ever so much –'

'No, no. Thank *you*. This sort of support is more valuable than you know.' She slapped me on the back and almost sent me reeling. 'Can't tell you how much it's appreciated, you know.'

Two hours and some three hundred signatures later, I decided Merlin would appreciate being taken out for a walk. To a lamppost.

'We'll pop home,' suggested Mum, flushed with excitement about her now bulging clipboard. 'Have a sandwich or something. I've got some liver sausage in.'

Once home, I went off to splash some cold water on my face, and when I returned to the living room, it was to find Merlin was rolling around the floor, with something brightly coloured clamped in his mouth. I pulled it from him. It was a threadbare Tellytubby.

'What's this?' I asked my mum, following her into the kitchen. She glanced up.

'Oh, that'll be Megan's, I expect. Thanks for rescuing it for me. They stayed here last night, and you know what it's like with little ones. So much paraphernalia!'

'Stayed here?' I asked, dabbing Merlin's dribble from it. 'What, the children?'

She nodded. 'Tracey, too.'

'Why?'

She was busy buttering bread. 'Oh, something and nothing, most probably, but one of the other mums had seen a blue Cavalier parked over the road for a while yesterday morning, and then again driving by at teatime. Tracey's husband – no, partner – or would it be common law husband? *Him*, anyway – he drives a blue Cavalier. She was a bit anxious about it, so I suggested they come here overnight. It had ladders on, you see.'

I rinsed my hands then pulled the milk from the fridge and splashed an inch into two mugs. 'Ladders?'

'He's a decorator.'

'Oh.'

'And he works locally.' She put down her knife. 'And I felt a bit bad, to be honest. It didn't really occur to me at the time, but we really shouldn't have let little Megan pose for the photo, should we? Only Tracey was off talking with the reporter at the time, and, well, we never really thought. I should have stopped them putting it in.'

'Oh, dear. That sounds like a bit of a worry. Have you told the police?'

She nodded. 'They've already got one of those – what is it? Restraining orders, that's it – on him, but they said it was good that we kept them informed. We're all keeping an eye out for them. I'm sure everything will be fine.'

She smiled, but I wasn't convinced.

Chapter 14

Ruth's friend Demelza was six feet tall, wore red stiletto boots and a dress made up of remnants, and arrived clutching a personal fan and a quarter bottle of gin.

'Ciao,' she said, proffering it. 'Ruth's doing the driving. Have you any tonic water, pray?'

We were a disparate bunch. Briony had arrived with her mother in tow, bless her, but given the short notice I'd not managed to corral many others; just the girl down the road who I sometimes walked the dog with and a few press-ganged stalwarts from work. Veronique, who had come straight from work herself, had already laid out all her Gunk on the dining room table. Oils, salt scrubs, night creams, day creams, creams you could slap on any old time, creams you should only use sparingly (if ever), shower gels, eye gels, lip balms and foot balms, micro-fine powders for the concealment of blotches, micro-pore patches for the removal of spots. Demelza swept past these as if a general surveying some tatty recruits, before plopping herself down next to Briony, who quivered slightly, like a stalk in a gale.

'Why Gunk To Go?' Demelza demanded now, sweeping her hair back and lunging at the nuts. She put me a little in mind of Morticia Adams. Kate would have thought her to die for.

'Well,' offered Veronique. 'It's, like, what we call our take away range.'

'Point taken,' Demelza shot back, volleying a peanut into her gaping gash of a mouth. 'Point taken. But don't the expressions 'to go' and indeed 'take away' signify that the purchaser comes to you – i.e. as in into your shop and indeed take away the goods? Isn't it a bit of a contradiction in terms to call the home delivery service 'to go'? Shouldn't it be 'to you' perhaps? She shot up a querying eyebrow.

'Yes, Like Sainsburys,' offered Briony helpfully. 'Sainsburys to you dot com. Ha ha ha ha ha.'

'Quite!' applauded Demelza. 'Like Sainsburys to you dot com. Good point. Valid point.' She nodded her head a few times and bestowed a slap of approval on Briony's back.

'I don't see what's wrong with "to go",' I said. 'You come here, you buy it, you *go* home with it. Where's the problem?'

'No problem *per se*,' she went on. 'Except that am I right in thinking that Gunk is the name of the shop you hail from, Veronica?'

Veronique looked confused. 'Er..Yes.'

'Therefore shouldn't your home delivery service be called something *other* than Gunk to go? Given that the gunk you sell in your shop could reasonably be construed as being gunk that goes, then gunk of the variety you have on display tonight is surely, more correctly, gunk that *comes?* Hmm? It's of no consequence, of course. Just playing with words. Just kicking the idea about. Hmm?'

'Oh, I see,' said Briony. 'Like – '

Demelza's arm shot out suddenly, veiling Briony (and her contribution) behind the swathe of purple material that was inexplicably trailing from the sleeve of her dress. 'And what is this evil looking contraption?'

Veronique, who had begun to perspire, now looked much relieved.

'Ah, now,' she said, lifting herself to commence her big spiel. 'That "evil contraption" as you call it,. is the Gunk Wonder Mask. It's revolutionary. It's –'

'A PVC eye mask, by the looks of it,' observed Ruth, squidging one in her hand. 'Filled with glittery water. What is it supposed to do, exactly?'

Veronique cleared her throat. 'As I said, it's revolutionary. If you look on the inside you'll see it's not PVC but a revolutionary new microporous capillary action material and filled with a revolutionary new formula of all-natural beneficial ingredients, and it works by actually… er… os*mos*ing these beneficial nutrients into the delicate eye area as you sleep. '

She paused here, either to take in a quantity of oxygen or to brace herself for dissent.

'Ah, osmosis!' barked Demelza, who seemed to respond to syntactical errors in an almost Pavlovian fashion. Briony's mother, who had been snoring throughout, woke up now with a start. 'There's a fine concept for you!' Demelza boomed at her. 'And here's another.' She lunged at a basket on the table, which was filled with an assortment of cosmetics, and which I belatedly realised had a ticket stuck in it, saying 'all lipstick's £1.99'. This she plucked up.

'Ah!' she said. 'The scourge of modern life. Call me Mrs Picky. Call me Mrs Ranty-pants even, but it's my belief that the misplaced apostrophe has a *very* great deal to answer for.'

'Blimey,' I said to Ruth, once I'd escaped to the kitchen to top up the Pringles and wine. 'Is she on something, or what?'

Ruth shrugged. 'She's a writer.'

I pulled a bottle of white from the fridge. 'That says it all then, does it?'

She nodded. 'Oh, yes. Indeed it does, Sal. There's just the two main types of writer, you see. Cardigan 'n' handbag or mad person, basically. Everyone's pretty much one or other.'

'Is that right? Which one are you, then? Or is that a stupid question?'

She crossed her eyes and blew out her cheeks. 'Of course. What's this?' She'd picked something up from the dresser.

'Oh,' I said, glancing over. 'It's mum's petition. I'm supposed to be gathering names for her.'

'Petition for what? Oh, I see –' She began reading. 'What refuge is this then?'

I handed her a copy of the letter my mum had written.

'I'm supposed to be wanging these off to anyone I can think of. They need to raise a deposit so they can buy the house.'

She read through the text. 'You know, you should give one of these to Demelza.'

'Give me one of what?' she said, sweeping into the kitchen.

'One of these,' Ruth said, handing one to her. 'Demelza's aunt is Collette Carr, Sal.'

'Really?' Colette Carr was a novelist of some note. Not only for the squillions of books she'd sold worldwide, but also for her outspoken public persona and well documented run-ins with the literary press. She was currently, so the papers had it, living in a tythe barn near Gloucester, with twenty seven geese, a tame llama and a goat. No cardigan. No handbag. 'That would be great, Demelza. If you don't mind.'

She scanned the letter, slurping at her gin as she read it.

'One thing, sweetie, if you don't mind me saying. A rather clunky split infin in para four.'

*   *   *

It was well past midnight by the time I managed to prise out the last of my guests. Which meant I had no time to do any of the prettifying things I'd had planned. Or indeed, to fret about the fact that I wanted to in the first place, which was becoming an almost equivalent obsession. But all was not lost. At least I had my Gunk Wonder Mask to melt my cares away.

The Gunk Wonder Mask would, the leaflet informed me, melt away not only my cares, but also every last vestige of superfluous fluid, making my eyes firm, youthful and sparkling, even-as-I-slept. And if used in conjunction with the Gunk Cooling Contour Geleé that Veronique had also thrust into my hands, it would miraculously smooth away all my crepitations, to boot. I wasn't sure quite how it expected to achieve this, but as suspension of rational scientific belief was one of the cornerstones of a healthy relationship with one's expensive unguents, I didn't much mind. It might, might it not? And it couldn't do any harm, after all. I slapped a large quantity around both eyeballs and fixed the mask carefully around my head. It felt a little tight, but I presumed this was intentional, and I lay back against the pillow to let the revolutionary osmosis-type action begin doing its thing on my face. Three hours now, if I was lucky, then an hour or so's anxious pacing, and I could whip it back on for a final couple of hours and embrace the day, if not free from all my Nick Brown anxieties, at least free from unsightly dark circles and bags. I fumbled for the light switch, re-plumped my pillow and sank into the embrace of a deep restful sleep.

Shortly after that the telephone rang.

I groped in the blackness for some seconds before I realised quite where I was. Or, indeed, where the telephone was. I seemed to have a fish on my face.

'Yes? What? Hello?'

There was a hissing noise and then a gruff voice said, 'Er, Mrs Matthews?'

I sat up now, awake. Who was this strange grunting person? I tried yanking at the Wonder Mask but it appeared to have welded itself to me. And there was suddenly a dreadful smell in the room.

'Mrs Matthews?' came the voice again, more coherently this time.

'Who wants to know?' I snapped, holding the phone in the crook of my shoulder, so I could wrestle with the poppers at the back of my head.

'Er…it's, um, Carl.'

'What? I can't hear you!' The poppers finally popped and the mask flipped on to my lap. My hand, inexplicably, was wet.

'*Carl,*' he said again, with more emphasis this time. 'I'm –'

His words were suddenly drowned out by a terrible banshee wailing. I held the phone away from my ear a bit. More grunting, and the wailing became a low moan. 'Hello?' said the voice again. 'Are you still –'

Good God! It was Carl!

'Carl? What on earth do you think you're doing ringing Kate at this time of night? It's twelve thirty two in the morning!'

There were more noises off. 'I know,' he said eventually. 'But I had to – oh, shit. Hang on –'

'Had to *what*, precisely?' I ranted. 'And does your mother know you're using the phone? And what on earth do you imagine Kate would be doing at this hour on a Monday night? And anyway, she's not even here! She's –'

'I *know*,' he said again. 'That's why I'm calling. I know she's not there. She's with *me*.'

My hand was wet, I realised, because my Wonder Mask was leaking . A trail of stinking golden slime was oozing down my T-shirt and beginning to pool in my crotch. God, what had they filled it with? Liquidised entrails? I yanked the duvet to one side and leapt out of bed.

'*WHAT!'*

'She's here. Right here. Beside me. She's not very well, Mrs Matthews, so I wondered if you could drive down and, um –'

'What! *Where*? Where *are* you? Not very well? What do you mean, not very well? Where is she? Put her on the phone!'

He put her on the phone.

'Muuueeeeeerrggghеyemmmshnotwelll mummmmmmeeeeee! Shycannnttttt….'

'*Kate?*'

'Shhbeenshick*evy*where. I caaanttt – muuu*uuummmmmmm*!'

Good grief! More wailing and shuffling.

'Carl? *Carl!'*

'I'm here. I – oh, shit! Hang on – nooo. Stand up! You're going to get it all over – oh, Kate! For *fuck's* sake, can't you –'

'Carl!' I snarled. 'What the hell is going on there? Where are you?'

'We're just up the lane from the Ferret and Firkin. In the bus shelter. I've been trying to take her back to our house, but she can't walk and I can't get any answer from my mum and she wants –'

More banshee caterwauling. Oh my God! My daughter in a bus shelter in the middle of nowhere! And a nowhere with Carl and an unsavoury pub!

'What the hell is she doing *there*? She's supposed to be at Amanda's!'

'Um –'

'So what is she doing with YOU? Oh, God! Right. Right! Stay *right* where you are. I am on my way!'

I then tripped over Jonathan's tennis trainers, which served as a pertinent reminder that I would not be on my way any time soon. I counted back. The Baileys with Ruth. The two – no! The *three* glasses of red wine! The glass of white wine while I was doing the nibbly bits, the half glass of white wine I took up to the bath with me…shit! I was standing here sober as sober, yet, technically speaking I was drunk! No, no. Not drunk. My head was so clear now you could triangulate the entire Pennine Way through it . But over the limit. Definitely over the limit. Oh, *great.*

I thrust my legs into jeans and pummelled my bare feet into trainers. I would just have to drive anyway. This was an emergency. I rattled down the stairs. But how could I? What if I got there and a panda car had already happened by and there was a policeman there or something? And I *breathed* on them? I could *not* drive. It was not responsible. I would have to call a taxi.

But the nearest taxi firm was miles away. And it was already a good fifteen minute drive to where Kate was. Oh, shit. I dialled them anyway.

'I need a taxi,' I said to the comatose woman at the other end of the phone. 'As speedily as you can, please.'

'Picking up from?'

I gabbled our address at her.

'Okey dokey.' I could hear a clatter of fingers on a keyboard. 'Now,' she drawled at length. 'Is that the Sandy Lane, Horsham or the Sandy Lane, North Chailey?'

'Gatwick. The one near Gatwick. The one off Carlton Road. How soon can you get one to me?'

Silence. Perhaps she'd dozed off. 'Now,' she said eventually. 'Let me *see*...Give us, oh, twenty-twenty-five, love?'

Twenty-twenty-five? Twenty-twenty-five *what?* Pounds? Oh, yes. Minutes. 'Twenty five *minutes?'* I squeaked. 'That's too long. I can't wait that long,'

'Best I can do, love.'

'Then, no. Thank you, but no.'

Hopeless. I *had* to drive. There was no option. My daughter was wailing and vomiting in a bus shelter and if rescuing her meant I had to go to prison then so be it. I would be going to prison anyway, because I was going to *kill* her.

Merlin was already all about by this time, clickety clicking around the hall and making inquisitive forays between my legs.

'*Will* you get away from me!' I barked, slapping his nose away. 'I am not a dog's bottom, OK!'

OK. First half glass of wine at half past six. Half past six to half past twelve – no. Call it one o clock. Six and a half hours. Six and a half hours at one unit of alcohol per hour meant six and a half units of alcohol metabolised. OK. Baileys. One unit. No. two. Ruth had poured it. Three glasses of red, one and a half of white. Say one and a half units per glass. One and a half times four and a half – no! Five and a half – no *six* and a half with the Baileys. Six and a half times one and a half. Which made...which made nine? Ten? Yes, ten. Two glasses of wine was OK. And two glasses of wine was about three units, so if you allowed three units, and took that away from ten then it left seven. Seven in six and a half hours. So I should be only over the limit by half a unit, shouldn't I? And if you made, say, a half unit allowance for the kettle chips and peanuts...yes. That would do it. So I was all right. Almost. *Almost.*

Satisfied that I must be at least *nearly* sober in order to deal with so many fractions while in charge of a motor vehicle I pulled out and zoomed off down the main road with Merlin in the back.

I had, however, failed to take the sensible precaution of getting Carl's mobile phone number so had to kerb crawl past several bus shelters en route before I eventually found them.

Kate was, I presumed, slumped out of sight inside the bus shelter. But Carl, by virtue of having hair the colour of a small gas explosion, was readily visible, and was leaning against the bus stop itself, smoking a cigarette. He pinged it into the kerb as I pulled up at the opposite side of the road, and shuffled forwards, hands stuffed in Jeans pockets.

'Er, look – 'he began, as I stomped across to meet him.

'Er look!' I snapped. 'I'll give you "er look!". What on earth do you think you're playing at taking my daughter to the pub and getting her drunk?'

I bustled past him and into the shelter. Kate, who was, indeed, a slumpen form, looked up at me with hollow eyes then reached her arms out towards me and burst into tears.

'I didn't!' whinnied Carl from behind me. 'She was completely ratted when I got there!'

He sounded like he was on the cusp of being sober himself. I patted Kate's back.

'Hmm,' I said, to indicate my disapproval anyway. He was probably very practiced at feigning sobriety. 'Well, can you give me a hand here please? I need to get her into the car.'

Kate's head rolled up again. 'I can walk,' she said dully. 'I think I've finished being sick now.' She pushed herself upright and staggered against me.

'I sincerely hope so, young lady!' I retorted.' What on earth do you think you've been doing? What have you been drinking?'

'Watermelon Bacardi Breezers,' she muttered. 'Not many. Uuurrrgh.'

We shuffled her out of the shelter. 'Not many?' growled Carl. 'You must have had ten between you. You could hardly see the table!'

'You? Who's you?'

'Amanda,' they both said.

'You were here with Amanda? What about rehearsals? Specifically, what about you sleeping over at Amanda's *house*?'

Kate didn't reply.

'She went home,' Carl explained helpfully. 'Her dad came to pick her up. They..er.. had an argument.'

We were weaving towards the car by now. Merlin's nose was pressed hopefully against the back window and I could hear him whinnying to get out and be part of the action. Kate's head pinged up again.

'You scumbag!' she cried suddenly, wanging an arm up and sloshing Carl across the chest with it. 'You want to *dump* me!'

Oh, Jesus. Not more of that stuff. *Please.*

She started crying again. 'You do! You want to dump me for *her*!'

Carl dodged a second assault. 'For Christ's sake, Kate! I do NOT want to dump you. I do NOT want to go out with Amanda. *OK*? I –'

'Hang on,' I said. 'Hang *on*. What was Amanda's Dad thinking of? Why didn't he bring you home as well? Why didn't he phone me? *Well?*'

Kate was now a slumpen form in the front seat of the car. Carl stooped to tuck her foot in. A tender moment, all told.

'I told him *you* were picking me up,' she muttered.

'Oh. Oh, I *see*. And did it not occur to you to run that one by *me*? I had a party tonight, Kate. I might even have been out. As it is, I've had – 'No. Perhaps I shouldn't mention the drinking. 'How on *earth* did you think you we're going to get home?' I finished. '*Well?*'

Kate shrugged again.

Carl put his hands on his hips. 'Quite,' he said pointedly. A picture of sorts was beginning to emerge. A rather embarrassing picture. An extremely embarrassing picture. Involving a drunken, raving Kate and the not-so-bad-after-all boyfriend who got stuck with the fall out. And there had certainly been fall out. There were suspicious looking flecks on his boots. I slapped the car door shut.

'So,' I said to him, digging out a watery smile. 'Can I drop you home, Carl?'

'Nah,' he said. 'It's not far. I'll be OK.'

He would too. He was a good foot taller than me and looked pretty alarming even in daylight.

'Um, well, thanks for, um…staying to look after her. I didn't realise – I mean, well. I'm sorry I shouted at you. You sure I can't drive you?'

He glanced over my shoulder and back.

'Nah,' he said. 'No sweat.'

Oh, the shame.

I got back into the car and stabbed the key into the ignition.

'Well,' I huffed. 'I just hope you feel thoroughly ashamed of yourself. You stupid, stupid *stupid* girl!'

Kate stared dully out of the windscreen and said nothing. Which left lots of empty airspace for me.

'That poor lad! What were you thinking of? You could have ended up in hospital! Not to mention court! I clearly can't trust you an inch! There's me thinking you're tucked up in bed at Amanda's house and all the time you're staggering round the streets making an exhibition of yourself and throwing up!'

The windows were beginning to steam up by now, what with the combined input of my ranting, Merlin's panting and the steam rising up from Kate's sick-splattered dress. I slid the heater knob to maximum and glared at the road ahead. Was there anyone in my life *not* giving me hassle right now?

Kate wiped a hand across her face and coughed.

And then she threw up again.

Oh, *great.*

Chapter 15

There is an antidote to the traumas of parental responsibility. It is called a hotel breakfast. A hotel breakfast with a very nice man.

I'd set the alarm for six, and showered quietly, so as not to wake Kate, but when I tiptoed downstairs to put the kettle on, she was already in the kitchen, sitting at the table, slurping from a mug of tea and munching on toast.

'Oh!' I said, peering into the teapot to find it stone cold and still harbouring yesterdays half finished dregs. 'I certainly didn't expect to find *you* down here at this hour, young lady. How is your head?'

She looked up at me as if I had just asked her if that big yellow thing in the sky was the sun.

'It's fine,' she said airily. I pointed at the toast in her hand.

'And your stomach?'

'A bit sore,' she conceded. 'But I'll live.'

'Oh, I'm quite sure you will,' I said, in my best 'holier-than-thou yet knowing absolutely *all* there was to know about the ravages alcohol excess could wreak' kind of voice. I wondered irritably how it was that she was able to drink a bucket of Bacardi and still be up at six eating toast, while I felt like the Gatwick Express had been rerouted through my ear holes. Stress. That was it. Stress and old age.

And guilt, of course. I put the kettle on and came to join her at the table.

'And are you going to enlighten me as to what that little performance was all about last night?'

She put her half eaten toast down and sighed.

'Mum, it was about nothing.'

No change there, then.

I tried a different tack. 'So did you actually *go* to your rehearsal?'

'Yes, of course I did.'

'But then you and Amanda had an argument.'

'Sort of.'

'What about?'

'Nothing.'

'No. *Not* nothing, Kate.' I waited. She waited. 'Well?' I said finally. 'About Carl, I presume?'

This seemed to strike a note of regretful recognition because she pulled an anguished face and plonked her head on the table.

She then yanked it up again, causing stray hairs and toast crumbs to take to the air. 'Oh!' she cried, eyes suddenly swimming with tears. 'She's *such* a bitch, mum!'

And out it all came. Namely that she had gone to rehearsals with Amanda and that Amanda had suggested they go to the pub for a drink afterwards with Janine (who was in the sixth form and had a Nissan Micra) and that once in the pub (and after the first flush of Bacardi had risen to their youthful cheeks, no doubt) Amanda had told Kate that she'd heard Lisa talking to Jemma in the church hall toilets and that they'd been saying that Carl was getting a bit fed up with Kate and wanted out. But when Kate (now much bridled) had gone into the pub toilets with Janine shortly after, Janine had told her that what Amanda said hadn't been true at all and that the truth of the matter – and that *everyone* else knew it – was that Amanda was desperate to go out with Carl herself and was spreading bad vibes about the place about him so that Kate would dump him and she could go out with him herself. And so Kate had gone back into the pub and asked Amanda what the hell she thought she was playing at and Amanda had got really nasty and said couldn't she see that Carl was sick of her and that, well, she hadn't been going to say anything , but that he'd said as much to *her* too, and that she was very sorry and all that, but Kate needed to wise up a bit (and so on). And just as Kate was retorting that no, it was *Amanda* that needed to wise up a bit and get her claws out of her – haarrruumph! – *best friend's* bloody boyfriend, Carl himself fetched up and was very surprised to find them all there. As, indeed, was Kate, as he'd told her he was staying in and revising with Andy for their Maths GCSE tomorrow afternoon, so what the hell were they doing down the pub? *Eh?* At which point Carl, who had indeed been revising for his Maths GCSE with Andy and who had only popped out for a bit of fresh air and a quick drink, told Kate she didn't own him and would she please, like, *back off a bit*. Which had Amanda, who was (apparently) even drunker that Kate, saying 'You see! You see! What did I tell you?' Which was making everyone really embarrassed and Kate, distressed, had shot off back to the loo for a wail.

She returned from the toilets to find that Janine had gone home and that Amanda was now standing at the bar with Carl and Andy and making a big show of being all friendly and 'I understand-y' and generally behaving like she and Carl had spent the last ten minutes planning their engagement, at which point Kate told her to sod off and went back to the table to swig another half bottle of Bacardi Breezer and sulk. Carl had then come over and said, 'Get a grip, can't you, Kate?' (or something like that) and told her that Amanda (who had Geography in the morning) had called her Dad to come and pick them both up. To which Kate responded that she'd rather sleep in a cess pit than sleep over with *her,* and that she'd already called her mum and she'd be there in half an hour. At which point Andy had said he'd better push off and get back to his quadratic equations, and then Amanda had left in a huff and it was just the two of them. And it was closing time. And Kate was feeling very strange and couldn't walk properly. And so on.

Carl had then decided (with some acuity) that he needed to get Kate out walking (after a fashion) in the fresh air, and preferably before the landlord started taking notice and asking them for ID. Which they had done for some time (interspersed with pauses for vomiting, wailing etc.), until it dawned on Carl that in fact I wouldn't be getting there any time soon because I had not, at any point, been actually phoned. And would doubtless be somewhat cross. At which point *he* got rather cross with Kate, but deciding the best thing would be to get her back to his place (it being nearer) he had called *his* mum instead. However, his mum, who slept like a corpse (apparently), had failed to answer the phone.

And so in the end he'd called me after all. And so I'd arrived. And now – *damn it!* – it was a quarter past seven.

'D'you think it's true he wants to dump me?' Kate sobbed now. '*Do* you?'

Having made a lightning re-appraisal of poor hapless Carl in the last six hours, I went and grabbed a bit of kitchen roll for her, and decided, in that hopeful, positive, mumsy way that one does, that, no, it wasn't true. I said so.

'However,' I added sternly, 'I think a) you should phone him and apologise, b) you *should* back off a bit, and give the poor boy some space, c) you should learn to trust him a bit more and d) you should learn that Bacardi Breezers are not Ribena and that as you are only sixteen, it is illegal for you to go into a pub and buy them.'

I chose my words carefully here. I had had more than a nodding acquaintance with acute gastro-intestinal irritation in my youth.

She wiped her nose. 'Almost *seven*teen, mum.'

'Kate, I am *almost* forty-two. But do you see me taking up macramé and bowls yet? No. You do not. There is no *rush*. You have decades and decades in which to experience the delights of post-alcoholic paranoia and remorse. There is *no rush*. Oh, and – where are we? E? –Yes, E. That you're very lucky you have such an understanding mother. If your father had been here you'd be dead.'

She shuffled over to the sink and ripped another sheet of kitchen paper from the roll.

'I doe,' she mumbled. 'I doe, Mum, honestly.' Her lower lip quivered and she put her hand to her forehead. 'Oh, God. I feel sick again now.'

So. There is justice after all.

Oh, blimey! And only forty five – no, *forty* – minutes in which to dress, put a face on, make my hair look half normal, and present myself to Nick Brown at the Meridien Hotel.

And my car smelt of sick. Oh, *great.*

After I had force fed Kate two glasses of water and put her to bed the previous night, I had gone back outside and scrubbed the inside of my car very vigorously. The passenger seat, the mat, the footwell, the outside of the glove compartment, the inside of the door. But it still smelt of sick. Badly. So much so that I had to drive all the way to the hotel with all four windows wide open and was greeted in the car park lift mirror by the sight of a completely deranged woman with hair that looked like it was a Harrier jump jet attempting a forced landing on an aircraft carrier. In the North Sea. In a gale. A very bad start to the day.

My acquaintance may only be slight, but it seems to me there is something reliably surreal and subterranean about the foyers of five star hotels. This one had all the usual attributes. A towering atrium, several vast expanses of well behaved water, click-clack receptionists with pony tails and talons who were always doing something with bits of paper and a stapler, and everyone being very *very* quiet. And despite there being clocks to tell you the exact time in ten countries, if felt spookily as if, in this place, time had stopped. There was, at least, one jolly family with an excitable toddler knocking about (what! Holidaymakers in our still haven of grave commercial important-ness!) but as his only foray into doing proper rampaging toddler stuff consisted of dipping one careful finger into the corner of one of the spooky black pools, and causing a *very* small ripple (and as he had a dummy in his mouth and was therefore unable to google and squawk at the top of his shrill voice about it), my breathless and crashy-bashy entrance was noticed by all. Heads turned on necks. Then turned back again, sniffing. I tried to pretend I was now in slow motion, and to glide smoothly on through, as if surveying a reef.

Nick Brown, fortunately, hadn't yet noticed me, as he was sitting on a length of couch-thing in a far flung corner, pressing buttons on his mobile phone.

Which was nice, because it allowed me a moment or two to soak up and be caressed by the great wash of healing endorphins that the act of seeing him now flooded so uncontrollably through me. He had never strayed far from the apex of my thoughts, of course, yet with all the traumas of the last twenty four hours, I was quite unprepared for how powerfully his presence could suddenly knock everything else in my life into touch.

My own presence was not long in making itself felt either, as I was in appallingly unfortunate footwear. A pair of spindly court shoes that worked well among the pink fronds of the new Drug u Like carpeting, but that on the resonant acres of mirror-like marble beneath me now, made my approach sound like someone was felling a tree.

He looked up, watching me teetering towards him with an expression that made my knees begin to buckle. Then stood, as if bringing himself to corporate attention. 'You're late!' he boomed heartily, in that way thrusting Americans do, and on which he had obviously based his management style. He then dipped his head, and pecked me lightly on the cheek. Oh, my. 'Another family crisis?' he added cheerfully. I hoped it wasn't because I still smelled of sick.

'Um, yes,' I replied, given that there was really no point in doing otherwise. 'I'm terribly sorry,' I added, pretending to adjust my right earring with my left hand so I could sniff my sleeve. 'My daughter's...er...going through a bad time at the moment.

Er…exam today. Usual crises. You know.' It wasn't true. Her next exam wasn't until Friday. But it would do.

'Tell me about it!' he said, putting his hand gently against my jacketed back and steering me towards the restaurant. He lifted the hand with the phone in it. 'My son – Will – just had a text from him. He's a fresher at Harvard.' He paused to beam slightly, bless him, then consulted his wrist. 'Jeez, it's twenty past three there. The guy needs to be in bed. Takes after his father, I guess. Anyway, shall we?'

Smiling indulgently (where Kate was concerned, this was a circumstance I had not had the luxury of enjoying in a long time – though there was, at least, *Starlight Express* to look forward to) he led me towards a large man wielding a snowy tea towel and a supercilious smile, who then led us in turn to a table in the far corner of the restaurant. It was fairly quiet – just the odd restrained cough and a sprinkling of big newspapers. Behind which, I guessed, various captains of industry chewed thoughtfully while considering the Big Issues Of The Day. I felt very suburban in my little coral coloured suit.

'Well,' said Nick, rubbing his hands together and smiling happily at me as we sat down. '*Isn't* this nice? And am I starving or what! What'll it be?' The man had sidled up again. 'Tea? Coffee? Hot chocolate?'

I opted for tea as I had quite enough stimulants on board as it was, and, once we'd placed our orders and been advised of the rules of engagement for the procurement of the breakfast buffet selection, he sent the waiter away. He was very bouncy. Very smiley. Very businesslike, this morning. I wondered if, like our last phone call, our meeting was being monitored and/or recorded for quality assurance purposes too. But perhaps I was just feeling unduly drugged. By sleep deprivation and lust.

Or love?

The cereals, fruit salads, cheeses, juices, croissants and so on were all laid out, in magnificent abundance, on a quadrangle of tables, extravagantly clothed, and dotted with implausibly stiff flower arrangements and towering jumbles of oversized fruit. What did they *do* with all this stuff after breakfast? We ventured across to graze upon the bounty before us. Him, a glass of juice and two croissants, me, a brace of diminutive pastries. By the time we returned to our table, the tea had already arrived. He poured me a cup, and smiled.

'So,' he said, stabbing his thumbs into a croissant. 'You.'

I liked the way he did that. No nonsense. Lots of crumbs. 'Yes. Me,' I replied.

'Indeed.' He smiled at me again, in an altogether less corporate fashion this time, before his eyes slid away and he cleared his throat. 'So, Sally.' He leaned forward, having corrected his expression again. 'The way these things generally work is that I now spend a lot of time now running through your appraisals and so on, and how your profile as an employee fits in with the Drug U Like human resource criteria, and then I spend even more time banging on about how-we-see-your-role long term in the development of Drug U Like's Optometry services to the UBP –'

'UBP?'

'Unsuspecting British Public – it's an internal thing. And, finally, I spend more time *still* telling you how exceptionally impressed we have been with every facet of your performance – productivity, attitude, level of expertise, interactive stroke people stroke time management skills and so on and so forth –'he ticked all these off against a finger as he spoke. 'But then I think you know most of that already, don't you? And as, basically, the bottom line here is that we'd like to interview you for the post of Optometry Manager, I thought I'd spare you the pitch and crack on with it.' He grinned. 'Of Amberley Park, of course,' he added. 'Not the entire Developed World. There you go. What do you think?'

He leaned back in his seat again and popped a hunk of croissant in his mouth.

I stayed hunched over my miniature *pain au raisin* and blinked at him.

'Me? *Manager?*'

His mouth was full now so he nodded.

'But what about Dennis?'

He flapped a hand as he swallowed.

'Oh, don't you worry about him,' he said, picking up his glass of grapefruit juice and taking a man-sized gulp from it. 'Not a problem. He told us very early on that he wouldn't be adverse to a healthy early retirement package and a chance to devote more time to his exhibition dahlias. Nice guy. Anyway, so no problem. Not relevant, Sally.'

I thought back to my first proper work meeting with Nick Brown and the fact that though I had said all the right things in response to all the usual where-do-you-see-yourself-in-five-years stuff (which had I been honest would have run as 'er, optometry? How should I know? I don't *do* life like that') I didn't recall having expressed any particular ambitions in that direction. And yet here it was. Being offered to me anyway. As if it were the most natural next step in the world. Strangely, it suddenly seemed as if it might be. Could be.

'I'm stunned,' I said.

'Excellent,' he replied, grinning. 'We like to keep the staff on their toes.'

Which was slightly unfortunate given the Ruth situation, but as she didn't seem to care a hoot any more, I decided that perhaps I shouldn't either. We exchanged a pointed look, and I finished mine with a smile, to let him know I wasn't about to rant at him about it again. He smiled back and sat forward.

'You'll want to think about it, obviously. Which is just fine. The time scale we're thinking is about twelve to fourteen weeks. You'd need to go on a couple of courses – neither involving outdoor pursuits this time, I hasten to add – just the standard stuff. Leadership skills, target-setting and so forth. And you'd need to continue with your practice, naturally. The branch isn't really large enough to support a full time dedicated manager, but my guess is that you'd want to do that anyway, right? And we'd probably bring in a trainee optom, and you'd need to oversee their professional development.'

'I'm stunned.' I said again, abandoning my half eaten pastry in favour of watching him instead. 'I suppose I just assumed Russell would –'

He shook his head then grinned at me.

'Which is an aspect of your leadership style that you *do* need to look at, Sally.' He spread his hands. 'Why ever *not* you? You're senior optom, you've been with the company a good long time now, you're very good at your job, you're committed, and most importantly, you have the support and respect of everyone I've spoken to.'

Why had *I* never thought of myself like that?

And thinking that thought made me realise something else. That Jonathan had never thought of me like that either.

‘Me included,’ Nick added, looking rather intently at me all of a sudden. My stomach flipped. ‘So,’ he said. ‘Do you think you might be up for it?’.

I sat there, gazing into his beautiful blue-ice eyes, and I thought ‘shall I tell him what I’m *really* thinking right now?’ Because right then, my thoughts were away with the fairies. In a meadow, I fancied, full of buttercups and poppies, in a long flowery frock, with his hand holding mine….. I lowered my eyes and felt the beginnings of a blush creep across my cheekbones. But it wasn’t just me. So much was being said here. Every time he dipped off his corporate line.

Another waiter wafted up and cleared a space for our breakfasts. His being pretty much everything you could fit on a plate, mine being two poached eggs; perfect whorls glistening on thick hunks of toast.

‘Yes,’ I said firmly, picking up my cutlery and smiling. ‘You know what, Nick? I do.’

There was a moment of silence, while a smile crossed his lips.

‘Great,’ he said at last, picking up his cutlery also. ‘That’s that sorted, then. Now we can get on and enjoy breakfast can’t we? So, tell me, what exam is your daughter taking today?’

In retrospect, I think it might have been the setting that doomed (if that is the word) this particular encounter, for we had an acre of table, a prettily placed sun shaft, hot coffee on tap and a congenial hour in which to do nothing more taxing than get to know each other a little better. We talked about him, we talked about me, we talked about all sorts of things. We even talked about the fact (me blushing furiously) that my car had recently played host to my inebriated daughter, and that if his intention was to come back with me to Amberley in it (which, alarmingly, it seemed it was – he had another meeting here tonight apparently, and might just as well leave his here and have a colleague bring him back), then he mustn’t mind the smell and must sit carefully on the green recycling bag I’d laid over the damp passenger seat so as not to infect my handbag.

One thing we *didn’t* talk about was my unfortunate shoes. (Unfortunate being how I would intermittently come to think of them as I lay awake in the small hours of the night following this fateful day.) Right now, as we exited the lift that had brought us back down to the ground floor, I just went ‘Yeeaargh!’

'Whoah!' Nick Brown said, as I lurched out of the lift, cannoning untidily into the side wall and now minus my left shoe. He made a timely grab for my arm and managed to spare me an intimate introduction to the carpet pile. Staggering a bit, I prised the heel from where it was wedged between the lift and the frame, pulled my dangling handbag strap back on to my shoulder then hopped on one leg blushing furiously while I tried put the shoe back on my foot.

'God!' I said, losing my balance and bouncing around like Tigger. 'Stupid shoes!'

'Here, hang on to me,' he said, putting his arm around my shoulder.

I slid the shoe back on to my foot and straightened up. His arm was still around my shoulder. A firm, warm, familiar weight against me.

'Must cut down on the early morning gin,' I twittered, laughing gaily to cover my sudden and electrifying recollection of our moment on the dune. I scooped the hair from my face. Felt a knot in my stomach. His arm was still around my shoulder.

'The gin, period,' he replied sternly. 'Can't have the management falling over drunk on the job. Not before lunchtime, at any rate.' He laughed as well. We moved away from the lift, along the carpet, towards the doors and the sunshine in the distance. I was walking just fine now, and yet his arm was still around my shoulder.

'Well, I'm sorry, but that's me off your promotion list then,' I answered, quick as you like and ho ho ho-ing again. 'I can't be doing with namby pamby rules and regulations, you know. Not if they interfere with my gin habit.' I swallowed. His arm was *still* around my shoulder.

And then, all of a sudden, I found I'd stopped laughing. And we had also stopped walking. I turned my head to look up at him.

'Nick, you still have your arm round my shoulder,' I said.

Oh, the surreal and subterranean ambience of a really posh hotel foyer. Except we weren't in the foyer any more, of course. We were now one floor below. Back in the cavernous carpeted expanse that led the way back to the car park, and which I'd jogged anxiously through not an hour and a half before.

I was gripped once more by the otherworldliness of it. The sense that we were held here, as if in a time lock or portal. Above us the hotel, dripping with the affluent trappings of lives extravagantly lived. Beyond us, outside, an ordinary car park. Ordinary life. We were stationary now. Suspended between the two. Still some yards from the doorway and standing in the half-light, adjacent to yet another extravagant floral display. There wasn't a soul around. I felt the knot in my stomach begin to unravel, sending tendrils of dangerous electricity through me. Not a soul. Just us. We were all alone.

'I know,' he whispered now, as I turned fully to face him. He wordlessly lifted his other arm so it, too, was now around me. And I couldn't seem to stop my own arms from participating. Up they shot, encircling the back of his jacket, like renegade eels I just couldn't control. My head tipped back too. Seems I couldn't trust *anything*. He seemed suddenly taller, but the distance was now shortening. He smiled as his head dipped.

'I know,' he said again.

At which point the thing we should have done – the thing that my extensive reading of some of the finer romantic gems in classic historical fiction would indicate persons in our situation might *sensibly* have done, would have been to draw apart reluctantly, sigh a little, swoon a little, effect postures of rigid embarrassment or dismay and continue on our journey to the automatic doors.

But I was no Anne Elliot. He was no Captain Wentworth. So I'm forced to report that we did no such thing.

Being, as we were, not a million miles from the support of an obliging wall, we staggered backwards, kissing each other as madly and hungrily as if global apocalypse or the departure of the last troop ship to the Normandy beaches was imminent, till we were right up against it, me panting, wall-side, him pressed hot and hard against me, a lather of tangled limbs, moans, groans and squirming, and utterly unrestrained, unbridled lust.

Until a gentle ping heralded the lift doors opening.

We sprang apart – pop! – and stared wide-eyed at each other.

'Oop,' he mouthed, untangling his fingers from my hair.

I was speechless. Breathless. Swimming. Steeped in a cocktail of desire and guilt. The lift disgorged a brace of middle aged men. I yanked my bag from my shoulder and began ferreting in it.

'– taken at face value,' one of them was muttering. 'Spurring's got a point. If we're talking bottom line here, my feeling's we have to start thinking *out*side the box. Get my reasoning on this, Graham?'

'Yeah, yeah,' the other man was saying through a haze of cigarette smoke. 'But come on, face it. Spurring's out of the loop. He's –'

The men wafted by, our eyes following them as they strolled off out into the sunshine, a thin sheet of smoke loitering at chest height in their wake. We continued to watch as one of them deposited his *Financial Times* on a side table (more exuberant flowers) just inside the doors.

And then they were gone. We looked at each other again.

'Dear me,' said Nick.

'Dear *me*,' said I.

He lifted my hand up and put it against his cheek.

'Yes,' he said softly, putting his lips to it. 'Dear you.'

Nothing like a big blast of radiation to turn a lightly fetid car into a seething morass of inhospitable fumes. Nothing like a big intake of inhospitable fumes to bring you to your senses and make you realise that no, you are not a celluloid heroine, but a real person, with a real life, and that you have just kissed, no, *snogged* – damn, it was the only word for it – someone other than your husband for the first time in eighteen long years.

'Ugh!' I said now, as the full extent of my family's olfactory contributions hit me like a slap around the face with a haddock. Nick, who had chivalrously opened the door for me, wrinkled his nose in disgust.

'Leave it here,' he said, closing it again firmly and locking it. 'Come in my car. I can drop you back here tonight.'

'Oh dear,' I said again, a tantalising parade of in-car clothes-off situations riffling alarmingly through my brain as if the flapping pages of a catalogue called *being ravished; a field guide*. My stomach flipped again. 'Do you think that's a good idea? I mean – 'I stopped. What *did* I mean? Did I mean that was that? 'I mean,' I said again, 'don't you think I should just –'

He was so *close* to me again. If I could just get a couple of feet on him perhaps I would be able to take a hold of myself and stop wanting to paw him so badly. He waited for me to finish whatever it was I'd been going to say, and as I failed to, (not knowing quite what it was I had wanted to say and feeling completely unable to formulate any utterance not starting with an extravagant sigh or a lunge at his shirt front) he took my hand instead and started leading me across to the other side of the car park.

'Tell you what I think,' he said firmly as I trotted breathlessly alongside him. 'I think you're right. It's an extremely *bad* idea, but I'm relying on you to keep your wits about you, and if I so much as *look* as if I might hint at the idea that we might make an unscheduled stop down a secluded lane somewhere –'he paused and took a breath here. 'Then please take immediate action and hit me over the head with your handbag or something. Or just slap me. Whatever. Oh, Sally – ' We had reached his car. He pressed the button on his key fob and the door locks clunked upward. His other hand was still holding mine and he squeezed it. 'Jeez. I am really *really* sorry. This is no way good. This is – '

I lifted a finger to his mouth to silence him.

'I can't,' I heard myself say.

He kissed it. 'Can't what?'

'I can't do that.'

'But you *have* to,' he answered.

What had possessed me? What on earth was I *doing* here?

'I know,' I whispered. 'But I *can't*.'

Chapter 16

'Oh, Sally! Oh, Sally, you've *never* seen anything so funny in your *entire* life. Really you haven't!'

Oh, *Nick*. Oh, God. What had I *done*?

Ruth had burst into my consulting room laughing so much I thought she might set off the smoke alarm, her gales of laughter reverberating like a volley of ping pong balls off the walls. I had got into work and been testing solidly ever since – a relief of momentous proportions as I could barely articulate the letters on my chart, let alone get to grips with making sentences. But now she had sought me out, and was twittering on about something that was clearly uproariously funny, but it felt like I was listening to her through a soupy pink fog.

'*Never*,' she said again. 'Oh, it was such a hoot! You can imagine her, can't you? Stomping around, screeching and yelling. My poor father thought the angel of death had come to lynch him. And her face!'

I grappled to make sense of her. 'What *about* it?' I had not even managed to establish what she was on about. I had not even quite established what day it was. All I had established with any clarity was *Five thirty. Back in the car park.*

'Well it was scarlet, of course! In a big livid stripe right across her face!' She paused for a second, then grabbed my wrist.

'God, there's a thought! You didn't use yours, did you?' She examined my face carefully. 'No. Of course you didn't. And DON'T. Whatever you do. They're obviously faulty. Oh, it was– '

My mind was a blank. '*What*, Ruth? *What* was faulty?'

'The Wonder Mask, of course! You had one didn't you?'

Of course. It suddenly seemed like a million years ago. I got my brain back into gear. 'Oh, *that*. Yes, yes, I did.' That. *Then*. A *billion* years ago. I nodded comprehension. 'And I did use it. Well, had *intended* to, but I had to go out and pick Kate up at God knows what hour, so I took it off again. And it split. I never smelt anything so vile. It –'

'I *know!* God only knows what was in there – at first I thought my Dad's colostomy – hmm, well.' She wrinkled her nose. 'Never mind about that. Anyway, I went and told Veronique this morning, and now she's in a right state, of course. Must have been old stock or something, mustn't it? Must have been degenerating or having some sort of chemical breakdown. I don't know what quite, but she's in a right old lather about it. She's sold about twenty of them, you know, poor girl. She's expecting to be sued now. So that's bang goes the Botox. Oh, but Demelza's face! What a picture! She was in a *right* old strop. She's supposed to be doing a workshop at the WriteRight group tonight, and she looks like – Er, Sally? He*llo*? Are you *with* us?'

'Er…what? Yes. Sorry –'I was trying very hard, but I kept slipping back into neutral.

There was a rap on the door. Russell poked his head round it.

'Sally?' he said brightly. 'Jonathan's on the phone.'

Where are we? Where *are* we? Monday? No. Tuesday. That's it. *Five-thirty. Back in the car park.* No! This is Tuesday. Tuesday morning. And I am at work. Everyone is behaving normally. *I* am behaving normally. Nick Brown is behaving normally. And Jonathan is on the phone.

I left Ruth regaling Russell with the details in my room and walked briskly out to the reception area. The receiver was lying on the desk by the computer. I swallowed hard, picked it up and put it to my ear.

'Hello?'

'Ah. There you are,' he said. 'All right?'

'Yes, I'm fine.' The words felt thick and strange coming from my treacherous mouth.

'I just thought I'd better ring and remind you about tennis. We've got our first home match tonight –'

'Oh. Yes. Of course.'

'Crawley Second team.'

'Of course.'

'So we'll be needing sandwiches. Or a cake or something? If that's not too much trouble, of course.'

I listened hard for traces of sarcasm, but there were none. It was a simple request, uncluttered by ulterior implications.

'Right. Of course,' I said again. 'No problem. I'll pick something up at lunchtime.'

'Unless you want me have Sylvia to get something from M and S up here. I'm sure she –'

'No, no,' I said quickly. 'I'll get a cake. No problem.'

I could see Nick on the other side of the shop floor talking to the area manager. Just off to their meeting, no doubt. I lowered my eyes before they locked on to his and made my mouth go into spasm like my stomach already had. I felt nauseated. Giddy.

'Anyway,' Jonathan was saying. 'You all right?'

He'd said that already. Twice in one phone call. 'I'm fine,' I said again. 'What time do you think you'll be home?'

'Oh, seven-ish, I imagine, traffic allowing. Quick cup of tea and I'll be on my way.'

'Only I might be late,' I said, thinking it suddenly. *Lucidly.* 'My car's at Gatwick. I had a meeting there this morning. I –'

'Well, whatever.' He sounded uninterested. It was really that easy. 'If you're not back before I leave you can always run the stuff down in the car later. No panic. Better go. See you later.'

'Bye.'

'Oh, and hey, hey, hey! More excellent news!' Ruth was beside me again, a box of pink Drug U Like contact lens cases in her arms. 'Had a letter from Woman's World this morning. They've asked me if I'd like to try my hand at a serial. How about that then? I mean, I know it's only a standard letter and everything, but it said 'dear regular contributor'. Fancy that, eh? A Regular Contributor! Me! Isn't that fab?'

'Fab,' I said.

She beamed happily at me. 'I've got to go for it, haven't I? And I had a chat with Michael first thing, and I've decided I might take a look at one of the part-time posts in the office here. I really don't want to move, and what with dad and everything – and he's said he'll help me out, the sweetie. So I can have a proper crack at it. I am *so* fired up right now about my writing right now. I really want to give it a go, you know? I've decided it's fate. This is my watershed moment. The whole Drug U Like takeover. It was obviously meant to be. To kick me out of my inertia. If I take a part time job it'll give me heaps more time to write . Anyway, the main thing is that I've really got something to aim for now, haven't I? Fab, or what? Hey, you OK?'

I nodded. 'I'm fine. Fab,' I said again. 'Really good news.'

Five-thirty. Back in the car park.

Five-thirty. Back in the car park.

And so soon. It felt as if I'd mislaid the whole afternoon.

'I was right,' I announced, as Nick Brown fell into step with me on the stairwell. 'I don't think getting in your car right now is going to be a sensible life-choice for me. In fact, I think it will be dangerous.'

His hand brushed my shoulder as he held the door open to let me pass. I was right. It sent seismic waves pulsing through me.

The car was sitting in wait. Almost a whole day had passed since we'd last been here, but I could still taste the last hungry kiss we'd snatched before leaving it. I bustled round to the passenger door and jumped in with my cake before he could come round and open the door for me.

He eased himself into the driver's seat and pushed the key into the ignition.

'I've been thinking all day,' he said quietly. The air was full of heat and leather. 'I've been thinking about you. I've been thinking what a complete ass I've been.' He turned. 'I really didn't think you'd be here.'

Oh, God. 'And I *shouldn't* be!' I lifted my hands to my face to shut out the clamour of raging guilt that was pressing in on me, then lowered them again and folded them together in my lap. It felt like I'd been in my suit forever. He started the engine and the car throbbed beneath us. I *was* here. Of course I was here. I was never not going to be here. It was a terrible, frightening thought.

'I told Jonathan I'd be late.' I said quietly. 'It's not even a quarter to six and yet I told Jonathan I'd be late. Why did I do that? I'm not going to be late. There's no reason why I would be late. Not *that* late. Only I'd already *decided* I was going to be late. Already *made my mind up*.' I glanced across at him fearfully. 'Why *am* I here? I should have got a lift from Ruth. I should have just left with her and had her drop me off. Only I couldn't bring myself to ask her because I knew she'd ask me why I'd left my car at the airport and I'd have to explain about Kate and her being sick and the car being so disgusting and you driving me to work and everything else and even though all of that is perfectly innocent and reasonable and not remotely suspicious, I couldn't do it. I just couldn't do it, Nick. My *face* couldn't do it. My whole body couldn't do it. God, what the hell am I doing here? I am married. This is *wrong*. I shouldn't be here. I shouldn't be doing this. Thinking the things I'm thinking and – 'I turned to look at him again and my body was suffused by new waves of fierce and uncontrollable heat. I put my head back in my hands. '…oh, God. I am thinking such evil, wicked things. But I had to – oh, this is *awful!*'

I stopped gabbling and took a few deep breaths while he slipped his card into the machine at the exit.

'OK,' he said calmly, as the barrier came up. 'Shall I take you to your car? Or shall we drive somewhere and talk?'

'Oh, I don't *know*! What will we talk about? That's exactly my point! I don't want to talk. I just want to kiss you and –' I turned towards him again, exasperated that I'd lost control of myself so utterly. He was looking straight ahead at the road, his expression unreadable.

'OK. So I'll just drop you at your car, then. Would that be best?'

'Yes. NO! Drive us somewhere. Let's talk.'

So we drove somewhere. A secluded lane, in fact. Ten minutes or so from the airport. A road going nowhere in particular, but with a parking space and with what was obviously a picnic area – a couple of wooden bench tables and an overflowing bin. And on the way there I took lots more deep breaths and tried hard not to think more than three steps ahead. Live for the moment. Wasn't that what my Dad always used to say? Live for the moment and bugger tomorrow. I had kissed him. So what? I had lived for the moment. But apart from that, I had done nothing wrong yet. Still time to salvage the rest of my life. The car rolled to a stop.

'Do people really do this?' I said, as he pulled on the handbrake and swivelled in his seat. I was feeling a little less panicky now we were distanced from the real world and surrounded by trees. God knew why, but I did. I lifted the cake from my knees and reached to place it on the back seat. 'I mean, do people *really* do this? You know, drive out to secret places and…and…' I flapped a hand in the air in front of me. 'You know –'

He glanced behind him. 'And make love in the backs of their cars?' he said. 'Yep. I guess they do. All the time.'

His words lingered in the air like voluptuous sirens beckoning from a rock. 'Nick, Do you – I mean, *have* you –'

He shook his head. 'Nope.'

'Me neither. I've never been unfaithful. Not once.'

'Nor me.'

'And I mean, it's not even as if I *have* been unfaithful – I mean, we only kissed, didn't we? So it's not as if – 'I sighed a heavy sigh. What was I *saying*? I plucked a fleck of dust from my skirt and felt the trembling of my legs beneath it. 'No. That's not true, is it? It *is* as if. It's *absolutely* as if. '

He leaned his head back against the headrest and stared into the distance. Then his mouth twitched.

'Up there is OK, Sally.'

'Not for me it isn't. That's the whole point. I've been feeling like this a good bit longer than you realise, you know.'

His head turned.

'How long?'

'*Too* long.'

'Since Wales? '

'Of course since Wales! Did you not *notice*? How could you not have noticed, Nick?'

He grinned. His first grin of this tortuous encounter. It soothed me. Like a plaster on a cut.

'Oh, yes,' he said. 'I noticed. But then I decided I noticed wrong.' He grinned again. 'No. That's not right. I knew I noticed right but I *told* myself I'd noticed wrong. A substantive difference.'

'To tell the truth, something strange happened to me the first time I clapped eyes on you. Almost like it *was* serendipity. Except I don't believe in all that nonsense. I just thought it must be my hormones.' He laughed at this, but then his expression became serious.

'I lied,' he said at last.

'Lied? What about?'

'When I said I didn't believe in all that stuff. I do.'

Just like Ruth. Fate. The Drug U Like takeover. Nick Brown flying in. My meeting him…my… 'Well,' I said crossly, 'that's all fine and very romantic and everything. But it leaves us *where*, exactly? Do we sit here and wait for more divine guidance to beam down and tell us what to do next?'

He considered me for a moment then dropped his eyes and pulled the keys from the ignition.

'Tell you what. Let's go for a walk.'

* * *

Walking. Not talking. Walking. That was the thing. Walking would be good. Space all around and fresh air in the lungs and sunshine and green leaves and views and perspective and the small matter of quite how I was going to deal with every single day after this one shunted away like a petal on the wind. We got out of the car and headed uphill, following a ribbon of well trodden pathway that wound away from the back of the picnic area. He stuck out a hand and I slipped my own into it as if it were the most natural thing in the world for me to do. Because it *was* the most natural thing in the world to do. To touch, to hold, to connect. I had not held hands with Jonathan since – since when? Since ever? No. Not quite ever. Since Kate was born and one of us always seemed to be pushing the buggy. How did we slip out of the habit so easily? I pondered, as we walked, about how it would be if I were to slip my hand into Jonathan's now. He would be embarrassed. I could almost *taste* his embarrassment. But worse – far worse – I couldn't even see myself doing it. I clutched Nick's hand more tightly and drew closer as we walked. My heart was so full of him I wanted to cry.

'Better?' he asked, as we crested the hill and paused to draw breath. The airport sprawled flatly in the distance, sun winking off metal as the toy planes taxied around. Beyond it, lay the cream bulk of Amberley Park. And beyond that, my home. The place where I lived with my family. All tiny. Unreal. All that felt real at this moment was the steady warmth of his hand in mine. It blotted out everything else.

I released it and took two steps backwards away from him. 'Marginally,' I said. 'No. Substantially. Better *enough*, all things considered. Enough to know that if I stand over *here* and you stand over *there* then everything will be just fine.'

He blinked at me. Knitted his brows in silent enquiry.

'There. You see?' I said, smiling wanly at him. 'Simple. Nothing to it. Proximity, that's the secret. Because if you take two steps towards me now, everything will go wrong again and I will fall in your arms and want you to sweep me up and tell me everything will be all right. But it won't, Nick.' I shook my head. 'Everything will be all *wrong*…' my eyes were smarting. My throat felt sore. 'Nick I'm *married*. I can't see you. I can't –'He frowned and took two steps towards me. Crushed me against his chest.

'You see?' I sobbed into his shirt. '*Not* better. Not better at *all*.'

'Oh, God. Don't cry, Sally. Please.'

'I can't help but cry!' I railed. 'I don't want to feel like this! I have a husband and children and responsibilities and…and…and I can't be *doing* with feeling like this about you. I just want to be able to go back to all that and be…and be…' I gulped at the enormity of what I was realising. '…and be quietly unhappy again.'

He held me against him tighter still. A plane roared overhead. A light breeze made the slender boughs above us creak.

'Well, I *don't*,' he said suddenly, his voice rumbling against my face. 'I've been quietly unhappy for most of my life. I don't want to be that any more.'

I pulled my face away from his chest.

'But you have to,' I said. 'It's what people have to do. It's what *I* have to do. Except I can't, Nick. That's just it.' I wiped my eyes furiously with the back of my hand, but the tears just kept coming. 'I didn't even realise I *was* unhappy. I mean, ours is no different to anyone else's marriage, is it? I mean, Jonathan and me –'I sniffed. Took a step back again, for safety. 'We're *OK*, you know. We just – well – been getting *on* with it. Like you do. You know?'

He grimaced and pushed his hands into the pockets of his trousers then turned to look out across the fields. We were feet apart now. Two statues on the top of the hill.

'Of course I know,' he said. 'I've spent most of my marriage doing just that, believe me. Getting *on* with it.' He fell silent.

Two lonely statues. 'So what's *changed*?'

'My wife. 'It was the first time I'd heard him utter those two words. 'My wife is what changed. She didn't want to get on with it any longer. She didn't want to live any longer with someone who didn't love her.' I could hear the heavy sigh that accompanied his shrug. 'Which is fair enough. Because it's true. I don't love her. I'd just been getting on with it.' He swivelled around and looked at me as if the words were physically hurting him. 'I have a son, you see. Who I love very much.' I stayed where I was. I just couldn't stop crying.

'So she left you?' I sniffed.

He shook his head.

'No. I left *her*. Practically speaking, at any rate. She asked me to leave. She didn't want me there any more.'

'So you came here.'

He nodded. 'I came here. I had always been coming here. *We* had always been coming here. But she didn't want to. She didn't want to leave her friends, and her family, and disrupt Will's education – and – and, Christ, why *would* she? For a guy who doesn't love her?' He took his hands from his pockets and spread them towards me. 'Would you?'

I shook my head. So he had come on his own. And here he was, standing not five feet away from me, lonely and sad and thousands of miles from the son he loved. And plopped down into *my* life, like the sugar lumps they used to give you to stop you getting polio. So sweet on your tongue as you crunched them. But with all that nasty tasting medicine along for the ride.

'And then I met you,' he said, moving towards me once again. His arms were back around me and I didn't resist this time. 'I guess I could have met any number of women. But I didn't. I met *you. Y*ou and your mad dog and that feisty way you have about you and your happy smile and your doggedness and your warmth and your….He trailed off, touching his fingers to my face and frowning again. 'And I don't know what to say, except if you want to stop this right now, you only have to say. Because you're right. I can't make it better. I can only make it worse.'

I was gulping back sobs now. I felt so weary, all of a sudden. Hot and tired and wrung out like a dishrag. All I wanted was to curl up into a little ball on top of this hill with him and wait for the storm to pass. His hands were drawing circles across my shoulders now. Gentle, rhythmic, calming strokes. I stroked him back, pressing my small tired body against his enveloping strong one. I was safe here, my face cradled in his hands, his lips warm against my wet cheek.

'I'm *sorry*,' he whispered. And then he was kissing me again. Kissing my forehead, my temples, my lips. Kissing my tears away. I could taste them on his tongue. Melting everything away as if nothing else mattered. Just him and me and here and now and the ferocious heat burning inside me again. It was as if a tsunami had suddenly taken hold of me and I could do nothing but hang on and ride it. *Everything* else was kicked back into touch.

'I'm not,' I mouthed, knowing, even as I said it, that storm clouds were gathering ahead.

Chapter 17

I would be sorry. As sure as I knew the sun shone I knew I would be sorry eventually. But I wasn't feeling sorry right now.

Chapter thirteen. Sexual Arousal.

My book says that women are like formula one racing cars. That the more work you put into the tuning, the better they go. I feel sure I've heard that somewhere before, but as it says it in a very learned looking font and includes all sorts of references, which are asterisked and annotated at the back, I presume it must have been said by someone who knew a thing or two, and not just some wag of a bloke down the pub.

My book also says that female sexual arousal is one of the cornerstones a couple must lay if they are to successfully relight the marital fire. Without sexual arousal (it says) sex is very boring for women, and it is no surprise that they find themselves remembering their Auntie Maud's birthday, mid-thrust.

I remember everyone's birthdays. Always.

Though I certainly wouldn't have today.

Nick had dropped me back at my car a little before seven, in some anguish, certainly, but rather more pressingly, in such a state of extreme and distracting sexual arousal that it felt as if my whole lower torso was being pneumatically drilled. We had kissed each other so much by this time that my lips were bruised. But that had been all. We had *only* kissed. We had talked a little more, but mainly we had simply held each other and kissed, and in a way that, by rights, shouldn't have been busying itself with anything that went on further south than my heart.

I got into my car, pulse still pounding away as I watched him stride the short distance to the automatic doors of the Meridien hotel. He turned as he went in. Waved. Blew a kiss.

And now here I was, driving into a giant red orb of sun, and in a state of arousal of such animal intensity that even the fetid fumes eddying around me were insufficient to loosen its grip. There was no way on earth that I could present either myself or my cake at the tennis club pavilion until serious steps had been taken to dampen it down.

I drove home slowly, judging things carefully. I needed to arrive after Jonathan had already left. I could not face him, feeling as I did. I had not felt like this for almost half of my life. If at all. Had I *ever* felt like this before?

Thankfully, the house, bar Merlin, was empty. Kate, obviously long since over her hangover, had left what for her was a fairly effusive missive, timed at 6.20, thanking me for my ministrations the night before, assuring me of her sobriety, and letting me know – she'd *had* tried my mobile – that she was being picked up by Carl and his mother and step dad and going with them to the multiplex cinema to watch Artificial Intelligence and have a pizza somewhere.

I freed my grateful feet from their long incarceration and padded upstairs. I could, at this point, have simply lain on the bed in the spare room, – not our room – closed my eyes and bade the image of his beautiful face to appear before me. It would have been enough. I was teetering on a cliff edge. But I didn't. I didn't want to. I wanted to hang on to this feeling. Savour it a while. Enjoy it as I walked around the bedroom, undressing languidly, hug its throbbing heat to myself as I turned on the shower. Let it race through my veins as the cold water hit me, and tuck itself away into every corner of my being. I wanted, in short, to save it for *him*.

That thought having been thought, I stood under the shower for ten minutes and soberly contemplated the rest of my life.

I was just about to leave the house when the telephone rang. My mother.

'Listen!' She started to read something to me. Some snippet she'd found in whatever magazine she'd been flicking through, about some screen idol or other who had fallen from grace with some other screen idol, causing much consternation in the film world and several thousand eager column inches. 'Can't help it? Tosh!' she snorted, as soon as she'd finished. 'Uncontrollable passion my eye! You wouldn't credit it, would you? These people have no shame. Why on earth do they get married in the first place? Five poor little kiddies between them and all they can think of is carrying on with other people on the side –'

I really didn't want to hear this right now. 'Mum, I can't stop. I'm just –'

'Oh, I won't keep you,' she said. 'I just thought I'd ring and let you know I've got things sorted.'

'Got what sorted?'

'For delivering my petition, of course! I spoke to someone at Charing Cross Police station earlier – such a helpful young lady – and they say I can have a slot on Tuesday. Is Tuesday going to be all right? I know you normally take your day off on Wednesday, but we've got the mobile hairdressers coming then.'

'What, *this* Tuesday? This one coming?'

'If that's going to be OK with you. I thought we could go up on the train. We'll need to get there in good time. You get given a fifteen minute slot, you see, and you can't miss it because of all the security procedures. You get taken in by a policeman.'

'What, you mean right to the door of number Ten?'

'Oh, yes,' she said breezily, as if hanging out with Premiers was a regular happenstance for her. 'They were very nice. You get to give it to the commissionaire there, and he'll pose for a picture, apparently. Isn't that nice? That'll be something for that man at the *Argus*, won't it?'

'Gosh,' I said. 'I never realised it was that simple.'

'Well, your father would turn in his grave to hear me say it, but I'm beginning to think I'll vote Labour next time round. Anyway, I plumped for half past twelve – emergencies permitting, of course – if something important happens they have to re-schedule you, of course – is that going to be OK with you?'

'Mum, it's a bit short notice to change my day off, to be honest. Does it have to be next week? Couldn't it wait till the week after?'

'I'm coming up to *you* the week after, aren't I? To help you out with Kate's show.'

I'd forgotten. I was forgetting everything right now. 'Oh, yes. Look, I really don't know, Mum. I promised Morgan I'd spend a day up in London with her soon, and I was thinking next week would be good. Jonathan's going to be away and –'

'So she could come too! And we could kill two birds with one stone, couldn't we? Have a wander round John Lewis and look at frocks after lunch, maybe. Look, will you try? *Please*? I'm sure if you tell your nice boss what it's for, he won't mind. How could he?'

How could he indeed. 'I'll try, Mum. OK?.'

'Oh, one thing,' she added. 'No banners, no placards, and no fancy dress.'

I put down the phone. Surreal.

*   *   *

It was still light when I arrived at the tennis club, the low sun emphasising the rich terracotta of the new clay courts they'd recently had laid. Jonathan, thankfully, was busy playing in a doubles match. I didn't want to have to talk to him. I didn't think I would be *able* to talk to him. I was outwardly calm, and showered, and functional, but inside it felt as if my whole body was quivering. Every time I thought of Nick, which was almost every second, the same heat would diffuse through my stomach as if a little ball of energy that couldn't work out what to do with itself.

I made my way around the back of the courts and into the pavilion. A trestle had been set up along the far wall and was already groaning under the weight of the cakes. I placed my shop bought offering at the far end. Away from all the puffed up and self important sponges, the lovingly cut sandwiches and glistening buttered scones. The products of loving wives, happier marriages. Stark evidence that mine was so lacking all round.

Then I scuttled off home and scrubbed the car once again, willing the sky to grow sufficiently dark that I could search out some constellation to tell Nick about.

Jonathan and Kate arrived home almost simultaneously.

'And,' I could hear Jonathan saying as they clattered in through the utility room together. 'I've got a bone to pick with you, young lady.'

I had not even paused to collect my thoughts about Kate. So much had happened in the intervening hours, that her misdemeanours of the previous evening almost seemed as if they'd happened to someone else. I had certainly not given any thought to it in relation to Jonathan, let alone what line of approach to adopt. Say nothing, was my first thought now. Let the thing be forgotten. After all, she'd had her own head to remind her.

Too late, was the second. I stopped loading the dishwasher and turned to greet them both. Kate caught my eye. I remembered her note. He must have read it. But just how incriminating had it been ? I mentally backtracked. *'Sorreeeee about last night. Am fine now, if delicate. Chastened but happy! Off out with Carl ....'*

'What about?' she asked him lightly, sloughing off her jacket and heading towards the fridge.

Jonathan put his racquets down with a clatter on the kitchen table. His forehead was pink and shiny still from the tennis. He frowned at her.

'About exactly what it was you got up to last night.'

Kate looked at me again while Jonathan stooped to pull his kit from his bag. I raised my brows to indicate I hadn't spoken to him. News, however, had obviously travelled fast.

'What?' said Kate again. 'What about last night?'

Jonathan assumed a severe expression and glared at her from the other side of the table.

'I took a call at work this afternoon. From Bob Hathaway.' Ah. Amanda's father.

'Tried your mother this morning – 'he pointed in my direction, 'but you weren't there, apparently.'

'I told you,' I said, feeling my neck redden. 'I had a meeting at Gatwick.'

'At Gatwick?' It was as if we hadn't spoken earlier. He hadn't been listening at all.

'A breakfast meeting. I told you. At the Meridien Hotel.' The words would never sound the same again. Jonathan rolled his eyes. 'Of course,' he said disdainfully. 'Your American chums. Anyway – 'he turned back to Kate. She had her face in the juice carton. 'What's this I hear about you and Amanda getting drunk?'

'I…er…' began Kate.

'They went to the pub after rehearsals,' I answered, before she could blunder in and antagonise him further with a spate of defiant denials. 'They went to the pub and they had a little to drink and I had to go and pick her up and bring her home. That's all.'

I waited for him to digest this. Which he did. And then spat it out again.

'That's *all?* And you didn't see fit to tell *me* about this? Like this morning? *Before* I had Amanda's father regaling me with my daughter's disgraceful behaviour down the phone?'

'I'm telling you now,' I said quietly. He ignored me and looked hard at Kate.

'A little?' he asked her pointedly.

'Look, Dad –' she began.

'From what I hear the pair of you could hardly stand up! And what the *hell* do you think you're doing going into pubs anyway? You're sixteen!'

I could see Kate's brain computing the number of times her parents had used those two words, and reaching the number 'too bloody often'. She inhaled through her nose and clenched her fists.

'For God's sake, dad! Almost *seven*teen, *OK*? And for your information, there is no law against seventeen year olds – or sixteen year olds for that matter – going in pubs. Not on this planet anyway. Not the one *normal* people live on.'

His face became redder. Oh, God. Off we went.

'Oh, right,' he snarled at her. 'Oh, right, young lady. So you're about to tell me you were not drinking alcohol illegally, are you? You're about to tell me that Amanda's father was imagining it when his daughter spent the night throwing up, are you? *Well*?'

More justice. I felt very slightly cheered by this news. Though not that much.

'Look,' I said. 'It's true. They *did* have too much to drink. And I have told Kate off, in no uncertain terms. And I'm quite sure Kate has learned her lesson. *Haven't* you?' I said pointedly to her, willing her to just shut her mouth and climb out of the gaping hole she was about to plunge herself deeper into. When would she learn that this sort of confrontation with her father was pointless? 'Jonathan, look, 'I said. 'We can talk about this later. I don't think there's anything to be gained by us rowing about it again now. Kate –'

He glared at me. 'Oh, right. So I'm not allowed to take my daughter to task when she behaves like a complete idiot, then am I? That's your job, then, is it?'

My turn now then. 'Jonathan, you weren't *here*. I told you. I have *dealt* with it. I –'

'Dad, I'm sorry, all right? 'said Kate, her voice far from sounding it. 'I have learned my lesson. I will not do it again. Now can't we just leave it?'

'No we will *not* just leave it, young lady!' He glared at me again. 'I'm supposed to believe that, am I? I'm supposed to trust you when all you ever seem to do these days is abuse that trust? What are you coming to, for God's sake?'

Trust. Such a powerful word. Kate narrowed her eyes.

'I told you –'

'Jonathan, *please*,' I entreated, dishwasher powder clutched to my chest. 'Can't we just leave it for *now*? Talk about it in the morning? We're all tired, and Kate and I have –'

'Oh, right,' he said, picking up the racquets again. For one terrible moment I thought he was going to throw them at me. But he didn't. Just shoved them under one arm and waggled the other one in the air. 'Oh, right,' he said again. 'None of my business then is it? Well, fine. You go ahead and undermine me. I'll leave you to get on with it then shall I? You're the expert, Sally. Don't mind me.'

'Look, I'm not saying that, Jonathan. I just think it would be better if we could sit down and discuss this calmly in the morning. That's all – '

'When it suits you, you mean. *Fine.*' He turned on his heel and marched back outside again. I could hear his car engine start up.

Oh *great*.

'Well done,' I said to Kate. Now your father's in a rage. 'Thanks Kate. Very good job.' Now she rolled *her* eyes.

'Well, *good*,' she spat. 'Good. Because I hate him.'

'Kate, you don't –'

'Yes I *do*!' She whirled around and slammed the fridge door shut. 'He obviously hates *me*. He never has a good word to say to me! He doesn't care about anything I do. He hasn't once asked me how my exams have been going. Hasn't ever asked me about my dancing. He hasn't even been to see me in a show since I was ten! All he ever does is criticise and moan and tell me I'm useless, and criticise my friends and tell me Carl's a waster – as if! – and drone on about how horrible young people today are. Well, thanks a *lot*! He knows nothing, mum! He knows nothing about me! He wishes he never had me, you know. He does! That's what it is. It's all *Morgan* this and *Morgan* that and Morgan the bloody other!. Just because she's so goody two shoes with her hoity toity friends and her brilliant career and…oohhhh! He makes me so *mad.*'

I was too tired for this. 'That's not true, Kate,' I said wearily.' It's just that he… well, he just doesn't know how to deal with you. He's doesn't really understand how to relate to you, that's all. If you could just try to see things from his point of view – he works very hard, you know, and he gets home tired and irritable, and if you could only use a bit of savvy and tread a little more carefully – '

She snorted at me. 'Why the hell *should* I, Mum? I get tired and irritable too, you know? I've just done a shedload of revision and some really hard exams and –'she gulped back a sob. 'Does he ever think of that? Does he ever think about *anyone* but himself? No. He does not. Look at you! Does it ever occur to him that *you* might be tired? No. You run around after everyone all the time – everyone! Him, me, Morgan, Gran – and you never get any appreciation from him. Not a bit! And yet you spend all your time defending him and pussy footing around him and letting him treat you like a doormat!' I began shaking my head. 'No, no,' she said, shaking her own. 'That's fine, mum. If that's the way you like it, then fine. That's your business. But just don't think I'm going to let him push *me* around like that, OK? '

She ripped half a dozen sheets of kitchen paper from the roll and stomped off to bed.

The air in the kitchen was ringing. All I could see of Merlin was his nose. I thought he might come out from under the table and nuzzle his head into my outstretched hand. But no. He knew when to keep his head down.

I picked up a plate – Jonathan's from earlier, presumably – and held it aloft, swung my arm back, took aim.

Then I dropped my arm. Dropped the plate into the dishwasher.

And reflected, unhappily, as I finished tidying the kitchen, that I was really rather good at being quietly unhappy. Getting on with it.

An expert, in fact.

Chapter 18

I didn't hear Jonathan come in. But when I woke at three thirty he was right there beside me, hogging the whole duvet and breathing regularly and deeply. Sleeping the sleep of the just, no doubt.

No such comfort for me. I slid silently from the bed and padded out across the landing into the spare room, a nagging anxiety crowding my consciousness, as it always did when there was tension in the house. And that seemed to be pretty much all the time these days, my own situation notwithstanding.

My *own* situation. The idea that there was a situation on the go and that I was its leading lady was making my mouth dry with fear. That I had spent a significant part of yesterday kissing another man was only the tip of this particular hunk of iceberg. It was everything else that scared me so much. The way my physical being seemed to be outside my control all of a sudden. The way I had become someone I suddenly didn't recognise. A selfish person, pursuing my own gratification despite so much of me knowing it was wrong. I'd never known guilt of this magnitude – hardly known it at all, in fact – yet it wasn't stopping me. Why?

The sky outside, as I had known it would be, was clear and bright, the stars winking down at me as I gazed out from the spare room window and wondered quite what it was I was going to do next. What I most wanted to do next was to go downstairs and text Nick, but every next thing I seemed to be considering right now just seemed like one more nail in my marital coffin. One more nail in my perception of myself. One more nail in my belief that I was a good person. It was pathetic. I would do absolutely nothing, that's what I would do. But I went down anyway. It was too hot upstairs.

When I got down into the kitchen, the floor bathed in the milky light of another almost full moon, there was already a message icon on the display. I felt my stomach muscles tighten as I pressed the button and read it. It simply said '*Hello. How are you? N.*'

I held the phone in my hand and stared at it for a good ten minutes. Then switched it off and put it back on the charger before the urge to communicate with him became so irresistible that it smashed my tenuous resolve into shards.

How was I? I was quietly unhappy. *Still* quietly unhappy. I walked wearily upstairs and back into the spare bedroom. Kate was right, I thought with dismay. I *was* a doormat. I was the prototype for doormats the world everywhere. It was a shock to discover this. I had never thought of myself in those terms before. I was just good at compromising, wasn't I? Just a good negotiator. A carer. A rescuer. A model of all those wholesome things psychologists prattle so enthusiastically about. A person who looked after other people. Not a doormat. A *carer*. And yet she was right. I spent so much time worrying about how everyone else was feeling, I had lost the ability to attend my own needs. And not only that, I realised with growing alarm, my whole sense of myself as a worthwhile human being was based on exactly those qualities. My usefulness to everyone else. I didn't even acknowledge I *had* any needs of my own. I didn't use the words 'me' or 'no'. Ever. Because I didn't want anyone not to like me. It was really that simple. Really that damning. Mother Teresa I was not.

But there was nothing to be gained from feeling sorry for myself. I left the bed in the spare room and returned to my own one. Then heaved on the duvet and clambered back under it. It was my bed, and I had to lie on it.

I only lay on it until twenty to seven, but by this time Jonathan was already downstairs. I walked down them taking mental deep breaths. The thing about arguments you go to bed on is not just that they don't disappear in the night, it's that they swell up still bigger, like canellini beans.

But Jonathan, much to my consternation, was not sitting in wait with a face like a mastiff, but calmly reading the sports pages of the Times, in reflective rather than pugilistic mood. It was as if he had assimilated the events of the previous night and instead of continuing on his 'I'm the head of this bloody family and what I say is testament' crusade (which would have been usual and given me scope to insert a little chagrin and righteous indignation into the proceedings) had decided to both pre-empt and disarm me by drawing up a ten point corrective strategy, which he aimed to implement forthwith.

‘I’ve made a decision,’ he announced gravely, but not aggressively. ‘When do Kate’s exams finish?’

I looked at him, trying to assess what new and unworkable regime was about to be wrought on my life. It was all very well him laying down the law, but he was never around trying to quash the inevitable mutiny. It had been thus since Kate was five. He raised his eyebrows in calm enquiry and I wondered anxiously how much of my own inner turmoil was creeping across the table towards him. Like a dose of CS gas.

‘Friday,’ I told him. ‘Her last one’s this Friday.’

‘Good,’ he said, nodding thoughtfully. ‘Excellent. That’ll work then.’

I went over to the teapot and took off the lid. ‘What’ll work?’

He glanced up at me and smiled. ‘I’ve decided she can come with me to Malta next week.’

‘*Malta?* With you? What – on your conference?’

He nodded again.

‘You’re quite right,’ he went on. ‘She and I are at loggerheads all the time at the moment –’he lifted a hand and held it out palm towards me. ‘– *my* fault,’ he said. ‘I’ve been very preoccupied with work just lately, and I think my lack of input is something that needs to be addressed. I think it’s time I stepped in and spent a bit more time with my daughter, don’t you?’

Well, *yes*, frankly, I thought. But didn’t say so. I wondered fleetingly whether he hadn’t in fact driven anywhere last night. Just lurked inside the garage and listened to her ranting about him. But no. I had heard the car crunch over the gravel. No. He had just been thinking. Like me.

‘Well, we’re clearly not getting on, are we?’ he said, in a tone that made me feel, however wrongly or rightly, that it was a state of affairs that was largely my fault. *Was* it my fault? I’d got so used to being left to deal with Kate over most things that this sudden appraisal of procedures and outcomes felt like a bit of an affront. What did he mean ‘needs to be addressed’? Was I not doing a good enough job?

But he seemed to read my thoughts. ‘Entirely my fault,’ he repeated magnanimously. ‘I’m obviously not handling things very well right now. So I’ve decided the best thing will be if she comes with me. I was talking to Paul Elliott the other day and he was telling me he was bringing his girls along with him. His wife’s got some college summer school she's going off to. So I thought 'why not?'. Kate gets on OK with them, doesn't she? Be a chance to enjoy a little quality time together. I think we've all been a little stressed out just lately. Do her good. Do us both good. What do you think?'

Do us good? I really wasn't so sure. And even less sure about this sudden use of such groovy right-on language. It was distinctly unsettling.

'Well, that's fine by me,' I said, fishing out a conciliatory smile and finding it not half as difficult to plaster on my face as I might have expected. I should, by rights have been bristling a little, both at the underlying inference that my parenting skills were, in his opinion, a tad on the *laissez faire* side, and the fact that he hadn't asked *me* along too. Which was a worry of itself. Implications mushroomed around me. A seriously serious worry. 'But I'm not sure Kate will be *quite* so thrilled,' I finished, both to steady myself, and before he ran away with the idea that his munificence would be greeted with undying gratitude. 'What about her rehearsals?'

There was also some post exam party to consider, but I thought it best not to go there right now. Jonathan closed up his paper and smiled back at me. A honeyed smile. A stuck-on smile. As if he were about to go off into the trenches and was putting a brave face on his imminent death.

'Missing a rehearsal or two won't *kill* her, Sally.' He looked at his watch and pushed his chair back. 'I'd better get going. Have a word with her, will you ?'He stood up then and smiled a proper smile at me. A rather wry one, in fact. 'Actually, no. Don't worry. I'll pop up and speak to her myself.'

So that was that sorted. Though it occurred to me as I unloaded the dishwasher how good we both were at skimming over the small scale pot holes of family dysfunction without ever landing in any of the gaping craters where our own relationship as a couple now sat.

'Well, thanks a lot, mum! That's just *marvellous.*'

Kate had appeared in the kitchen shortly after Jonathan had left for the surgery, mouth curled in contempt.

'This is nothing to do with me,' I said, removing the last mug from yesterday and starting to load up again with the breakfast things. I would be late for work if I didn't get a move on.

'But couldn't you have *stopped* him? Talked him out of it? Why on earth would I want to go galumphing off to Malta with Dad? I can't imagine anything more dire!'

'The Elliott girls are going.'

'*Quite.* I mean, don't get me wrong. They're very nice and all that. Just terminally boring, that's all.'

'Look, it's only for a few days, Kate, and it'll be good for you to spend a bit more time with your father.' I realised I was simply parroting out Jonathan's line but lacked the energy to do more. Or the will.

'Yeah, right. And what about rehearsals?'

The conference, as it turned out, was only to be a four day affair, so Kate would only have to miss one rehearsal and would not miss her precious end of exams party at all. So my heart wasn't exactly bleeding for her. On the contrary (and chipping away at my fragments of resolve still further) it occurred to me at least two hundred and seventy five times that both husband and younger daughter safely out of the country equalled danger zone situation with Nick Brown.

Oh, God! I thought, as I said my goodbyes to Kate and the dog and reversed out into the lane and off to work. This was no way to live. I was suddenly so, so, *so* excited. I was bubbling with excitement. Fizzing with excitement. Where had my head gone? Where was the person who normally lived here?. This was surely not how things should be. This unpredictable see-sawing between euphoria and terror. My resolve, clearly, was about as potent a force in my life as a pop sock. I felt like I'd suddenly been slit down the middle. That there we two of me now .

Thankfully, however, Nick was to be back in Brighton for what was now left of the week. Drug U Like were launching their flagship UK store there – our own turn would come a few weeks down the line. Which meant I wouldn't have to look at him at least. Which meant I would have space and time and a chance for thinking and reflection and all the other serious and sensible things that I knew I should be doing but for which I seemed to have lost the ability. I could read my book. Think about my marriage. Try to get a handle on what it was I should *do*. But just thinking these things made me think about Nick, which made me feel so *fizzy* again.

I rattled on down the A23, dreaming up scenarios in which we would meet, fall into each other's arms and declare our undying love for one another, all the while in another bloody poppy strewn field. And having decided my resolve had been found wanting in so many departments that it was all but moribund, I abandoned any immediate plans to take it to task. Until it felt a little stronger, at least. Instead I resolved I would return his text message instead. Just as soon as I fetched up at work.

'*OK*,' I typed feverishly as I sat in my car in the bowels of the car park. '*But missing U already. Where U? How U? LOL, S xxx*

I sent it off and smiled a little smile as I put on my lipstick in the rear view mirror. It was the beelzebub smile of a fallen woman. I smiled it again. Felt the bubbles fizzing up. Felt the delicious heat of expectation suffusing through me again. Imagined Nick – where was he, I wondered, *right* now? On his way into work? Tucking into yet another hotel breakfast? Already in a meeting? Most likely, I thought. With his mobile tucked into the inside pocket of his jacket. The little message icon waiting for him. *Me* in his pocket. I kissed the phone before I slipped it back in my bag.

As I got out of the car I spotted Dennis sauntering towards me, raincoat folded over his arm, briefcase swinging from one hand.

'You're looking very chirpy,' he observed. 'Cat got the cream, eh?'

And *whump!* I was back down at the other end of the seesaw. Oh, God. This was no way to live.

Chapter 19

But live I did. Live I must. Mrs Sally Matthews back in her kitchen. Normal service resumed.

And it was surprisingly easy. Despite everything inside me being in a state of near-chaos, outside life went on as normal.

On Saturday morning I got a letter from the Drug U Like UK Head Office, to let me know that following my recent meeting with Nicholas Brown, Human Resources etcetera etcetera, they were now inviting me to attend an interview for the post of Optometry Manager, Amberley Park, the following Friday week at eleven fifteen. It was to take place at their southern area head office (map enclosed) and I was to take along with me an up to date CV and report to a Mr Monroe.

Both Kate and Jonathan expressed about as much interest as they had when I'd become senior optom, i.e. sufficient to but not excessive. Kate expressed mild surprise, Jonathan mild disinterest. My job was my job. He did teeth, I did eyes. And apart from (what for him seemed, at any rate) a modest increase in my salary, nothing much in his sphere of interest had changed. Had he been effusive and excited and all the things it now occurred to me he might reasonably have been expected to be – even if it was little more than a polite display – I think I would have found things a little harder to deal with. As it was, every small moment of minor neglect had become a counter-weight to balance my burden of guilt. Enough, I well knew, and the scales would surely tip. It was only a matter of time. A shameful admission and a scary one. Even so, that was how it was.

I had been sensible up to a point. I had not told Nick about Jonathan and Kate leaving the country on Sunday evening. Even manic as I was (and I was) the one thing I knew I must *not* do was to tell Nick I was going to be alone for four days. That way lay danger and hob goblins and triffids, not a few of them sprouting from the rich peaty compost of my own wicked thoughts.

I had no misconceptions about myself on that score. And I knew as surely as night follows day that bad things followed bad people around. It was karma. Whether I believed in it or not.

But sensible *only* up to a point. Bad, to a greater degree. My reasoning on the non-contact equals safety score was decidedly woolly, for we had been sending each other flurries of text messages all week. I was like a child with a new toy to play with. And this was a deliciously enjoyable game.

How I managed to go about the ordinary business of being a sensible forty year old person while conducting this juvenile text correspondence I didn't quite know. But there were two things I did know. One was that had I come across such toe-curling bilge on *Kate's* mobile I would most certainly have been sick in a bucket, and the other – the more pressing and pertinent of them – was that I should be getting ready for some seriously bad karma, because I'd become a very bad girl.

'*Sally* –'he'd sent. 3.45 am Saturday. '*Am back home tomorrow. Amberley Monday. Monday Night? Maybe? When/where? Yes/no?*'

'Jesus, Kate!' Jonathan barked now, scowling theatrically. 'What have you got in here? Bricks?'

It was just after five on Sunday afternoon, and we were toiling along the concourse in the South terminal at Gatwick, Kate plugged into her Discman, a portion of the din that must have been crashing against her eardrums following her around like a swarm of angry bees. Jonathan was pulling both cases.

'Books' she yelled back (as one does when in headphones). 'I thought I'd better have something to do.'

'Kate,' I chided. 'You'll have a *lovely* time. Really you will.'

She turned round and gave me her best withering look. 'Yeah, right, mum. So why don't *you* go instead?'

But teenagers, for all their sneery superiority are actually very easily impressed. There was an almost palpable lifting in Kate's spirits once she realised she was cruising past the Economy crocodile, and heading for the Business Class check in instead.

'Cool,' she observed. 'Mum, get this bit of carpet!'

I waved them off confident she'd have a fine time in Malta. And then there was one. And I really shouldn't go there.

I got home from the airport a little after six. The sun was still up and my heart was still pounding. I would take Merlin for a nice long walk to calm down.

I drove out to the Ashdown forest, to lose myself in the gorse and bracken. There was a little low cloud bubbling up on the horizon and the beginnings of a chilly breeze in the air. I let Merlin off the lead and began the long haul up to the top of the far hill, hoping the heavens wouldn't open in the meantime.

I had just reached the summit when my phone peeped in my pocket.

'*Hello,*' I read. '*Just arrived home. Where are you?*'

I stopped on the footpath. Merlin was rootling in a tussock up ahead. My freedom felt like a great burden all of a sudden. Especially as the tang of foliage and uncompromising terrain put me so much in mind of our exploits in Wales. How tempting it was to just tell him. Right now. How lovely to have him come here and find me. But I mustn't. I knew that if I told Nick I was out here on my own there was a very real danger of him doing just that. I could not have that. I could NOT have that.

'*Out walking the dog,*' I replied, resolute and decided. '*Legs aching. Puffed out. And so on. How was Brighton?*'

His message came back immediately.

'*Very dull. Wish I had a Merlin to walk. Where are you walking*?'

I paused here and waited while another wave of treacherous desire washed over me.

'*Here and there,*' I typed back. '*Over hill and down dale.*'

'*Be nice to join you. Here and where*?' came the response.

It was a rhetorical question. It had to be. For all Nick Brown knew I was yomping across the downs with my entire extended family, half a dozen neighbours and the man from the Happy Shopper in Lingfield, but it did serve to crystallise the situation I was in now. That of being a woman at large with a dangerous passion. And having thought this I realised I was quite, quite wrong and that it was not in the least rhetorical. What was I thinking? He wasn't stupid. Were I *really* out walking with Jonathan or Kate, I'd hardly be sending him text messages, would I? I would, I resolved (oh, so much resolving!) have to try a little harder, stand a little firmer. And, above all take *very* great care not to let slip I was alone. I switched the mobile off and slipped it into my pocket. This *wasn't* a game. Not at all.

*　　　*　　　*

But my resolve being what it was (pathetic, intermittent, flimsy, ethereal – pants, basically) I felt entirely unequal to the task of having to keep shoring it up all the time, and as soon as I clapped eyes on him on Monday morning I could almost hear it shattering into a million pieces around me. Who was I kidding? I was completely in thrall to him. It was greatly fortunate therefore that the seeing was done in company. Namely the short meeting he held at the Amberley offices first thing on Monday and which related to the up coming in-store festivities that would accompany the 'big push' on August tenth. Funny how corporate bodies so often seemed to want to glorify their commercial endeavours with doughty references to war. But then, Drug U Like *were* an American firm. Perhaps they thought it would bring in a few World War Two veterans and thus shift a shedload more specs.

Nick Brown could sell me a time share in Thetford. I watched him work, watched him talk, watched him move, watched him breathe, all with the same breathless compulsion.

'How you?' he mouthed as we shared floor space around the coffee machine afterwards.

'Terrible,' I whispered, smiling coyly up at him. I couldn't help it. He just made me act that way.

'Later? Something?' He mouthed, shrugging minutely as he reached across me to get a plastic cup.

'I don't know,' I said. 'Um…'

And then Russell was there, flapping his in the air.

'Come on. Shift up, Matthews. Stop hogging the Cona. And I bet you've already pinched all the custard creams, haven't you?' He turned to Nick. 'You have to watch her like a hawk around biscuits.'

Nick smiled and walked away. I took the bourbon as well.

And then he was gone, and presumably into several lengthy meetings or a space pod to Jupiter, because I didn't see or hear from him again that day. But that was fine. That was OK. This was space. Which was what I really needed. Space and time to think everything through.

Even so, when by six thirty and I was ensconced in the familiar yet suddenly changed surroundings of the pub with Russell and Ruth, I couldn't help feeling a stab of anguish that he'd not sent me a message since our brief conversation in the morning. Was he worried I was avoiding him? Keeping his distance? Waiting for me to make some sort of move now? *What?* This was like being Kate's age again.

'Here,' announced Russell, sliding his buttocks on to a squat bar stool and slurping the top off his pint. 'You know what I heard this morning, don't you?' We shook our heads. 'Kevin from pharmacy is apparently shagging that Susan whatshername from the canteen.'

'No!' said Ruth, pausing with her own pint halfway to her lips. 'Susan Taylor?' Russell nodded. 'But she only got married last February, didn't she?'

Russell nodded. 'Incredible, isn't it? If it hadn't been Michael that told me, I wouldn't have believed it myself. '

'God,' said Ruth, taking a sip now. 'How depressing.'

'Russell shrugged. 'I don't know. I doubt Kevin sees it like that.'

'But she's married! How could he?'

Russell grinned again. 'Listen to Mrs Prim! Never seemed to stop you.'

I felt myself cringing on Ruth's behalf. I wished they would change the subject, and fast.

'D'you want a punch in the face?' she asked him.

'Rumours,' I remarked, adding a yawn for emphasis. 'Just people who've got nothing better to do. So, Ruth. Any more sales since last week?'

'As it happens, yes,' she said. 'A twist ender for *Coffee Time*. Three hundred squids. So far so good.'

'You've got a moustache,' observed Russell, reaching to wipe it from her lip.

She slapped his hand away. 'Oh, piss off,' she said.

So far so good.

I was getting frighteningly adept at going-though-the-motions. I'd always imagined people who had affairs lived in a state of constant hyperventilation and anxiety, but it was obviously not so. On the contrary, I found myself strangely enervated by the time I got home, almost as if energy had been seeping out of me all day, leached away by the steady drip-drip of my guilt.

I dumped the training manuals I'd brought home to gen up on, poured myself the remainder of Jonathan's Claret and gave Merlin the cold half-pizza I'd earmarked for reheating but which I could no more face eating than I could face eating the plate. Eating, I decided, was becoming a chore. Still, I thought, I had shared a packet of peanuts in the pub with Ruth earlier, and as I'd recently read a book in which the heroine managed to exist for 300 pages on little more than pork scratchings and red wine, I figured it would do. Then I showered and went to bed. I was so tired. All this resolving and vacillating and worrying had worn me out. And if I went to bed early, I reasoned, then I would at least get a few hours in before I was woken by the infidelity fairy and obliged to spend an hour thrashing about with my conscience before taking my mind off down avenues of sexual speculation and up softly lit *cul de sacs* of carnal excess. Yes. I would sleep now. So far so good.

The peep-peep of my mobile woke me with a start. I turned my head to find the phone still illuminated greenly on the bedside table beside me. I picked it up and pressed the button.

A message from Nick. '*Hello.*'

Just that. I wriggled up to a sitting position and rubbed the sleep from my eyes. It was not much after midnight. I had been asleep less than two hours.

'*Am azzzzzleep,*' I typed, wide awake now. '*What time do you call this*?'

The answer came back almost instantly.

'*Asleep in bed?*'

'*In bed.*'

'*And on the phone*?'

'*On the phone.*'

'*On the phone in bed*?'

'*On the phone in bed.*'

Then a two word response. '*And alone*?????'

I stared at this message for ages. *Ages*. In reality only a few moments, most probably, but if so, it felt like the longest few moments of my entire life. This was it. This was a going-through-the-motions situation no longer. This was real, and scary, and now in my hands. I didn't know how he knew, but he knew. He *must* know. I swallowed. Everything in my hands. Everything dependent on the decision I made now. I threw myself back against the pillows and glared at the phone in my hand, willing it to ring. Willing it to take things *out* of my hands. But even then, I could elect not to answer it, couldn't I? There was no decision to be made here. There was only one thing to do. I deleted the message and turned off the phone. Lay back against the pillows and closed my eyes. But inside my head they were still busy seeing him. I opened them again. Wisps of pale cloud scudded across a charcoal and ink backwash. The phone, temporarily extinguished beside me, was no more than a small chunk of plastic and metal, but it was almost as if it had become my executioner. I battered my pillow a bit and lay my head on it once again. Closed my eyes once again. That was the thing. Close my eyes and try to sleep. Ridiculous. How on earth could I sleep? I rolled over, smelt the familiar scent of Jonathan's aftershave on his pillow. Now I *really* could not sleep. Get up then. That was the thing. Get up. Go downstairs. Talk to the dog. Look at the stars. But there were no stars out. Just the granite sky and a dispiriting drizzle. Coming down in bright speckles against the white glare of the outside light. Go downstairs. That was the thing. Make some tea. Go back to bed. Go through the motions. Get *on* with things.

I sat up and pushed the duvet irritably from over me. Scooped my hair from my face and sighed loudly. This was no good. It wasn't going to work. The other me was having none of it. The other me was having *him*.

I snatched up the phone again. Switched it back on. Half an hour had passed but he'd sent nothing more. I scrolled down the menu. *Send message*? It prompted.

Yes. Send message. *A*. Stop. *L*. Stop. *O*. Stop. *N*. Stop. *E*. Stop. Full stop. *YES.*

The front doorbell rang thirty two minutes later.

The rain had all but stopped by now and a sharp rise in temperature was pulling the moisture from the earth, lending a misty soft focus to the dripping shrubs in the front garden. It was now one seventeen in the morning. This couldn't be happening and yet it was. His hair was damp. His expression was serious. His crystal eyes bored into mine.

Then dropped. Became veiled by those impossibly thick lashes. I felt too overwhelmed by him to speak. 'It's OK,' he said, pocketing his car keys and glancing at me sheepishly now. 'I parked at the end of the lane and walked.'

I peered up and down.

'Right,' I said, beckoning. I felt like a gangster. 'Come in.'

He came in. We stood in the hallway looking at each other. I had taken off my night time T-shirt and replaced it, frantically, with a pair of jeans and another, smaller T-shirt. And then prowled around the house like the caged beast I'd become. I was naked beneath it. My feet were bare. I gripped the carpet with my toes to stop myself from swaying. He seemed to fill the whole hall.

'I don't know what I'm doing here,' he said. 'I just –'

'How did you know?' I interrupted him.

'Ruth,' he said, following me as I turned and walked into the kitchen. 'Just in passing. We were talking about the weather. She happened to mention you'd drawn the short straw. Malta, was it? Your daughter and…well, it doesn't matter. I did.'

It didn't matter. He was right. And he was *here*. I licked my dry lips.

'I wasn't going to tell you,' I said. 'Self preservation. Resolve. All that. because I knew if I told you –'

'But then you did anyway.'

In any other circumstance I would have found myself blushing. But not this one. I nodded. 'Yes,' I said slowly. 'I did.'

There was nothing much of use either of us could say at this juncture. I knew this because I had rehearsed it many, many times since Jonathan had announced his Malta idea. Countless times. And there was nothing to say. The only thing that could reasonably be said was that as both of us were fully aware of the gravity, the seriousness, the very *wrong* nature of the circumstance in which we had now placed ourselves, we really should not be here at all. We *knew* that. Yet we were. Looking at each other across a kitchen and failing to articulate these thoughts to one another, lest they swell up and smother us in guilt. Lest they force us to do the right thing. So we continued to stand there and gaze into each other's eyes as if, by the intensity of our need for one another, our guilt could be dissolved away.

It couldn't. It didn't. 'Well, here I am,' he said finally.

'Yes,' I replied. 'And here *I* am. Tea?'

He laughed at this. A nervous laugh that caused Merlin to stir in his basket and lope across the kitchen for a sniff of this unexpected guest.

'Tea I have,' he said, stooping to ruffle Merlin's neck. 'It was a cup of sugar I was after.' He looked so ill at ease all of a sudden.

I shook my head. 'Sugar I don't have. I'm sweet enough already.'

'OK, milk, then.' The words were mumbled. Then he took himself off across the kitchen and peered out into the back garden. 'Or flour. I don't know. Whatever you've got.'

I went over and looked out into the garden with him. There was nothing to see but our own reflections. Two ghostly faces peering in through the window at us. His image looked suddenly grim.

'What?' I said, turning to study his real face.

'I should go, shouldn't I?' he said.

I swallowed. 'Yes,' I said. 'Of course you should.' *Should should should.* Such an un compromising word. I gripped the draining board, anxious now. 'But you won't, will you?'

He nodded. 'I will,' he said, reaching into his pocket once again. 'I will if you say. It's not too late.'

I reached out and halted his hand with my own.

'It *is*,' I said. 'It's way too late.'

He glanced down at my hand and looked intently at me. 'It's not,' he said quietly, taking it and holding it. 'Not at all. Look Sally, you have a lot at stake here. My fight's done. My future's already mapped. You've… 'he cast his eyes around him. 'Look, I don't want you to do anything you're going to spend the rest of your life regretting. I didn't come here to seduce you. Tell the truth, I feel really uncomfortable right now. I didn't think – hell, it was a crazy idea. I just wanted to *see* you. But now I'm here…'

He stopped talking and stared out of the window again.

As his hand was still linked in mine I jiggled it. 'Now you're here?' I prompted.

He turned back to look at me again. His eyes seemed more glittering and translucent than ever. Almost as though, if I looked hard and long enough, I'd be able to see into his soul. Such ridiculous tosh, but I couldn't seem to help it. Still I waited. He sighed. A big, heavy sigh. 'Now I'm here, Sally,' he said, dispelling my fanciful notions in an instant. 'Now I'm here, I just feel like a prize shit.'

'You're not that!' I said, becoming fearful now of the anguished look in his eyes.

'No? Standing in some other guy's house and wanting to make love to his wife? What was I *thinking*? Jeez, Sally, this was not a good idea.'

I let go of his hand and wrapped my arms tightly around him instead, but he was rigid and unyielding. Hopelessness trickled through me. He was wearing the same suede jacket he'd had on the first time I met him. Velvety against my cheek. The colour of toffee. Scented with *him*.

'You're not that,' I said again. 'Any more than I am. It's just, well, circumstance. You're right.' I looked around me. At Kate's show poster on the wall. Jonathan's beer tankard glinting down at us from the dresser. The card with the date of Merlin's next injection, pinned lopsidedly to the cork notice board that hung by the door. And the ever present guilt. Which was rolling thickly in around us like hill fog. 'This is not a good place to be. Let's get in your car and drive somewhere instead, shall we? You know. Talk for a bit. I don't know. *Anything*. Only don't look at me like that. Please.'

He put his own arms around me now and drew me close against him.

'Back seat of the car, is it?' he said softly, stroking my hair now. 'I'm not cut out for this Sally. I can't do this to you.'

I pulled myself away from him and felt my unhappiness harden into a tight knot of anger. 'Nick, you already *have*! All right, so you go now. What then? What do I do then? Go to bed? Sleep? Get up? Go to work? Come home again and repeat the process the next day and the next day, and just carry on as if none of this ever happened?'

'Sally – '

I spread my hands, exasperated. 'Well I *can't,* Nick. I've spent almost every waking moment since I met you trying to do exactly that, and I can't! I don't want to! There, you see? So you're wrong. It *is* too late. I've already crossed that threshold, don't you see? And much as I hate myself – much as I wish I was a better person – a person who *can* do all those things, a person who can subjugate their own desires for those of everyone around them, I've discovered I'm not up to the job. So if you think I'm going to let you walk away from here now, then…..' I dropped my hands now and let them hang at my sides. 'Nick, you can't do that to me.'

The words out now, I stood there before him mute and horrified.

But however much of a taste they had left in my mouth , I had needed to say them. To make this all real. So much time spent agonising over what to do and all of it had been pointless. I was a human animal and I wanted this man. I shouldn't, but I did. It was half past one in the morning and my thought processes were pin-prick sharp. There was no point in trying to ferret out my other self any more. She was long gone, and now I had a stark choice. Goodness and unhappiness or happiness and guilt. Both states new territory, unfamiliar pairings. I should opt for the former but I wanted the latter. It was as simple as that.

'I won't,' I said again, pulling my new self to attention and hooking my hair behind my ears with shaking fingers. 'So you are going nowhere. I'm going to make us both a cup of tea and we are going to sit right down here and talk about it. In fact, no. We are going to go and sit in the garden and talk. It's stopped raining. It's not cold. And besides, we can go and sit under the umbrella on the patio anyway. Yes. Yes, that'll do. We'll sit there. OK?'

He blinked at me, nodded contritely. Exhaled.

'OK,' he said at last, with a trace of a smile. 'OK, Sally. So. Where are the mugs?'

But we didn't get as far as the garden. We certainly didn't get as far as the talk. We didn't even get as far as the mugs.

'Ah, mugs,' I'd said, as he stood before me, brows raised, achingly beautiful. Incredibly, here. Unbelievably, mine. 'Right. Mugs.' But as soon as I had begun the small action of directing this man in my kitchen to the dishwasher I realised with a breathtaking sense of inevitability that something organic was happening between us – moreover, that it had been quietly happening all the time we'd been talking – and that tea was the very last thing on my mind. I put my hands on my hips.

'Do you *really* want a cup of tea?' I asked him.

He shook his head. 'Nope.'

'Coffee?'

He shook it again. 'Nope.'

'*Anything*?'

He shook it a third time. 'Er…nope.'

'Me neither.' And in less time than it takes for a biblical cock-crow, we had covered the four strides of quarry tile between us and were now back where we'd been not half an hour before, except this time the mechanics of sexual chemistry would not be diverted by our tedious machinations.

'I'm so sorry,' I panted as I slid my hands under the lapels of his jacket and prised them up and back over his shoulders. 'Oh, Nick, I'm so sorry I shouted at you. It wasn't your fault. It was me. I *made* you come here.' I squirmed against him, pulling his head towards me to crush his mouth against my own.

'No!' he breathed, still kissing me while he shrugged his arms from the sleeves of his jacket and I began grappling with the buttons on his shirt. 'It *was* my fault. I shouldn't have come. I should have stayed away.' His hands were in my hair again and his breathing was becoming shallow. 'I was going to, *really*, but –'

The jacket fell to the floor with a flump. 'I would have *killed* you!' I gasped, as his hands rippled down my backbone then slid up inside the back of my T-shirt instead. 'Oh, God, Nick, you have no *idea* how much I've –'

The buttons undone now – one, two, three, four – I yanked the shirt from inside his jeans and freed the fifth with a flick. 'How *much* –'

'I think I do,' he murmured from somewhere near my clavicle. His lips were hot against my neck now, and his hands were back around the sides of my T-shirt. He peeled it up and over my head in one fluid movement. He gaped at me. 'Oh, God, Sally, I think I *do,*' he said again.

I could feel my chest pumping under my breasts as he stared at them. Then his hands were there too and his mouth back on mine. I could hear something tap tap tapping against the table leg.

'Yikes!' I said, realising. 'I forgot about the dog!'

I pulled reluctantly away from him and shunted Merlin out into the utility room.

'Oh, God – *jeans*,' gasped Nick again. He'd already ripped his shirt from his shoulders, and now crushed me against his bare chest as I fell back into his arms. I could hear the dog whining outside. Hear the sea in my ears. Feel the strength in his arms as he caressed me.

'Jeans?' I asked distractedly, as I grappled with his belt.

He growled. 'Yes, *jeans. You,* in jeans. No top on. Just jeans. Oh, *God*. That *really* does it for me.' He pulled me towards him and got his hand on the rivet.

'That does it for you?' I said, freeing his buckle and hooking my trembling hands under his waistband. I could feel the baby soft hair against the backs of my fingers, the taut bulk of his stomach muscles tensed underneath.

'God, Sally,' he murmured. '*You*. *You* do it for me,' his lips nuzzling my ear now, his hand on my zip.

'There's nothing underneath them,' I whispered back feverishly, fumbling with his fly buttons , leaning back to see. 'God, Nick! Why d'you *wear* these things? Are they impossible or not?'

He nibbled at my earlobe. '501's,' he explained.

I could hear the smooth zzzziiiipppp of my fly being undone now. The smooth feel of his hand sliding over my hip. The smooth sound of his moan as the other slid down my stomach.

'Oh, *Nick* –'My own hands were still struggling with his buttons. 'Is that the brand name?' I panted, as his fingers inched lower. 'Or – oh! Oh, *Nick*! – Oh, God! – Oh, *drat*! Or the minutes it takes to get the bloody things off?'

'Hang on,' he said, sliding mine deftly down over my buttocks, breathing hard and fast against the side of my head and beginning to grind his hips against me. 'Let me do that, OK?' He swung his head back now and grinned at me wolfishly.

'Remember the motto, Sally. More haste, less speed.'

I wriggled my jeans down and stamped my legs from inside them. Haste didn't do it justice. I was a desperate woman.

'Oh, Sally –'he moaned again, as we struggled with his.

Our eyes locked. 'Come *on, Nick!*' I breathed. 'Get those *off,* will you!'

And there we were, suddenly, naked and panting, clothes puddled around us, eyes dark with desire.

'Sally – you're sure?' he gasped.

'Yes,' I said.

'Really?'

'Now', I said.

'Here?' he said.

'*Here*,' I said. '*Now*.'

I gripped his head, kissed his lips, mouthed the words through it.

'Make love to me, *now*, Nick.'

So that's what he did.

A quarter to four and it is just getting light. And I have re-discovered sex.

We're somewhere else now. I open my eyes and look around me. I see the coffee table, a mound of magazines, a stump of candle on the mantelpiece. Things look so different from here.

And a delicious warmth. I'm lying on the sofa, his sleepy bulk curled close and solid beside me, stirring a little as I move, one hand cupped round my breast. We're covered by the throw from the other sofa and the fringing round the edges is tickling my nose.

I twist around to face him and slide a hand slowly along the curve of his hip bone. His eyes blink and then open. Sleepy eyes. So blue. He blinks again, looks at me, smiles slightly, says nothing. Plays a finger over my stomach. I feel the muscles of his legs contract as he eases one of them gently between my thighs, grunting slightly as he heaves his body above me once again. There is a pounding in my ears. I feel my lips part and the sweet heat of his tongue against the inside of my mouth. The fire in my groin as his hand slips soundlessly up the inside of my thigh. My arms snake over his buttocks, crushing them to me as he begins nudging now against me, the low hiss of his breath against my face growing faster, as his thrusts become stronger, more urgent, more deep.

Still we say nothing. Just look. Just keep gazing at each other. He plants one careful hand by my head and rears upwards, the throw shrugging off and slipping noiselessly from his back. He mouths my name now, and his movements start to quicken, my pelvis arching to meet him, my body tensing to enfold him, while his hand moves in darting circles over my breasts. His head dips to meet mine as I reach up to kiss him, grasping his neck, pulling myself up against the arm of the sofa, our eyes still wide open as the first waves of orgasm begin to pulse through us, racing through our bodies, shining bright in our eyes. His neck muscles tense, and the spasm as he climaxes floods me with a new rush of impossible heat. Then he sinks down against me, lips soft against my cheek now, and I hold him in my arms while the shudders fade away.

A quarter to five and the day is fully dawned. I have re-discovered sex. I feel sated and adored. But I've discovered something else. Something horrible.

Remorse.

Chapter 20

Tuesday. Tuesday proper. Tuesday real life. Tuesday *woe*. No. Woe is Wednesday's child, isn't it? Whatever. Ten to ten and my mother has arrived.

And I am exuding sex. I can *feel* it. I can feel it inside me, outside me, wrapping its fragrant fingers around me, squeezing from my pores and riding bare-back on my breath. I *am* sex. Sex on legs, sex on-a-stick, sex personified. I am languorous and silky-limbed, voluptuous and wanton. I have the remains of a rosy bloom still soft on my cheeks.

'Hullo,' says my mother, raincoated on the doorstep and carrying an umbrella. 'You wouldn't think it was June, would you? I had to have my blow heater going last night.'

She shakes out her umbrella and steps past me into the hallway. She has only walked the twenty yards from her car to my door, but she has her perm to think of. She cannot risk any frizz, bless her. She has to look her best for Tony.

I watch her trot along to the kitchen but linger in the hall long enough for my heartbeat to slow a little. Goodness, is it going to be like this all day? This feeling of imminent exposure? It's all right, I reassure myself, she cannot tell. She cannot *see*. But how could anyone possibly *not* see what has happened to me? Every time I think of the enormity of what I have done, adrenalin whooshes up inside me and zips about all over my body, making my fingers and toes tingle and hijacking my physiology so comprehensively I think I might, at any moment, keel over and faint. And I have been thinking about what I have done almost constantly since Nick left at five.

Remorse. So this is what it feels like, then. I study myself in the hall mirror. My hair, freshly washed, hangs in bouncing coppery scythes on my shoulders and my eyes, though they have absolutely no business to be doing so, stare confidently back at me, glittering and defiant. So whatever it *feels* like, it looks something else entirely. For the me in the hall mirror is not me at all. She's a hussy, a slut and an unfaithful wife. The real me turns away, shrinking from her gaze.

'Well!' I hear my mother exclaim to the dog. 'What have we *here* then? What have we *here*?'

I scuttle anxiously along the hall. Oh, God. Something of Nick's? Boxer shorts? No. He wasn't wearing any. His mug! But I washed up his mug, didn't I? And anyway, it's *my* mug, isn't it? And how on earth could anyone extrapolate sex on the kitchen floor from the sight of a mug on the draining board? Ridiculous. Insane! Yet this is my *mother*. This is my mother and I fear the awesome acuity of her maternal nose. And not for the first time in my life, I find myself dismayed at the fact that my Mother has always had *carte blanche* with my drawers. That there is no cupboard in my house she would feel it inappropriate to rummage in. How did this happen? Did she, or anyone else, for that matter, never consider that my storage was my business?

It is a metaphor for the rest of my life. I see that now. People around me simply making assumptions about what'll be good for me and my own pathetic after-the-event inability to point out that, no, this is *not* what I want. From unsolicited cakes to weekend-long visitations by relatives to Christmas presents of fridge jugs and recipe book rests. This, then, is what *really* frightens me. The absolute transparency of my life to date. How everyone else always knows where I am, what I'm doing, how I'm feeling, what'll be good for me. And how at odds that state of affairs is with the pre-requisites for becoming an unfaithful wife. Which are many and varied and involve, above everything, the careful preparation of a seedbed of privacy for the easy propagation of secrets and lies.

'What?' I say, arriving in the kitchen and plucking Merlin's lead from its hook.

But she is not rootling among my utensils. She is not on the floor scouring my crevices for evidence. She is too busy giving my dog an erection. What *is* it with my mother and dogs? One look at her bearing down and threatening to tickle their tummies and they all – sex and breed entirely regardless – seem to prostrate themselves and splay their legs for her. She waggles a little bag.

'Oh, just some choc drops for Merlie. But only if you're a werry werrry werry good boy, though.'

'I have to take him out,' I say, suddenly nauseated by the sight of my mutt's hairy bits. 'What time was the train?'

'Half past ten,' she informs me, giving him a playful tap on the nose with the choc drops. 'So don't be too long, will you?' She straightens. 'I'll sit and do my crozzle while I wait.'

Once outside, Merlin straining energetically at the lead, I stride out powerfully, letting the warm drizzle wet my face.

I still cannot believe it, and yet it is true. Not five hours have passed since I was writhing on my own kitchen floor with Nick Brown. A part of me is clamouring to go back into the house, turn the shower to hot and scrub away at the memory, but a greater part is already plotting and scheming. Five hours without him already feels like too long.

I feel for the phone in my pocket, pull it out, take hold of it. Form the words of my message as I walk down the lane. *Hello... Get to work OK? If you're there, call me. Out walking the dog, S XXX*

I continue to walk. Up the wide road at the end of our lane, down the next, over the stile and on into the slim strip of woodland that borders the farmland beyond, where I let Merlin off the lead and watch him bound off into the damp ferns. I've taken him on this walk many times over the years, night and day, week in week out, its route so familiar I could do it with my eyes shut, every fallen tree, wildflower and crop duly noted, the times the blackberries and wild rose hips are glossy and ripe. It's a calming and comforting ten minutes of solitude. An intake of fresh air.

Nick's message arrives ten minutes later, just as I'm about to turn back into our lane once again. I check the time and linger on the corner to read it.

'*In a meeting. Ring you in 45 mins xxxxxxx*

Standing there, my nostrils now full of the sharp scent of a summer morning I wonder at the utter insanity of the course of action I have just taken. The fact that at every juncture where I could have said no I've said yes. The unbelievability that the trajectory of my life could have been so radically altered in just a few short weeks. I feel like I've outrun the state troopers and crossed over the border. Become exiled from ordinary life. This thought, chillingly, thrills me a little.

And the peonies outside Mr Metcalf's squat bungalow nod velvety assent as I hurry back home.

I suggested we drive my mother's car to the station, ostensibly because using mine would have meant moving hers out of the way anyway, but in reality because I was, even then, thinking one step ahead. We arrived at the station car park fifteen minutes later, just in time to grab a pair of coffees and head up to the platform.

In some ways I was glad to be with my mother today. Whatever my worries about her domestic penetration, at least I was not at work, facing Ruth. Though I was more confident Ruth wouldn't find any clues, she had a way of looking at me that sidetracked evidence and simply demanded my honesty. So it is with really close friends.

The train glided smoothly up to the platform and minutes later we were heading north, towards London, me staring out at the sage backdrop of a rainy-day landscape and my mother, who had laid out all her travelling Tupperware, busily embroiled in her crossword clues. I deflected her offers of corned beef sandwiches and Wotsits, and tried to lose myself in sleep. We were just beyond Caterham when my mobile phone rang.

I reached for the phone and moved to my feet in one fluid movement. A simple process as I had already decided this was what I would do. Just as I'd already decided what it was I would say. Everything in the planning. That was the thing.

'It'll be Ruth,' I mouthed to my mother as I pressed the answer button and snaked my hips around the table. I stepped out into the central aisle. 'I've been expecting a call from her. I'll go out and talk to her in the corridor.' I tilted my head to indicate out of the window. 'Problems with reception.'

Fortunately, my mother knew as much about mobile phones as she did about Plate Tectonics so she nodded as if she did know and returned to her crossword while I weaved my way quickly up the carriage.

Nick had just come out of his meeting and his voice was low.

'Where are you?' he asked. 'On the train?'

I assumed there were other people around because there was a background hum of noise. Or was it just the rush of blood in my temples? It sounded like he was walking somewhere.

'Yes,' I replied. I had already told him about my trip with my mother. 'I guess we'll be back about six. I'm not sure.'

Our short conversation was already bristling with sexual static. A woman in a raincoat squeezed past me. 'So I'll meet you at the station then, shall I?' he said. This too, we had already arranged.

'That'll be fine.'

'Have dinner somewhere, maybe? Would that be good for you?'

That would be good for me. That would be very good for me. But I didn't know what to say to him all of a sudden. My words kept getting sidetracked by the input from my loins. Sexual arousal. How could anyone keep feeling like this and still function?

'I'll call you then, shall I?' I managed finally. ' Once we're on the train home?' I could hear the fade in and fade out of his breath as he walked. 'About five, then? Something like –'

'Sally,' he interrupted softly. 'Are you all right?'

'I'm fine.'

His voice dropped lower still. 'I mean, all right about *this*?

'Nick, of *course* I'm all right,' I replied, anxious to reassure him, the tenderness in his voice giving me a new surge of feeling. One of pure, unadulterated happiness and joy. I could feel a smile in my voice. I hoped he could hear it. 'I'd hardly be standing in a train corridor arranging secret assignations with you if I wasn't, would I?'

He laughed. 'So that's a yes, then?'

'Nick, you *know* it is. God, Nick, I –'But then I had to stop myself suddenly. 'I'll call you at the end of the day, OK?'

I pressed the end call button and stared out unseeing through the rain. I'd very nearly told him I loved him.

My mother glanced up from her crossword and smiled as I sat down again. How uncomplicated her life seemed to be.

'All right, my love?' she asked me. The Tupperware boxes had gone now and in their place was a packet of snack size Mars Bars. She tapped it with her pen and shunted it towards me.

I shook my head and wedged myself back behind my side of the table.

'Fine,' I answered.

'And Ruth?'

'Oh, Ruth's fine too. Except – '

She was in the middle of doing an anagram, the paper before her dotted with random letters, all written in capitals in her neat hand. I waited while she finished filling in a clue. She looked up. '– except that she's a bit down right now. …..what with work, and her dad being ill … you know?' The lie came out so smoothly, so seamlessly, so *effortlessly*, that I was forced to confront another unpalatable fact in a day already so overburdened with them. That I really *wasn't* the person I thought I was any more. And I was clearly no longer the person everyone around me thought I was either. Or maybe I was. Maybe that was actually the real point. Maybe the good person they all knew and trusted was actually not me at all. Maybe I'd been living a lie all this time.

I embellished it with another.

'She's asked me round for supper,' I told her. 'You don't mind, do you? I know we were talking about fish and chips or something, but, well, what with…well, her dad went home yesterday and she sounded like she could really use some company, and I really feel I have to be there for her at the moment, you know?'

I waited for my mother to look peevish about this, as I knew any display of pique on her part would make me feel immeasurably less of a complete cow than I did right now, but she didn't. Instead, she nodded her head knowingly and looked for all the world as if having supper with me had been the very last thing on her agenda.

'Poor thing. It must be very hard on her. Jack Braithwaite – you know, or maybe you don't –he had a colostomy end of last year. Terrible business. Crohn's, I think it was. Or maybe Irritable Bowels?' The man in the seats opposite shot across a startled look, to which my mother was entirely oblivious. 'Or was it polyps, or something? What's its name? You know, that growth thing people get. Anyway,' she tapped her pen on her paper. 'A growth of *some* sort. I'll have to ask Betty. – well, anyway, he's been finding it really difficult, poor love. Yes, fine. Of course, dear. No problem. Tell you what. I'll drop you round there when we get back.'

I shook my head quickly, having anticipated even this. Lying was a frighteningly straightforward business once you got the hang of the techniques involved . 'Oh, there's no need, mum,' I trotted out easily. She's going to pick me up from the station herself. Save you worrying. On her way home from work.'

Horribly simple. And simply horrible. But my heart simply refused to care.

'It's certainly a nice day for it,' my mother remarked as we emerged from Westminster tube station. The rain had cleared now, the sky a poster paint turquoise above Big Ben. 'It's a shame you couldn't persuade Morgan to come too. It seems like ages since I've seen her.'

I wasn't altogether sure why I hadn't been able to. I'd thought she'd be pleased to meet up with us for lunch. Especially for a chance to see her gran. They had always been so close.

'She's very busy at work right now,' I said, herding my mother on to the crossing on Whitehall. 'It's difficult to get away, what with work being so busy, and everything else she's got to do at the moment.'

Morgan had sounded flustered even, which wasn't like her at all. The strain of it all, no doubt. And who could blame her? It was a big thing to organise, a wedding. Even so, it wasn't like Morgan to let things get on top of her. Histrionics and short temper were generally Kate's department.

'Anyway,' I said now. 'That doesn't mean we can't find you an outfit, does it?' We crossed the road and started walking up towards Downing street. 'So. What's the drill?'

A surprisingly simple one, it turned out. Delivering a petition to ten Downing Street, it seemed, was just a case of making an appointment to do so. And as long as you didn't come in fancy dress, as she'd told me, or carry placards, use loudhailers, wear slogans on your clothes or plan any elaborate stunts, you were made very welcome. You didn't *actually* get to see the man himself, of course. But you did at least get a glimpse of his hallway – which my mother felt was almost as good.

We approached the constable guarding the wrought iron gates to find not only that he had my mother's name written on a sheet he carried, but also that he knew exactly what we were here to petition about.

'Any press with you?' he enquired, smiling.

'Oh, lordy!' said my mother. 'I should have thought of that, shouldn't I? Oh, what a missed opportunity!' She glanced across to where another group of petitioners were standing, complete with a gaggle of people with microphones and a man with a furry sound boom. She tutted. 'What a twot. I should have told that man from the Argos to come with us, shouldn't I?' She considered for a moment. 'But tell you what, Sally. I bet if I –'She thrust her bag into my hands. 'Hang on right there.'

And then she was off like a whippet, raincoat tails flapping. And heading back, moments later, with a big smile on her face, and dragging along a man with a mike.

The policeman looked at his schedule and then back at me.

'Your mother?'

I nodded.

'She's a bit of a one.' he tapped his list. 'She works at this refuge then, does she?'

I shook my head. 'No. Lives next door.'

'Well, she should,' he said, grinning as she approached with her captive. 'Don't think I'd mess with her any.'

I felt fidgety and irritable by the time the train pulled up at Oxted. My mother, still flushed by her near-Blair experience, was like a terrier with a frisbee, and had been twittering excitedly to anyone within earshot almost all the way back, including an elderly gentlemen who'd got on at East Croydon, for whom she'd recited almost all of her impromptu interview, as well as pressing upon him a copy of her save-the-refuge letter and the remainder of her bag of mini Mars Bars.

But my mind was now elsewhere. We'd delivered the petition, we'd got the photos to prove it, and, yes, there might even be a line or two in the Standard, but even so I wondered how long it would now sit in an in-tray, along with all the others that must fetch up all the time. I chided myself for my negative thoughts. It was a great, unselfish thing my mother had done today, and yet all I could think about was me.

That was it really. That cruel juxtaposition. My mum slogging her guts out to do something good, something *selfless*, and me, busy – what was the word my mum had used for it? That was it – carrying on.

Carrying on. What a horrible turn of phrase. Was that really what I was doing with Nick? I racked my brains for other, less damning terminology I could apply to what we were doing. Carry on. Fling. Affair. Bit on the side. They were all so yeuchy and squalid. What I wanted to say was that I'd fallen in love. But I wasn't seventeen and the words sounded stupid, even when I said them to myself. Melodramatic. The stuff of Ruth's tales.

Nick's car was parked in the station car park. I could see it as we crossed the footbridge. I pushed my hand into the pockets of my jeans as I walked and let the fizzy, unspeakable, carrying-on-type feelings that I could do nothing about percolate up through my stomach.

'Now, are you sure I can't drop you?' my mother was saying. I hoped he wouldn't be standing in the booking hall. I didn't think I'd be able to stop myself from running into his arms and whispering appallingly rude things in his ear. But he was nowhere to be seen.

I kissed my mother's cheek and shepherded her hurriedly towards the exit. 'Ruth'll be here in a minute,' I said. 'You get off home. I 'm going to pop into the Spar for some wine.'

'You won't forget to put the film in?' she reminded me.

'First thing,' I said. 'I'll have them in the post to you before lunch.'

She lingered. 'And don't forget to get the big prints. And get two copies, while you're at it. I'll send some to your Auntie Beryl in Hove. She'll like that. Oh, and be sure to tell Jonathan to have his Secretary get the Standard, won't you? The man did say it might go in tomorrow.'

I kissed her quiet and reminded her about the traffic. 'Don't want to get stuck in a jam, do you?'

She kissed me back.

'You're a sweetheart, you are, darling. An absolute sweetheart. Thanks for today. Give my love to Ruth, won't you?'

I wondered, as I watched her clack away over the concourse, if she'd feel quite like that if she'd known the truth.

Canoodling. There was another one. Well, sod it. So be it. I was just turning to head back towards the station car park when I felt a tap on my shoulder.

'Boo.'

He was standing behind me. Holding a bunch of flowers.

Pinks. With a sprig of something limp and ferny thrown in. 'They're gross, aren't they?' he said, smiling happily. 'But they're strictly gestural, so don't hold them against me. I just really wanted to buy you some flowers, is all.' We started walking towards the car park. Him and me and the flowers still cradled in his arm. I couldn't take them from him, because someone might see.

'They're lovely,' I said, wanting to hold them against him very much.

'So. Hungry?' he asked.

'Not in the least.'

'Me neither. So. What shall we do instead?'

'Um…let me think. Nope. I can only think of one thing.'

'Me too. So. D'you want to come back to my place?'

'See your etchings?'

'Absolutely.'

'I'd like that very much.'

So be it. Off we went, in his car, back to his place. And made love, on the rug, on the floor, in his hall.

Nick's apartment – for it was very much 'apartment'. Not at all 'flat' – was situated on the edge of Oxted, in a large converted Victorian house. It was on the first floor, with its own front door at the side. Provided at minimal expense by the powers that be at Drug U Like, apparently, who had, it seemed, no shortage of largesse where their thrusting UK task force were concerned.

We had moved, by now, to the living room – a high ceilinged expanse of blond strip-wood flooring, with cream coloured walls and a pair of low leather sofas. At the far end, French doors led out on to a small balcony, which had a view over the largely lawned garden. Beyond that a swathe of intensely green trees seemed to go on for miles, unbroken. He'd made me a cup of coffee. Rich dark coffee that tasted almost of chocolate. He'd also made toast for us, two slices of which I'd already eaten. I was sitting at one end of a low leather sofa, reduced now, sartorially, to a T-shirt he'd lent me, my legs outstretched and my feet in his lap.

Shame on you, Mrs Matthews, in your knickers and T-shirt, eating toast for your dinner and having sex on the floor.

Nick was just finishing his third slice of toast.

'Marmite I miss,' he observed, licking his fingers one by one. We had showered together in his small black and white tiled bathroom. There were expensive looking bottles on the narrow glass shelf, and the towels, of which there were many, were fragrant and snowy. He had one around his waist now, the edges falling away half way down his thighs. His legs were crossed at the ankle. He was twiddling his toes.

'Can't you get Marmite in America, then?'

He shook his head. 'Not easily. I guess if you were to look hard enough. You kind of get out of the habit.'

'You'll have to stock up then,' I said, licking my own fingers.

'Oh, I'll get round to that kind of thing before I go back, no doubt. I generally do when I'm here. Mind you, it's getting more and more difficult. There's only so much tomato puree you can shove in your shoes without – Sally? What is it?'

I had put a cushion over my face. I lowered it again.

'Do we have to talk about this? I don't want to talk about this, Nick.'

He shook his head and put his plate on the coffee table.

'No,' he said, stretching out along the sofa towards me. 'We don't have to talk about this at all. Not at this moment.'

'But we'll have to sometime, won't we?'

He put his feet up on the arm of the sofa and lay back against me. 'I imagine. That rather depends on you, I think.'

'When do you go back?'

His head swivelled. 'Hey! I thought you didn't want to talk about it?'

'I don't. But now I'm all agitated about it I can't *not* talk about it. It's like when you get a raggedy edge on a nail. You keep nibbling at it. When?'

'I finish up here end of July.'

'Oh, God –'

He clasped my hand in his. 'Hey, you know, I don't *have* to go back then. There's a permanent HR job here if I want it. It's just that, well, I hadn't *planned* on staying. But Sally –'

'Oh, God,' I said again. 'I don't want to talk about this. We shouldn't talk about this. No, no, no.' I leaned forward and slipped my fingers underneath the fold of his towel instead. 'Tell you what. Let's not talk at all.'

But my not talking plan was about to be vetoed. Nick pulled his lips from my own. 'Sally,' he said. 'I don't want to worry you, but there's something going on in your bag.'

I clambered up to get my handbag from the table and pulled my mobile out. Two missed calls. And one of them was Morgan. I rang her back.

'Mum? Where are you?' She sounded tired and cross. Snappy. Not like herself at all. 'I've been trying to get hold of you for *ages*. Did Mr Poselthwaite get you in the end? I gave him your mobile number but he said he couldn't get through. Where *are* you? Where have you been?'

I've been up to London to visit the queen. So that would be the other missed call. Mr Poselthwaite. Who on earth was Mr Poselthwaite?

'I'm at Ruth's,' I said, a little too quickly, as Nick padded silently out to the kitchen with our plates. Who was he? Who *was* he? Oh, yes! The penny spun and clattered to the floor. The marquee man! The man who was supposed to be calling this evening to measure up and cost the marquee! 'Oh, God, Morgan! I'm sorry. I completely forgot!'

'Oh, *mum*! How could you forget?'

And would have done so already. An hour back. Obviously *had* done. Oh, *dear*. I could hear her irritable sigh. Why was everything was so amplified by guilt? 'Look, I'll call him back now, shall I? When will you be home? Perhaps he can call back or something. Oh, mum, *honestly*. How could you *forget*?'

Twenty minutes later, Nick had dropped me at the end of the lane. I then walked the fifty or so yards to my house, still clutching the flowers I wouldn't be able to put in a vase anywhere, still fretting about quite how I'd managed to forget Mr Poselthwaite, still wondering what on earth I was going to do next.

The doorbell rang half an hour later.

But it wasn't the hapless marquee man with his tape measure. I opened the door to find someone else on my doorstep. It was Ruth.

'I saw you,' she said.

Chapter 21

I had, I judged, about three seconds in which to gather my face into order and formulate some sort of credible response, and I squandered every last one of them. In the production, instead, of a violent blush. Perhaps I was turning into a cuttlefish.

'Saw you in his car,' she added, stepping smartly over the doorstep and looming in front of me with an expression that, even in the midst of my small panic attack, I could see held gleams of both salacious delight and stern disapproval. But Ruth didn't do disapproval. Hadn't up to now, at any rate. But perhaps there were some things even Ruth disapproved of. Me, for instance. Right now. There was, of course, no need for her to qualify the 'him'. We exchanged a look instead. It was a given. Oh, yes.

She moved past me and took off her jacket, plopping it over the newel post on top of mine.

'I was on my way home from Tesco's and I saw his car. And you *in* it, Sal. And I thought 'funny. What on earth is Sally doing in Nick Brown's car at half past seven on a Tuesday evening?' And then – don't ask me why. Call it the product of a febrile and writerly imagination – It suddenly occurred to me that whatever you were doing had absolutely nothing to do with work. It doesn't, does it? *Does* it? Sal, what were you *doing*?'

I shut the door behind her and could think of nothing sensible to say.

'Ruth, I –'

She put her hand on my forearm.

'Sal, look, tell me this is none of my business if you like but, Christ! What the hell's going on?'

I could think of nothing to say to that either, so instead I asked her if she wanted a glass of wine or a cup of coffee and walked on heavy legs into the kitchen, her and anxiety both hot on my heels.

She plonked her handbag on to the kitchen table.

'Well, Sal,' she said, chattily. 'So it's really true, then?'

I had my back to her, reaching for wine glasses. Perhaps it wasn't too late. Perhaps I could invent some meeting or other. Perhaps I could tell her I was helping him with his buy-one-get-one-free profit projections. Perhaps I could come over all indignant and huffy and – yes. I would do that. That would work. I turned around. 'What do you mean,' I spluttered. 'So *it's* really true? So *what's* really true? What's 'it's'? *It's?* What on earth are you talking about?' And so on. I put the glasses down and slid a bottle of red from the rack on the corner of the worktop but it was one of Jonathan's poseur wine club ones. I pushed it back in again. And pulled out a Sainsbury's discount Merlot instead. That would do. 'It's? *Honestly*, Ruth. You *are* a case. What on earth are you on about? *It's,* indeed. He was just giving me a lift, that was all. He'd seen me at the station and stopped to see if I wanted a lift. Is there a law against that, or something? I mean – 'I stopped here, partly because I was already thinking the lady was protesting way too much, but also because it was evident from her expression that she knew perfectly well I was talking utter bilge. She was standing in the middle of the kitchen with her arms folded across her chest and one eyebrow slightly raised. She looked like Jeremy Paxman skewering a minor politician. And then she began nodding as well. It was a pathetic attempt and both of us knew it. 'Oh, God. All right. Yes. *Yes*,' I said sadly. 'You're right. It really is true.'

Ruth pulled out a chair and sat on it, looking disarmingly pleased with herself.

'Well, bloody hell.'

'Quite.'

'I mean – how long has this been going on?'

'Not long. I mean, if you're thinking –'

She rubbed her hands together. 'Oh, believe me, I'm thinking all sorts of things, most of them involving lower torsos. But – God! it's all beginning to make sense. No wonder you were so crabby about the idea of me getting my claws into him.'

She said this entirely without malice or pique. Indeed, she was grinning now.

'Ruth, it wasn't before –'

She flapped a dismissive arm. 'Oh, forget it. I'm well over that particular crush. Well over, believe me. In fact I was only thinking the other day how very fetching that new guy in – well. We'll see. No. Not a problem. He's all yours. So the way I figure it, you're the one with the problem. Or not, of course, depending on your viewpoint. What's the deal then? 'She accepted the glass I held out to her. 'Is it serious?'

Is it *serious*? What an expression that was! Yes, of course it was serious! It was about a serious as an event could reasonably be! I had had sex with someone other than Jonathan. Three times now. Three times! Eighteen years of quiet, unremarkable, unblemished fidelity and then three frantic couplings in less than twenty four hours – two of them on the floor! Oh, yes. What was happening to me right now was serious all right. Whether what was happening to *us* was serious – I didn't know. I had no yardstick with which to analyse the rollercoaster of emotions I was experiencing right now. I just knew they were terrifying. That I wanted him – *ached* for him – and it was terrifying me. But did I feel as I did about Nick because of Nick? Or was it because of Me? Me and Jonathan? Me and my impending menopause? Me and my twitty, half baked notions of romance? No. It *was* him. It was *him*. It was a chilling thought, so I poured myself a hefty slug of wine before answering.

'Yes,' I said, pulling out another chair and sitting down on it. I felt poleaxed. 'It's extremely serious. Call me anything you like, Ruth – infatuated, obsessed, smitten, overwhelmed — but that's about the size of it. Yes.'

She slid her glass across the kitchen table towards me. I only half filled it because she was driving.

'Well, bugger me, Sally,' she said, smiling.

But it was nothing to smile about. Every perfect jewel of a moment of the last two and a half hours had now become dulled by the dirty stain of my guilt.

'Quite,' I said again.

'And?'

'And what?' I pressed my fingers against the sides of my temples. 'I feel terrible. I don't think I've ever felt so terrible. I don't know what to *do*, Ruth.'

I could feel myself growing very close to tears.

She took a sip from her wine and looked carefully at me. 'Hmm,' she said. 'Well that really depends on how you feel about extra marital shenanigans really, doesn't it, sweetie pie? Which is obviously not the way *I* always thought you felt about it.' She shook her head. 'What a turn up. I really thought you were happily married, Sal. All tickety boo and sorted. But are you? I mean, lustful obsessions about the Anglo American Treaty aside, *are* you? Honest answer, now. Do you *love* Jonathan?'

Shenanigans. Another hateful expression. I swallowed the lump this damning question had forced into my throat. 'That's just it. I don't *know*. Every time I start to think about it, it really scares me. I don't *want* to think about it. Because every time I do the answer seems so obvious. No. I don't. But how could that have happened? How can you fall out of love with someone so comprehensively without even realising it was happening?'

She shrugged. 'Same way as you can fall *in* love with someone, I suppose. It just happens. Catches you unawares.'

The telephone rang than. It was the marquee man, to remind me what a failure I was as a parent as well, and let me know he'd been held up at a costing in Horsham and that as it was almost dark there wasn't much point in him coming round again now. He'd come tomorrow instead, if that was all right. I said yes, it was all right and wrote MARQUEE MAN 7.30 WEDS in big letters on the back of a Christian Aid envelope and took it back into the kitchen. Ruth was still sitting there. Expectant. Wanting details.

'So,' she said. 'Wales. That was it, wasn't it? That was when it 'just happened' for you guys, was it? You've definitely been a bit peculiar since then. Bit of a gleam. Bit of an edge to you, lately.'

'Nothing happened in Wales,' I said, then immediately thought better of it. What point was there in pretending to her? I shook my head. 'No,' I said. 'That's not true. It had *already* happened. Not sex. Nothing like that. Just that I guess it was then that it really dawned on me how I felt about him. It was like, *wham!* It was like I'd been going around with shutters over my eyes all my life. It was almost like it had taken me over physically, you know? Not a conscious thing at all. I didn't seem to have any control over it. I just had this overwhelming sense of, I don't know, *need*. Of connectedness. This awesome sense of inevitability, of it being the strongest, truest, most intense – '

'Yeah, yeah. And you felt like you'd known him all your life. Or in some other life, maybe. That you were made for each other. That it was meant to be. That it was –'she clutched a hand to her bosom. '– don't tell me – written in the stars?' She put the hand back on the tabletop and tutted. 'Sal, I *know*. I write this stuff. Bloody hell, I *live* this stuff. It's what makes the world go round. *Comprendez?* I *know*. But though it pains me to be the one pouring a bucket of yesterday's dishwater on your lofty musings, I think you'll find that's just plain old lust. You know, spelt S.E.X. Or 'phwoarh!', perhaps. You can tart it up with all the hearts and flowers and adjectives you like, but the bottom line is still sex . You fancied the pants off him. And he fancied the pants off you.' She smiled. 'It *feels* romantic, I'll grant you. It works well in Woman's Weekly, I'll admit. But it's still basically about sex.'

I blinked at her, my tears now arrested, my mind lucid. 'God, Ruth, you make it sound so *tawdry.*'

'Oh, piffle!' she said. 'Tawdry? There's nothing tawdry about it. It's *normal*, Sal. It's human. And God knows, I'm no expert, but I'd imagine that if you've been shagging the same guy for eighteen years, and this is the first time you've tasted forbidden fruit, it could even be classed as pretty damned restrained. I mean, I know there's the odd wrinkly that raves on about their fantastic sex life with the guy they got it together with just after the Boer War, but I'm afraid I don't see it. I certainly don't see it around me. People aren't made that way. Look, I know what you're thinking. You're thinking, how would she know? She just lurches from one hopeless infatuation to the next – but it seems to me it must be bloody difficult getting a sweat on over the guy you've been sharing basic bodily functions with for half your life, even with the best will in the world.'

That was true, I thought sadly. It *was* difficult. It was very difficult. Nigh on impossible in fact. But you just got on with it, didn't you? Made the best of it. Didn't you? Didn't everyone? I could do the routine – the sporadic and perfunctory sex, the intermittent, nice-cup-of-tea orgasms. But this wasn't about the realities of long term libido sustainment. It was about the fact that far from being the best in the world, my will, since the moment I clapped eyes on Nick Brown in that lane, had simply turned tail and run away. I sipped some more wine.

'You're right about that.'

'I know I am,' she said. 'Which is why people find themselves lusting after other people all the time. It's basic biology, Sal.'

Basic biology. Was that all this was? My body having a last frantic sexual mutiny before osteoporosis and crepitude kicked in?

'Biology?' I echoed, not believing it for an instant.

'Biology,' she confirmed. 'So what the hell? Join the human race. Go with it. Have a fling with him. Shag him senseless. Get it out of your system while you've got the chance. As long as you're scrupulous about keeping it quiet, where's the harm? What Jonathan doesn't know can't hurt him.'

'What – just like that? Have an affair? Ruth, how can you suggest something so *clinical?*'

She shrugged. 'Tawdry, clinical. God, you have a rarefied take on sex, Sal. What is it? Once a month with the Laura Ashley curtains drawn, the lights all switched off and no mention of body parts allowed?' She laughed, very heartily. Then scrutinised me carefully. 'Ah, but that'll be a 'no' as of just lately, then, will it?' I managed a smile. 'Look,' she said. 'I don't mean to devalue it. I'm just a pragmatist. I'm not saying having an affair with Nick Brown would be the ideal. The ideal would be that you didn't have the hots for Nick Brown in the first place, and that you and Jonathan shuffled on through life together without it even *occurring* to either of you to shag someone else. Great. But likely? I think not. The thing is that the concept of fidelity in perpetuity probably worked just fine when everyone dropped dead before they were forty, but that's not the case any more, is it? People live longer. Relationships wear out. When you think about it logically, the only purpose of sexual attraction is to get men and women together to pass on their genes. It's not written in the stars that they should stay in love for all time. Just long enough to make their babies and rear their children. After that, well, like I said, they used to drop dead. These days they stock up on viagra and HRT and yeehah! Round two. Why not?'

'Seahorses mate for life, don't they?'

'So that's your template, then, is it? That because seahorses mate for life you have to do likewise? But you're not a seahorse. You're a *woman*, Sal. And, remember, you've as good as done the child-rearing bit.'

Ruth, of course, had not yet had children. Didn't she realise? The child-rearing bit *was* for life. 'But, OK,' she went on. 'Say that *is* your template. Then fine. Like I said, have an affair.'

I shook my head. 'I can't *do* that.'

'Why not?

'Because I simply couldn't *bear* it. It's not about sex, Ruth. That's the whole point. You're right. You're *absolutely* right about the sexual attraction, of course you are. But that isn't what makes this so dreadful. Don't you see? If it were simply that I felt sexually frustrated, I could just give myself a good slapping – or a vibrator even – and get *on* with things with Jonathan. It really, really isn't about sex. That's the whole point. That's the reason I'm so frightened. It's about everything else. All the other things we're not doing very much of – being friends, being loyal, being committed, respecting each other, enjoying each other's company, having consideration for one another, nurturing each other – '

'Blimey! You've been doing a bit of thinking, haven't you?'

'But don't you see? If we had all that then the sex wouldn't matter at all, would it? If I loved Jonathan – if I looked at Jonathan and felt all those things were a part of my life, if I felt Jonathan truly loved *me*, then it wouldn't matter that we didn't fancy the pants off each other any more, as you put it. Because sex wouldn't be *about* sex. It would be about love. Making love would be exactly that. An expression of love. An expression of –'

'Whoah! OK. I think I get the picture.' She lifted her hand and spread her fingers before her. 'OK, so the basic situation as I see it is that you've got the hots for Nick Brown, big time,' she was ticking them off as she spoke. 'You think you've fallen in love with him, you know he's not going to be around very long, but nevertheless you've still got this big panoramic picture all sorted where you float off into the sunset and grow old together – making love once you're too old and shagged out for shagging, and jam when you're both completely decrepit – you think it's something you have absolutely no control over, you think it's something, moreover, that you're not going to *get* over, you're certain you don't love your husband any more and your pretty sure he doesn't love you.' She put her hand down and nodded sagely at me. 'You're right. It is serious,' she said.

Chapter 22

Ruth had stayed another hour and been all the things you could wish for in a friend. Consoling. Sensible. Calm. Non-judgemental. Non-judgemental, above all. I was so weary of judging myself. So tired of finding myself wanting. I had, as I'd known I would, finally caved in and cried. Noisily, snottily, self-pityingly, *endlessly*, and she had sat and comforted me till I had run out of tears and then made us both a cup of coffee.

And then she had gone home and I had taken Merlin for a walk in the dark and, feeling better for being out and under the same black spangly sky as he was, I had sent Nick a message of star stuff and kisses, and without waiting for a response, or even considering phoning him for fear of what I might say, I took myself off up to bed.

I had slept for a scant two hours when I woke with my head full of horrible conviction. Ruth was right, I decided. Fidelity in perpetuity might sound like something worthy and trite that belonged on a crest or a mission statement, but it was also the thing I had promised, in a church, all those years back. That was the deal. That was what marriage was about. I was in love with Nick Brown and I didn't love Jonathan. But what of it? That was the deal.

It was one thirty, and raining again. Sheeting down in metallic rods. I went downstairs to the kitchen. The Christian Aid envelope was still sitting on the kitchen table where I'd left it, and I picked it up now, feeling wretched again. It was such a little thing, having forgotten about the marquee man coming, and yet it felt like the talisman for all the sins I was committing. Against my husband, my marriage vows, my responsibility to my children, my responsibility for my *family* – so many people's happiness and well being, all of which I was subjugating for my own selfish needs.

Ruth had talked more. Not about selfishness. On the contrary – she had talked about responsibility for *self*, and the right to individual happiness, self determination, personal fulfilment, and lots of other right-on feel-good stuff that turn of the century fidelity-challenged society soothed itself with when their guilt got too much. And though I was all too aware of her relative inexperience in matters of marriage and children, I too had found her words seductive and soothing. I'd joined a new club now. The failed. The unfaithful.

But that was then, and in my vulnerable, small hours state I could now see it for what it was. Excuses. Justifications. A large-scale attempt to absolve the guilty now the guilty numbered enough that they could get together and whine about their lot. There were the wronged and the wrongdoers, and I had become one of the latter. I had no excuses. If my happiness would make so many others unhappy then how could I *expect* any rights?

Purposely ignoring my mobile, I pulled my diary from my bag and added Mr Poselthwaite to it. Then flicked over to the pages for notes at the back. The dress fittings, the cake, the invitations, the limo. My mother's Downing Street photos. My interview – was Friday really only two days away now? –The costumes I'd still to finish for Kate's show next week. So much to do. So many things to get organised. All of them a part of the fabric of my life and yet none of them seemed anything to do with *me* any more. I felt like an impostor in my own family.

I reached for my bag again, and this time I did pick up my phone. Nick's answering message was long and loving, and had been sent only half an hour ago. He was out on his balcony, he said, and it was raining again. And he was worried about whether I was coping OK, because he wasn't sure he was, and he wanted to talk.

His words made me start crying all over again. But we still had one whole night before Jonathan returned. And resolved though I was that it should be both our first and last together, I wasn't about to give it up.

'You have a fabulous view of the stars from here.'

Funny that Ruth's words of gung-ho abandon should have had such a contradictory effect on me. I felt like someone addicted to a forty a day habit who had made a pact with themselves to kick it, and soon, but who was equally determined to eke out their last cigarette.

He was standing close behind me, arms loosely around my waist, the hairs on his chest tickling my back. I had discharged my marquee responsibility, and spent a fruitful hour in the garden with the very chatty Mr Poselthwaite, while he'd measured and tutted and measured again. Then I'd phoned Morgan and left a message on her answerphone to let her know everything had been arranged OK and that he'd be back round the following week with his quote.

I had then walked and fed Merlin and showered and re-dressed and then driven myself, tingling and uncertain, round to Nick's.

He was cooking when I'd arrived, gloriously badly. It was such a novelty, being around a male person who had the run of his own pepper mill and fish slice. More delightful still that he was so utterly inept. He was no chef. Which pleased me absurdly, and had me clucking and reaching for utensils, until his indignant refusal to let me help him made me realise, with a start, that this was what I did. I took people and cared for them. Made up for their deficiencies. But not this person. He was having none of it.

'You,' he'd said sternly, 'will sit on that stool. And you will eat a breadstick and watch me and look sexy and sip that (I held a glass of white wine in my hand) and make approving noises where appropriate. I will not learn if I don't make mistakes. Here was someone who didn't require mothering. Would I, I wondered fleetingly, be similarly pugnacious if I was attempting to put up a shelf and he offered to deal with the drill? I rather thought I might be. Funny, this constant re-analysis suddenly of the ground rules we'd based our marriages on. I felt like a new person. That I'd sloughed off a carapace and emerged shiny and new underneath. I wondered about his wife. Imagined her holding court in her kitchen and dismissing his ineffectual offers of help. I wondered how early such demarcations took hold. But I didn't wonder for long. There was something so compelling and endearing about his endeavours that once he'd finished doing battle with his bolognaise sauce, I had been so overcome with emotion and desire that I had insisted he put everything in the oven to keep warm while we went and made love in his bed..

And now we had eaten his spaghetti and lumpy sauce and defrosted profiteroles that were still icy in the middle and fed the last of the breadsticks to each other. We were still clad in two of his towels. I had fixed mine around my waist as he had, because it thrilled me so much to be a sex object and not a domestic appliance for a change. And because he would touch my breasts from time to time with the same gentle, loving, uncomplicated tenderness with which I would caress Merlin's ears. We had taken our mugs of coffee out on to the balcony. A different coffee this time. One flavoured with hazelnut. He nuzzled his face against my neck.

‘Uh-huh,’ he said. ‘Pretty neat, isn’t it?’

We continued to gaze out at the twinkling panorama. The night was perfectly still. Rainless and tar black. I wished I had more and better words to describe it, but nothing seemed up to the job. Beautiful. Breathtaking. No words were worthy.

‘I wonder if we’ll ever really know what’s out there,’ he said. ‘In our lifetime, I mean. I wonder if we’ll ever make it beyond our solar system.’

I shook my head. ‘I don’t think so. Do you? And you know? I’m glad, in a way. I like the fact that we know so little about the universe. Wouldn’t it be disappointing if we rattled off to another constellation and found it was just the same as here? Petrol stations, supermarkets – ‘

‘Branches of McDonalds.’

‘Exactly. Besides, we *do* know what’s out there.’

‘We do?’

I turned around to face him. ‘Of course we do. Neverland, silly.’ Where I felt we were now, in fact. For the moment, at least. He smiled. ‘That sure takes me back.’

‘Second star to the left and straight on till morning.’ I wished us there, badly. ‘Hang on. Or was it right?’

He grinned. ‘Oh, for sure.’

‘Yep, you’re right. It *was* right. Except the only thing is I don’t want it to be morning. I don’t *ever* want it to be morning, Nick.’

He turned me around again and dipped his chin into my neck, cupping a breast in each hand. ‘OK, then,’ he said, pointing at the night sky. ‘So how about we go off and explore somewhere else instead ? How about second star on the right, then take a left at Mars, then go round the mini roundabout just after Mercury, then straight down the dual carriageway until we hit Venus.’

‘Why Venus?’

He laughed. ‘Because she’s the goddess of love, of course, dingbat.’

‘That sounds much better.’

‘Yes, doesn’t it? Here –’

He took my mug from me and placed it with his on the table. Then swept me up suddenly. Just like that. Legs and all.

‘It’s one hell of a journey,’ he said, carrying me inside. ‘So we’d best crack on, don’t you think?’

*   *   *

When I woke, at five, I didn't know where I was. The light from a streetlamp formed window pane squares across the far wall. He was lying close beside me, one leg curved over mine, his features suspended in sleep.

I shook him gently awake. Watched his eyes blink open.

'I can't see you any more,' I told him.

His eyes stayed open. Unblinking now.

'I'm dreaming, right?'

I moved my head against the pillow slightly.

'No.'

His lips formed an 'O'. 'It's a nightmare then, is it?'

I moved my head again.

'Yes.'

'That's it?'

'That's it. I can't do this, Nick.'

He lifted his arm and tucked one hand behind his head. His hair had sprung up into lots of tiny curls as he'd slept. I had this at least. This beautiful memory. He frowned at me. 'There's nothing I can say, is there?'

It wasn't really a question.

Which was fine, because I couldn't answer him now anyhow. His face swam in front of me, distorted by my tears. He pulled me close to him.

'I love you, Sally. You know that?'

'That isn't much help.'

'I should have told you already.'

'I should have told you.'

'That you love me?'

'I love you.'

He hugged me, tight as could be. Tight till it hurt. 'But you're leaving me anyway.' His voice sounded strange.

'I have to.'

'You don't have to. Sally, you *don't.*'

Straight on till morning. 'Yes I do.'

Chapter 23

It's so easy to make judgements about people. To criticise, blame and condemn the unfaithful. Easier still to have a set of rules and morality in place and to cite them, with a tut, at those who fail to meet them. I recalled the day David, the man who used to be practice manager at Sandals when I was a new trainee, announced to us in the staff room that he was transferring to another practice because he was leaving his wife for someone else. I remembered how much I had liked David. I remembered how much he'd helped and supported me when I was new. I remembered what a nice man he was. Yet I also remembered how he had left the staff room and how the mutterings of disapproval had ricocheted around the space, burgeoning and intensifying with every utterance. How irresponsible he was. How wrong it all was. How not-on it all was. How could he? We'd all chorused. How could he be so selfish and cruel? How very slugs and snails and puppy dogs tails-ish a thing it was that he had done. I remember I had joined in. I knew nothing of his wife, his marriage, his situation, yet I judged him along with everyone else. I mainly remember how we'd all been so polite and impeccably behaved in his presence, yet how readily we'd turned the knife on him as soon as his back was there to be stabbed. To my shame, I don't think I ever really stopped to wonder about him. Whether he was all right. Whether we had any right to pass judgement on his actions with such breathtaking surety. Whether he was carrying quite enough guilt around with him already. Because to most of us who are not in unhappy marriages, the precipitate actions of those around us who are, are just another rather distasteful example of the selfish pursuit of their own ends. So much judgement, based on so little knowledge. I wondered how he was now.

Fidelity was all about sex, of course. It didn't matter what went on in your head as long as you remained sexually faithful. Which struck me as a bit of a farce. Having secret sex with other people for recreation – playing around – might be *called* infidelity, but on its own it was something far less serious. True infidelity, it seemed to me, was not about having sex with someone else. It was actually about having love for someone else.

Which was not the best job-lot of cheery thoughts with which to be greeting your husband and daughter from Gatwick airport at tea-time on a Thursday afternoon, but as that was the one that was lodged in my fore-brain, that was, of necessity, what I was thinking. But, blinking now at the 'baggage in hall' sign above me, I knew I must step smartly off the rollercoaster now and fix myself firmly back on the flat, grey tarmac of my life.

I wondered if they'd notice my swollen eyes.

Kate was already on her mobile as they came through the arrivals door towards me. Talking to Carl, no doubt, to arrange their next date. I envied her her freedom from care. She looked tall, beautiful, bronzed, serene. Jonathan was lugging both cases, as ever, and a small flame of compassion lit somewhere inside me for this man, this greying and rather dignified man who knew nothing of what was going on in my heart. I smiled and waved my arm about enthusiastically, as if the action might slap me back into some semblance of order. But it was if I was doing it underwater, through a mask.

Kate, as I had dreaded but expected, went out only half an hour after we arrived back home. No longer than it took her to press her bag of dirty washing upon me with exhortations to pleeeease wash her black jeans and jacket before the end of exams party the following night. And then it was just us. Him and me, him and her. Because as far as Jonathan was concerned it was his reliable and faithful wife who was sitting opposite him at the kitchen table, eating the chicken and salad I'd hastily prepared and sharing a decent bottle of wine. And why would he not? It was an ordinary Thursday. Apart from a suitcase in the hallway and some duty free gin – Bob and Androulla were due to arrive Saturday and they drank it by the bucket – in all other respects it was a straightforward evening. Duty had taken up where my heart had left off.

But there was one thing about ordinary married life that was beginning to loom large over our evening. I could feel it, even as Jonathan passed me the pepper, commented wryly on the state of the government's policies on Railtrack, laughed a little too heartily when I made some small joke. And even as his absence of irritability and his lack of curt rejoinders was looking like a bit of welcome relief from the gruntiness of his company on a normal Thursday evening, I was already feeling beneath for its real root. I knew very well why he was being nice to me. It was because he wanted to have sex.

We finished our supper, watched a dreary programme about the storming of some twelfth century castle or other, and then the tail end of a made for TV movie that had lots of post-watershed shots of people having sex in unlikely locations. It was about then that chill fingers of panic begin to press against the hard knot of pain inside me. But before I could grab the remote and expunge it, Jonathan announced that he'd had enough television and that he thought it was about time to toddle off to bed.

'You coming?' he asked me. For this was the shorthand.

Rusty, I found myself thinking. Wasn't that what secretaries put on job applications? Fifty words per minute typing and rusty shorthand. Life, work, stress, tennis, aches, pains, cricketing injuries, gruelling extractions, the M23, flood, fire, there being an R in the month, me being out, him being away; Whatever the reason the net result didn't vary. There wasn't a lot of sex in our marriage. Sex was a B-list recreational activity that filled in a gap in his schedule. Something to do once a fortnight or so, when there wasn't a more pressing fixture on the cards. The trouble was, it had ever been thus. I had met and fallen in love with a man who was still grieving for the young wife he'd so tragically lost and stumbling miserably through the minefield of single parenting. Was it any wonder his sexual appetite was slight? And what about me? The naïve, rather timid, somewhat self-conscious me? I'd been, of course, what any adoring young wife would be. Patient, understanding, and largely undemanding. And then we'd had Kate and we were both little interested. It was all so painfully obvious now it made me wretched to consider it. Such folly. I'd been too young, too inexperienced, too *stupid* to realise that it didn't have to – wasn't supposed to – be this way.

But sex was a part of a marriage, like any other, and we had not had sex now for three or four weeks. Sex was due. And that was all there was to it. He was hovering by the door jamb, one hand in his pocket.

I nodded and turned to finish clearing the kitchen. Yes, I was coming, I said. I wouldn't be long. I toyed, for some minutes, with the idea of lingering. Just long enough that he'd give up and go to sleep. But something told me that tonight this plan would be fruitless.

I could do this, I told myself. I have to do this. I *have* to.

So slowly, compliantly, on my two guiltily feet, I took myself off up the stairs. Up to bed.

He'd turned off the lights and drawn both sets of curtains. And even before I had climbed in beside him, engaged in this loveless love we'd be making, I knew, as surely as I knew anything, that I'd never want to do this with Jonathan again.

Time flies when you're having fun, they say. But they are wrong. The week – this one short week in my life—had felt like a life in it's own right. Friday dawned, recollection flooded through me, and with it a dull ache the like of which I had never felt before. Would I feel like this now, every morning, forever?

'You're up early,' Jonathan commented as I pattered around the bedroom, opening cupboard doors and inspecting their contents. I would wear my blue suit. Conservative. Sombre. But with my pink blouse. Drug u Like would approve.

'It's my interview today.'

'Interview?' He rolled over in bed.

'Yes,' I said, stupidly grateful for his absence of memory. His lack of interest. I was stockpiling shots of guilt-vaccine. The better to make all the guilt go away. I didn't know what to do about the pain. 'My interview for manager. It's at eleven fifteen.'

'Oh, yes,' he mumbled. He had elected not to go into the surgery until after lunch and was obviously intent on staying in bed for a while. He squinted across at the alarm clock. 'But it's only seven.'

I ripped the cardboard packaging from a new pair of tights.

'I know. But I'm going into work first. I have to make some extra copies of my CV.' I had to do no such thing. I simply had to get out of the house.

He grunted and nodded, eyes still half closed.

'You haven't forgotten you've got to go and pick up that Wagner CD from Spillers, have you? I promised Bob I'd have it here for him when they arrive. D'you know if they managed to get it in OK?'

I didn't. Bob and bloody Androulla. Whatever else I needed in my life right now, it was not them for the weekend. I nodded.

'No. But I'm sure they will have,' I said.

He smiled sleepily. 'Well. Good luck, then.'

I nodded. 'Thanks.' Though I wasn't sure what he was wishing me luck for.

The offices now occupied by Drug U Like inc. were in a tall mirrored building just outside Crawley, in one of those business parks where fountains spewed chilly spray over architecturally sculpted arrangements of neatly clipped grass. I pushed the revolving door open and walked across similarly shorn acres of pink carpeting to where a trim receptionist, dressed uncannily like me, smiled a welcome from behind her desk.

Nick had sent me another text message, wishing me luck and saying I didn't need it, and telling me he didn't know how he was going to function without me, that he was hurting, that he was sorry, but that he understood. Then N for Nick, and seven capital X's in a row. I had stood in the car park and counted each one.

There were two other applicants for the post, one of them a guy I was on nodding terms with and who was senior optom from a smaller branch in Croydon, and the other a woman who was a manager from somewhere up north who had moved down south with her husband's job and was looking for a transfer. And me. Who had moved to somewhere else altogether and who was looking to find her way back. The receptionist put a tick against my name and directed me to the eleventh floor.

Strangely, I was not in the least nervous.

Which was presumably why I got the job.

'Well, well, well,' said Russell, handing me my drink and genuflecting flamboyantly. Sweetly, they had both demanded that I go with them to the pub for a celebratory drink. He tipped his head. 'Are we going to have to call you ma'am now?'

'Absolutely!' said Ruth, who was almost as pleased for me as if she'd got the promotion herself. How selfless and precious her friendship was. I was so glad she wasn't going to leave.

I sipped at my drink and tried hard to pretend I was as happy about my promotion as they both presumed I'd be. Well, not both, really. I had already told Ruth I intended to stop seeing Nick. She'd thought I was crazy. But then, she would.

We hadn't stayed long celebrating at the pub, however. Russell was off to the cinema with his latest acquisition – a girl from cosmetics, of whom Ruth violently disapproved.

'Really, Russ,' she'd chided him in the pub car park. 'She's barely out of school!'

'She's nineteen!' he protested.

Ruth sniffed. 'A very *young* nineteen.'

Russell pulled his shades from his jacket pocket. 'And I'm a very young twenty nine,' he said, putting them on.

'You said it,' said Ruth. She seemed to have it in for poor Russell tonight.

He swung his keys from his hand. 'And what's that supposed to mean?'

Ruth hitched the strap of her handbag on her shoulder and sniffed.

'It means it *figures,* Russ. Obviously way too young to handle a real grown up woman.'

Russell pointed his key fob and unlocked his car. He looked Ruth up and down. 'What on earth makes you think I'd want to?' he said.

And then I went to Tesco. Where I wandered, sightless, up and down the aisles, gathering the things I'd need for the weekend. Jonathan, thankfully, wasn't in when I got home.

'He's gone off to his tennis club committee meeting,' Kate informed me as she helped me unload the shopping. She was glowing, her tan setting off her luminous young skin, her spangly black jeans like a starscape themselves. 'He said to remind you about the CD. Oh, and Debbie rang to say if you got a moment she'd be really grateful if you could do a bit of work on the Electra costume, because the zip's gone again and she thinks it might be better if we use hooks and eyes instead.' She patted my wrist and grinned. 'I said you would, of course. Oh, and I nearly forgot. Morgan rang as well. About meeting up with you or something? Wanted to talk to you, anyway.'

'What about? Did she say?'

Kate shook her head. 'I think she was hoping you'd be able to go up next week. Something about her dress fitting ? I told her I didn't think you'd be able to, what with my show and everything. She sounded a bit off about it, but no surprise there. She's been a right rat bag lately.'

So why had she not met up with me and my mother last week, then? 'Oh, come on, Kate,' I said. 'She's just stressed, that's all.'

She pointed at me, suddenly. 'Why've you got that suit on, by the way? Not like you to get all poshed up.'

'I had my interview.'

'Oh, yes! Of course you did. Sorry. Did you get it?'

'I got it.'

'Wicked, mum.'

She gave me a hug and my eyes filled with tears. Whoosh. Just like that. This was no way to live.

I drove her round to Amanda's and let her happy chatter soothe me. Then back, under a violet sky, along the very same lane where I'd first met him all that time ago. I slowed up on the accelerator. So long ago now. Yet the twin furrows that had been made by my tyre tracks were still there, where I'd made them. Two muddy dips in the flower flecked grass.

I was crying properly by the time I was back in our lane. Still crying as I pulled frozen prawns from the freezer. Still crying while I stood and marinated the meat.

I poured myself a Pimms. Well, I'd been promoted, hadn't I? And then a glass of amaretto while I finished off the cheesecake . And I cried into that as well.

Chapter 24

Bob and Androulla. Bob and bloody Androulla. I should have seen the writing on the icing on the cake.

Saturday evening in the jolly Matthews household. Saturday evening and a jolly dinner party in the jolly Matthews household. What fun. And we had got on to the wedding, of course. Androulla was big on weddings. I don't think she ever really got over the trauma when her own progeny, Richard, decided to get hitched. A boy I remembered mainly for his exhibition burping (and who was now a gingery thirty something and a biscuit wholesaler in Leeds) he had zipped off with his girlfriend and got married on the sly with two council workers as witnesses. So I should have realised Androulla wasn't going to let this one slip by her. We were never *not* going to talk about the wedding.

'Oh, dear. That *is* a pity,' she said in saccharin tones while perusing the order of service. The latest in a long line of perusals. She had been perusing, tight lipped, for most of the evening. She had already perused most of the contents of Morgan's wedding file, from the cake (a bit modern?) to the fireworks (a touch pretentious?) to the pew allocation (Sally, *really* – tinkling laughter – the Pattersons at the *front*?). She peered at me over the grapes Bob was passing to her. 'A pity you didn't think to consult me about the service first, Sally. I could have told you about the hymn.' Hymn? Consult? What was she on about now? 'Shame on you Jonathan,' she went on, frowning at him. 'How could you forget about the hymn?'

Jonathan, ruddy from too much port already, slurped from his glass and shrugged.

'Oh, I've kept well out of it, Andy' he muttered. 'Am *keeping* well out of it.' He and Bob exchanged a grimace.

'Good man,' said Bob.

'What *about* the hymn?' I said.

'Praise My Soul, of course,' she finished, putting the sheet back in Morgan's plastic file and closing the popper with a snap. She laced her fingers together. 'Praise My Soul The King of Heaven. Did you never think to mention it, Jonathan?'

He looked non-plussed. 'Er, nope,' he replied.

'Mention what?' I persisted, growing irritated now.

Androulla smiled sweetly at me.

'That we'd always said it would be the one Morgan would have on her wedding day. It's rather special, you see.'

'Special?' This sounded ominous.

'Well, perhaps it's not for me to say (which meant it was). I'm only her *God*mother, after all. But you remember that conversation, don't you Jonathan? When we were down in Cowes? Of course you do, darling.' She twittered for a moment.

I looked hard at Jonathan. 'Cowes?'

'Er, vaguely,' he said.

Androulla drew her one-hair-wide eyebrows together. 'Vaguely? Tut tut. How could you have forgotten? Tut! Still, I suppose it's not for me to – '

A lot of tutting for someone who was so busy supposing she should shut up about it. '*What's* not for you to say, Androulla?' I interrupted.

'Oh, it's nothing. Just seems a shame, that's all. If you'd only given me a ring, Sally, I could have stopped you before you went and – well. Never mind.' She looked like she was minding very much, however, her shrivelled lips now pursed in disapproval.

'What *about* it?' I said again. 'What about Praise My Soul? What's the big deal about Praise My Soul?'

Androulla sniffed. And put on her 'well I didn't want to make a point of it but now you've made me' face. She was very good at those.

'Well, it's just that it was Tricia's favourite, you see. She'd had it at *her* wedding, (she looked simperingly at Jonathan), as did her mother before her, and her mother before her. It's a tradition in the family. We'd always said Morgan would have it too, of course. Tricia used to tell me how much she was looking forward to…well, you can imagine how much it *matters*, can't you? That Tricia will still be able to look down upon her daughter and…well. As I say, I do feel it would be remiss of us not to respect her wishes.'

Remiss? Looking down? Upon? *Wishes*? Oh, *please*. And this tosh from a woman who, to the best of my knowledge, had not set foot in a church since her best bloody friend's funeral. And silly me. To imagine we'd *not* get round to talking about Tricia. *You should have consulted me* indeed. I was getting unimaginably, dangerously cross with her now.

'Oh, well,' I said, rising from the table. 'Can't be helped. Morgan's chosen now. Immortal Invisible and Love Divine.'

But Androulla was not to be deflected from her cause.

'Ah,' she said. 'But at *that* point she wasn't aware –'she paused here, to roll her eyes heavenwards. I could feel my knuckles clench around the plates in my hand. '– just how much it *meant* to her mother, was she? Hmm, Jonathan? Yes?' She pulled her napkin from her lap and smiled at me. 'But don't worry. I'll have a word with her.'

'Androulla, 'I said levelly. 'There's really no point. The hymns have already been chosen.'

'Well, that's as maybe, Sally. But I still think Morgan should be made aware, don't you? I mean, who are *we* to deny her the chance to pay tribute to her mother's memory?'

I am not one of life's arguers. I am Mrs non-confrontation personified. I am a negotiated settlement on legs. Or at least I thought I was. Being in love with Nick Brown, I have decided, has done curious things to my temper.

The pasta fandango I could cope with. My fault. Silly me. I should have realised Androulla would be on some twitty prohibitive diet or other. She had made ludicrous unscientific exploitative diet – sorry – health management regimes a career. The no-wheat nonsense. The dairy embargo. Wasn't that what homo-sapiens *ate*? She'd have me boiling up nettles for her next. And how long, I conjectured, before she started paying visits accompanied by portable oxygen and a tube up her nose?

The pillow debacle I could cope with also. Who am I to come between a woman and her stuffing preferences? And it's no bother *really* to drive off into Crawley to replace my shoddy guest bedware with duck down and goose.

But I could not cope with this. I could not.

'By which you mean *me*, I take it?' I said, with a quickening pulse. I started gathering up cutlery. 'Anyway, it's academic. Everything's already with the printers.'

Androulla leaned behind her and scooped up her handbag from the floor.

'Now you're being silly,' she said, as if I was five. 'Anyway, I don't doubt they'll be able to change it. Leave it with me. I'll have a little word with Morgan in the morning and then I'll get on to them for you first thing on Monday. I'm sure we'll be able to sort everything out. Do you have their number to hand?'

A little nuclear warhead exploded somewhere inside my head.

'No,' I said. 'I don't have their number to hand. And you don't need it anyway, Androulla, because I don't need you to ring them.'

'But –'

'But nothing,' I said, slapping the lid down on the butter dish. 'The hymns have already been chosen.'

I was being completely unreasonable. Of course I was. Why the hell *shouldn't* Morgan be given the opportunity to change her mind about her hymns? It was her wedding wasn't it? It was pathetic of me to dig my heels in like this, and yet, curiously, it was that very knowledge that drove me on. For this was not about hymns. It could equally well have been the pillows. This was about us. And she knew it.

Two pink spots appeared on her leathery cheeks. 'Now you really *are* being silly,' she said, refusing to meet my eye now, and still rootling in her bag for a pen. 'It'll be a terrible shame if –

I could feel a violent heat in my own cheeks. 'A shame if *what?* If I don't let you turn Morgan's wedding into a memorial service? A shame if I don't let you hijack the day? Tell you what. Why don't we just go and dig her up and have done with it?'

Everyone's mouths dropped open. Jonathan winced. I was being outrageous and cruel but I couldn't seem to stop myself. 'Why not, eh? *Eh?* Tell you what. How about if I just don't turn up at all. Then I'll be out of the way and you can erect a little Tricia effigy and make a speech about her after the toasts. Would that suit? I'm sure you'd do a fine job, Androulla.'

I banged the four cheese plates on top of one another and stalked off to the other side of the kitchen. Why oh why hadn't we eaten in the dining room? At least then I'd have a reason to escape.

'Well, that's lovely, I must say,' she said. 'I mention this one little thing, and you fly off the handle!'

I whirled around. 'It's *not* one little thing! It's *never* been one little thing! It's everything. The flowers – oh, dear, I think Tricia would have wanted roses. The guest list – yes, you're right. Terribly remiss of me to have forgotten to invite Tricia's second cousin from

Godalming. The bloody invitations, even – God! What was I thinking! How could I possibly forget to make mention of her name somewhere on them! A footnote, perhaps. From Jonathan and Sally and Tricia-her-*real*-mother who'd just love to invite you except – oops! Darn it. She's been dead twenty years.'

Jonathan stood up.

'Sally!' he barked at me.

He could bark all he liked. 'And don't you Sally me!' I spat. 'You, of all people, should be with me on this! How dare she come into my house and tell me how to run my own daughter's wedding! How dare she!'

Androulla, hot pink under her diarrhoea coloured tan, stood up as well. And now she did look at me. With enough venom to fell an elephant. 'But she's *not* your daughter! And I think it's high time you accepted that there are other people who have a right to – '

'A right to *what?* Come on, tell me. Tell me what exactly gives you the right to come in here and treat me like a second rate bloody surrogate mother. I would *really* like to know. Because she's not *your* daughter either!'

'Now you're being ridiculous, Sally.'

'I am *not* being ridiculous. I am sick and tired of you criticising me. You never let up, do you? It's always been the same! 'I think you'll find Tricia would have done things *this* way, Sally. 'Are you sure you should be doing that *that* way, Sally?'. How do you think that's always made me feel, eh? Well, I'll let you into a secret, shall I? She's been dead twenty years! *Twenty!* Morgan barely remembers her! And you can wipe that expression off your face right away. It was nothing to *do* with me, OK? I didn't kill her. I didn't bury her. I certainly didn't try to take her place. But Morgan was three! Take some reality on board will you? I *am* Morgan's mother, how ever much it pains you. Oh, and for your information, it just so happens that she chose Love De-bloody-sodding-vine for *me*.'

I banged down the cheese platter and fled the room at that point. Before I took the grape scissors and chopped her into tiny pieces. Jonathan, predictably, was after me moments later, his feet heavy and staccato on the staircase.

'What the *hell* was all that about?' he hissed at me the minute the bedroom door was shut behind him.

'*What?*'

'You! Lashing into Andy like that! What the hell did you think you were doing? She's in floods!'

'Good!' I snapped. 'About bloody time too. If I never see the witch again it'll be way too soon!' My hands were still shaking. I couldn't believe how angry I was. Give me one excuse, I thought. Just one. And I will be out of the front door before you can say fairy fucking Godmother.

'That was bloody obvious. What the hell got into you? How could you be so vitriolic? The poor woman! She was only – '

'Poor *woman*?? How could *I*? Jonathan, the woman is monstrous! Don't you see that? Have you *never* been able to see that? Don't you realise what she's about? She's never forgiven me, never!'

'Forgiven you for *what*, for God's sake?'

'For *existing*, you idiot! For coming into your life and stealing her little girl away from her!'

'*What?*'

'God, you really don't see it, do you?' I shrieked. 'You never have!!'

'What the hell's got *into* you?' he said again, eyes bulging with shock. 'I've never heard such ranting! Christ, Sally, she was only trying to help, for God's sake! I know full well she drives you up the wall at times, but that's *your* problem, not hers.'

'*WHAT?*'

'You heard.'

'Oh, yes. I heard. But I'd like to know quite what you meant by that. What did you mean by that?'

He didn't speak for a second. Long enough to make me realise he was going to say something I wouldn't want to hear. Which he did.

'*Your* problem,' he said again. 'The chip on your shoulder has always been so bloody massive you can't see it. *Stealing*? For God's sake! You're paranoid! '

'*WHAT?*'

He drew a hand over his forehead and exhaled noisily. 'Look,' he said, waggling a finger in front of my face. 'She's *not* trying to take over. She just wants to be involved. She *is* Morgan's Godmother. Don't forget that. Why can't you let her? What the hell difference will it make to you to let her get involved a little? You're always complaining you have too much to do – so let *her* do some of it. If you don't like her suggestions all you have to do is say so, for God's sake! Not reduce the poor woman to tears! What's the *matter* with you?'

'What's the *matter* with me? God, Jonathan, you really don't have a clue, do you? Just say so, eh? Ri-ight. Just like that. God, you make me so *mad*!'

He stared at me. It was true. He really didn't have a clue. It felt like a punch.

'Look,' he said, lowering his voice now and frowning. 'Come back downstairs and let's sort this out.'

'Absolutely not,' I said. 'No way. Not a chance.'

'But you can't just –'

'Oh, yes I can, Jonathan. You just watch me.'

My expression must have told him he was wasting his time. He turned on his heel and marched out of the room.

A dismal ending to a miserable week. And an inauspicious start to the next one. Had I an atom of intelligence, I might have seen it coming. And I might have stayed in bed for the duration.

We had made up in – us grown ups – after a fashion, in the morning, in that over-polite and rather nauseating way that grown ups are required to do. It was a necessary evil. Right though I was about bloody Androulla, I still had to be a grown up. Yes, she hated me. Yes, I had stolen her little girl from her. Yes, it was all to be expected. No matter that it was actually *her* problem, in fact. It was not my fault that she'd not been able to have another child after Richard. Or anything to do with me that she should become a full time nanny to Morgan when Tricia had died. Or that the four of them (in Cowes, *dar*ling) had agreed that should one couple die then the other would adopt their precious babes. Or that she saw Tricia's death as largely the same scenario, except in the sleeping arrangements.

Grrr . It was nothing to *do* with me. I was still in bloody college. But in Androulla's head that made little difference. I came, I stole, I conquered. There was nothing to be done about it, except make up and be polite. But *only* after a fashion. I would, I'd agreed, speak to Morgan about the hymn, and I would, should she wish it to be changed, try to change it. But only because by then I'd already spoken to Morgan, who, as expected, cared about Praise my Soul not a jot. A pyrrhic victory, perhaps – I had now morphed, I knew, into Mrs Nasty from Bitchville, particularly in Jonathan's somewhat myopic eyes – but I didn't care any more. I was sick of it all, I was hurting for Nick, and I'd had enough rows to last me a lifetime. Or so I thought.

Morgan's absence of care in the matter of memorial hymn selections, however, had not been out of deference to me. She'd asked me again if I would come up and have lunch with her, and had sounded dismayed when I'd said I couldn't manage it. Yet she wouldn't elucidate why.

'Don't worry,' she'd said, with an edge of irritation in her voice. 'It was nothing important. I guess you're up to your eyes in it with Kate's big production.'

I ignored the tone. 'You said it!' I answered brightly. 'But, tell you what. I've got Wednesday off next week. How about I come up early and we spend the whole day together? Lunch, shopping – whatever you want to do.'

'Wednesday,' she repeated. 'I don't know. I'll have to see. Yes. Why not?' She sounded distracted.

'Morgan, look, if it *is* something urgent, I really wish you'd tell me – '

'No, no,' she replied. 'Just some things I wanted to run through with you. That's all. If you're too busy, they'll just have to wait, won't they? Wednesday week. Fine.'

'You're *sure?*'

'I'm sure,' she said firmly. 'Nothing important. *Really*. I'll see you on Friday for the show. OK?'

I put down the phone with the unsettling impression that her 'nothing' was something I should be worrying about.

On Tuesday, however, I received the final invitation list and table plan from her in the post, together with a chirpy, much-more-Morgan-like note. Perhaps it *was* nothing. I gave the list a read through. On our side the usual suspects (plus bloody Androulla on the top table, the COW), and on Cody's, a mind boggling, tongue twisting selection of double barrelled, unpronounceable names.

'What about Carl?' asked Kate, who'd come home from her rehearsal in her usual artistic high-dudgeon.

She sat down beside me. 'Where's he on this plan?' She pointed at the A4 sheet and frowned. 'He's not on there,' she said. 'Why not?'

I had, in fact, addressed this problem already, when Morgan and I had first run through the guest list. As it was, I now felt Carl *should* be invited. Contrary to Morgan's opinion that he was a yob and a low-life, he had turned out to be a perfectly OK young bloke, and Kate was clearly serious about him. So what that she wasn't quite seventeen? It may well turn out she'd get through half a dozen Carls before settling down with someone. But on the other hand it might not. Plus I felt she could do with some like minded support among the Cholmondley-Wotsits and Flibberty-Giblets. There'd be precious few people there she had anything in common with.

But Morgan had been adamant. For a start, she'd pointed out, he'd be as good as on his own. Unless we wanted to stick him on the grandparents table, or slot him into a group of Morgan's media friends. Which was, she'd said firmly, an absolute no-no. He could come to the disco, and that was final. And, anyway, what was wrong with that?

'Because, well, because he isn't, Kate,' I said now. 'There's only so many people can be accommodated in the marquee and we did say it would be – look, he *is* invited to the disco,'

'Oh, right. Well that's really nice. Really sisterly of her.'

'– and I'm sure he wouldn't want to come to the wedding himself anyway. I mean, you'll be on the top table and busy with all the formal stuff, and, I mean, who would he sit with? Gran? He'd be a bit stuck out on a limb, wouldn't he? And is it really going to be something he'd want to spend –'

'Mother! That is *entirely* beside the point! He's my boyfriend! How could she not invite him?'

'Kate, look. I know he's your boyfriend, and I know he's very special to you, but it's simply not possible for us to invite everyone who happens –'

'To be as insignificant as the bride's sister's boyfriend. Well that's fine, Mum. Just fine. I'll leave you to tell her she can find another bridesmaid. If he doesn't go then neither do I.'

So then I had a row with Morgan.

'No,' she said snappily, when I called her on the Wednesday morning. 'Absolutely not. Tell her to stop being so precious. I'm not having some loud mouthed spotty oik at my wedding and that's final.'

This was so unlike Morgan I was open-mouthed with shock. And Carl was not loud mouthed or spotty or an oik. I said so.

‘That’s not the point, Mum! I don’t want some bloke I don’t know from Adam leering out from my wedding photos, thank you very much. Just because he happens to be the yob Kate’s currently infatuated with. No.’

I wasn’t altogether sure this wasn’t more to do with the Hillbilly-Twiglets and Mabelthorpe-Sprouts, and Morgan’s anxiety that someone like Carl would show her up. Or, indeed, the ‘nothing’ she wasn’t talking about. I didn’t say so. Instead I said, ‘couldn’t we find a space for him somewhere? Just to keep Kate sweet? There’s no point having all this bad feeling over something so unimportant, is there? Perhaps we *could* squeeze him in on Gran’s table –’

‘No! It’s *my* wedding, mum,’ she went on. ‘Not hers. And as far as I’m concerned it’s up to me who I invite. Isn’t it?’

Not quite. ‘Er, largely,’ I said carefully.

‘So it’s not.’

‘Well, yes it *is*, but we also have to consider – ‘

‘Fine then,’ she said. ‘Invite who you like. Invite the East Grinstead W.I. if you want to. Don’t mind me. I’m only the bride. Do what you like, mum. *Fine.*’

And then she put down the phone.

I called her straight back but the line was engaged. Not a bit like Morgan at all.

On Wednesday afternoon, she rang back and apologised, and said we’d look at the seating plan when she came down on Friday night to see Kate’s show. Though not to me – I was at work – but to my mother, who was by now installed with us and on backstage-duties (and who I hadn’t – thank the heavens – had any rows with as yet).

She’d then phoned me at work to let me know, bless her. She too had noticed that Morgan sounded a bit strained, and not like her usual sunny self.

‘But it’s just wedding nerves,’ she’d reassured me when I got home that evening. ‘Never known a wedding yet that didn’t cause family arguments. Don’t worry, dear. It’ll all come out in the wash. Now then, I’ve hunted high and low, but I’m all out of red cotton. D’you think anyone’s likely to notice if I finish off this torn gusset with the taupe?’

Thursday was row free, thankfully, though somewhat hectic on account of the fact that Kate’s first show was that evening, so I had to work through my lunch in order to leave early. I was losing weight at an alarming rate. It was all being gobbled up by the thing in my stomach. The worm of pain that was eating away at me. Nick hadn't been at Amberley at all during the week, and though on Monday I had thought this to be a good thing, I was wrong. Each day without him was worse than the last, and I was getting to the stage now where I felt that if I *didn't* see him, I would quite possibly just curl up and die. Every new row seemed to make me shrivel further. Just *see* him, that was all I asked. Just a restorative glimpse. I wondered for the eight-millionth time since last Friday whether he'd be coming to the Drug U Like dinner. I didn't know the answer and there was no one I could ask.

'Of course he'll be going,' said Ruth, on the Friday. 'Absolute certainty, I would imagine. But what good will that be to you? You'll have Max with you, won't you?.'

This was her latest appellation for Jonathan, after I'd told her about the weekend's debacle. She had found the whole business uproariously funny, and had taken to calling me the second Mrs de Winter. And Androulla was Mrs Danvers, of course. Quite so. The thought was very satisfying, somehow. Though I hoped she wouldn't be urging me to leap off a balcony and plunge to my death any time soon. Hoped, but hadn't ruled out. I shook my head.

'Jonathan's not coming,' I said. 'He's running some Dental tutorial in Brighton on Saturday, so he's staying down there for the night.'

Ruth tutted at me, grinning. 'Too much bother to zip back, eh? That's *highly* convenient for you.'

'No it *isn't!* Ruth, I *told* you. I have made up my mind. I have absolutely no intention of seeing Nick again.'

'Yeah, yeah. And I'm a vestal virgin.'

I wished she wouldn't keep doing that. I was feeling wobbly enough about it as it was. How many times had I picked up my mobile this week? How many times had I nearly caved in? Oh, God. *Billions*. It was like a disease. I tutted at her irritably. 'I wish Jonathan *was* coming to be honest, because at least then I wouldn't feel so vulnerable, but he hates that sort of thing. No. That's not true. He likes that sort of thing, but only in its right and proper format. Him big shot professional, me dutiful little wife.'

When I got home from work I fully expected to find Morgan there, but she still hadn't arrived.

‘Friday evening traffic,’ suggested my mother, who was once again beavering with a thimble on her finger, the contortions of the Debbie Davies Dancers having put paid already to many a badly sewn seam. ‘Don’t fret so!’ she said soothingly. ‘You’re looking peaky enough as it is. Go and take the dog for a tinkle. She’ll *get* here.’

‘Probably decided she can’t be bothered,’ observed Kate as I clipped on Merlin’s lead. ‘Probably too busy hob nobbing with her posh London friends to faff with something as provincial as our little show.’

‘Kate, how can you say that?’ I chided. ‘Gran’s right. It’s probably just heavy traffic, that’s all.’

But by the time I had returned from walking Merlin she still hadn’t arrived, and I began to find myself wondering if Kate wasn’t right after all. Morgan had said more than once this week that she was up to her eyes in it. But to just not turn up. No phone call or anything. It really wasn’t on. Yet another thing to worry about. Why was it that it took being a mother to understand the simple fact that mothers *worried?* Oh, God – why was life doing this to me? This week of all weeks. Was it payback time? *Was* it karma, perhaps? I tried calling her several times, but there was no answer from either her flat or her mobile, so I had to content myself with leaving a message, plus a note in the kitchen with directions to the community hall, after which we set off there ourselves. Starlight Express. How I wanted to be on one. With Nick. Second star to the right, please, driver. And straight on till we get someplace else.

I had never seen *Starlight Express*, and it was more enjoyable that I had perhaps expected, my previous exposure to the Debbie Davies Dancers having been an ambitious re-working of the Tempest, set, bizarrely, in a post-holocaust London and featuring a variety of unusual costumes, many of which seemed to be made out of plastic lemonade bottles, and which rattled and squeaked with such violence and regularity that they drowned out best part of the script . Oh, and the sound system exploded in Act two.

So, scope for improvement, and they all did magnificently. The scenery stayed up, no one fell over, no one fluffed their lines, the costumes hung together and no bottoms were laid bare, and nothing, as far as the audience could tell anyway, spontaneously combusted or broke. Indeed, so slick and polished was the production that the only small blip in the proceedings was when just at the big scene between Dinah and Diesel, my mobile phone went off.

I pulled it from my bag as soon as the show ended. The call had been from Morgan. She'd left a message on voicemail.

'She's not coming,' I told my mum as we made our way back to the car park with Kate's costume shortly after. The dining car herself was staying on for half an hour to soak up the plaudits with her friends. Amanda's dad would be bringing her home. Her wonderful performance had made me more tearful still.

'Well, there wouldn't be much point now, would there?' She waited while I opened up the boot, then lay Kate's costume carefully across it. I followed suit with her hat. 'No matter,' she said brightly. 'I doubt Kate really cared that much. And perhaps she can come down tomorrow instead.'

'She didn't say so.'

'Well, you can ring her in the morning, can't you? No point fretting about it now.' She paused at the side of the car, looking at me over the dew-frosted roof, her hair made orange candyfloss by the streetlamp behind her. 'Are you all right, dear?' she said suddenly. 'You haven't seemed yourself at all just lately. Is it Ruth?'

'Ruth?' It took a moment for me to work out what she meant. So it is with liars. I put my car key in the lock.

'Are you worrying about her?'

I shook my head, feeling dreadful that I'd made such a big deal of it.

My mother tipped hers to one side and looked at me thoughtfully.

'Something else, then?'

I shook my head again. Shrugged. 'Really, mum. Nothing. Nothing in particular.'

'Well,' she said, with an expression that made it clear she wasn't fooled in the least,'You're doing way too much, you know.'

'Mum, I'm *fine*. Anyway, you're a fine one to talk.'

'I'm *retired*, Sally. I have no one to look after, no house to run, no family to organise, no job to worry about and nothing else to do. I watch you, you know, rushing hither and thither, never a minute to yourself. You need to slow down a bit. Stop running around after everyone –'she paused to smile. 'Me included, I'm ashamed to say. Look, I know it's a busy time and there's lots to arrange, but it *will* happen. You don't have to organise every little thing yourself. Darling, the world won't end if you leave it to look after itself for five minutes, you know.'

I nodded. Swallowed hard. Got into the car. How could she know it already had?

Chapter 25

How I would have loved to tell my mother. How I would have loved to sit down in the car at that moment and just let it all out. Not because I felt it would change anything. Not because I thought it would help with anything, but simply because I knew she'd forgive me. That she'd love me not an atom less after the telling.

Nick *was* to be at the dinner, as it turned out. I knew this because Mr Monroe (the area director, and he of the interview) had telephoned me at work on Saturday morning to let me know that as we were both 'going solo' as he put it, he wondered if I'd mind if he took me off Mr Brown's table, and allow him and his fellow directors the benefit of my company instead. They were sharing a mini-bus. I said that would be fine and gave him my address, my heart thudding at this disquieting news. If he'd not been going I would have felt safe. Were he going and sitting on my table, it would have felt dangerous. But there and *not* there, as in not within reach, would be frustrating, difficult, exquisitely painful. I wondered if Nick himself had had anything to do with it. I wondered if I shouldn't just get on and stop wondering. Yes, that would be best. Put him out of my mind.

A sensible decision all round, I figured. Out of my mind. Out of my life. Out of my unhappy little universe.

By the time I had returned from work, my mother and Kate had already left for the community hall, leaving me a precious hour of solitude before girding my loins – with something steely and unbroachable, ideally – and heading off to the dinner. I had about as much interest in going as I had in particle physics, but as it looked like my career was now blossoming in direct relation to the withering of my heart, I knew I must make some sort of effort.

And still no word from Morgan. What *was* going on with her? I checked the phone five times before leaving the house. Something was wrong. I could sense it so keenly.

And my senses were not, it seemed, wrong.

My mobile rang halfway through the main course. Not wishing to suffer the same embarrassment as I had the previous evening, I had switched it to vibrate, so it took several seconds and an astonished guffaw from beside me before I realised what was going on.

'Good grief!' said Mr Monroe. 'Do you keep a pet gerbil in there, Sally?'

He was pointing to my evening bag, which I'd placed on the table in front of me, and which was now making juddering progress towards the cruet. I put my cutlery down and picked it up. The phone inside zizzed a bit more.

'It's my mobile,' I said. There was a ripple of laughter. Someone started telling a joke about two rats going into a pub.

I had pulled the phone from my bag by now, but it had already stopped. Missed call, it said. I checked the register. A number I didn't recognise. Yet some instinct made the hairs on the back of my neck prickle. I glanced across the table to respond politely to the punchline. Nick, on the table next to us, was looking my way.

'Excuse me,' I said, smiling and pushing my chair back. 'Might be my daughter or something. You know what it's like.'

They did, they said. So I made my excuses and threaded my way out of the function room. There was something *badly* wrong. I could feel it.

The phone was ringing again by the time I got to reception. I was right. There was.

'Mum? Oh thank Goodness!'

It was Morgan. And she was crying. Crying very hard.

'Morgan?' I said, panic rising in my throat. 'What on earth is the matter?'

'Oh, Mum –'she sobbed.

'Morgan, what *is* it? What's the matter?'

'Oh, mum,' she said again, between gulps. 'Mum you've got to come – '

'Come *where*? Morgan, what's happened? Is it Cody?'

I could hear her ragged breathing.

'Yes, yes it is. *Please.* You have to come. Leman Street. It's – that's right, isn't it?' she was speaking to someone else now. I could hear a low rumble of assent. A male voice. 'Leman Street Police Station –'

'*Police* Station?'

'*Yes*,' she sobbed. 'Oh, mum! I've been arrested.'

I gripped the phone tighter. What on earth – what on earth –

'*Arrested?* Morgan – *why*?'

The floor seemed to be moving beneath my feet all of a sudden. I walked half a dozen paces on wobbly legs and sat down heavily on a sofa. Morgan was still crying, taking in air in huge gulps.

'*Why?*' I said again. 'What on earth has happened? I couldn't begin to imagine what possible reason there could be for my daughter to be at a police station. An accident ? Oh, please no. Not an accident.

She sniffed noisily. 'It's drugs. It's *drugs.* I've been arrested for possession of Ecstasy! I don't even know anything about it, Mum. Really I don't . It's Cody. It's to do with Cody ! He's been – Oh, God, Mum. He's disappeared! What am I going to do? I was just –'She dissolved into speechlessness and sobbing once more.

It was too much to take in. 'Right,' I said, taking deep breaths and trying to get my head together. 'I'll phone your father – '

'*Noooo*! No, Mum, *please.* Don't tell him. Don't phone him. Don't. I couldn't bear it. Please. Just come. Please come. Please just come and get me out of here. I can't –'she broke into sobs again.

I took another deep breath. He was in Brighton anyway. There was no practical point in phoning him. 'Calm down,' I said. 'Calm down. I'm on my way. I'll go and get the car and I'll be with you as soon as I can. What's the address again?'

'I don't know! It's near Fenchurch Street. You know Fenchurch Street?'

In the city. I could find my way there.

'Whereabouts?'

'Hang on,' I heard her talking to someone else, then a different voice came down the phone. A policeman, I presumed, who told me in flat, matter of fact tones exactly where to go. I scribbled his directions down on the back of my invitation card. Yes, I could find my way to Tower Bridge. Yes, I knew the city a little. Yes, I was sure I could find my way to Leman Street. He gave me the station number and told me to phone if I got lost. And then he was gone and so was Morgan.

'Is something wrong?' Another voice. Another male voice. I turned around. It was Nick's.

Seeing him, standing there in his dinner jacket and pink bow tie, it was all I could do not to fall sobbing into his arms. But that would be no use to anyone, least of all Morgan. I stood up, pushing the card and the pen back into my bag.

'I have to go.'

'Go? What's happened? Sally? Are you all right? You look ashen.'

His hand hovered somewhere near my elbow. I stepped back a pace, brain whirring with unanswered questions.

'I'm OK,' I said, grasping for some strength to put into my voice. 'it's just that I've got a problem to sort out.' Yes. That was it. A problem. Jesus. Morgan arrested. It was unthinkable. 'Morgan,' I said. 'I have to –'

'Sally, for God's sake! What's *happened*?' Now he did take hold of my arm. 'You look terrible! What's happened?'

'I'm OK,' I said again. 'I just have to go to London to get – '

'*London?* What, *now*?'

I nodded. 'Morgan's in some sort of difficulty. So I've got to – will you tell Mr Monroe for me? Give him my apologies and everything? Only I'd better get going because it's already gone ten and –'

'No,' he said, putting his hand on my other arm too. 'I will not. Not until you tell me what's going on.'

'I can't–'

'You can. I'm not letting you leave here in this state. No way. Tell me what's happened. What's *happened* with Morgan?'

His eyes were staring steely blue into mine. His hands were still firm on my arms.

'She's been arrested,' I said.

'*What?* What for?'

'For possession of Ecstasy, by all accounts. Something to do with her fiancé. Nothing whatsoever to do with her.' The words came out in a crisp staccato tumble, pushed ahead by the bile that was rising in my throat. I swallowed hard. 'And now I have to go.' I shook his hands from my arms and turned towards the exit, but he was still there, hand on my shoulder now, stopping me.

'Is your husband coming to pick you up?'

I shook my head. And then regretted it. If I'd simply said yes I could have gone by now. But it was too late.

'He's away,' I admitted. 'I'm going to get a cab to take me home. Then I can pick up my –'

'I'll take you,' he said.

'There's no need. There's a cab rank –'

'No, no. I'll take you to *London,*' he said.

'Don't be ridiculous.' I started walking towards the foyer. My fingers were shaking. Vibrating, like my phone. I balled my hands into fists. 'I 'm quite capable – '

'I know that, Sally.' He was still behind me. 'But I'll take you anyway. I can't let you drive all the way up there at this hour on your own.'

I whirled around to face him again.

'Don't be ridiculous!' I said again. 'I'm not a child!'

He looked hurt.

'I never said you *were!* But I still can't let you – '

'There's no 'let' about it, Nick! I am going. So would you please just tell Mr Monroe for me? Please?' I started walking again. He did likewise, matching my stride.

'Sally, don't be silly. Let me drive you. It'll be much quicker if we take my car. And besides, there's no way you can drive anywhere in this state.'

'I am *not* in a state.'

'Yes you are. You look like death. You're shaking. Please, Sally – let me do this for you.'

'Nick, please. I don't *want* you to come with me, OK? I can sort this out on my own. Really. It's very kind of you to –'

He looked more hurt still. Then stern. 'Sally, I am not being kind, OK? I am being sensible. I am being concerned. I know full well that you don't want me to take you, and I know full well *why* you won't let me help you, but you are being ridiculous. I have my car here. We can be there in little over an hour. There's just no sense in you hiking all the way back home to pick your car up when mine is here. Is there? *Is* there?'

What was the point? He was right.

'OK,' I said. Damn him. 'OK, OK, *OK!*'

I let him go back in and explain in the vaguest terms possible that one of my family was unwell and that I had to get home. Not the detail, but just that I had a small family crisis. He led me round to the car park and I was soon back in his passenger seat, headed for London and whatever we'd find there.

Within minutes we were on the M25.

I felt numb with fear. 'This is all my fault.'

'That's ridiculous,' he said calmly. 'How on earth can it be your fault?'

I grasped the bag in my lap. 'It *is* my fault. I should have seen it coming. She's not been herself for weeks. I should have gone up there last week – I should have – Oh, God! I'm so selfish! I should have spent less time worrying about *me*, that's what! *You*, quite frankly. *Us*, in fact. If I'd just – 'I couldn't speak any more. All I could think of was that Morgan would go to prison and that it would be all my fault. I had failed her utterly.

He turned to glance at me. 'Sally, don't do this to yourself. It – whatever it turns out to be, which I'm sure will be far less dreadful than you imagine – is not your fault. In any case, she's said she's done nothing wrong, hasn't she? And I'm quite sure she's telling the truth. Let's just get there and play it one step at a time.'

'How would *you* know? How the hell would you know? For all you know she could be running a heroin empire!'

'Do you think that?'

'No, of course I don't!'

'Then neither do I.' He continued to stare at the road.

'Oh, God. I'm sorry. You're right. I'm sorry, Nick. I just can't get my head round it. I just can't –'

'I know.'

'And I should have called Jonathan.'

'D'you want to call him now?'

I shook my head. No. No, I didn't.

When we got over Tower Bridge the streets were quiet and dark. He parked the car down a side street and walked with me up the steps to the station entrance. I had calmed down a little. This was Morgan. Honest, good, sensible, law-abiding Morgan. Everything would be all right. I would sort things out. Bail her out? What happened in circumstances like these? My last brush with the police had been over a decade ago, when I'd come along to some road safety talk at Kate's junior school. This was so very different. So frightening. There was a uniformed policeman manning the front desk. He looked at me enquiringly, taking in, I could see, the ridiculous sparkles, the spindly evening shoes, the little sequinned bag. I must have looked like a reject from a Chicago audition. In that place, with its unforgiving fluorescence, its acres of lino and Formica. I marched up to the desk and told him who I was. His manner changed perceptibly, to one of mild boredom. Just another parent come to rescue their miscreant offspring from an everyday unpalatable mess.

They showed me into a little room, lit like an operating theatre. And then, minutes later, Morgan came in.

She looked terrible. She was wearing a tracksuit, much crumpled, and had mascara running in sooty trails down her cheeks. She looked tiny and scared. I leapt up to hug her. She too had lost weight. It had only been a matter of weeks since I'd seen her, but she looked so changed. So fragile.

My presence had her bursting into great heaving sobs again.

'Oh, mum, thank god. You can tell them now. Please tell them. I haven't done anything wrong. I don't know anything! I didn't know anything about it!'

The policewoman who had brought her in gestured that we sit down.

'They've arrested Cody as well now!' Morgan was wailing hysterically. I tried to still her with my arms. 'They've found him! They've arrested him too, mum! Oh, God, mum! What's going to happen?'

I looked at the policewoman. She seemed kind, if a little detached. As you would be, I thought sadly. She nodded at me.

'He fetched up here half an hour ago,' she told me. 'And we've taken him into custody, so Morgan here is now free to go.'

'She is? But you arrested her. What was she arrested for?'

'It's standard procedure, Mrs Matthews. Where drugs are found on premises then everyone on those premises is arrested as a matter of course. But Morgan hasn't been charged with anything. She's made a statement for us, and we're satisfied that she isn't involved in any way. We may need to talk to her again at some point, but as of now, as I said, she's free to go.'

I squeezed Morgan's hand. 'Oh, thank God. But what about the drugs? What'll happen now? What will happen with her fiancé?'

'His father is on his way, apparently. Look, I'm sorry, but I really can't discuss this with you.'

'But what about Cody? Can we see him?'

'He's being interviewed at present, but if you –'

'*No*,' sobbed Morgan. 'I don't want to see him. I don't *want* to see him, OK? Please, mum. Just take me home.'

'But what about the drugs?' I said again to the policewoman. 'Will Cody go to prison?'

Stupid, stupid questions, but I couldn't think what else to do. The policewoman smiled in a gentle sort of way. 'As I said, I'm afraid I can't discuss that with you, Mrs Matthews. Thank you for coming to collect your daughter. I think it's best that you get her home now, don't you? We'll be in touch in due course.'

Nick was still sitting in the front of the police station when we returned, sipping from a polystyrene cup of something. He put the drink down and stood up as we approached.

'This is Nick Brown,' I said to Morgan. 'He works with me. He was at the dinner tonight, and he very kindly offered to drive me up here.'

The words sounded stiff and unnaturally formal. Morgan nodded, dull eyed, then extended an arm to shake his hand.

'I'm so sorry,' she whispered, always polite. My heart was breaking for her. For this awful thing Cody had done to her. If he'd walked into the station at that moment I think I would have killed him stone dead on the spot.

Nick raised his brows enquiringly and reached into his pocket for his car keys.

'We need to go back to Morgan's flat,' I told him. 'If that's OK. To get some things for her. Clothes and so on. He was nodding his head. 'It's not far. Only Docklands.'

'Not a problem,' he said, opening the door for us both.

'I'm so sorry,' said Morgan again.

It took twenty minutes to drive to Morgan's, the streets here busier with Saturday night traffic and the spill out from various clubs and bars. She let us in. Her flat was in a minor state of chaos.

'They just came in' she said. 'It was awful. Just came in and started turning everything over. They already had a search warrant. I couldn't take it in. I was so scared.' She ran her hands over her forehead and seemed to pull herself together She looked around her as if trying to make sense of our being there now also. 'Would you like a cup of coffee?' We both shook our heads.

'Just get your bits and bobs together and we'll get you home, darling,' I told her gently. 'Shall I help you?''

She shook her head. 'I need a shower. Would it be OK if I had a quick shower? I feel so dirty – '

I started to tell her not to worry. That she could shower once she was home, but I stopped myself. She probably *needed* a shower. She probably felt soiled. That she needed to wash it away.

'Perhaps we will have that coffee then, eh?' Nick suggested. 'Keep us awake.'

'Right,' I said, leading him into her little kitchen. 'Coffee. Yes. That's the thing. Come on.'

I filled the kettle and directed Nick to the cupboard.

'What a business,' he said, slipping off his jacket and hanging it over the back of the door, over her Amnesty International carrier bag holder. Such a good person. Such an honest person. How could this have happened to her?

'What a bastard. I can't believe it. I simply cannot believe it. I mean he was always such a – 'I stopped. 'No. I don't know that at all. I know nothing about him. All I know is that – *God*, what a mess. I mean, her *wedding*. It's only three months away.' I could feel tears springing unbidden into my eyes. So many horrible implications. Nick was standing across the kitchen from me. A distance of only a matter of feet. He was tapping a teaspoon against his palm.

'I know.'

'Oh, Nick, I wish you weren't here. It feels all wrong. It feels'

'It'll be all right,' he said firmly. 'He'll make a statement and it'll all be sorted out. You'll see. And better now. Better she's found out now, at least. Better than afterwards.' The kettle boiled behind me, belching great clouds of white steam into the air. He was spooning coffee into mugs now. 'Come on,' he said crossing the kitchen with them and lifting the kettle from its rest. 'You need a cup of coffee.'

I watched him pour hot water into both mugs. Watched the tendrils of steam dance and fade. Watched him stirring in milk with his big strong hands.

'What I need is a hug,' I said.

We got home a little before two in the morning. Morgan had slept for much of the journey and I had to shake her gently awake once the car was parked on the drive. I helped her to the front door – she was weak as a rag doll – while Nick brought her case in from the boot.

And my mother was still up. I was just putting my key in the lock when the hall light came on and the door opened wide, spilling light all around us. She was in her dressing gown, all smiles.

'I thought I'd wait up and – oh! Gracious! Morgan! *You're* here!'

She stepped back to allow us in, hand clamped around Merlin's collar.

'I'll put this here then, shall I?' Nick asked, stooping and placing the case just inside the door. I nodded.

'Oh!' said my mother again, glancing at us both. 'Are we all right?'

This was, I presumed, directed at Morgan, who, fully awake now, was once again crying.

I shook my head. 'Not really,' I said wearily. 'Put the kettle on, will you, Mum?'

She let go of Merlin's collar and enfolded Morgan in her arms instead, clucking and stroking her hair.

'Right,' she said, with the absence of fuss for which I loved her so much. 'Let's get you in the warm.' She glanced at me, and nodded minutely. 'Come along, Morgan love. Let's get you sitting down.' She started off down the hall with her, Merlin trotting behind. I turned to Nick, who was by now back on the doorstep. My stomach was all churned up again. Over and over and over and over. When would I stop *feeling* like this?'

'I'll get off then,' he said. He looked tired.

'You don't want another coffee?'

He shook his head.

'Better not.' He turned to go.

'Thank you *so* much,' I said, reaching for his hand and wishing I could pull him back in over the doorstep and keep him beside me forever. He stopped on the step and looked into my eyes for a long, long moment. I squeezed his hand briefly and then let it drop.

'Thank you,' I said again.

He opened his mouth. 'Sally, I –'

'Please, Nick. *Please*.'

'OK,' he said quietly. He held my gaze for a moment more, then he turned and walked back to his car. I shut the door, very quickly, behind him.

Chapter 26

It had been almost four before we'd put Morgan to bed. For once she'd started talking it seemed she couldn't stop. Despite her shock at the events of the previous evening, it seemed she had had her suspicions about Cody for some time. Nothing tangible really, just that his behaviour seemed erratic, just a feeling he was keeping something from her. Her first thought had been that he was having second thoughts about the wedding, but as the weeks had gone on she'd come to the conclusion that his problems were more about money than anything else. There had been his car – he'd always driven a rather swanky BMW, but one night three weeks back he'd turned up to collect her from her office in an ageing Ford instead. And then there had been his ever more frequent disappearances. He'd be out of the office for long spells, and though his work, as far as Morgan knew, made him fairly autonomous, he'd become increasingly difficult to pin down.

More tellingly there'd been young guys calling at her flat. On one occasion one had turned up there at midnight, demanding to know where Cody could be found.

She didn't at that point know a great deal more. Only that he'd gone to work on Friday morning, from her place, and that he hadn't arrived and had not been seen since. She'd spent much of Friday and Saturday trying to track him down. It was only the arrival of the police on her doorstep that had put all the pieces of the jigsaw into place.

'I thought he'd been killed,' she said now, her voice tiny. 'I stood there and just held my breath, waiting for them to tell me. But they didn't. They just asked to come in then showed me some paper and said they were going to search my flat. I've never been so scared. Never.'

'And they definitely found drugs?' I said. 'At your flat?'

The policewoman I'd spoken to had been unforthcoming on that point, except to say that they'd already found drugs at Cody's. Morgan nodded.

'Oh, yes.' She spread her hands and sighed. 'This great big plastic bag full of pills. God, I don't even know where they found it!'

My mother shook her head slowly but said nothing.

'And then they arrested me. It was completely unreal. The older one – the one with the moustache – started saying 'you don't have to say anything' and all that stuff. I couldn't take it *in*.' She shook her head. 'And then they took me off. No time to do anything, get anything. Nothing. He just picked up one of my jackets from the back of the sofa and said 'this do?' and next thing I was in the back of a police car. It was so degrading. How could he *do* that? How could Cody do that to me?'

As it turned out, we weren't long in finding out. I had decided there was no point ringing Jonathan in the small hours, but I telephoned him as soon as I woke the next morning, and he was back in the house before ten. I had braced myself for some serious ranting, but in this really big thing he was uncharacteristically calm. The first thing he did was to call the police and the second was to tell us that Cody had been released on Bail during the night. By teatime it was evident, following Jonathan's subsequent conversations with Cody's father, Morgan's subsequent conversations with Cody himself and our subsequent conversations with Morgan herself that our jail-bird speculations were probably wildly inaccurate. Cody was in trouble, certainly, but their main target was the man he'd become involved with at work, and who had, it seemed, quite a little empire on the go. Cody's clean record and co-operation would stand him in good stead. But though a custodial sentence had been pretty much ruled out, there would be no wedding happening come September. Morgan could cope, she'd announced tearfully, with being married to someone with a drug problem, but she couldn't, and my heart went out to her at this point, be married to someone who told her lies.

By bedtime it was evident that Cody had other ideas. He had rung up on no less that eight occasions, the last of which Kate had picked up, en route to bed. She put her head round the living room door.

'It's the Drug U Like man,' she announced, rather gaily.

From Morgan this elicited a watery smile. From me, who had half risen from my armchair by now, a furious cochineal blush.

'Well, it's not such a big deal, really,' observed Russell in the pub on Monday night. 'Half the population have probably taken drugs at some time in their lives. Sounds to me he's just been a bit of a prat, more than anything. I mean, you head down most nightclubs on a Saturday night and you'll find any number of people dealing E. It's pretty common, Sal. And, hey. Could have been worse. It could have been coke, given he's a toff.'

This, to my utter consternation, had been the verdict of Morgan herself not twenty four hours earlier. That the experience she'd been through had been harrowing in the extreme, but that it was only E. That it could have been worse. *Only*. I felt like I'd been beamed here from Mars. I had tried to persuade her to stay for a couple of days but she'd been firm. She had work to go to, a big media campaign to get organised, and she needed to get home to get things sorted out. Home meaning *her* home. I was struck once again by the simple truth that her life was not with us any more, but in London. She went off early with Jonathan, with promises to call me in the evening – and reminded me we were supposed to be meeting up the following Wednesday.

So here I was, plopped back into my own life, with a new sheaf of things to do. Or un-do, it now seemed. My mother, likewise had toddled off back to Eastbourne. Looking forward to a bit of peace and quiet, she'd said. Or what passed for that in her hectic life, I guessed. I felt very lonely, all of a sudden. Kate would be off out with Carl, no doubt, and the one person I could talk to was out of bounds.

'Finish that,' Russell said now, 'And I'll get you a refill.' He stood up and smiled as I drained my glass of wine. 'Only difference between us and them, you know, is that our drugs are legal. That's all.'

Ruth rubbed her hands together then jiggled a finger at me.

'Your life,' she said, 'is one long round of crises and disasters. I'm going to have to write it some day, you know.'

'Hmm,' I said, thinking how much I'd like to get drunk now. 'Just make sure you give it a happy ending, then, will you?'

When I got home from the pub, Merlin was the only living thing in the house. Since finishing her exams Kate had become a bit like the Pleiades. Always on her way to or from somewhere. Only visible out of the corner of your eye. There was a note from her on the kitchen table to say that Jonathan had phoned and to call him back later. And something else. A text message from Nick, which said, '*Just wanted to check in and find out if all's well. Much love, N.*' I decided the best thing I could do under the circumstances was not to reply. I erased it instead. As you do. I was hurting so much I didn't know what to do with myself, but I was getting better at this. Slowly.

Wednesday dawned fine and clear and all the things one would wish for at the beginning of the school summer holidays. Unless you were me, of course, shrouded in clouds. The train was packed, delayed, sweaty and, well, all the things you could expect at the beginning of the school summer holidays. Given the above. Which kind of suited, somehow.

By the time I had emerged from Oxford Circus tube station and threaded my way through the slow moving syrup of tourists to the restaurant, I was almost forty five minutes late.

I'd phoned ahead to warn her, so when I got there Morgan was already sitting at a table, a menu open in front of her and a bottle of wine in a silver bucket on a stand at her side. She saw me, and reached across to pull it out.

'Are you driving? She asked as I approached.

'No,' I answered, slipping off my jacket. 'Briony was going into Oxted so she dropped me at the station. I'll grab a cab at the other end.

'Good' she said, filling my glass almost to the rim. 'Because I've taken the afternoon off work and I feel like getting seriously drunk.'

It was good to see Morgan looking more like herself again. Smart and polished in her slim fitting suit. There was a slight edge to her voice, but why wouldn't there be? I sat down and opened my menu also. This was nice. This was good. This would be a tonic for us both. Perhaps I would get tipsy as well. Why not? The smiling waiter, anxious to regain the initiative after being pre-empted by Morgan's actions plucked my napkin from in front of me, shook it out with a snap and spread it carefully over my knees.

'So,' I said, picking up my wine and sipping it gratefully. It felt good to be away from home for a while. 'That's the plan then, is it? Not a good move in my experience. The last time I drank in quantity at lunchtime I came home with a motor powered juice extractor.'

She smiled. 'Shopping I can do without, Mum. I am all shopped out. I thought we might just sit here and talk. Maybe take a taxi down to Tate Modern later. There's a new exhibition I fancy taking a look at. If I can still focus by then.'

Her laughter sounded slightly forced.

'So. How's things with Cody?'

She shrugged.

'Cody is – well, I'd say as well as can be expected. He's lost his job, of course, but that was on the cards anyway. And for the best, in my view. He's looking at courses.'

'What, college?'

She nodded. 'His father's fairly unimpressed, but he's going to take him on part time for the moment.' Cody's father was a partner in a big architectural practice.

'And you?'

'I don't know yet. One step at a time.'

'But the wedding's definitely off.'

She shook her head. 'Not off. Just postponed.' She toyed with her fork. 'I can't just leave him, Mum. I love him. I know what Dad says is all sensible advice, but I can't take it. I love him.'

I had barely spoken to Jonathan since his brief rant on the Sunday evening about it. No change there, then. And then he'd gone off to London, returned late on Tuesday, and had gone this morning before I was up. All of which suited me right now. If I didn't have to see too much of him I could at least toy with the prospect that spending the rest of my life with him and without Nick would be bearable. One row, one put-down, one cross word just now and I knew I would snap. 'What *did* dad say?'

'All the usual stuff. That he's no good, that he'll do it again, that I can do better for myself, that I should keep my options open, that there are lots of other pebbles on the beach etcetera. All of which is probably true, but entirely meaningless. I'm not after another pebble. I've chosen the one I want. It just needs a buff and a polish, that's all.'

I liked her metaphor, but I wasn't so sure of the sentiment. 'It's never a great idea to think you can change someone, Morgan.'

She was on that like an exocet.

'Who said anything about changing him? I don't want to change him. I'm talking support, respect, giving him a chance to be the person he *is* instead of the person everyone thinks he *should* be.

That's what's crippling him. He's been stifled by everyone's ridiculous expectations of him. If I'd got engaged to someone who then got diagnosed with MS or something, would anyone expect me to dump him? I don't see it's much different. He just needs some space to find out what he wants to be.'

And get through the court case, of course. I didn't want to think about that right now. 'Well,' I said, thinking what a wise and thoughtful human being my daughter had become. 'You certainly seem to have thought things through.. 'And it's your life.'

'That's what I said to Dad. And at the end of the day, I'll have to live with the consequences. He's not a bad person, mum. He's just – he just got himself into a mess, that's all. Hooked up with some idiot people. I don't think Dad really understands that, you know? The pressure. The pressure to *be* someone, achieve all the time. You know, all he always wanted was to go to horticultural college. But his father was having none of it. No son of mine – you know the drill. I think there's a fair amount of soul searching going on chez Southgate right now. But yes, off as in off in September. One step at a time. We're going to see how things go for a few months, and have a re-think after Christmas. His solicitor thinks he'll get community service – did I tell you? – but then, well. Move out of London even. If he gets on to a course, we could be talking moving right away. I think he's asked for a prospectus from some college in Scotland. Which is fine. My skills are pretty portable.'

My daughter talking about community service as if it were just a different kind of Saturday job. Such breathtaking confidence. Far from being traumatised she seemed positively energised. Had she stepped off a rollercoaster *she* didn't want to be on? I tried to imagine Cody as Alan Titchmarsh and Morgan swapping her slick suits for wellies. Though it would never have occurred to me, I could suddenly see it. She topped my wine up, even though there was barely an inch gone from it. The bottle, I noticed, was already almost empty. The waiter was back again. He tipped the remainder into Morgan's glass and upended the bottle in the ice.

'We'll have another of those,' she said.

'My, you're on a roll.' I watched her as reached for her glass once again. She was looking composed and assured but there was an edge of fragility about her too, somehow. Not brittle exactly, but as if she was made of newly blown glass. One tap at a weak point and she'd shatter.

'Funny,' she said, as if reading my thoughts and anxious to prove them wrong. 'I don't think I've felt so sorted in months. Strange, isn't it? I should be feeling wretched and yet all I feel is this overwhelming sense of relief. As if I've taken control of my life again. You know?'

'And Cody's, by the sound of it. And I don't think it's strange to feel like that at all. But I wish you'd told me sooner, Morgan. Why didn't you tell me what was going on? If you'd only told me – if I'd only known how serious things were, I'd have – '

She flapped away the end of my sentence.

'I wouldn't have told you, mum. I thought I would, but, in the end, I knew I wouldn't. What difference would it have made? It was something I had to sort out for myself.'

The wine was beginning to find it's way into my veins. 'By getting arrested? Fairly dramatic means!'

She laughed again. 'But it did need to happen. I can see that now. I've spent far too long trying to pretend everything was OK. Letting you trundle on with the wedding arrangements.... Anyway, it's done now. If I'd told you and dad it would have been all too easy to let you take over and cancel the wedding.

'Even so, I wish you had told me. We should have been having this talk weeks ago.'

'Well,' she said. 'We're here now, aren't we?'

The waiter came back with the wine and then another bustled up for our order.

'It's all horrendously expensive, Morgan. I can't possibly let you pay for all this.'

'Tough,' she said. 'Anyway, we're celebrating, aren't we?'

'Celebrating? Well, I suppose, in a strange sort of way –'

'Not me! *You*. Your new job, of course.'

It seemed like a million years ago. I said so.

'And you never even told me! Trust me to have to find out from Ruth.'

'I had a lot of more important things on my mind at the time. Ruth? How come Ruth told you?'

'When I spoke to her.'

'Oh –'

She raised her glass. 'So here's to you. Great news!' She took a sip. 'But one question.'

I raised my brows, slightly tipsy. Vaguely smiling. Certainly unprepared for what was coming.

Which was 'What's going on with this Nick Brown guy, Mum?'

Chapter 27

Oh, God. Here we were again. My stomach did a triple salko and landed with a splat somewhere near my shoes. 'I beg your pardon,' I said, forming the words out of sandpaper. 'Nick Brown? The guy from work? What about him?'

Here *again*. Just when I'd thought I could wriggle off the hook. Just when I thought I could swap deceit for depression, guilt for wretchedness and passion for regret. Just when, in short, I could start addressing the next bit; the *getting on with things* bit, here we were again. I felt I'd been skewered to my seat.

'Yes, of *course* Nick Brown from work,' she said, sliding her glass across the table a little so the waiter could top it up. Our starters arrived. I looked down at mine. It looked back benignly. My arm was laid lightly across the table, holding the stem of my own glass. I could feel my pulse hammering in my wrist. This could be nothing, of course. Some other supposition. About my job, perhaps. Something like that. Or perhaps she'd read something in the papers about Drug u Like. Or perhaps….. perhaps, perhaps, perhaps. There was no perhaps about it. I knew *exactly* what she meant. I heard a delicate, cut-glass laugh issue forth. It was mine. I added an enquiring smile to it. A theatrical lilt to my voice. And then I said, 'And?' loaded with meringue. 'What *about* "Nick Brown from work"?'

Morgan looked momentarily uncomfortable. As if considering the possibility that she'd jumped to some slightly embarrassing conclusions and would now have to recant in the face of an irate mother. Or perhaps not.

'Well,' she said. 'I just rather got the impression that –'

'Oh, really?' I said cheerfully. 'That sounds intriguing. What impression was that?'

Her face changed again. Damn. My fault. My *fault*. I had jumped in too soon. Why did I *do* that? Why didn't I just let her carry on feeling silly? I could feel my own expression configuring itself into the beginnings of its inevitable betrayal.

She jabbed her fork into a scallop.

'The impression,' she said, in a much firmer voice, 'that something is going on between you. That's what.' She popped the scallop into her mouth and chewed on it as she scrutinised me.

I picked up my own fork. What to say next? What? *Think. What?* Think. I thought. But not for long enough. Morgan swallowed her fishy little sea creature. I ate a piece of lettuce.

'Why?' I said.

She looked at me more earnestly now. 'Lots of things,' she said, leaning slightly forward and lowering her voice. 'You telling me you were at Ruth's when you weren't, for one thing. The way you've been out so much just lately. The way you've *been*, period. The way –'

'I have been busy and I have been stressed, Morgan. It's hardly surprising that – '

'The way I saw you and him in my *kitchen*.' My fork stopped halfway to my mouth. So did Morgan's. 'Mum, he had his *arms* around you.'

That one small moment of tenderness. That one chaste embrace. Was this the bad karma I'd been waiting for, maybe? I put the fork back on my plate and drank some more wine. I must get some water.

'Morgan,' I said stiffly. 'There is nothing going on with me and Nick Brown.' This much was true. No it wasn't. Yes, it *was*. I picked the fork up again and pushed something else into my mouth. Some sort of mushroom. It tasted of carpet. Morgan's hand stayed where it was.

'Don't lie to me, mum. I've had enough of being lied to. I'm right, aren't I?' This new forthright Morgan was frightening me. I continued to eat, shaking my head as I did so. Another piece of carpet. A leaf. A liliputian potato. This was my daughter. This was *Jonathan's* daughter. This was not someone I could even *begin* to contemplate discussing my infidelity with. Perhaps if I continued to stuff enough food in my mouth I could ride it out till I thought up a credible response. I did so.

'There's no point,' she went on, her voice becoming more brittle. 'I'm not stupid, Mum. Anyone could see. It was so *obvious*. I tried to shrug it off at the time. I decided he was probably just comforting you or something. I decided maybe you were just upset and he was – '

I swallowed my mouthful of undergrowth. 'I *was* upset! Wouldn't *you* be upset? He *was* comforting me. That was all he was doing, Morgan. He's a friend. A good friend. And that's all there was – all there *is* to it. I'm not – '

But she carried straight on as if I hadn't spoken at all. 'But then the more I thought about it, the more it all began to make sense. Please tell me the truth, Mum.'

I put my cutlery together. One last try. Damage limitation, at least. Then perhaps we could get this subject wrapped up and finished. Oh, the irony of being confronted with this now. When there was no longer anything to tell.

'Morgan, I *am*. He's just a friend. That's all. Yes, I like him very much, and yes, all right, I enjoy his company, and yes, I have seen him socially a couple of times. But as a *friend*. Like Ruth.'

She blew a small polite raspberry. Like a Parisian lady. *Pish*! 'I don't think so,' she said.' Mum, he was kissing your *hair*!'

'Morgan, you've got this all wrong –'

'You're saying you haven't, then?'

'Haven't *what*?'

'Kissed him.'

'Morgan, what *is* this? Of course I haven't!'

She sat back in her seat and considered me for a moment. Then leaned forward again. Her pupils, I noticed, were dilated. Was this why she'd decided to get sozzled today? The better to confront me? 'Mum, you are a hopeless liar,' she said. 'It would be comical if it wasn't so…so awful.'

Unless you are trained in the art of resistance under torture or tanked up with psychedelic drugs, there are only so many times you can gabble insincere denials at a person without the law of diminishing returns kicking in. I had, I could see with absolute clarity, just reached the limit of mine.

'All right,' I said finally, conscious that I had already taken too much wine on board on an empty stomach and that it was surely about to be my downfall. But I couldn't think of anything else to say or do. 'Yes,' I said. 'I have kissed him. No, I am not seeing him any more. It happened. It ended. That's all there is to tell. Subject closed.'

'You don't look like you mean that.'

Ah. Subject *not* closed, then. I held her gaze. 'It's the truth, nevertheless.'

'Did he end it?'

'No. I did.'

'Because it was just a bit of fun? Because you went off him? What?'

Either of those two would have done. Either of those to would have put paid to her scary conjecturing, but, liar and deceitful person that I undoubtedly was, I couldn't seem to articulate them. I swallowed. 'Because it was the only thing to do.'

She looked satisfied.

'So it's not ended at all, then.'

'Morgan, it has.'

'Not here.' She touched her chest. It wasn't a question. Where did this daughter of mine develop such sharp intuition? Not from her father, that was for sure. I shook my head sadly.

'No.'

'Do you love him?'

'Oh, for goodness sake, Morgan –'

'I thought so.' She was beginning to look belligerent now.

'Morgan, I really don't want to talk to you about this. Can we get some water?'

She lifted an arm to call a waiter in that languid way that beautiful young women can do with impunity, as everyone is already watching them anyway.

Then she dropped it and folded her hands together on the table cloth. She was still wearing her engagement ring, I noticed. 'It's as bad as I thought then,' she said gravely.

'What on earth do you mean, "as bad as you thought"? What exactly *have* you been thinking? Since when have you been analysing my every movement and –'

'Mum, I'm not stupid,' she said again. 'I know exactly how things are with you and Dad.'

Worse on worse. 'Oh, really?'

The waiter fetched up. Morgan pointed her fork at me. 'Still or sparkling?'

'Still.'

'One of each, then, please. Yes, *really*.'

I drank another gulp of wine to stop my mouth from desiccating while I waited for the water. Perhaps I could say I was going to the loo and go and get on a number twelve bus.

‘Morgan,’ I said, quietly, sadness pressing in around me. ‘I really don’t think it’s any of your business.’

‘Of course it’s my business!’ she said indignantly. ‘You’re my parents!’

‘I know that. It’s just – look, you really don’t know anything about it. Marriages are – well, they’re complicated. It’s easy to form an impression about someone else’s relationship, easier still to leap to conclusions, but you don’t *really* know, I can assure you. Never. Your father and I are just fine, OK? I won’t deny that we’re not the last of the red hot lovers, but we’ve been married a long time and, well, that’s par for the course for a lot of people. More than you probably imagine. It doesn’t mean the institution of marriage is about to be dragged to its knees’. I tried to look wise and world-weary, the latter, unsurprisingly, being effortless. ‘Morgan, please don’t concern yourself with this, OK? Concentrate your energies on your *own* relationship.’

She gave me a sideways glance. ‘Yeah, right.’ She sounded like Kate.

‘But if you’ll take one piece of advice from me, I’d want it to be that you must make absolutely sure you’re certain before you marry Cody. Be sure. You’ll be a long time married. Think long and hard about what you want and –’

‘Did *you* do that? Did you think long and hard when dad proposed to you, then?

‘Yes,’ I said. ‘*Yes.*’ I looked hard into the eyes of the little girl who had figured so prominently in my thinking back then. Whatever regrets I was living with, this young woman was not one of them. ‘Look, Morgan,’ I said. ‘I really don’t want to talk about this.’

Tough. Because she *did*. Particularly in the small matter of my woolly thinking. I was beginning to speak in Kashmiri goat. Just what was I trying to say, for God’s sake? ‘But you’re not *happy* together, are you?’ she said, palms up, eyebrows raised. ‘Look. On the one hand you’re telling me to think hard before making any decisions about marrying Cody – fine. But on the other hand, you’re telling me I’ll probably be unhappy after a few years in any case. You’re talking nonsense, mum!’

Which was true. ‘Look, Morgan,’ I tried, ‘it’s not as simple as that. You have to accept, sometimes, that, well it’s not always going to be the way you thought it would, maybe. That there will be times when you wonder –’

'And how come you never said all this six months ago, eh? You're just proving my point, Mum. It is serious, isn't it?' She looked at me earnestly. 'Do you think you'll leave dad?'

'*Leave* him? Who said anything about *leaving* him, for goodness sake? Morgan, you're being ridiculous. I don't know what's brought you to that conclusion, but you can just unconclude it right away, OK? I told you. There's nothing going on. Your father and I –'

'But you would, wouldn't you? If it came to it. I mean, not necessarily for this guy, but – '

'What do you mean 'if it came to it'? You talk as though I'm already setting a date! Morgan, just because I'm – because I'm, well, up in the air a bit right now, does not mean –'

'I knew it,' she said, shaking her head. 'It was bound to happen sometime.' She pulled her napkin from her lap and stood up suddenly. 'I have to go and have a pee.'

She went then, off to the ladies, her slim legs, glossy in tights that were not quite black but almost, drawing admiring glances from all the tables nearby. I sat and stared unseeing at my half finished food, wishing myself a million miles away. The waiter came back with the water and cleared our plates away. What had I ordered for my main course? Ugh. The thought of eating any more made me feel like throwing up. But that was nothing compared to how I was going to be feeling shortly. *Oh*, no.

When Morgan returned, freshly lipsticked, but with a flush on her cheeks and a grim set to her mouth, she downed the last of her wine and refused more. Which seemed sensible. She was no longer quite sober.

'The thing is,' she said, apropos of nothing except perhaps whatever dialogue she had been conducting with herself while sitting on the loo, '–the thing is –'She shifted in her seat. 'Look, you're quite right. It *is* none of my business, but the thing *is*,' she said again, 'I *know*.'

'You know what?'

She looked down at the tablecloth.

'About you and dad. About what *happened*.' Happened? What did she mean by "happened"? But she rattled straight on without pausing to explain. 'And I know how awful it must have been,' she was saying, 'but it meant nothing. *Really* it didn't. I mean I know it went on a long time, and I know how that must have made you feel, but it didn't mean he didn't love you, you know. It didn't. It was just a fling, Mum. Just something and nothing. Just one of those infatuations – yes. Infatuation. That was the word he used. Just one of those things that *happen*. And I always thought – well, I've been waiting, I suppose. I always thought how *I* would feel in that situation and whether I'd be able to do what you did. Just forgive. Trust. Get the marriage back on track. Love him still. *Stay* with him. All those things you've just been telling me people do. That's what it's all about, isn't it? But I never believed it. I never thought you'd stay with him. I always thought the day would come when – well. I mean, you're so much younger than him, and pretty and clever and – God! I can't imagine how *I* would be in that situation.'

I think the Pinot Grigio must have dulled my responses, because at this point I should surely have been shrieking or jabbering or tossing back the rest of the bottle, but instead, all I seemed to be doing was staring at her. Fling. *Fling*. The word had eased itself head and shoulders above the others. I felt suddenly clammy. As if my brain had at long last caught up with my ears. 'Morgan, *what* situation?'

She leaned back a little while the waiter placed our plates in front of us. That was it. Goat's cheese and asparagus tartlet. Why had I ordered *that*? It looked like a leak from the bottom of a bin bag. He moved off again. My head was beginning to swim now. Morgan picked up her cutlery. 'Mum, you don't have to pretend. I *know* about Constance, OK? Daddy told me. I mean, he didn't actually *need* to, of course, but –'

'You do?'

'*Yes,*' she said. 'I've known about it all along, Mum. Well, not *all* along, obviously, but since I've –'She stopped. Moved her wine glass half an inch across the tablecloth. Then yelped, 'Oh, God!' and slapped her hand to her face. She looked stricken. Horrified. A second crawled by. 'Mum, you don't – oh, *God!*'

I prodded the sludge on my plate with my knife. 'You're right. I didn't know,' I said.

And now she would have to tell me.

It was a remarkably short and unprepossessing tale. Constance Perkins was an actress of some celebrity, apparently. That I couldn't bring her to mind was most probably because I didn't subscribe to TV Quick. She was currently (apparently) playing the proprietress of a hairdressing salon, in a crummy soap set in some swish London Mews (think El Dorado with drizzle), and of which, for reasons that have always eluded me, my mother was particularly fond. Back then, however, for this was four years ago, she was starring in some worthy west end production of the sort of play that gets lots of glittering reviews but no one, bar striving young thespian hopefuls, actually goes to see. This had been about the time when Jonathan had gone into practice with his colleague in London.

So, in short, he'd fixed her teeth, and she, *bless* her, had paid him in kind.

It had gone on for two and a half years. (The affair. Not the play. That bombed a now pleasing two months in.) A simple arrangement . He would see her on Monday nights – sometimes on Sundays too – when working in London at his practice. That was all. She was merely his mistress. Until being merely was no longer deemed sufficient, and she'd left him to marry her third husband (apparently), the cheesy presenter of some second rate quiz show. And I had known nothing about it. At all.

Morgan was breathless after the telling. Skewered to *her* seat, in fact.

'I thought you knew,' she finished wretchedly. 'I really thought you knew.'

It could have been the third glass of wine I'd sunk, but by now I felt strangely detached. 'So how did you find out?' I asked.

'I saw them.' I nodded. She was an observant girl. 'I called round to his flat after work one evening and I saw them getting into his car. Nothing specific, but it was just a bit too touchy feely, you know?' She hesitated. Blushed. 'Anyway,' she went on in brisker tones, 'I phoned him at the surgery the next day and asked him who she was.' She smiled slightly. 'He's an even more useless liar than you. He gabbled a bit. Gave me a load of nonsense about her having a crown fitted or suchlike – none of which I believed, but there was nothing else to do but accept it. But being a suspicious soul, I kept an eye on him a bit – I was working in Cavendish Square then, remember? –'I nodded. I did remember. I remembered how nice I'd thought it was that Jonathan – poor lonely lamb up in London – would have Morgan working nearby. They could meet up for lunch. They could have dinner together. How nice, I'd thought. Save him being on his own. What a *bastard*. 'Anyway,' Morgan finished. 'a couple of weeks later I saw them together again. He admitted it then.

'And that's all there is to tell. I said I wouldn't tell you. He said *he* would. I thought he *had*. He always said there was nothing serious about it, Mum. Just that he was very attracted to her, and that the feeling was mutual and that it just sort of, well, happened.'

I thought briefly of myself and Nick and that moment by the lift. These things didn't 'just happen' at all. Not if you were happy. 'So why isn't it *still* happening?' I asked. 'Assuming it isn't, of course.' How would I know? How would I bloody *know*?

'No, *no*! It's *long* over, Mum. Honestly.'

'How come?' I asked again.

She looked anguished. How had the twenty year old Morgan *dealt* with all this? No wonder she was so tuned into my every movement. 'I think they got to one of those her or me situations, you know?' She looked at her plate. 'And so that was that.'

Now I did drain my wine glass, and my water glass too. 'Lucky me, eh?' I said. Lucky me. How very magnanimous of Jonathan.

Morgan reached across the table and put her hand on my arm. 'Mum, you can't leave him. You can't. He loves you. He *needs* you. It would kill him if you left him. Mum, there really wasn't any choice to make, you know. *Ever*. It was just one of those crazy things – '

'Did *he* tell you that?'

'He couldn't help it, I don't think.'

'Did he tell you that too?'

She shook her head. 'It was just –'

'Just what, Morgan?'

She lowered her eyes. 'Just that you know what really struck me about her? That she looked so like… well, like my Mother.'

We made the exhibition, because there seemed little else to do. And jolly good I'm sure it was too. A retrospective – that's what they're called, aren't they? – of some dead abstract painter who'd come back into fashion (as opposed to dead-abstract painter, which school would doubtless be in fashion the following week), and whose oversized gloomy daubings provided the perfect backdrop to the one act drama I had now found myself in. But the reality was that Morgan's had perhaps been the worst shock of the day. She had been so sure I'd known, and so convinced everything she'd observed in our relationship since was a consequence, and now the fact of my ignorance had hit her in the face she was terrified she'd just sealed the envelope on my divorce petition. It took a great deal of firm reassurance to persuade her that, no, it wasn't so. That it didn't make any difference. That it was all in the past, and no longer relevant. That I certainly wasn't about to invoke it as reason for some undignified tit for tat emotional revenge. That I certainly wasn't about to leave Jonathan. And Nick? Well, things like this happened, didn't they? Just like it had with her father. It had been my own 'fling', as it were. Ha ha ha ha ha ha *ha*.

So I'd lied yet again.

Oh, and I bought Kate a poster.

When I got home I trawled through the Sunday papers for the TV listings. There it was. Four days a week *Parker's Yard* was on apparently. And, yes. Today was one of them. I looked at the kitchen clock. Not long to go then. The inside of my head felt like it had been stamped on by a diplodocus. Water. More water. That was what I needed. I ran the tap and filled up a pint glass of the stuff, but two swallows in and I couldn't face drinking it. Drink was what I needed. Drunk was what I needed. Yes. I'd get drunker. That would be the best thing. I poured myself a large Pimms, hacked up a lemon, plopped it in the glass, swirled it with my finger, knocked back an inch, prised off my shoes, called Merlin to attention, went into the living room, sat down on the sofa Nick and I – no, don't *go* there – tucked my feet under my bottom, knocked back another inch, and we settled down, woman and dog. To wait.

Chapter 28

She could have been called lots of things. Susan. Joyce. Tabitha. Dolores. But, no. She was called Constance. Which struck me as rather spooky and apposite. Not only because I was on my second Pimms. Not even because she was about as constant as a yesterday's paper in a typhoon, certainly not because she was a second rate actress (she was) playing a second rate hairdresser in leather trousers, but because Constance, of course, was the name of Lady Chatterley. Who was famous for having had a lover. Though *his* name was – what *was* his name? I couldn't seem to recall it. Only that he wasn't in the least bit like Jonathan, being a son of the soil and having a hut in the woods and a flat cap and string round his trousers. Or perhaps that was Worzel Gummidge. Whatever. He certainly didn't go off to work in a suit. Constance Chatterley on the one hand. Rebecca de Winter on the other. And *me* (I thought). The second Mrs de Winter. She, of course, being equally famous. For not having a first name at all.

I'm not given to sneering as a pastime. Not for me the 'ooh! I can't *stand* her' pronouncements about people that fetch up on the television, but that I have never even met. I don't do that stuff. Yet I believe that had you glanced in at my living room that evening you would have found yourself peering at the face of a woman for whom the superior sneer is the expression of choice. It was with this novel set to my features that I watched the second half of *Parker's Yard.* There had been a commercial break in the middle, during which I was encouraged to take heed of the fact that my dog could be glossier, funkier, lustier and doggier if I were to switch to Binga-bonga Compleat (or something). I thought perhaps I should write up the list of ingredients and send them to Androulla, pretending they were a new diet, for a laugh. That being the sort of laugh I thought funny right then. And then I sat and I watched and I thought.

I thought mainly that there was something unexpected going on here. Something interesting. Noteworthy. Curious. The fact that while I watched Constance Perkins and her plank-like pronouncements in the matter of a misguided root-perm, my instinctive, gut-based, organic response was to want to punch her in the face, hit her around the breasts with a frying pan and tell Heat Magazine that I'd heard on the grapevine that she was riddled with genital warts. Which was grotesque of me, surely. How could I hate her? How could I bring forth such bile for Ms Constance Perkins when I was a chess piece carved from the very same wood? What right had I to feelings of anger against her, when I was practising the very same strokes myself? Unable to fathom a reason – unable to *reason*, full stop – I scratched Merlin's ears and saw *Parker's Yard* through to its (decidedly) bitter end. Then I wondered, in an almost dead-abstract fashion, whether Jonathan would be expecting dinner when he got home from his Tennis club AGM. I had already abandoned dinner myself. If I was lunching with Morgan (so my reasoning had gone) then I certainly wouldn't want dinner. This was still so. I had dined on my lemon. And as Kate was out – where *was* she? Oh, yes. Staying at Amanda's – there seemed little point in preparing some brownie point meal just so Merlin could snaffle it down at half past eleven. Jonathan, I thought loftily, could make his own dinner. Have some cake, maybe. And eat it, too.

It was just gone eight thirty, and having satisfied myself that Ms Constance Perkins was old and wrinkly and had a neck like a fallen down football sock, I decided I would do something else instead.

I went and riffled in the box at the top of Jonathan's wardrobe. And yes, she *did* look like Tricia.

One of the commonest causes of insomnia, it's noted, is excessive alcohol intake. It's caused by the body's internal regulatory system becoming aware of the chemical changes that occur when the alcohol level in the bloodstream has dropped. Any change in the body's chemical balance can be sufficient to coax it from sleep. I don't know if this is true or not (I drink, I wake up, I don't drink, I wake up) but suffice to say it was really no surprise to find myself staring at the ceiling at half past two.

Another of the commonest causes of insomnia is having something pretty damned important to keep you awake. And the pondering of two and a half years of completely undetected infidelity would surely challenge the somnia (if that is the expression, which I concede is unlikely) of even the most dog-tired grizzly bear. Thus excessive alcohol intake was, in a way, a blessing. Though I would most certainly wake up at some small hour and grieve, I would sleep like a corpse until then.

.Jonathan had come in at nine thirty, by which time I had cleared the dog hairs from the sofa, the Pimm's bottle from the worktop, and my head of any ridiculous ideas that I would confront him about what Morgan had told me. Which were small in number in any case. Not only because I had promised Morgan, but also because what purpose would such bloodletting serve? And there *would* be bloodletting. Of that I was sure. The thought had been almost sobering. Indeed by the time I had dispatched the last of the contents of my glass I had become so anxious about the bloody and terrible aftermath I was certain would follow such a revelation – from *both* regiments – that I elected to go to bed ultra-early, in the hopes that I'd be fast asleep by the time he got home.

I hadn't been, not quite, but I'd obviously absorbed a little of the Perkins technique, for when he put his head round the door and said 'hello' I was breathing in wisps and sprawled across the bed, limbs arranged as if I'd been jettisoned recently from a passing high-altitude jet.

And then I had slept. And now I was awake. And Jonathan was in bed snoring beside me. I lifted the duvet gingerly from over me and padded across the room in my T-shirt. The moon was a half crescent of creamy luminescence, backlighting a haze of high, feathery cloud. I glanced back to the bed, to this stranger I lived with, and felt cold stirrings of sobriety and misery begin to tug at my up-to-now maniac brain. Nothing had changed and yet everything had. It was true. I'd been right. Jonathan didn't love me. And despite the other promise I'd made to Morgan not twelve hours ago, my instinctive, three a.m., almost hysterical reaction was that I wished beyond every wish I'd ever, *ever* wished that I could be with the man who did.

But I couldn't I wouldn't I shouldn't. There. If I repeated those words to myself often enough, perhaps they would stop my fingers from creeping ever closer to my phone. I went downstairs and now I did drink some water. Three glasses full, standing at the kitchen sink, staring out into the night and looking for starlight. He didn't love me. Had never loved me. Not in the way he had loved his first wife. I was simply the woman who rescued him from his misery. A wife to take care of him and a mother for his child. Morgan's words swirled in my head. It meant nothing. *Really*. It was just an infatuation. It would kill him if you left him. There was never a choice to be made. Well, she was right about that. How could there have been? There was only one woman he would leave me for, and she was six feet under not three miles from here. No. That was wrong. He couldn't leave me for Tricia. Because he'd never left Tricia in the first place. I drank some more water and swallowed this truth along with it.

I went back to bed, then, and lay sleepless till sun up. The loneliest woman in the world.

But loneliness in the face of having done the right thing was a feeling I thought I could cope with. And had the benefit of being like a bobbly old blanket. A whole lot more comfortable to live with than guilt.

Thus went my thoughts when I woke the next morning. I had faced up to the acid test and I had not been found wanting. I had looked into the deep well of my conscience and, despite the siren call of my newly absolved feelings for Nick, I had taken that vital step back from the precipice. I had remained true to the promise I'd made Morgan. I was not going to unravel my marriage and family. Like Jonathan had done (for I was certain-sure love for *me* didn't figure), I was going to stay with my spouse and get over Nick Brown. I had ended my fling. I would do the right thing. Happiness of the kind I had glimpsed so beguilingly was simply not a God-given right.

But being all things to all men, and a rock and a stalwart and a person who does the right thing in the face of difficult moral decisions and so on, clearly takes its physical toll. As does round-the-clock crying.

'Christ, you look like shit,' observed Russell gaily, as we half-collided in my consulting room doorway a little after eleven . I paused long enough for him to register that I was not going to grace this comment with a sharp and profane riposte, and he leaned forward to inspect me more carefully.

'Russell,' I said eventually. 'Do you think it will be appropriate to be passing such comments once I am Manager of Amberley Park?'

'Absolutely not,' he said, plunging a hand into the breast pocket of his suit. 'But you don't need to worry. Got my interview date this morning.' He'd been invited to apply for the post of senior optom in Redhill, and it looked like the job was as good as his. He mimed a little plane taking off with the letter. 'And then I'm outta here.' He nudged me playfully. 'Go on. Admit it. You're gonna miss me, aren't you?'

Yes, I thought. *Yes*. I am. Very much.

'Russell, don't kid yourself,' I told him gravely. 'Believe me, I'm counting the days.'

'Well, I shan't miss him in the slightest,' puffed Ruth as we sat and went through the special offers together. 'Not in the least,' she went on. 'Be nice to be able to come into work without someone looking down my cleavage and passing judgement on my clothes sense, and taking the piss out of me all the time.'

I sighed. I couldn't seem to stop sighing all of a sudden. Was this the future for me now? A life of regretful exhalations? Would they erect a little monument to me? 'The mysterious woman who sighed'? 'But I couldn't seem to help it. I think it was the pressure of having so much regret inside me. So much to think about. So many reasons for feeling sorry for myself. So many decisions I could be making but the knowledge that the only one that mattered any more was the one I had already made. Damn Jonathan. Damn him. How dare he let Morgan find out about Constance bloody Perkins. How dare he put in place a chain of events that meant *I* knew about Constance bloody Perkins. How dare he marry me at all.

How foolish of *me* to marry *him*. I sighed again. 'I find all this very unsettling,' I said, pretending to myself that there was something inside me other than rocks and finding I could just about manage. 'Everything changing. Everyone moving on. I know it's progress and promotion and inevitable and everything, but it's still a bit sad.' I was talking on auto-pilot. Merely trotting out words. I felt, very keenly, that my world had collapsed. Morgan gone, Kate not so very far behind her, Merlin growing older, Ruth changing her job, Russell leaving altogether, my mother busy with her protests. And then just Jonathan. Just Jonathan and I. 'Nothing'll be –'

Russell poked his head around the door.

'Phone for you, Sally. It's Morgan.'

I had expected Morgan to call, of course, so I was word perfect and prepared.

'I'm sorry to ring while you're at work, Mum,' she said. 'But I just wanted to – you know. Is everything all right?'

'Everything is fine,' I said smoothly. 'The subject is closed, and I don't want to hear any more about it. What about you? Do you have a head like a prune in a bucket? You deserve to.'

'I'm OK,' she said.

'Good.'

'Mum – '

'Morgan, I really have to go. I've got patients waiting.'

'I know,' I'm sorry. I just –'

'Well don't, OK? As far as I'm concerned you never even told me, OK?'

Ruth was still on her knees in the contact lens cupboard when I got off the phone. Work. That was the thing. I had patients to test and referral letters to write and I also had to sort out a thing called a game-plan to present at my induction morning the following week. Lots and lots to do. That was the thing. Carry on. One day at a time. Being sad successfully was all about not thinking long-term. About splitting your day into manageable chunks. Just get through this. Just get through that. Just get through the other, ad nauseam.

'Hmm,' she said, glancing up. 'There's a thing.'

'Thing?'

She said hmm again. 'You heard of a band called Kite?. Russell's got a spare ticket for them tonight that he wants to offload. Some crowd of his from five a side football are going and one's dropped out. The question is, can I be bothered?'

'I don't know,' I said. 'D'you like Kite?'

'Vaguely. In a hum along but don't buy the CDs sort of way. Much more to the point, do I want to spend and evening with Russell and half a dozen of his tanked up, testosterone fuelled pin headed cronies?'

'Well, put like that, er…yes?'

'Hmm,' she said, twiddling a pack of disposable lenses. 'Hmm.'

'Hmm, indeed,' said Dennis, who had arrived with Colin, the Store manager, clutching some posters. We'd been sent a big package of publicity material, for the official Drug u Like launch on August the tenth.. 'I don't think I've ever really come to terms with this colour scheme. Rather you than me, Sally. He unrolled one of the posters and squinted at it. 'These Americans might have streamlined the business but they have an alarming tendency to overstatement. By the way, have you had the dates for the course they're sending you on yet? I was speaking to Adam over at Crawley earlier. He said it was farcical. Lots of jumping up and down and shouting yes!yes!yes!, apparently. Don't quite see how that's going to help him run anything.'

I nodded. 'I still have to sort that out with –' I swallowed the next sigh because I knew it would be a big one. 'Nick Brown. Is he due in any time this week?'

Dennis was in the middle of checking his watch. 'Nick Brown?' he said, drawing his brows together. 'He's gone, hasn't he?'

'Gone?'

He nodded.

'Finished here, certainly. I think he's gone back to San Diego, hasn't he, Colin?'

I watched Colin nod. Could feel Ruth's eyes upon me.

'Oh,' I said. 'Oh, right.'

'Anyway, I think it's David Harrington you need to speak to about the course. He's taken over the scheduling and so on. His number should be on your letter. If not, give me a shout and I'll get it for you.'

We watched them stride off across the shop floor and then I felt the pressure of Ruth's hand on my arm.

'Is that *true*?' she said.

I shook my head. 'I knew nothing about it.' My voice seemed to have gone as well.

'But – '

I got to my feet. 'I knew nothing about it,' I said again. 'Nothing.' I picked up the box of record cards. 'Look, Ruth. D'you think you can take this lot downstairs for me? I need to go somewhere and weep for five minutes.'

She too was on her feet then, and jogging back along to my consulting room behind me. I was walking with giant's strides, the tears sloshing so much in my eyes that I could barely see out of them any more.

Ruth closed the door behind us.

'Gone?' she said again. 'Just like that! But didn't he – '

'Ruth I *told* you. I stopped seeing him. How would I know?'

'Yes, I know, but –'

'Oh, God, Ruth. I can't believe it.' I pulled a wodge of tissues from the box by the sink. 'I thought I was going to be able to – oh, Ruth –'I wiped the tears away angrily. 'Oh, God, Ruth! *Gone*. Just like that. Without even saying goodbye. I feel like I've been hit in the stomach.'

'Oh, Sally,' she said. 'I'm so sorry. But I thought you'd already decided to –.'

'I had. I *have*. I thought I'd do the right thing. I thought I'd be strong and – and now – Ruth, he's *gone*. I can't believe it. I mean I know it doesn't make any difference, but – *gone*. I don't even have a photograph of him.'

She put her arms around me.

'Perhaps it's the best thing,' she said. 'I mean, he was always going to be going sometime, wasn't he? Perhaps it'll be easier if he's not here. Perhaps, you know, with Jonathan, perhaps things will get better.'

I shook my head and blew my nose noisily.

'Not a chance,' I said. 'Not an earthly, Ruth. Things just got a whole lot worse.'

We went out to lunch soon after. I couldn't eat, but I let her drag me off anyhow. I knew I'd feel marginally better once I'd escaped from work.

'Bloody hell,' she said, once I'd finished relating my sorry tale. 'That's certainly a shock. Oh, you poor thing. Listen, d'you want to come over and spend the evening with me tonight?'

I shook my head. 'No, no. You go off to your concert.'

'Bugger the concert. I –'

'Ruth, *really*. I'll be OK.'

She snorted at me.

'OK? You call this OK? Look at the *state* of you! I don't think I'd be OK if I'd just found out my husband had been shagging some tart for two years!'

Heads turned. I buried my face in the muffin she'd insisted on buying for me and wondered if being in a state was something I could adopt as a fashion statement so that people could get used to it and wouldn't feel the need to comment on it all the time. 'It's not that,' I sniffed. 'I mean it's all ancient history. It doesn't *change* anything –'

‘Doesn’t change anything?’ She pushed her empty plate away and plonked her elbows on the table. ‘I don’t see how you figure that one out. It changes everything! I mean, all this time you’ve been banging on about doing the right thing, and he was cheating on you all along.’

‘But it still doesn’t *change* anything.’ I sounded like a stuck record.

‘Of course it does! It means you don’t have to feel guilty! It means you’re *free*, Sally. You have every right to –’

‘It’s not about rights, Ruth. It doesn’t *work* like that. Oh, I know it might work as a handy plot-twist in your stories, but this is *real* life. You can’t package it up so neatly. Oh, it would be all too easy to decide Jonathan’s affair somehow cancels mine out, but it’s all in the past. The real point is that he didn’t leave me. Didn’t leave *us*. So it doesn’t make me feel any better about what I’ve done, Ruth. Doesn’t make me feel I’ve somehow climbed a rung higher on the moral ladder. Doesn’t make me feel as if it suddenly gives me the right to leave him. It’s not about leaving *him*. It’s about tearing my family apart. It’s about the girls.’ I pushed my own plate away and stood up to gather my things together. ‘Besides, it’s all academic. It’s too late now anyway, isn’t it?’

She glared across over the table at me, then snatched up her own bag and stomped out into the walkway ahead of me, batting plastic weeping fig fronds out of her way and scattering startled shoppers.

‘Oh, will you stop all this self-righteous whimpering, girl! Listen to yourself! Your eldest is an adult and your youngest as good as. You carry on as though they were a pair of toddlers! D’you think they’d see it like that? Really? That it would be better for you and their father to hang around together in misery till you’re a pair of shuffling crones scowling at each other just because you’ve got some cock-eyed idea it’ll be better somehow? *Better?* Credit them with a little intelligence, for God’s sake! Don’t you get my point at all? God, Sally! Sometimes I wonder if you’re inhabiting the same planet as everyone else. You’ve been –’

‘Ruth,’ I said miserably, ‘you’re shouting at me.’

She whirled around and jabbed a finger towards me. ‘I know that, Sally. And I’ll tell you something else. If I didn’t love you so much I’d give you a bloody good slap as well.’

We went back to the office and I had a full afternoon's testing ahead of me. Back to back patients and the reassurance of sameness. 'And *blink*. And look *up*. And look *down*. And *blink*.' Good. Hypnotic. Robotic. Thought-free. If I had to spend one more minute dissecting my situation I thought I might just lie down and die.

Chapter 29

Not dissecting my situation was beginning to look like the answer. The waves of sadness kept washing over me, but I knew I could cope if I just made an effort to ignore them. Wall to wall happiness wasn't a right. Thursday. Friday. One day at a time.

But not ignoring them was not an option with Ruth around. She sought me out as soon as I got in on Friday morning, and insisted on knowing how I was. As friends do.

'Miserable' I told her. 'Er, let me see. Heart-broken. Wretched. Empty. Yes, definitely empty. Lost. Sorry for myself. Discombobulated–'

'Come again?'

'It means disturbed. Disconcerted. But sounds so much better than either, don't you think?' I switched on the light box then went over to hug her . 'I'll *live*, Ruth, I'm sure. Thanks for asking. But end of consultation, OK? So. Tell me. How did last night go?'

Her face changed then. The furrowed brow of the concerned friend being replaced by a barely suppressed smile of happy bemusement.

'I don't know,' she said, grinning. 'I'm still too discombobulated to tell.'

I smiled too, taking my cue from her. 'Why?'

She leaned across to shut my consulting room door.

'There was no one else there,' she said obscurely.

'No one else?'

She shook her head. 'No. Just us. Just Russell and I.'

'What happened to all his mates then?'

'There *were* no mates. Oh, he gave me some clap-trap about how he was supposed to be meeting up with them somewhere, but he didn't show the least enthusiasm for doing so.'

'Perhaps he decided it would be too much hassle. Were the band good?'

'I don't know. We never went.'

'Never went?'

She shook her head again. She'd put her hair up in a spring clip, and little tendrils of it curled prettily around her chin. 'We stayed in the pub all evening. And talked. And talked. And, well, talked, basically. Who'd have thought it? Me and him, *talking*! Anyway,' she said. 'That's what we did. And we're off for a curry this evening.' She stood up and smoothed down the front of her skirt. Who'd have thought it,' she said again. 'Eh?'

Who indeed. 'You and Russell?' I said. 'Not me, for starters. But now I think about it, why *not* you and Russell? Do you like him?'

She winked at me as she opened the consulting room door. 'You know what, Sal? Derr brain and loudmouth and infuriating jackass that he is, I have to say yes, I rather do.'

Amazing how two people can live in the same house, sleep in the same bed, share the same bathroom and yet manage to co-exist on such a superficial level. Amazing, but do-able, obviously. But even as I consoled myself with the fact that I was but one statistic among many I wondered how well or how long we would manage it once Kate had left home as well. Would we begin taking an interest in bonsai? Get a budgie? I had a momentary vision of Jonathan taking up a new sport – bowls perhaps, or koi carp breeding or growing exhibition dahlias like Dennis did. Gradually replacing the possible with the actual. Anything to spare us the uncomfortable business of having to communicate about abstracts and thoughts. We would, it seemed however, have a chance to try it on for size.

'You absolutely *have* to let me go, or I'll die,' Kate was saying on Saturday morning, in her usual considered and understated way.

She had returned home from sleeping over at Amanda's with the news that six of them – four girls, plus Carl and Andy – had been invited to spend a week at Janine's father's friend's caravan in Cornwall.

'Newquay?' asked Jonathan warily. 'Isn't that the place I've read about? All surfing and sex, I've heard.'

'Oh, *honestly*, Dad,' snorted Kate. 'Where do you *read* this stuff? Please let me. I've been working *so* hard. I deserve a break, don't I?'

As Kate had spent much of the preceding three weeks when she wasn't out having fun, either in her bed or on her bed or on the floor by her bed or at Amanda's – on *her* bed, no doubt – this didn't hold a great deal of weight as a reason, but as I had been a teenager myself, I knew how debilitating such activities could be.

'I don't know,' he said. He had not been a teenager. Not ever. 'I'm not altogether sure the idea of you and boys on your own in a caravan is such a good one,' he said. About as good an idea as his one of being on his own in a flat in London once a week, come to think of it.

'Dad get *real,*' she said. 'Mum, tell him. I'm almost –'

'Yes, yes. Nearly seventeen,' he said testily. 'As you never tire of telling us. But being nearly seventeen is not the same as being eighteen, and all the while you live under this roof –.'

Kate rolled her eyes. 'What about Janine's parents?' I said. 'Are they going to be down there in their caravan too?'

'Over the weekend, maybe, I think. But what's the big deal anyway? Janine goes down on her own all the time. They're cool about it. It's not like we're going to be having orgies all day. Just hanging out and chilling and –'

Jonathan pulled a face that made it plain he considered the idea of hanging out and chilling to be just another variation on the same unsavoury theme. 'Quite,' he said. He picked up his paper. 'I'll think about it,'

Kate put her hands on her hips. 'For, like, how *long*, exactly? I have to let Janine know by –'

'Kate, I will *think* about it. End of discussion.' He opened the paper and retreated behind it.

Kate tossed her hair back and stuck out her tongue, then flounced off out of the room.

'I don't see that it'll be a problem,' I said once she'd gone. 'It's hardly as if they're going to be doing anything they haven't had every opportunity to do already.'

I began clearing the breakfast things. The paper rustled a little. 'May even have *done* already, in fact.' It rustled a little more. 'Could do perfectly easily *any*where, in fact. Jonathan I think there's a trust issue here, don't you?' The paper was lowered. He looked at me grimly.

'That's your department,' he said.

Which struck me, as I walked up to Kate's room, as a great deal more pertinent than he knew. I tapped lightly on the door.

'Well?' she said. She was – *quel surprise* – lying on her bed. The poster I'd bought her at Tate Modern was now stuck above the head of it. It had an eerie, sinister quality about it. I didn't think I'd ever be able to look at it without being reminded of horrible things.

I sat down on the bed beside her. 'Kate, Carl *is* your boyfriend. So let's be honest, shall we? We're not just talking all mates hanging out together, are we?'

'Mum,' she said, groaning. 'Do we *have* to do this?'

'Yes,' I said tartly, feeling all frazzled and tearful again all of a sudden. Could I really do carpet bowls and floristy and crosswords? Aunt Sally. That was me now. 'We certainly do, young lady,' I trotted out anyway. 'Unless you're about to tell me you and he spend your time playing scrabble. Kate, this is important. This is –'

'Yeah, yeah, yeah, mum. We've had this conversation. Don't ever take drugs and don't ever get pregnant. I *know*, OK? I'm not a child, you know.'

'I know, but –'

'So you don't need to give me a lecture on contraception, OK?'

'I wasn't about to tell you about contraception, Kate. God, if you don't know by now you never will. I just wanted to…well. Kate, *have* you slept with him?'

She looked at the ceiling. 'Not yet.'

And do you love him?'

She looked at me now. Her face was Drug U Like pink. 'Mum, what *is* this?'

'Well, *do* you? I just want you to think about it, that's all. Just want you to, well… you're only sixteen, Kate. I just want you to think about…well, just don't be too ready to, well, get yourself too involved with…*give* yourself to someone if you're not *absolutely* sure it's what you want. You have a long life ahead of you – university, perhaps, and you'll be meeting other boys, and I just would hate to think of you making a mistake that will –'

'Mistake? Mum, we're not talking getting engaged here, you know.'

'Exactly, Kate. *Exactly*. Which is why I just think you should –'

'Mum, it's only sex.' She sat up.

'But it's *not* only sex, Kate. Making love is –'

'Sex, mum.' She sat up. 'Look, mum. What exactly are you trying to say? That I should save myself for Mr Right, or something? Be a virgin till I'm thirty? What?'

But I couldn't articulate what it was I wanted to say, because I didn't even know. Only that if I tried I'd start crying. So instead I rattled round her room gathering up socks and plates.

'Just don't do anything you don't want to do,' I mumbled finally.

She snorted. Then grinned. 'Mum, like, when did I *ever*?'

On Wednesday morning I had to leave early because I had my induction morning at the Drug U Like area office. I left Kate packed and ready and refrained from starting up any more ditzy conversations with her.

'It's *cool*, OK, mum?' she said, as I left. Which had to be good enough, I supposed.

The irony wasn't lost on me that it had been exactly a week ago that I'd been making my way up to London to see Morgan. Exactly a week ago when I last lived in a state of blissful ignorance in the matter of my husband's soap opera life. Exactly a week ago that everything had seemed so straightforward. Sad, but nevertheless straightforward.

An awful lot of thinking for someone who was supposed to be finding her way to a conference room in a building the size of a football pitch, and without benefit of a map. Which was probably why it wasn't until I felt a tap on my shoulder that I was aware that someone was coming up behind me. That and the dense pink carpet of course.

'Sally?'

To my distress, I had by this time begun to find the exact details of his face a little difficult to recall to mind, but the voice, clear and distinctive in the air conditioned space, was still as recognisable to me as the sound of my own . I spun around, stunned.

'Hello,' he said. 'You lost?'

Nick. Here. Just standing in front of me. Looking at me. Smiling at me. *Here*. I swallowed.

'I thought you'd gone, ' I spluttered finally.

'Gone?'

'Back to San Diego. Dennis said you went back to San Diego last week.'

He shook his head.

'Next week,' he said. 'I go Tuesday. Well,' He smiled wryly. 'I say Tuesday, but it's at some god awful hour in the morning so it might just as well be called Monday. Still, hey – don't sleep much anyway, eh?' He raised his eyebrows enquiringly. Then , seeing my expression presumably, let the awkward grin slip from his mouth.

'Anyway,' he went on, 'he's got his dates muddled. I've been here all week. You know. Tying things up.'

'You are going back then?'

I felt cold. Despite the heat of the morning I could feel goosebumps on my arms. He nodded again. 'Looks like it.'

'Oh,'

'I've pretty much decided against going for the HR development job here – well, what with everything… '

He shrugged. I shifted the strap on my handbag.

'Yes. Well. Best thing. Back to see Will, and –'

I ground to a halt, upset beyond measure by this small intimacy. This little affirmation of closeness. I so wanted to hold him. Just once more.

He looked at me carefully. 'How are you?'

'OK,' I said, snapping myself to attention. 'I'm supposed to be going off on my Management training course in a fortnight. And I'm –'

'I didn't mean that,' he said quietly. 'I meant how *are* you?' He stopped in the corridor. To see.

I spread my hands. 'I'm…well, I'm OK. I'm here. I'm all right. I'm –'

A door opened just ahead of us and a woman holding a box file came out of it.

'Ah,' she said. 'That's handy, Nick. I was just coming down to see you. Don wants a word if you've got a minute.'

He moved the sheaf of papers he was carrying from one hand to the other and pushed his fingers into his hair. His watch face glinted at his wrist.

'I'll be right along,' he said. 'I was just on my way there now.'

She smiled and retreated. I remained suspended in wretchedness. I started walking along the corridor.

He did likewise. 'Where are you supposed to be?'

I consulted the letter in my hand. My fingers were shaking. 'Conference room four,' I told him.

'Come on, then. I'll show you where it is.'

This was simply too painful a situation to contemplate. 'Don't worry,' I said. 'You go off and do whatever it is –'I started flapping my hand in the direction of the office door we'd just passed. He glanced back.

'It's not on this corridor,' he said, still striding alongside me. 'You have to get around to the other side of the quadrangle then take the –'

I stopped.

'Nick, I'm sure I'll manage to find my way.'

'Sure?'

No. *No*. Not at all. But I knew if I didn't get away from him now, then I would not find my way *any*where, ever again. I gazed up at him and looked squarely into his eyes. 'I will, Nick. Somehow,' I said.

I left him then, standing in the middle of the sun-flooded corridor. As I turned the corner I glanced back to wave. But by then he'd already gone.

I bought him a jar of Marmite.

I recalled little of the morning, even less of the afternoon. Only that by the time I arrived home at six it felt as if the sun – which had burned with such relentlessness all day – was eating its way into my very soul. Jonathan was sitting in the garden when I got there, a glass of beer at his elbow and the Telegraph open on his knees. I felt gripped by an almost convulsive need to be somewhere else. Anywhere else.

Dogs have many uses. Pausing only to call out a brief hello, I slipped upstairs to change into jeans and then took mine out for a walk. A long walk. We walked down the lane, through the woods, across the edge of the wheat field, down the bridle path that led across to the farm buildings themselves, then on down the lane towards Lingfield, where there was a generally well-stuffed local shop. I hadn't set out with the Marmite in mind, particularly. Just a card, or something. Just *something*. But as soon as I saw it, sitting squat on the shelf, I knew I could send nothing else. I bought the Marmite, a jiffy bag, a pack of plain postcards, and a little book of self-adhesive first class stamps. Then I parcelled up the marmite, wrote *Good Luck* on the postcard. Thought again, added *Goodbye* and seven tearful kisses, sealed it in the jiffy bag, kissed it, hugged it and put it in the letterbox. It landed with an audible thump at the bottom. Too late for tonight's collection, of course. But it would go off tomorrow. And he could take it home with him.

Home. A long way for us both.

*   *   *

I was just putting my key in the front door when I heard the phone ringing.

I unclipped Merlin's lead from his collar and reached for the receiver.

It was my mother.

'Oh, hello dear,' she said jauntily, cutting through the fog in my head. 'Glad I managed to catch you. I just wondered. Have you got any plans for this weekend?'

I have no plan for the rest of my life, I thought miserably. Bar nursing my heart and being quietly unhappy. Which was a plan of sorts, I supposed.

'No,' I said eventually. 'I'm working Saturday, and I think Jonathan's got a tennis match Sunday. Kate's away, of course. I imagine I'll be spending most of it continuing to un-arrange Morgan's wedding.'

'Oh good,' she said. 'I mean, not *good*, of course, but I was wondering if you fancied a trip down to Eastbourne. I have a bit of spring cleaning to do.'

'Spring cleaning?' I asked. 'In *July*?'

She cleared her throat and sent a little tinkly laugh down the phone. Her jauntiness sounded rather forced, all of a sudden, even to my heavily dulled senses. 'Well, you know me –'she began.

'And?' I said sternly.

'Well, dear, it's just that my living room's – well, it's in rather a state at the moment and I'll need some help moving the furniture.'

'Mother, can you be more specific, perhaps?'

'Well… it's just that there's been a bit of an accident.'

'*What?*'

'No, no,' she added quickly. 'Not *that* sort of accident. Nothing to worry about, darling. Just that – well, there's…um… paint everywhere.'

'*Paint?*'

'It's OK. It's only emulsion. It washes off all right. I've already done some. It's just that, well, it spilled, you see, and there's…well… rather a lot of it.'

This conversation was becoming surreal. 'Mother,' I snapped. 'What on *earth* have you been doing? What on earth were you painting?'

'Er…the living room, mainly.'

'The living room! For goodness sake, what are you painting your living room for? What were you thinking of? If you'd wanted it decorated you should have rung me and asked me –'

Typical. Off on one of her mad schemes again. Probably been watching too much Home Front. For some reason, the notion made me feel a little bit better. The thought of a day with her a whole lot better. A day away from home. Away from Jonathan. 'Honestly, Mum!' I said, tutting back at her. 'You are priceless, you know that?'

'I know, dear,' she said, sounding relieved. 'But, well, there you go. You know what I'm like. Are you free? *Could* you come down?'

'Yes,' I said, blinking back a new spate of tears. 'I'll be there first thing Sunday, OK?'

Yes. I would go down and help her spring clean. I really needed my mum right now.

Chapter 30

'Mum, what the *hell's* been going on?'

I should have known. I should have known when she'd phoned me. I should certainly have realised the moment I arrived at the house, because I couldn't get my front door key to work. I'd still been struggling to get it back out of the lock when she opened it for me, her expression apologetic. I followed her inside with some trepidation. There was no evidence of any decorating endeavours. No stepladder, no roller, no brushes or sponges. Just paint. In quantity. In very pale pink.

'Um..' she began. I looked around me in horror. There was paint *everywhere*. On the carpet, the sofa, the bookcase, the coffee table. Crusted on the cushions, pooled around the chair legs, spattered on the pictures, sprayed up against the wall. There was even paint forming an impromptu pink bogie on the face of my gran, whose photo hung by the door.

'God, mum!' I gasped. 'What on earth has *happened* here? It looks like someone has just been in here and literally chucked the stuff around!'

Which was, it turned out, because it had.

'It was him,' she said, perching on the edge of the sofa.

'Him?'

'Tracey's husband.'

'*What*? You mean he just came in here – in *your* flat – and flung a tin of emulsion all over your living room?' I was at a loss for words.

She shook her head. 'Not flung. He kicked it apparently.'

'*What?* But why? When? God, Mum, why didn't you tell me?'

She folded the tea towel she held in her hands.

'On Tuesday,' she said. 'He'd seen her. He was working just up the road, you see, and he saw her come in here. And he followed her –'

I felt suddenly fearful. '*What?* But what about you? What happened? Was he violent? What did he do?'

'I wasn't here,' she said. 'Tracey had just –'

'*What?* What do you mean, you weren't here?' I interrupted her. 'How come Tracey was –'

She looked aggrieved. 'I do wish you'd stop squeaking '*what?*' at me, dear.' She unfolded the tea towel again.. 'She had a key. She'd just –'

'*Wh* – Sorry. But a *key,* mum? What on earth did she have a key to your flat for? Mum, what possessed you to –'She stood up and started heading for the kitchen. I stomped after her. 'Mum, what on earth were you thinking?'

'Look, Sally,' she said, turning around and looking defiantly at me. 'I know it was stupid. So you don't need to tell me. And all the locks have been changed, and the police have arrested him, and there's really no point in going over it all again. I *know* it was silly of me, but what else could I do? Poor mite. She's been scared witless *–witless* – and what with – well, anyway. It looks much worse than it was, apparently. Polly had seen him go in, and she called the police straight away. She was on him right away anyway, and they were there in minutes. And the little ones weren't there or anything. Megan was at school and the baby was next door. Tracey had only popped in to pick up her library books. It's done now. At least she knows he won't be bothering her any more.'

I wished I felt as confident about that as my mother sounded, but then I thought of Polly and her tattoos and her boots, and felt a little better. I didn't comment.

'But *why?'* I said instead. 'Why the paint?'

She shrugged. 'Just an unlucky coincidence. He'd been on his way back from his van apparently. He was painting in a house up the road. Just my luck, eh?' She grinned at me. 'My tapestry went for a burton.'

'Oh, *no*!'

'Oh, no nothing. Glad to see the back of the wretched thing, quite frankly. I was getting sick of the sight of it. I was beginning to think it was going to see me out. Besides, I can't help thinking it wasn't such a bad thing, as it happens. If he hadn't had that bucket of paint to kick…'

'You're making me feel very anxious, mum. What if he comes back? What if –'

'Sally, he's *not* coming back. Going to prison by the sound of it. And besides, he doesn't know me from Adam, does he? It just happened to be my living room he tracked her down to. Could have been anywhere. Anyway, Tracey's gone up to Northampton now. She's got a sister up there and she's taken them in. Best thing, I think. Though why it takes something like this before families actually do something, I don't know.' She shook her head and pushed up the sleeves of her cardigan. 'Anyway, enough of that. Now. Cup of tea before we start? I have some more rather exciting news.'

Which was true, as it turned out. On Saturday morning she'd received a letter from Collette Carr. Pledging her support and saying she'd be more than happy to help with publicity where possible. And enclosing a cheque.

'Wow, mum! Ten thousand Pounds!'

Just like that. I made a mental note to go buy her whole back catalogue sometime soon.

My mum was nodding happily. 'Isn't it amazing? And it's all thanks to you. Polly's already called her, and she said she'll be happy to give us a quote as well. Polly's going to put it on the refuge notepaper.'

'That's *really* something,' I said, feeling full of pride. 'And not *at all* to do with me. It was your idea, mum. You who wrote the letter. You who did the work.'

'Yes, but you got it to her. You will thank Ruth as well for me, will you?' She slipped the cheque back into the envelope. 'Restores your faith in people, doesn't it?

There is nothing like an extended bout of arduous scrubbing to chase all your demons away. Admittedly, there is nothing like an extended bout of arduous scrubbing to rip all your nails out, give you big oozy blisters and take all the skin off your knuckles either, but I considered that a small price to pay for half a dozen precious hours of being otherwise engrossed. Perhaps I should take up scrubbing as a hobby.

We worked pretty solidly through the day, and true to my mother's prediction, the paint did, in the main, come off. There were a few casualties, certainly, but the only major one was the sofa, which my mother hated anyway. She would, she said, treat herself to a new one. No she wouldn't, I told her. Now I had my promotion *I* would treat her to one. Once the light had begun to fade we decided we'd go for a walk along the sea front and pick up some fish and chips on the way home. We headed off along the promenade, picking pink paint from what was left of our fingernails as we walked.

'God, I'm weary,' I said, as we reached the front.

'Hmm,' she said. And you're not looking any better.' We made our way down on to the shingle so Merlin could have a paddle. 'How are things with Morgan?' she said. 'Is she coping?'

I was grateful for the direction of her thoughts. I nodded. 'Remarkably so. You know, it's almost as if she's happier now than she was when the wedding was still going ahead. So perhaps Cody's arrest was serendipity, even. He's applying to do a degree in Horticulture next year.'

'Horticulture? What on earth would he want to do that for?'

'It's what he always wanted to do, apparently. He's hoping to get a place at Keele University.

'Keele? What, in Staffordshire?'

I nodded. Merlin came back with his hunk of driftwood and deposited it at my feet. I picked it up and hurled it across the beach for him. 'And if he does, they'll move. Morgan seems to think she won't have any problem finding a job up there, so –'

'That's an awfully long way away.'

'I know.'

She sighed. 'It never used to be like this. Families stayed together.'

'It's not so far. Five hours. Six at the most. But, yes. You're right. Not popping up for lunch distance. Still, if she's happy…'

My mother stopped and picked up a pebble.

'But you're not,' she said.

'Mum, I'm *fine*.'

'Fiddlesticks.' She stopped and turned to look at me. 'You're about as fine as a wet day in Worthing. I wish you'd tell me what the matter is, Sally. I worry about you, you know.'

She tossed the pebble into the foamy shallows. We walked a little further along the shingle in silence, stooping every so often to throw the stick for the dog. I wondered if maybe I *should* tell her. But what was the point? What was there to say? It would only worry her even more.

'We used to push you along here in your pram, your dad and I,' my mum said suddenly. 'Not down here, of course. Up on the prom. We were always great ones for walking. All the way to Holywell and back sometimes. We used to stay in that little guest house in Cambridge road. D'you remember that?'

'Vaguely,' I said. 'I remember the model village.'

Merlin came back with the stick again, and my mother wrestled it from his mouth, before flinging it ahead of him. 'I'd love another dog,' she said. 'To walk with.'

'You could get one. A small one.'

She shook her head. Too much of a tie. Besides, I've got Merlie here to visit me, haven't I?'

I nodded, feeling tearful again all of a sudden.

'Do you get lonely?' I asked her.

'Lonely?' She turned to look at me. 'Why d'you ask that?'

I brushed at my eyes, grateful for my sunglasses. 'Dad's been gone such a long time. *Aren't* you lonely?'

'Of course I'm lonely,' she said. 'But you learn to cope. I'm not unhappy, if that's what you mean. Way too busy, for one thing!' She chuckled.

'But did you never think – never hope –'

'What, that I'd meet someone else?' She shook her head and scooped another pebble from the shingle. 'There was never any point. When you're dad died I knew that was it for me, really. I loved him too much, you see. And when he went, well, that part of me went along with him. I'd never be able to love anyone else like I loved your dad. Didn't even want to have to try.' She lobbed the pebble into the water. 'So, no,' she said. 'It wouldn't have been fair.'

Jonathan, who had been at a tournament in Horley, rang midway though the evening to let me know that if I wasn't planning to be back until late he might as well get off up to London as sleep at home and have to crawl up there in the traffic in the morning. So there was really no rush to get back. Would there ever be?

When it got to ten and I was dozing off on the sofa, my mother decided to take charge.

'Sleep here tonight,' she said firmly. 'It won't take a minute to make a bed up for you, and there's no point in driving all that way back to an empty house, is there? I can get you up nice and early for work.'

I thought of her lending me one of her winceyette nighties. Of waking in the morning to hear her pottering in her kitchen. Listening to the dreadful local radio station she liked. Her popping her head round the door with a cup of early morning tea and a Digestive biscuit. I thought I would rather like to be her little girl again. For one night, at least. It would feel safe. Ordinary. Reassuring.

So that's what Merlin and I did.

Chapter 31

There are lots of safe, ordinary, reassuring things one can do when one is suffering from emotional overload and heartbreak and another of them is the management of curtains. Why had I never considered this? Why had I never realised that the reason ordinary, sensible, dependable people – people like Briony, in fact – did not go off the rails and get themselves embroiled in dangerous passions was precisely because they did the sensible thing and kept themselves busy with curtains.

I am busy with curtains right now. Briony's Mum's room's curtains, specifically, as they were seriously dusty and she has had to have-them-down. And I have been asked, on this cheerless Monday evening, to help her to have-them-back-up. This is on account of the sprained wrist she sustained during the having-them-down bit earlier in the week, which does indicate that despite my enthusiasm for curtains right now they are not entirely without pitfalls. Briony's mum's room smells sweet, faintly sickly. It has little lace doilies over every conceivable surface and a sepia photograph of an unsmiling family group scowling out from her darkwood dresser. There is a large print copy of a Catherine Cookson novel on the bedside table, the cover redolent of a time when women scrubbed their own doorsteps and knew right from wrong. I wonder if and when my own mother will submit to the dictates of old age and stop storming around and getting embroiled in disasters. But then I think about her holed up and doing tapestry in a spare room – my own, most probably, so dust would clearly be an issue – and I send a silent prayer of thanks that it is probably not yet.

'It's her lungs,' Briony explains. 'Nothing much wrong with them, but she gets very twitched about dust. It's Dad's emphysema. It was the mines that really did it, of course, but there's no telling her that. I wouldn't normally go to the bother of washing curtains this often, but if I don't do hers she gets a bee in her bonnet. And, fair do. They've not been down in six months.'

Six *months*? My curtains have not been down in six years. I must, I decide, pay more attention to my soft furnishings. Soft furnishings and their husbandry could become the lynch pin of my life. I could get my carpets steam cleaned, I could have my loose covers Scotch guarded. I could spend many a contented hour sewing contrasting piping cord round all my cushions. Oh, and I could scrub.

'Are you OK?' I hear Briony say now. 'Sally?'

Curtains. That's the thing. I shall become a good and reliable housekeeper. For if you take away my heart what else is there for me to be?

'Dust' I quip. 'Bit of dust in my eye, that's all.' Here, hand me up that one and I'll get this end hooked on.'

When we come back down to the sitting room, Briony's mother is sitting in the dark with the television off. The only light in the room is that still filtering palely through the slight chink in another set of curtains, these swagged and rouched and colour-matched with the sofas. You could cosh a prop forward with the tie-backs.

'There's been a noise,' she announces with a warble in her voice.

Briony flicks the light switch back on.

'A noise, Mum?

'I thought it was coming from the television so I turned it off. But it started up again. It's not the lights.'

Briony strides across and picks the remote control from her mother's lap, then puts the television back on as well. 'You're missing your programme, aren't you? Why didn't you call me? What sort of noise?'

Her mother tuts. 'A buzzing noise. I didn't like the sound of it. It stopped but then it started again.'

'A bluebottle?' says Briony.

'Or a car alarm?' I suggest.

She shakes her head.

'No it wasn't. It was in this room. Very loud. Very buzzy.'

'The smoke alarm, maybe?'

Briony glances upwards then shakes her head.

'That doesn't buzz. It peeps. Perhaps it was something *on* the telly, mum. In a programme, or something.'

Briony's mother shakes *her* head now. 'I told you, it started up again after I turned the television off. I didn't like it. I don't like strange noises.'

‘Well,’ says Briony, with her infinite patience. ‘It’s stopped now, mum, so no need to worry. It was probably just –’

‘I don’t like all these electrical things around the place. You never know if they’re – there we are! There it goes again! Listen!’

We listen.

‘Oh, yes, I can hear it,’ begins Briony. ‘A sort of –’

Tropical insect in bean tin-type buzzing. ‘I know what it is,’ I say, picking up my handbag. I fish around in it. ‘It’s my phone.’

And it is Jonathan. What is *he* ringing me for?

I push the connect button.

‘Where are you?’ he growls.

I’m so taken aback by the tone of his voice that I can’t remember for a moment.

‘Pardon?’ I say instead, flustered.

‘Where *are* you?’ he says again. If such a phenomenon actually existed, the hairs on the back of my neck, by this time, would be standing to attention and waving at me. Briony and her mother look on politely.

‘What d’you mean, where am I? I’m next door.’

‘Next door?’ the words come out in spits, like bacon.

‘Yes. I’m helping Briony with –’

‘Next door? Really? Honestly?’

‘Honestly! Why on earth –’

But he has put down the phone.

And then the one in Briony’s hall begins ringing.

‘Fancy that!’ she says gaily, going off to answer it.

Briony’s mother looks up at me suspiciously. ‘I don’t like electrical things,’ she says.

I look at my own phone, which says six missed calls. I switch it back to vibrate. I’m inclined to agree with her. Even more so when Briony comes back into the sitting room.

‘Goodness me, you’re in demand tonight, Sally!’ She cocks her head. ‘It’s Jonathan, of all people! For you.’

For me. Jonathan. Jonathan 4 Sally. I walk out into the hall on feet that are suddenly as heavy as lead. A rush of heat floods my face. A rush of anger is not far behind.

‘Is this some sort of joke?’ I ask him levelly. ‘Where are *you*?’

His voice is less sharp now, but not so you’d notice. Unless you’d been married to him for eighteen years, of course.

'I'm at home,' he says.

'*Home*?'

Home? Jonathan? On a Monday night? 'Yes,' he barks.

'How come?' I feel cold.

'Why do *you* think?' I feel colder. '*Well?* Are you coming or not?'

At the junction of our lane and the main road there's a bus stop. I can't remember the number of the bus that stops there, or, for that matter, its destination. Only that the buses stop running at about nine in the evening. I know this because it's one of the many reasons why I spend so much time ferrying Kate around. It is half past nine. It is not, therefore, an option. I could walk, of course. I could walk in any direction and in time, with luck, I would be somewhere else. Brighton, perhaps. Or Croydon. Or, if I strike lucky and sprout some wings, a suburb of Neverland perhaps. I don't much care. I don't think I've ever felt such a powerful, passionate, overwhelming need to be somewhere else at this moment.

Nevertheless, I fetch up at our door because that is where my legs take me. I don't need to use my key because the front door is already open. Jonathan is framed in the light from the hallway, Merlin beside him, a grim Hammer horror silhouette.

I don't know what to say to him. It's impossible to know what to say in such a situation. How does one feel one's way back into a conversation that has been put on hold for the best part of two decades? He, clearly, doesn't know either. So he stands back against the door to let me walk past him then shuts the door quietly behind me. Here we are, shut in and alone with each other. The air is shuddering with unspoken thoughts and thick with the backed up resentments of years. I can smell drink on his breath. I feel trapped. I want to scream.

'Well?' I say instead.

He moves past me and heads off towards the kitchen. Merlin and I follow. There is a bottle of malt whisky open on the kitchen table, an empty glass beside it. He splashes another half inch of drink into it and puts it to his lips. Then he lowers it. I watch mutely while his expression hardens further.

'I've spoken to Morgan,' he says suddenly.

I watch Merlin turn circles underneath the table. 'And?'

He grimaces at me. 'And I've driven home, of course. And now I'd like you to tell me what the hell is going on.'

My immediate thought – the thought that crowds out every other cognitive process in my brain – is that I should tell him nothing. That whatever Morgan has told him, I should deny everything. Keep things on track now. Settle down. Do curtains. What *has* she told him?

'What's going *on*?' I echo. 'Jonathan, I –'

'Let's not play games, Sally,' he says, as if talking to an infant. 'What's going on between you and this – this – this *man* you're seeing?'

Well, that's that one answered then. So there's little point in denying it. But I can certainly tell him the truth.

'I'm not seeing him any more,' I say.

'What's that supposed to mean?'

'What I said. I'm not seeing him.'

'So you're not denying you've *been* seeing him?'

'No.'

He blinks at this conversational dead end. Then clears his throat and picks up the glass from the table. He tips the rest of the whisky into his mouth and puts it back down again. I feel frightened. Not because I think he's going to hit me or anything, but because I can already feel the fabric of my existence fraying. That the safety net of long established routine is unravelling beneath me. That I'm going to fall at any moment into a void.

'For how long?' he says.

'Not long.'

'*How* long?'

'A few weeks.' He looks relieved at this. Which strikes me as a huge misjudgement where feelings are concerned. It took no time at all, after all.

'And?'

'And I'm not seeing him any more. You must know that. Morgan must have told you that.'

'She told me you'd said that but that she didn't believe you.' He looks at me through slightly bloodshot eyes. How drunk is he? How long has he been here? 'Are you telling me she should have? That *I* should?'

I feel suddenly as if I have already fallen. And that I'm now at the bottom of a big, craggy rock face and that the summit is shrouded in cloud.

'Whether you believe me or not isn't relevant, Jonathan. It's the truth.'

'OK,' he says. 'Then *why* not? If not, why not?'

How many times am I going to have to answer this question?. 'Because I'm married to you.'

'That's not a reason.'

'It's the only reason I can give you right now, Jonathan, so I'm afraid it'll have to do.'

There is, sometimes, a little road noise in the kitchen but at this moment the silence is so dense and woolly you could pluck handfuls from around you and ball it in your fist. Jonathan pulls out a chair and sits down at it, then puts his face in his hands. I don't know quite what to do, so I wait, gripping a chair back. He lifts his face again, rubbing his fingers across his temples.

'Have you slept with him?'

'Yes.'

'Are you in love with him?'

I pause to swallow the bitter taste of the untruth before I utter it. 'No.'

There is another silence and this time I let it wash over me. Merlin is beside me now, his flank pressed close against my thigh.

Looking at the table, Jonathan says, 'Do you love *me*?'

'Jonathan, I – it's –'I spread my hands. 'I don't *know*.'

'Jesus,' he says, so quietly that I can hardly hear him. '*Jesus*. I can't believe this is happening to me.' He looks up at me now, his eyes glittering. 'How many times?'

'Christ, *what?*'

'How many times have you slept with him?'

'God, Jonathan, that isn't important!'

But he ignores me. '*Where* have you slept with him? *When*? When did all this happen?' There is a tremulousness about his voice that is entirely unfamiliar to me. 'Who is he, Sally? Who *is* he?'I am shaking my head now. 'Come on, *Tell* me. Please. I need to know. When did you meet him? Who *is* he? What the hell did he think he was playing at? Christ – you're my wife! Sally, you're– 'He's up on his feet now and moving across the kitchen towards me. I can feel the dog tensing against my leg. 'Christ !' He bats away Merlin's face with his hand. 'Get away, will you? Damn dog!'

'Don't hit him!'

'I wasn't hitting him!'

'Yes, you were!'

He's not listening. 'Who *is* he?' he hisses, a foot or so from me now. Merlin retreats, whimpering, back under the table, his claws rat-a-tatting on the quarry tiles. 'Where does he live? How could you do that? How could you –'

'Jonathan, stop this! It's not important! You do not need to know, OK? None of that's going to help anything! All you need to know is that I'm *here!*'

He is standing so close to me now that I can feel the heat coming from his face. There is a tic at the corner of his jaw.

'Not important! Of course it's important! You breeze in here and tell me you're sleeping with another man and you tell me it's not important! Christ –'He raises an arm and I lift my own instinctively. I am truly frightened now. He is not a person I know any more. My action seems to shock him and he looks at me, horrified. Then he sits back at the table and lays his head on his wrists. His shoulders start moving. And with a jolt I realise he's crying.

Accepted wisdom would have us believe that the thing to do when someone dear to you is crying is to put your arms around them and make consoling noises and tell them that everything will be all right. Accepted wisdom has a lot to be said for it, but in the space I had been now granted two things became clear to me. One of these was that Jonathan *was* very dear to me – a simple and gratifying moment, made no less intense for the fact that the man I loved, *truly* loved, was not this one – and the other was that to move on to the safe ground of consoling and touching and saying everything would be all right would be an absolute mistake. Cue another eighteen years of not talking to one another. Cue status quo. Cue a shed load more quiet unhappiness. Cue curtains. We needed to move forward. I needed *not* to hug him. Instead, I pulled out a chair at the other end of the table.

'Shall we talk about Constance Perkins? I said.

His head remained on the table a moment more and then he lifted it.

There was no surprise in his eyes. Only pain.

'What's the point,' he said dully. 'What the hell can I say to you?'

'You could start by saying sorry –'

'Christ, Sally. You must know that! I'm here, aren't I? God, you can't imagine how sorry –'

'*OK*,' I said, the bile rising in my throat. 'You could start by telling *me* about *her*, maybe. You could start by explaining what *you* thought you were doing. You could start by –'I stopped. Start by *what,* exactly? He was right. It was pointless. Valueless. Useless. 'No,' I said quietly. 'Let's not talk about her. Let's talk about something much more to the point. Let's talk about Tricia instead.'

His head snapped back. And in doing so it became instantly clear that we didn't even need to. Eighteen long years – no – twenty since she'd died – and his expression, that tiny spark of anger in his eyes, told me everything I needed to know.

'What?' he said, staring at me. 'Christ, Sally! *Tricia*?'

'Yes, *Tricia*,' I said again, fury welling inside me. 'The *real* other woman in your life!'

'Oh, for Christ's sake, Sally! What's the point in going *there*?'

'Don't Christ's sake me, Jonathan. Don't you dare say that to me! She's the *real* reason we've come to this! Can't you see that? Jonathan, she's the *whole* point!'

He looked at me coldly then suddenly stood up.

'I can't talk to you any more,' he said.

For some minutes after the front door slammed behind him I stood and stared bleakly at my reflection in the kitchen window. The air in the kitchen smelled stale and cloying. He had been drinking. He had drunk God only knew how much. I marched back across the room and seized the bottle from the table. Still two thirds full. Was it full to start with? No. No, it was already opened. When Bob and Androulla came. That was it. A new sound reached me. One that I recognised. The motor on the garage door. I ran out into the hall and yanked the front door open again. His tail lights were just curving out towards the main road.

And then there was silence. A hollow one this time. And I didn't know what to do. I had reached a full stop, and I didn't know how to begin the next sentence. I simply didn't know what to do next. There was a wetness against the back of my hand, and I sank to my knees, burying my face in the musty folds of Merlin's neck, my dog who loved me. Loved me above all else.

But I couldn't just sit there forever. I had to do something. But what? Where had he gone? Should I just stay here and wait for him? Get myself together? Go to bed? What? I took myself back to the kitchen and made myself a mug of good strong coffee, gave Merlin a dog biscuit and sat down to think.

She had been buried in the cemetery at St Mark's church. Buried, not cremated, so there'd be a grave to visit. Somewhere for Morgan to place childish posies on her birthday, on Morgan's birthday, on the anniversary of her death. I had been there only once before – at my insistence, we'd married elsewhere – yet as I pulled up in the quiet lane that led to the churchyard it was as if that day had been mere moments before this one. Nothing had changed. The trees had grown taller, the bushes a little bushier, but it was a view that had not changed substantially, I guessed, in the several hundred years since the church had been built. I locked Merlin in the car and walked carefully along in the darkness. No moon tonight, though a thick spread of stars, casting a pearl wash over the silver tinged stone. The church clock said twenty past one in the morning. Where had the time gone? Had it really taken me three long hours to arrive at the truth that had brought me up here?

I spotted Jonathan's car almost immediately. He'd parked a little way further down the lane, the car listing half up on the grassy verge. I put my hand on the bonnet as I passed. It was cold. So he'd been here a very long time.

Tricia's grave was at the far end of the churchyard . I passed gravestones of every conceivable type. Old slabs of crumbling stone, grey-green with lichen, black marble, white marble, nibble-edged granite. It wasn't cold, exactly, just chill with the sombre taint of death in the air.

He was standing still as a monument himself, head slightly dipped, hands in pockets. He turned at the sound of my approach.

'I'm sorry,' he said as I drew alongside him.

Tricia's grave had been an elaborate affair. A sturdy headstone topped with an angel, the dates that recorded her truncated existence and the words '*most beloved*' carved in a large curling script. I had brought Morgan here when she was just six and her mother had been dead for three years. We had brought flowers – a little pot of pansies, I remembered, that we'd dressed up with some ribbon and a Happy Birthday note. Whose decision had that visit been? I couldn't now remember. Nor did I need to. Whether Jonathan's, or mine, in an effort to please him, it mattered little. All I recalled was a small girl, uncomprehending and happy, skipping over graves on a bright winter's day. I looked down at Tricia's grave now. No pansies. No, now there were roses. Red roses. A big bunch of them, set in the rose bowl that had come with the gravestone. A few were still buds, the majority in bloom, all carefully arranged in the mesh. I stooped to stroke one of the velvety petals. Not a weed, not a grass tuft to be seen.

'How often,' I asked quietly, 'do you come here?'

Jonathan took his hands out of his pockets and drew them both through his hair.

'It varies. Once a fortnight or so.'

'When?'

'God, Sally, does it matter?' He stepped back and started walking away. I followed. The grass was growing dewy now. It spangled as I walked. Jonathan always bought me flowers for my birthday. Once a year. Lilies, carnations, freesias. Never roses.

'Yes, it does matter. It matters very much, Jonathan.' I looked back at the grave. 'Tell me.'

He continued to walk through the maze of graves towards the gate. Big assured strides along a well-trodden route.

'It doesn't matter,' he said again.

I caught up with him, then. 'No,' I said. 'You're probably right. The details don't matter, do they? Just the – I turned to look at him. 'Just the fact that you do, Jonathan. Just the fact that you *still do.*' He walked on now, but I stopped and looked back. All those graves. All those lives lived and now long extinguished. The timeless process of bereavement, grieving, the cherishing of memories, and of time then moving on. Of *people* moving on. And there was Tricia's grave, as trim and well tended as the day it was laid. Jonathan was standing by the gate now, waiting. He was stamping his feet. Glancing around him. Uncomfortable, I realised, at being in this place with *me*. I felt suddenly as if it was trespass to be here. That this was their place. That I had no right.

I took a deep breath, filling my lungs with the damp night air. Well, so be it. It was true. I *shouldn't* be here. Because I was alive. I *felt* alive. My heart was still pumping blood around my body and my body was still whole and youthful and *living.* As was he, though he'd had to come this far to discover it.

I walked the last few yards towards him lighter of foot than I could ever have imagined, Morgan's anxious words only catching me up as I reached him. But she was wrong. It couldn't possibly kill him if I left him, because just as my mother had said to me yesterday, that part of him died on the night Tricia had. I got to the gate. Met his eye and smiled at him. No. Wrong word. Not died. Had simply been chained to this graveyard. Had been so since the day he had settled for a substitute. Someone to take care of him. A mother for his child. I wasn't about to kill him. Far from it. He could move on now. But not with me. I was about to set him free.

'I can't stay with you, Jonathan.'

'I know that,' he answered.

'I can't stay with you because you don't love me enough. *Can't* love me enough.' It was such a small thing to say but such a big thing to contemplate. Perhaps that's why it had taken me so long to do. That and finding out there was someone who could.

'I do love you, Sally. It's just – 'He glanced back up the way we had come. 'No,' he said sadly. 'Not enough. I know that.' He pushed his hands back in his pockets. 'Are you going to come home now?'

I shook my head. 'Not yet. I'm going for a drive. You go home to bed. We'll talk tomorrow, OK?' He started to protest, but I waved my hand to stop him.

'I have my phone. I have Merlin with me. I will be fine. Please go home.'

He looked at me for a moment, then nodded, accepting, and set off down the lane back to his car.

I looked up at the stars, remembering Ruth's ranting. I could see what she meant now. I'd at last had that slap.

Chapter 32

What DO stomachs do? Do they lurch? Flip? Somersault? Tie themselves in knots? Sitting in my car in the stillness that followed after Jonathan had driven off, I pondered this descriptive conundrum awhile. Because, though I was at a loss to describe it, something of a gymnastic persuasion was certainly happening to mine. And the reason it was happening to mine was because for the first time since that night in that lane all those months back, I could finally see my way clear. I could imagine a life different to the one I'd lived so far. I could imagine myself being loved.

At the end of June one of the brightest constellations in the sky is Lyra. I could pick out Vega at its centre, blinking down at me from its vantage point high in the heavens. It was now ten past three. A ridiculous time to be up for most people. But I wasn't most people and neither was he. I picked up my phone. The numbers on the display leapt out at me, as if welcoming me back into the sensation of a forgotten embrace. I pressed the connect button and waited for the ring tone. I would find out what time his flight was. That's what I would do. It didn't matter that he was leaving now. I would see him and hold him and tell him I loved him. What happened next I was happy to leave to providence. Or fate even. I didn't care what you called it. Only that I was happy that it would guide me. Guide *us*. I felt freed from the shackles of not believing in destiny. Able to accept that some things were meant to be, that some things *were* written in the stars.

The phone rang on. And then a voice answered. *The Vodafone you have called is not responding. It may respond if you try again later...* Rats. *Rats*. I nibbled the aerial. Perhaps reception was bad. Perhaps he was in a tunnel. Perhaps, I thought, heart thudding anxiously inside me, he was already in the airport and had switched off his phone. I put my key in the ignition and then thought better of it. I should send him a text message too. If I sent him a text message his phone would beep at him as soon as it was switched on again, wouldn't it? Yes, that would be best. Send a message, then *get there*. I scrolled down the menu with feverish fingers. Write messages, it said, the cursor blinking at me. '*Nick, it's me,*' I typed out. *'I'm on my way to the airport. I need to talk to you. Meet me?'* Oh, God, meet me *where*? Which terminal? *Which*? North, I decided. It had to be North. He was flying BA, wasn't he? Or *was* he? Oh, God. Yes, North. Must be North. Go for North. '*Costa Coffee?*' I typed. Would Costa Coffee be open? Would *anything* be open? Oh, why wasn't he *there*? '*Or MacDonald's*?' I suggested. Then I typed '*on my way!!!*' and added seven kisses. One for each of the seven sisters. I started the engine, placed the phone down beside me, switched on the headlamps and set off down the lane.

Déjà vu.

The road was big, wide, empty, dark. All the things that country lanes generally are at night. It was flanked by tall trees, all in full leaf now, a dense black filigree against deep inky blue. He hadn't called back. No message. No nothing. It was now twenty to four. His words kept returning. 'At some ungodly hour so it might as well be Monday'. Supposing I was too late? Supposing he *had* already got to the airport? Supposing – my heart sank – he was already on the plane?

No, he couldn't have, I decided. It was too early, surely. *Way* too early. Long haul flights didn't take off in the middle of the night, did they? Another thought occurred to me. Supposing he was still at home? God, why hadn't I thought of that? Yes, that was it, *surely*. Packing, most probably. Supposing he was there and hadn't heard his mobile? Why hadn't I thought of that earlier? Stupid, stupid. I pulled over, taking care not to drive my wheels up on the verge. I would try him at home. As I pulled into the kerb, Merlin began whining, turning circles on the back seat and nudging at my neck. How long since he'd been out now? God, poor thing! *Hours*, must be. I opened the car door and climbed out. He bounced out behind me and yomped off to cock a leg at the nearest tree. Home number, home number, where was Nick's home number? I kept scrolling. Not under 'Nick', my devious little brain reminded me. Not under 'Brown' either. I kept on scrolling. That was it. Under S. S, for Star. Up came the digits. I pressed call and waited. Ring ring, ring ring. Oh, *please* be at home.

But he wasn't. Not even the answerphone message. So final. So definite. So uncontestable. He'd already gone. Gone in every sense possible. He'd even switched off his answerphone. I imagined his apartment, now shrouded in darkness. I imagined him winging his way back to America. I imagined him chalking us up to experience. I imagined his heart mending. His thoughts turning elsewhere. His – oh, God. Gone gone *gone*. The airport. I absolutely must get to the airport. I slid the phone into my pocket and looked around for Merlin. No sign. He'd been there only moments ago, hadn't he? And yet now he was nowhere to be seen.

I peered into the trees. 'Merlin! Come on!'

I scanned the length of the verge.

'Merlin! Come *on*!'

I glanced wildly around me.

'*Merlin! Come on!*'

I ran round the car, up the road, down the road, up again.

'*Merlin!* Where *are* you? COME ON!'

Never tempt fate and name dogs after wizards. Abracadabra. Mine had disappeared.

Swearing, my mother always told me, was the province of the illiterate. Profanity the refuge of the syntactically impaired. Not her words, exactly, but I always took her meaning. Only people with inferior vocabularies swore.

And me. 'Bloody stupid *fucking* dog!'

There was no one to hear, of course, so it didn't really count. But it made me feel marginally better.

'MERLINNN!!!!!!!' I called again. What the hell was I going to do now? I had two options. Go and find him or leave him and go. To my shame I gave a microsecond's thought to the latter, which is presumably what happens when you start affixing swear words to much loved pets. But bloody stupid dog that he was, he was *my* dog, my much loved pet, and therefore he had to be found. I yanked my bag from the passenger footwell and the keys from the ignition, then slammed and locked the door and set off in pursuit.

It must, I decided, have been a wild animal. Merlin, for all his failings in the mud on the kitchen floor department, was not a dog given to absconding. A squirrel maybe, or a fox. But whatever it was, there was no sign of it now. I started off up the lane in the direction I'd last seen him.

Five to four. Five to *four*, I thought as I ran. He would almost certainly be at the airport by now. You had to check in about a fortnight before take off these days, didn't you? And ungodly hours couldn't mean much after six could they? OK. Keep calm and be sensible. You will find your dog and make it to the airport in time. And if you don't make it to the airport in time it will not be the end of the world. Don't be silly. Just remember that –

'MERLINNNNNNNNNN!!!'

–That he has not gone into outer space, merely to the other side of the Atlantic ocean, which is not so far really. Only – oh, *God* – *thousands* of miles. No. Don't be silly. He's still working for Drug U Like, isn't he? *Is* he? Did he say that? He wasn't going for the HR job. Yes. He said *that*, but did he say – *did* he? No, no. Of course he's still with Drug U Like. And even if he isn't, you can still find out his address from someone – from who? – from *someone.* And you can write him a letter. Or send him an email. And you can tell him all about it – oh, how he'll laugh! – and then you can send each other more letters, and ….and what? And be pen pals? And – oh, *God*! But I need to *see* him! So *badly*. Don't be silly. *Not* the end of the world. You can save up all those vouchers you get in Tesco and swap them for air miles, and some day, *some* day, you can go out and visit him and you can–

'MERLINNNNNNNNNNNNNN!!!!'

–You can sort everything out and – and – but he lives in *America*, for God's sake! You can't sort anything out! He'll be there and you'll be here and – and at this rate still stumbling through the undergrowth just off the A bloody 23, most likely. It isn't fair! If this is what fate has in mind for me, well fate can go fu–

'Yeeeow!'

I hit the ground running and hit the ground hard. When I opened my eyes and spat the grass from my mouth, my dog was standing on me, licking my face.

I didn't kill him.

I didn't even smack him. Despite the dog training school's stern lectures about the importance of negative re-enforcement, I was just so grateful to have him back that I threw my arms around his flank and held him in a vice like grip till I could struggle to my feet and get my fingers under his collar.

'You,' I said, as we rattled back along the verge towards the car, shedding undergrowth like a pair of fugitive scarecrows, 'will find yourself dispatched to Battersea dogs' home if you so much as *look* like you might pull a stunt like that again. You hear me?'

I unlocked the car door and Merlin slithered in guiltily. Twenty past four. Twenty past *four!* I couldn't have been more awake if I'd downed fifteen expressos. Oh, why, oh *why* hadn't he answered my message? Come to that – come to that – oh, bloody, *bloody* dog – where the hell had my phone disappeared to?

'Sorry, love. This one's full right now. You'll have to go back to the South Terminal car park and get the monorail back up.'

It was now ten to five. I had looked everywhere. In my pockets, in my handbag, in the footwells, in the boot, up the lane, down the lane, under the car, in the lining of my coat, in my handbag again. Everywhere, in short, that a phone might fetch up. But mine was nowhere to be seen. I had toyed with throwing myself on to the wet grass again and simply expiring with frustration, but attractive though the idea was, it would have been a senseless waste of valuable time, so instead I hurled myself back into the car and drove to the airport is if my very life depended on it. Which, as far as I was concerned, it did. And now they wouldn't even let me in. '*What?*'

'Sorry love. Busy time. You know how it is. Just take the slip road back out and follow the signs.' How *dare* so many people go on holiday right now? More bad karma. More *bloody bad karma*. The man in the neon peered into the car. 'You flying, love?'

Only in the face of all common sense. I shook my head. 'No. No, I'm not.'

'Leave your dog in the car then, will you, my love? Its chaos enough in there as it is.'

The last of the stars were just beginning to slip behind their veil of daylight by the time I made the South terminal car park. It seemed like such a bad omen, morning sneaking up on me like that. But I was here at least. There had to be *some* chance. Some tiny chance.

I shot like a missile down the moving pavement that led the way into the south terminal, scattering sleepy holiday makers and bored businessmen alike. Airports were just too big, I decided, conscious as I sped across the clicky-clacky concourse, of the suspicious looks my dishevelment were gathering as I ran. There was a monorail train, thankfully, just about to leave, and I plunged through the closing doors puffing and panting and pulling bits of muddy grass from my clothes.

Standing in the blackness of the monorail terminal I could see I had a fair thatch of grass in my hair as well. I couldn't give a damn. Some tiny chance. *Please.*

We clattered on round to the North Terminal and once spewed from the train I shot off to departures, casting wildly around as I ran. The departure boards were many and complicated. This flight to there, departing gate twenty seven. That flight to the other, gate one million and two. I realised with a start that I didn't even know which airport he was flying to. Did San Diego even *have* an international airport? If not, would it even be up on the board? I ran my eyes up and down the lists several times. They told me nothing. I may as well have been reading the football results.

And there was little point anyway. If he'd gone then he'd gone. On the other hand, if he was still groundside, there must be *some* chance he'd still be at Costa Coffee waiting for me, mustn't there? Or MacDonald's. Some chance. Some tiny chance. *Mustn't* there? Couldn't chance be on my side for once?

I had just skirted Tie Rack when chance caved in and helped me. In the shape of a distant blur of brown up ahead. No, no, not brown. Tan. Tan – or, yes. Toffee. I quickened my pace. A tan suede jacket. *A toffee suede jacket!* But moving away fast. I filled my lungs with air.

'Nick! I bellowed. 'Nick! I'm *here*! Nick, WAIT!'

The world paused for a month while he stopped and turned round. With his mobile in one hand, held to his ear, and a cup of Costa coffee in the other.

Chapter 33

I threw myself at him in the middle of the concourse. As with the dog, it seemed the only thing to do. 'Oh, God, Nick! Thank God! Where have you *been*?'

He held tight to his coffee. 'Right here!' he said waggling his phone at me. 'More to the point, where have you been? I've been trying you constantly. Why didn't you answer your phone?'

'Oh, God, I lost it. And I've been in such a panic! I'd been trying for hours! 'Your mobile, your home –'

He shook his head at this. 'I left there yesterday. I had to go to a meeting, so I stayed at the Meridien last night.'

'But why didn't you answer the mobile?'

'It never rang. I guess you must have called while I was showering or something. But I got your message just fine so I headed straight here to wait.' He was grinning at me now. 'And boy, did I wait. This is my third. Where d'you get to?'

We walked back to the coffee shop arm and arm and I told him. I told him about Jonathan, I told him about Tricia, about Morgan, about my mother, about Merlin running off. He got me a coffee and we sat down in a corner. I felt giddy. Stupid. Delirious. But Nick's smile was gone now, and he took both my hands. 'Jeez, Sally. It's so good to see you.'

'It's so good to see you as well,' I said. And in saying so, everything suddenly caught up with me. The morning had come now and with it, reality. And the future. A scary, scary place. What *now?*

'Forgive me,' I went on, 'if it seems like it's *not* good, but I'm afraid I'm going to burst into tears now. Have you got a hankie or something?'

He reached across to another table and plucked a handful of napkins from a holder.

'I'm sorry,' I sniffed. 'I'm sorry, but – God, what *now*, Nick? What happens *now*?'

There was so much tenderness in his eyes that if I hadn't already been sobbing I would have started up. 'What happens now,' he said, handing the napkins to me, 'is that I put my arms round you and hold you very tight and don't mind in the least that you make a mess all over my shirt, and then you blow your nose and then we talk. Deal?'

Which made me laugh, but then weep all the more. 'But your flight!' I snivelled, burying my head as directed and wondering how I'd ever manage to let him go again. 'Nick, what about your flight?'

'What about it?'

'Well, aren't you going to miss it? It's getting on for six –'

He shook his head.

'Oh, I changed it last week. I don't fly till a quarter to eight. They screwed up in travel. Had me routed via Amsterdam, for some bizarre reason. So we have a while at least, don't we? Though I guess you need to be in work in a couple of hours anyway, and you still have to take Merlin home.'

'But what can we *say*?' I said, scrumpling the napkins in a ball against his chest. 'Nick, what do we *do*?'

He considered for a moment. 'Well,' he said finally, 'the way I see it is that right off I tell you I love you more than you can possibly imagine and all the while I'm pinching myself because three hours ago I thought you'd broken my heart and then I tell *you* to pinch me as well – just to be certain – and then – this bit happens kind of naturally – we kiss and we hold each other and you tell me everything's OK now and that I'm *not* dreaming this and that you *do* love me and that we're going to be together after all, and then I tell you again – just in case you hadn't heard the first time – just how very *much* I love you, and then we kiss a bit more and then I tell you again. We sort of keep on in that vein till a sunset fetches up. And then we go off and live happily ever after. That kind of stuff. It's all pretty standard. Corny, but standard. I'm sure we'll get the hang of it.'

Which made me weep even more. I was weeping fairly uncontrollably by now.

'Well?' he prompted. I couldn't speak. 'That's, like, your *cue*? Jeez, Sally, I don't know. Really I don't. I come *all* this way – '

'Down a hotel corridor.'

'Down a *long* hotel corridor. And have drunk enough coffee to keep me awake till mid-August –'

'Oh, God, I *do* love you, Nick. I love you so much that I when I think I was this close –'I put my finger and thumb together '– *this* close to letting you go the thought scares me like you wouldn't even begin to believe. But how *dare* you make me laugh at a time like this! Nick, I can't just up and go and live thousands of miles away. I *can't*. There's Kate and Morgan, and my mum, and Merlin, and – and there's, well, Jonathan to think of too. There's *so* much to sort out. I can't just –'I gripped his shirt front. 'And I can't ask you to either. What about *Will?* I mean – '

He pulled away slightly and looked sternly back at me. 'Six hours fifty five minutes.'

I sniffed. 'What?'

'Is the average flying time between Boston and San Diego.'

I sniffed again. 'Boston?'

'Will's at Harvard, remember? On the other hand –' he dropped his arms from my shoulders now and took both my hands in his. 'The average flying time between Boston and Heathrow – you can't fly into Gatwick from Boston, but I made an allowance for driving time, OK? – is only six hours *twenty five* minutes.'

I stared at him. 'You worked all that out?'

He nodded, a touch bashfully. 'As you do. Got to have something to occupy your mind when you're lying in bed night after night unable to sleep because you've fallen in love with someone who is married and lives on a different continent to you. It's a fairly intractable problem.'

'You mean you'd come back here? You mean, for good? I mean, with him being there, and –'

'Sally, that's my whole point! He'll be *nearer*. Not in miles perhaps, but practically speaking he will. For the next fours years at least. And, well, I didn't want to bring this up, but my mother'll be pleased. She's been in a mood with me since 1982. You'll like my mother, Sally. My mother will certainly love you.'

'But what about your career?'

'I guess I opt for the HR job here after all.'

'Just like that?'

'No. Not just like that. Sally, I never turned it down, you know. I'm only going on vacation right now. Nothing's sorted yet.'

'On vacation?' I squeaked. 'But your flat –'

'Is still there, dingbat. Look, the plan was that I would look at what's on offer over there, sort out my domestic situation, and – well. It's decided now, isn't it?' He pulled a blade of grass from my fringe and kissed my forehead. 'You've decided it for me. So you'll go off to work, and I'll go get my plane, and we can talk every day – and before we know it, I'll be back.'

'How long will you be gone?'

'Two weeks? Say three. Three weeks, at the most. Do you think you can wait for three weeks?'

'I've been waiting every week of my life for you, Nick,' I said gravely. 'I think I can manage another three.'

He pulled something from his pocket and slipped it into my hand.

'Guess I won't be needing this after all, then,' he said.

I looked down at the little jar of Marmite I'd sent him. A warm black nugget in my palm. 'So you got it –'

'I got it. Though I have to say it'll be a relief not to have to sneak it past customs. I spent an hour being grilled at Newark once on the strength of a crummy packet of Oxo cubes. Tell you what,' he said. 'Save it till the day I get back. We can have it on toast.' He chuckled. 'It can be a toast to *us*.'

I winced in his arms.

'Ruth was right,' I said. 'You *should* have a licence.'

He laughed. 'Can't be helped. And you should worry. Sometimes I burst into song.'

'Best not. Don't want you getting arrested.' Oh, God. So little time. Perhaps I should arrest him myself. I tightened my grip on the back of his jacket. 'Oh, Nick. I wish we had longer.'

'So do I, so do I.' He glanced at his watch. 'But we don't. Twenty past six. And I'm boarding at seven. So we'd better crack on.' He pulled me tight against him now, chasing all the horrors away. I buried my face in his shoulder, drinking in the scent of him. 'Sally,' he said, stroking my hair now, 'I love you so much. More than you can possibly imagine. I love you so much I – yeeow!! *Jeez*! What was *that*?'

Morning had come but all the stars had stayed out for us. I lifted my face from his shoulder.

'Your pinch,' I said, knowing I could embrace the day as well now. 'Come on then, Nick. Get your act together, will you? That was supposed to be your cue…'

THE END

Coming soon by Lynne Barrett-Lee

A modern twist on Cinderella

Radio Wales DJ Jack Valentine finds a lost trainer on a station platform. With echoes of Cinderella, he appeals on his show for its owner, Hope Shepherd, to come forward.

Hope handles publicity for a Cardiff based charity, Heartbeat. Encouraged by colleagues to secure Jack Valentine to raise the profile of an upcoming fun run, she reluctantly heads for the studios.

The attraction between Hope and Jack is immediate but, bruised and battered by their recent divorces, they are reluctant to risk romance again.

Barefoot In The Dark is a bitter-sweet novel about taking the first steps towards trusting again. But when love at first sight is the last thing you're after, is a fairytale ending an impossible dream?

ISBN 1905170378 Price £6.99

Lynne Barrett-Lee is the author of four novels and has also been selected to be part of the new Quick Reads Initiative with her book, *Secrets*.
Lynne lives in Cardiff with her husband and three children.

For more information please visit
www.lynnebarrett-lee.com